Believe It Or Not

MAPLE PRESS

Believe It or Not

Published by : Maple Press Pvt. Ltd.
4675 A/21, 1st Floor, Ansari Road,
Daryaganj, New Delhi–110 002
☎ 011–41513581
Email : info@maplepress.co.in
Website : www.maplepress.co.in

Printed By : DD Offset Printing Press, Noida

PREFACE

Human knowledge is an ever expanding process. Today, we are in such stage of civilisation that there are millions of new informations coming up in every passing second. You miss a plethora of new facts/information when you blink your eye for once. We live in the age of information. We have to make a close observation of everything happening around us as a true seeker of knowledge. The hunger of knowing something new is the only remedy to keep our life going in this highly competitive world. In fact, in today's world, the one who knows more than his fellow-beings is considered superior. He is respected by all and delivered a good position in job sector. Thus, the society is in the process of a sharp classification between persons who knows more and persons who knows least. Having a sound background of everything in and around the world has become the cardinal principle of becoming a successful man in life. This book is an effort to give a big push to the ambitious students of this generation. It consists of a great deal of informations, which we are something quite amazing that we come across for the first time. Every information in this book is of great use in our life. It will give you a vivid impression of the world we live in and its flora and fauna. It also give a great deal of knowledge about the universe, we are on the process of exploring. Hope the reader will find it fruitful and inspiring. Wish you all the best!

Believe It or Not

1. We all know about the 'honey mushroom'. But we were not aware of its large and invasive size. The researchers investigated on this unique fungus and found out that this fungus was responsible for

killing large groves of evergreen trees. They cut into an infected tree and they found spreading white filaments, *mycelia*, whose function is to draw water and carbohydrates from the tree to feed the fungus. A large number of samples of the fungus were collected from a widespread area and its DNA was analysed. And the result showed that it turned out to be from a single organism.

2. Anaconda holds the world record for its massive size. It has earned the famed title, 'king of snakes'. Though the Asiatic Reticulated Python (Python reticulatus) holds the world record of 33 feet for length, yet the girth of the anaconda is far bigger. Anacondas are big enough to swallow an adult man as a whole! Generally, Anacondas are found in the wild hanging out in rivers hunting for their

prey. They are usually known as solitary creatures of somewhat shy nature and not many of them are easily seen. They are very well camouflaged in the swamps and bogs in which they thrive. It has been reported by some early European explorers of the South American jungles seeing giant anacondas up to 100 feet long and some of the native peoples of the South American jungle have reported seeing anacondas up to 50 feet long. Anacondas have the ability to remain partly hidden in the water that make it difficult to estimate its complete length accurately.

Anacondas are members of the boa constrictor family of snakes. This is obvious because of their habit of killing their prey. This family of snakes kill their prey by coiling their large, powerful bodies around their victims and squeezing until their prey suffocates to death. Then the snake unhinges its jaw and swallows the victim whole. They are slow moving snakes.

Anacondas have teeth but they don't use it for chewing. They just use it for holding onto their prey, preventing them from escaping. Some snakes have venom in their two extra long teeth (called fangs), which they use to kill their prey. But Anacondas' teeth are not venomous. They rely on their enormous size and power to subdue their victims.

3. The name of the river 'Dead Sea' sound strange infact it is called the Dead Sea, because in reality nothing lives in it. It is almost six times as salty as the ocean. This sea is completely landlocked and it gets more saltier with increasing depth. At about 130 feet (40 metres) deep down the river, the seawater comprises about 300 grams of salt per kilogram of seawater. Below 300 feet, the sea has 332

grams of salt per kilogram of seawater and is saturated. Salt precipitates out and piles up on the bottom of the sea. In such salinity, no living organism can exist. There is no seaweed or plants of any kind in or around the water. There are no fish or any kind of swimming, squirming creatures living in or near the water. The water in the Dead Sea is deadly to all living things. Even if a fish, accidentally swims into the waters of Dead Sea from one of the several freshwater streams that feed the Sea, is killed instantly. It's body is quickly coated with a preserving layer of salt crystals and then tossed onto shore by the wind and waves. The shore of the Sea is covered with white, crystals of mineral salts.

The Dead Sea bears this unusual quality because the sea is continually fed from the rivers and streams coming down off the mountains that surround it. And we know that, the only way water gets out of the Sea is through evaporation. Moreover, Dead Sea lies in one of the hottest parts of our planet. Therefore, when the water evaporates, it leaves behind all the dissolved minerals in the Sea, making it salty. Hence, the water does not escape the Sea as it traps the salts within its shores. It is impossible to find any living creature in such a salty water because no life can adopt to such living conditions.

4. Can you believe it that Leonardo da Vinci's 'Mona Lisa' is the most valuable object ever stolen? The masterpiece was stolen from the Louvre, Paris, France, on August 21, 1911. Finally after nearly two years that it was recovered in Italy in 1913. Vicenzo Perugia was charged with its theft.

Leonardo da Vinci
(1452-1519)

5. Lawrence Doyle Conklin of USA has a record of being transferred maximum number of times in different prisons. In a period of 27 years, he was shifted 117 times to 53 different prison facilities in the USA. He was imprisoned in 1971 and moved from prison to prison till his death on September 12, 1998.

6. The biggest criminal gang in the world is knownas 'Yamaguchi-gumi' gang of the yakuza. It is a Japanese criminal organisation, which has 30,000 members. This gang had certain characteristics that were common to all its members. For example, Hiroyuki Suzuki who was a former gangster and has now become a priest, has typical yakuza characteristics, such as tattoos and cut-off finger-tips.

7. Tirupati temple in Andhra Pradesh is famous worldwide because more than 2.2 million dollars are raised each a year through the auction of hair sacrifice of the pilgrims. The hair is collected from the pilgrims to the Tirupati Temple in Andhra Pradesh, India. The temple attracts an average of 30,000 visitors per day. Pilgrims

donate their hair as a form of sacrifice. There are 600 barbers employed by the temple who shave the pilgrims' heads. They are available 24 hours a day.

8. Can you believe that the statue of Liberty is not just a mere fasci-

nating building but it is actually a token of gift that was gifted by the people of France to the people of United States of America. It is officially known as the 'Liberty Enlightening the World'. It was sculpted by Auguste Bartholdi and engineered by Gustave Eiffel in 1886. The statue stands 151 ft. tall and weighs 225 tones.

9. The world's costliest outfit was sold for $66,112 at Sotheby's, London, England on September 16, 1998. It was the same dress, which was worn by Geri Halliwell for the Spice Girls' 1997 Brit Awards performance. Peter Morton, the owner of the Hard Rock Hotel in Las Vegas, Nevada, USA bought it and created the history.

10. The biggest mosque in the world is Shah Faisal Mosque, which is near to Islamabad in Pakistan. It can accommodate 100,000 worshippers in the prayer hall and courtyard. A further 200,000 worshippers can offer their prayers in the adjacent grounds. The mosque covers the total area of 47 acres, with the covered area of the prayer hall taking up 1.19 acres.

11. Graca Machel is famous for being the first lady of two countries. She married Samora Machel, the president of Mozambique in

1975. But the president was killed in a plane crash in October 19, 1986. On July 18, 1998, she married Nelson Mandela, president of South Africa. Hence, in this way she is known as the first woman to become 'first lady' of two different countries.

12. A major earthquake in Taiwan that struck on December 9, 1999 killed an estimated number of 2,400 people. The most surprising fact is that 80 days after this massive earthquake, a cat was discovered alive in a collapsed building in Taichung, Taiwan. The cat was immediately admitted to a veterinary hospital, where it made a full recovery.

13. Can you believe that the playback singer Kumar Sanu recorded 28 songs in a single day in 1993. All the songs were recorded for Sterling Records and Cassettes at the Musicians Studio at Mumbai.

14. Sayeed Jaffrey is renowned for being the first Indian to give most appearances in International films. In 1998, he started acting in international cinema and British television. Till date, he has appeared in 18 international films such as *A Passage to India* and *Gandhi* produced in 1982. His current project includes UK's longest-running soap opera, Coronation Street. Since 1977, he has acted in 100 Hindi films and 1 Punjabi film.

15. On September 25, 1999 Gordon Cates of Alachua, Florida, USA kissed 10 monocle cobras and a 15-ft. king cobra consecutively.

16. On April 5, 1999, a kissing contest was held in Rabin Square, Tel Aviv, Israel in which 107 couples took part in the event. Karmit Tsubera and Dror Orpaz won and created the record of kissing for 30 hours and 45 minutes.

17. Li Jian Hua of Jiangshan on December 17 1998, in China, lifted a 50 Kgs of a column of bricks hanging from a clamp joined to his ear. He held the weight for 9.3 seconds. Similarly, Walter Arfeuille of Belgium on June 9, 1996 pulled eight railways passenger coaches bearing a total weight of 493,563 lbs. He travelled a distance of 10ft. 6in. along a track, with his teeth.

18. The world's largest mug is 20ft. high with a diametre of 14ft. and a weight of 3.5 tons. Parnassus Event of India built it in 1998. It was unveiled at Bangalore Palace, India, on August 14, 1998.

19. It has been said in olden times that cinnamon was the attar used by Queen of Sheba to captivate King Solomon.

20. Cloves because of their shape are considered an aphrodisiac for males, especially in Asia i.e those drugs that are responsible for arousing or increasing sexual desires. Parents in Indonesia believe in planting a clove tree when a son is born to them. This ritual is performed to wish that both will prosper as they grow up together.

21. Ginger is related to the family of the gladiola. The ginger's pure white blossoms are thought to be a love potion because a woman wearing the aromatic bloom is so alluring. It was brought by Egyptian traders to Rome as an aphrodisiac.

22. Do you know Ancient Persians used to put almonds in jars with flower petals before using them in desserts so that the almonds are perfumed.

23. Tomato is often referred to as the love apple. Tomato received this designation not because it was originally considered an aphrodisiac, but because of a hearing problem. The Spanish called it 'manzana' or apple because that is what they thought it was. Earlier tomatoes were yellow in colour, so Italians called them pomod'or - apple of gold. Later, a Frenchman touring Italy asked for the name of this unusual ingredient and misunderstood it to be pomme d'amour - love apple. The misnomer rapidly spread throughout Europe and

became synonymous with the juicy red fruit ever since. So, this is how tomato by the name of love apple became famous.

24. Can you imagine the distance travelled by a dolphin depends on its food intake? The speed at which a dolphin spends a minimum of energy and hence can maintain for a long time is about 8 km/hr. Also, Dolphins sleep about 8 hrs/day that means 16 hours are left to travel for them. Hence, it means a dolphin can travel up to 128 km/day.

25. A blue whale weighing approximately 160 ton is equal to 30 bull elephants or 1830 adult humans. A blue whale calf can swim 22 mph. It can drink about 130 gallons of milk per day. It gains up to 200 pounds per day during its nursing period. A blue whale has a special quality of producing the loudest and the lowest sound of any animal: 180 dB and 10- 20 Hz.

The size of its eye of a small teacup and their external ear is the size of the tip of a pencil. It has a big tongue, which is about the size and weight of a full-grown African elephant. Its heart is compared to the size of a Volkswagen beetle.

26. In a recent study on whales, a sperm whale's stomach was cut open and to great astonishment 28, 000 tiny squids were found. Similarly when other sperm whale's stomach was cut, boots, wire, buckets, plastic bags and sand were found inside.

27. In order to keep themselves warm in cold, icy waters, whales have, under their skin a very thick layer of Blubber. This helps in Thermal Insulation and also acts as a food storage.

28. Sperm whales have an average lifespan of 60 or 70 years of age. Males reach their physical maturity at 45, while females reach maturity at the age of 30. They also use their sonar to identify and capture prey. They also use it to stun their prey.

29. The blue whale in Latin is referred as Balenoptera musculus. The term 'Musculus' means 'winged mouse'. Linnaeus himself, developer of the biological classification system, named it in 1758, as a joke. The whale society is a matriarchal one, therefore, one will

always observe sperm whales are directed by the biggest female.

30. Whales cannot drink ocean's salt water, therefore, they don't swallow salt water; they use their baleen to strain it out. An adult blue whale can accommodate up to 10,000 gallons of water, which is equal to 256,000 glasses of water in its mouth.

31. Whales do not have good vision under water. They have very good hearing and use a system known as echo location, which utilises a series of sounds and echoes to help them find their way and their food.

32. A Whale's foetus has hands and fingers, which fuse together before birth.

33. In a recent study of Whale and human brain studied under microscope, it was found out that the structure of a dolphin's brain is as advanced as that of a human's brain.

34. In 1300-1700 A.D. mummy flesh was ground into powder and used in Europe as medicinal aids. The Egyptians believed in mummification because they thought if you wrapped the deceased body up it would preserve it and you could go into the afterlife.

35. Cleopatra, the queen of Egypt was the last pharaoh before it fell to Rome in 30 B.C.

36. Honey contains vitamins and antioxidants, but is fat free, cholesterol free and sodium free. It has the ability to attract and absorb moisture, which makes it remarkably soothing for minor burns and helps to prevent scarring. It is a natural energy booster as it provides a concentrated energy source that helps prevent fatigue

and can boost athletic performance.

37. The reason behind honeybees collecting nectar from flowers and blossoms is to make sufficient food stores for their colony over the winter months. The nectar is converted to honey by the honeybee and stored in the wax honeycomb. It keeps them warm, as bees cannot survive in winter season. They do not die out over the winter. They feed on the honey they collected during the warmer months and patiently wait for spring. They form a tight cluster in their hive to keep the queen and themselves warm.

38. A single little brown bat can catch 600 mosquitoes in just an hour. Bats are exceptionally vulnerable to extinction, because they are the slowest reproducing mammals on earth for their size. Most produce only one young a year.

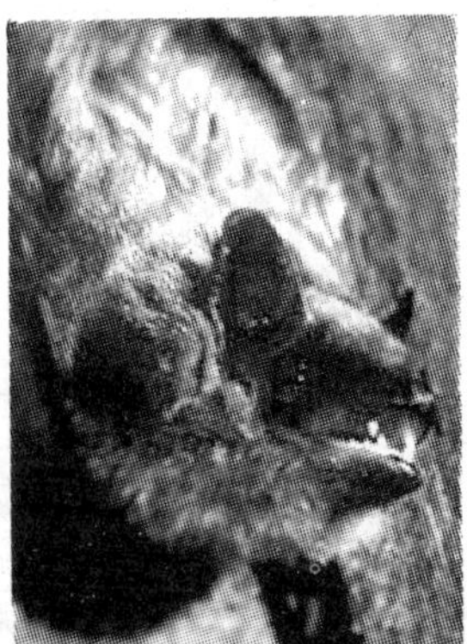

39. Can you believe it that 12% of Scientists in America are Indians; 13% of Xerox employees are Indians; 17% of Intel employees are Indians; 28% of IBM employees are Indians; 34% of Microsoft employees are Indians; 36% of NASA employees are Indians; and 38% of Doctors in America are Indians. Isn't it amazing?

40. Christopher Columbus was attracted to India in 16th century because of its wealth.

41. India is the largest democracy in the world, the 6th largest country in the world and one of the most ancient and living civilisations (at least 10, 000 years old).

42. The game of snakes & ladders was created by the 13th century poet saint Gyandev. It was originally called Mokshapat. The ladders in the game represented virtues and the snakes indicated vices. The game was played with cowrie shells and dices. Later through time, the game underwent several modifications but the meaning is the same i.e. good deeds take us to heaven and evil to a cycle of rebirths.

43. Indian railway system is the largest employer in the world, employing over a million people!

44. Takshila was the World's first university established in 700 BC. More than 10,500 students worldwide studied in this university.

More than 60 subjects were taught here. It was built in the 4th century.

45. Acupuncturists consider that to control appetite, there is a point on the head that you can press. It is located in the hollow just in front of the flap of the ear.

46. In ancient China, doctors were not allowed to see their female patients naked. To circumvent this prohibition, doctors on house calls brought with them a small ivory carving of a woman's naked body. This carving was passed into the curtained bedchamber of the ailing woman along with instructions on how to mark the troubled organs. The statue was then handed out through the curtains and the doctor made his diagnosis on the basis of the markings.

47. The Insulin used to treat diabetes in human beings is taken from pigs and sheep. The substance produced in these animals is exactly the same as that found in the human body and has precisely the same sugar stabilising effect.

48. The great Yankee slugger Babe Ruth, who began his career as a pitcher, had a favourite pitching trick that has rarely been duplicated. He was able to throw two Baseballs in such a way that the balls remained parallel to each other all the way from his hand to the catcher's glove. Ruth was famous for this stunt and would demonstrate it on request.

49. In the year of 1905's Football season, eighteen men were killed in college games in the United States and 159 were permanently injured. This was because, at that time Football players wore only light equipment. Punching, linking arms, gouging and kicking were all part of the action and the entire team was allowed to line up on the scrimmage line. At least a quarter of all games, reports tell us, ended in mob brawls. In 1905 the Reverend David Buel of Georgetown University reported that one unidentified team had been taught to 'strike their opponents in certain delicate parts of the body so as to render them helpless'. The large number of deaths and injuries that year prompted President Theodore Roosevelt to establish the National Collegiate Athletic Association, which instituted regulations designed to make college Football a less lethal sport.

50. A space vehicle must move at a rate of 7 miles per second to escape the earth's Gravitational pull. This is equivalent to going from New York to Philadelphia in about twenty seconds.

51. Many scientists believe that Gold exists on Mars, Mercury and Venus.

52. The Sun provides our planet with 126,000,000,000,000 horsepower of energy every day. This means that 54,000 horsepower is delivered to every man, woman and child on earth in twenty-four hour period of the day. This amount of energy equals only about two billionths of the total energy broadcast into our solar system by the Sun each day.

53. A crocodile can't move its tongue and cannot chew. But its digestive juices are so strong that it can digest even a steel nail easily.

54. An ant can lift object weighing up to 50 times its own weight.

55. Pearls are found in oysters. The largest pearl ever found was 620 carats.

56. Oysters are provided with an additional facility to change from one gender to another and back again depending on which is best for mating.

57. A hippo can open its mouth wide enough to fit a 4 foot tall child inside.

58. A human's scent membrane in the nose is about the size of a postage stamp. A dog's is about the size of a handkerchief. Its olfactory lobe is also 4 times that of a human.

59. Can you imagine that a man named Charles Osborne had hiccups for 69 years.

60. If there is an increase of carbon dioxide in the surrounding air, a mosquito will become restless and start flying around.

61. Leather has enough nutritional value to sustain life for a short time.

62. A sneeze travels out from your mouth at over 100 m.p.h. The highest recorded 'sneeze speed' is 165 km per hour

63. The Grand Vizier of Persia in the tenth century Abdul Kassam Ismael, carried his library with him wherever he went. Four hundred camels carried the 117,000 volumes of books.

64. It is really amazing to know that Alexander Graham Bell, the inventor of the telephone, never phoned his wife or his mother. They were both deaf.

65. An American cow called Fawn was not afraid of flying. In May 1963, she was swept up by a tornado and carried half a mile, only to land safely in another farmer's field. Five years later, another

tornado carried her over a bus. She survived this too and lived to the ripe old age of 25.

66. An Octopus has 3 hearts!

67. Apple pips contain cyanide. There once was a man who really liked the taste of apple pips, so he saved up a cupful of them and ate them in one go and promptly died of cyanide poisoning.

68. Astronauts are not allowed to eat beans before they go into space because passing wind in a spacesuit damages them.

69. Try out the fact that chewing gum while peeling onions will keep you from crying.

70. Chocolate is not given to dogs as it is lethal to a dog because cocoa beans contain theobromine, which is poison for dogs.

71. Do you know Cockroaches' love eating the glue on envelopes and on the back of postage stamps?

72. Dall's porpoise never sleeps, elephants sleep two hours a day, horses nap standing up and Sitatunga antelopes can sleep submerged.

73. Each king in a deck of playing cards represents a renowned king from history: Spades - King David, Clubs - Alexander the Great, Hearts - Charlemagne and Diamonds - Julius Caesar.

74. One wrinkle is created from every two thousand frowns.

75. It is really amazing to know that fish talk to each other. Some of them communicate by making noises in their throats or by rasping their teeth while others use their swim bladders to make sounds.

76. If a person has two thirds of their liver removed through trauma or surgery, it will grow back to the original size in four weeks time

77. Observe this fact from now onwards-If a statue in the park of a person on a horse has both front legs in the air, the person died in battle; if the horse has one front leg in the air, the person died as a result of wounds received in battle; if the horse has all four legs on the ground, the person died of natural causes.

78. It was mandatory in Ancient Egypt that if a surgeon lost a patient while performing an operation, his hands were cut off.

79. If the government has no knowledge of aliens, then why does Title 14, Section 1211 of the Code of Federal Regulations, implemented

on July 16, 1969, make it illegal for U.S. citizens to have any contact with extraterrestrials or their vehicles?

80. Iguanas and komodo dragons have two penises. Actually they have a single penis, but it is split in two (pretty much 'Y'-shaped.) This organ is known as a hemi-penis. Snakes also share this interesting feature. Apparently, the dual penis is meant for the ease of left-handed or right-handed mating.

81. In 1386, a pig in France was executed by hanging, for the murder of a child.

82. In Alaska, it is allowed and legal to shoot bears. However, waking a sleeping bear for the purpose of taking a photograph is prohibited.

83. Irn-Bru is a soft drink that is more popular than Coca-Cola in Scotland. When McDonalds opened in Glasgow and did not sell Irn-Bru, it was considered an insult and the restaurant was subsequently boycotted.

84. Recently an anticrime law was passed in Texas, stating that criminals are required to give their victims 24 hours notice, either orally or in writing and to explain the nature of the crime to be committed.

85. You cannot drive even a single lane in a dirty car in Russia. It is a criminal offence and the offender is heavily penalised.

86. It is said that when Black Beard the Pirate was beheaded his headless body danced around for eight minutes before finally collapsing to the ground.

87. One cannot keep dog as a pet in Iceland as it is against the law.

88. The flag of Libya is the only flag in the world with a solid, single-coloured flag — it's green.

89. Louis IV of France had a big stomach, which equalled the size of two regular stomachs.

90. Many species of bird copulate in the air. In general, a couple will fly to a very high altitude and then drop. During their descent, the birds mate. Sometimes the couple gets too involved and SPLAT!

91. Honeybees die after they sting people. This is because our skin is elastic, unsuitable for their stingers, which are meant for harder inelastic skins. Their venom glands are also torn out in the process. Hence, they die.

92. It's surprising to know that native speakers of Japanese language learn Spanish much more easily than they learn English. Whereas native speakers of English learn Spanish much more easily than they learn Japanese.

93. No animal, once frozen solid (i.e., water solidifies and turns to ice) survives when thawed because the ice crystals formed inside cells would break open the cell membranes. However there are certain frogs that can survive the experience of being frozen. These frogs make special proteins, which prevent the formation of ice (or at least keep the crystals from becoming very large), so that they actually never freeze even though their body temperature is below zero degree Celsius. The water in them remains liquid: a phenomenon known as 'super cooling'. If you disturb one of these frogs (just touching them even), the water in them quickly freezes solid and they die.

94. The Titanic sunk on her maiden voyage on 15 April 1912 and in this tragic accident over 1,500 people died. But it is astonishing to know that fourteen years earlier a novel, which was published by Morgan Robertson, had already foretold this disaster. The book described a fictional ship named 'The Titan' which is the same size as the Titanic and which crashes into an iceberg on its maiden voyage on a misty April night.

95. The Canadian two-dollar bill has the picture of the flag flying over the Parliament building. The astonishing point is that the referred flag is an American flag.

96. The world's most powerful fire engine is the Oshkosh fire truck. It is used for aircraft fires. It is so much powerful that in just 3 minutes, it can spray enough foam to cover a football pitch.

97. Isn't it surprising to know that only female mosquitoes bite whereas male mosquitoes only drink water and plant juice.

98. The Declaration of Independence was signed on July 4. Only John

Hancock and Charles Thomson signed it. Most of the rest signed on August 2, but it's astonishing that the last signature wasn't added until 5 years later. To add to more surprise, the original copy of the Declaration of Independence is lost. The copy which is in Washington D.C. is what is a holograph i.e. it is a handmade copy of a document and is not the same as a laser produced hologram.

99. In medieval Europe, people used to drink gold powder mixed in with water to relieve pain from sore limbs.

100. Pigeons die if they are fed uncooked rice. This is because either their stomach can't handle the carbohydrates or it swells in their throats and chokes them.

101. Pigs don't have sweat glands. Hence, they don't sweat and in order to keep themselves cool they roll around in mud.

102. Point Roberts is a city in Washington State. It is cut off from the rest of the state by British Columbia, Canada. To travel from Point Roberts to the rest of the state or vice versa, the visitor needs to pass through Canada, including Canadian and U.S. customs.

103. We see Polar bears' fur white, but actually they are not white but they are clear. In reality, their skin is actually black. But since their hair is hollow and act like fibre optics, it directs sunlight to warm their skin.

104. A fly can also be dangerous. Pope Adrian VI died due to choking after a fly got stuck in his throat while he was drinking water from a fountain.

105. Rats are very cautious beings. They are quick to understand that if their food is in an exposed area, they don't consume it there, they usually carry or drag it to their hiding place.

106. Watson and Crick had established double helix DNA model but very few know that it was Rosalind Franklin who did all the experiments, but died before she could be acknowledged for her work. Watson and Crick's credit is just that they merely took her results and interpreted it.

107. Have you ever noticed that why birds fear Scarecrows? This is only because of the human odour emitted from the clothes.

108. Do you know that scorpions die or can be killed by pouring vinegar over them. They'll 'snap' and sting themselves.

109. The only country with one train station is Singapore.

110. Before going to their expedition to walk across Antarctica, Sir Ranulph Fiennes and Dr Michael Stroud drank neat olive oil in order to gain body fat.

111. In every country, soldiers salute with their right hand.

112. There are some large clouds, which can store enough water for 500000 showers.

113. The country with three official capitals is South Africa. The capitals are Pretoria, Cape Town and Bloemfontein.

114. President Stalin was only five feet, four inches tall. His left foot had webbed toes and his left arm was noticeably shorter than his right.

115. Alaska has the highest percentage of people in the world who walk to work.

116. It has been observed that a cat falling from the seventh floor of a building has about thirty per cent less chance of surviving than a cat that falls off from the twentieth floor. This is because it supposedly takes distance of about eight floors for the cat to actually realise what is occurring and how to correct itself. At about that height it hits maximum speed and when it hits the ground it's rib cage absorbs most of the impact.

117. The famous poetess Sylvia Plath attempted suicide many times but always failed. Her last attempt to kill herself in which, she succeeded was at the age of 31 when she put her head in an oven. Another interesting fact about her life is that Sylvia Plath's husband, Ted Hughes, who was also a famous poet, was married three times and two of the women he married committed suicide.

118. The Amazon rainforest produces half the world's oxygen supply.

119. We have such a big amount of carbon in the human body that it would be enough to fill about 9,000 'lead' pencils.

120. The amount of energy liberated in the form of light in a supernova explosion is so much that the explosion can be seen even during day!

121. An average person would take seven minutes to fall asleep.

122. The biggest bell is the 'Tsar Kolokol' cast in the Kremlin in 1733. It weighs 216 tons. It is not rung now because a crack has appeared on it. The bell was being stored in a Moscow shed but it caught fire. To save it the caretakers threw water on the bell. The water hit the superheated metal and a giant piece immediately cracked off, destroying the bell forever.

123. The biggest Pyramid in the world is actually about sixty miles southeast of Mexico City, Mexico. It covers more than forty acres.

124. The Boston University Bridge (on Commonwealth Avenue, Boston, Massachusetts) is the only place in the world where a boat can sail under a train driving under a car which is also driving under an

airplane.

125. The children's nursery rhyme 'Ring-a-Round-The-Rosies' actually refers to the Black Death, which killed about 30 million people in the fourteenth-century.

126. The cockroach will be the only creature to survive a nuclear war because it has a high resistance to radiation.

127. The Eiffel Tower in Paris equals the weight of over 1000 elephants.

128. Though it is said that every individual differs from each other in their fingerprints but it has been observed that the fingerprints of koala bears are virtually indistinguishable from those of humans. It is so much so that they could easily confuse fingerprint experts at a crime scene.

129. Philippines is the only country whose flag is the only national flag that is flown differently during times of peace or war.

130. A banana or an apple emits enough gas, which can help an orange ripen.

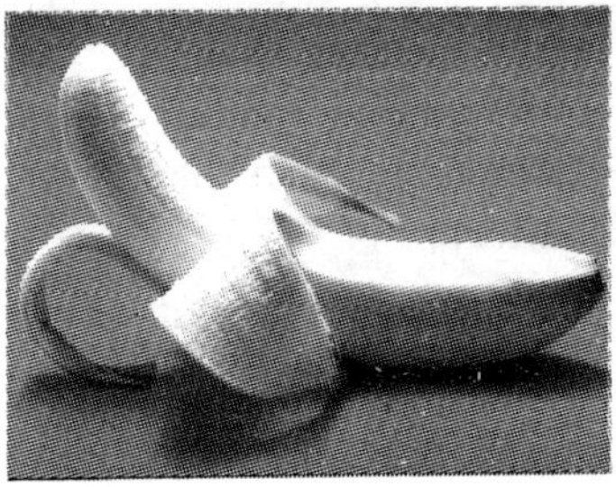

131. It is considered that the sex genes determine gender of an offspring but this is not the case with reptiles. The gender of Reptiles are determined not by the sex genes, but by the temperature in which the egg is incubated. There are certain temperatures fixed that will produce a male and vice versa for a female.

132. The highest number of children born to one mother was recorded to be 69. The mother gave birth to 16 pairs of twins, seven sets of triplets and 4 sets of quadruplets.

133. The maximum growth rate recorded of bamboo plant is three feet (91.44 cm) per day.

134. Usually we see rivers flowing in a single direction but the Hudson River along the island of Manhattan flows in either direction depending upon the tide.

135. All the human bones are connected to each other in the body but there is only one bone i.e. the hyoid bone in throat, which is not attached to another bone.

136. The light from computer screen streams at us at almost 186,000 miles per second.

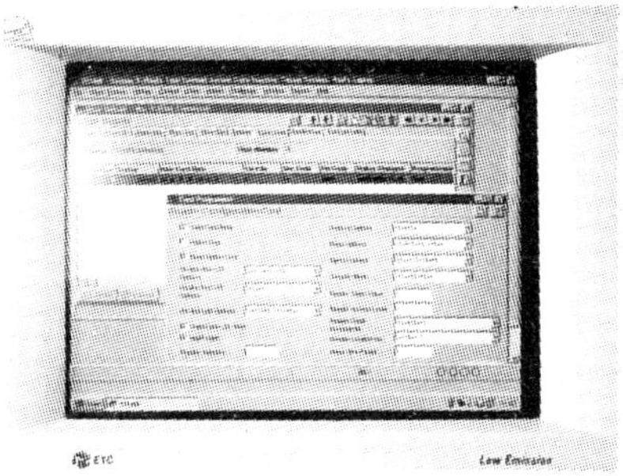

137. The Madagascan Hissing Cockroach is one of the few insects who give birth to live young offspring rather than laying eggs.

138. The male praying mantis cannot copulate while its head is attached to its body. The female initiates sex by ripping the male's head off.

139. The national anthem of Greece has the maximum number of verses i.e. 158 verses. No one in Greece has memorised all 158 verses.

140. The New York in its telephone directory had 22 people by the name of Hitler listed before World War II but there were none after.

141. Creosote bushes in the Mojave Desert are the oldest living thing on earth. These flowering shrubs are 12,000 years old.

142. The actual translation of the nursery rhyme Ring Around the Rosey is a rhyme about the plague. It says infected people with the plague would get red circular sores ('Ring around the rosey'...), these sores would smell very badly, so common folks would put flowers on their bodies somewhere inconspicuously, so that it would cover the smell of the sores ('...a pocket full of posies'...), People who died from the plague would be burned so as to reduce the possible spread of the disease ('...ashes, ashes, we all fall down!')

143. In September 1993, Ramón Blanco was the oldest man to reach the Mount Everest, the world's highest peak. He was then 60 years old.

144. The Astronauts can only take pecan nuts as food to eat in space.

145. Rabbit and parrot are the only two beings that can see what is happening behind them without turning their heads.

146. The opposite sides of a dice cube always add up to seven!

147. Magellan named the Pacific Ocean. He named it so because the ocean to be named was calmer than the Atlantic Ocean.

148. Do you know what is special about The Pentagon, in Arlington, Virginia? It has twice as many bathrooms as is necessary. This is because when Pentagon was being built in the 1940s, the state of Virginia still had segregation laws, which stated separate toilet facilities for blacks and whites.

149. The phrase 'rule of thumb' is not what we actually mean it today. It was actually an old English law. The law stated that one couldn't beat his wife with anything wider than his own thumb.

150. The Ramses brand condom is named after the great pharaoh Ramses II who fathered over 160 children.

151. The Ribbon worm to avoid starvation starts eating itself.

152. Do you know how did the practice of saluting started? The salute of uniform bodies (e.g. army, police) originated from knights who lifted their visor to show their face to a royalty.

153. When macho people crack your knuckles, a sound is heard. This sound is actually the sound of nitrogen gas bubbles bursting.

154. Can you imagine that the Soviet Sukhoi-34, strike fighter has an

attached toilet in it?

155. The starfish are the only animals without brains.

156. The term 'the whole 9 yards' came from WWII fighter pilots in the South Pacific. When arming their airplanes on the ground, the .50 calibre machine gun ammo belts measured exactly 27 feet, before being loaded into the fuselage. If the pilots fired all their ammo at a target, it got 'the whole 9 yards'.

157. McDonald's is the world's largest chain of restaurants.

158. A mathematics teacher in Madison, West Indies owned the world's smartest pig, who memorised the multiplication tables up to 12.

159. There are two kinds of camels. One is the Arabian that lives in Western Asia and Northern Africa. It has one hump. And the second kind is called Bactrian, which has two humps and lives in Mongolia and Chinese Turkistan.

160. Scarlet Pimpernel is a flower that can foretell about the weather situations. It indicates about the weather in the following manner. If the flower is closed up, this means rain is coming and if it is opened up, it means the day will be sunny.

161. A species of spider called the demodex folliculorum lives at the root

of people's eyelashes, but it does not harm anyone.

162. There is a species of parrot in New Zealand which loves to eat the rubber strips that line car windows.

163. Science is considering the fact that there is about 200 times more gold in the world of oceans, than it has been mined in our entire history.

164. Thomas Edison, the scientist who invented light bulb, was himself afraid of the dark.

165. Parthenogenesis is the process of reproduction without having sex. Turkeys have this ability to reproduce without having sex.

166. Virginia Woolf, the renowned writer wrote all her books standing.

167. Walt Disney got the name of his famous cartoon character Mickey Mouse after Mickey Rooney, whose mother he dated for some time.

168. Watching an hour-long soap opera burns more calories than watching a three-hour baseball game.

169 Wearing headphones for just an hour will increase the bacteria in your ear by 700 times.

170. Plague spread was brought on a merchant ship, which contained rats that were infected with the disease from Tana in the Crimea to Messina in Sicily in the year 1347. Earlier the Bubonic Plague, carried by fleas on the rats, attacked the lymphatic gland system and caused swelling. Pneumonic Plague attacked the lungs. The Black Death plague went through Sicily to Italy and then throughout Europe and England. The population dropped low by as much as 50%.

171. It takes five years to yield first consumable fruit after a coffee seed has been planted.

172. When a giraffe gives birth to its baby, it falls from six feet height and that too without being hurt. A giraffe is usually six feet high.

173. If a dead sparrow is immersed in liquid, it will make a sound like a crying baby.

174. It took about 200 years to recognise potatoes as a food, in Spain.

175. Many of us would have observed that when we put a seashell to our ear, we hear the sound of the waves. Actually, these are not sound of the waves but the echo of the blood pulsing in our own ear.

176. A child is born with 300 bones. The number of bones is reduced to 206 when he becomes an adult.

177. A stomach produces a new layer of mucus every two weeks or it will digest itself.

178. Chinese Emperor Shi Huang-Ti had built a network of 270 palaces. He had linked all these palaces by tunnels. He did so because

he was afraid of assassination. He used to sleep in a different palace each night.

179. In 213 B.C., the Chinese emperor Shi Huang-Ti ordered to destroy all of China's books. So, China has a very few collection of its earlier literature. Shi Huang-Ti did this because several writers used to criticise him.

It was only through the efforts of a few brave teachers and scholars that some of the earlier literature of China survived. It was after 150 years that the surviving books were brought from their hiding place.

180. The Sui, who ruled China briefly around 600 A.D., constructed the Grand Canal, a waterway 100 feet wide, lined with roads and trees and stretching for 1,000 miles. It took 25 years to complete the canal, at a terrible cost of human life. It is estimated that almost 5.5 million people were involved in the construction and out of these 2.5 million died due to the harshness of the working conditions.

181. We might think that the Canary Islands might have got its name from the Canary bird but in reality the name was derived from the wild dogs that the Romans found when they landed there. They called the island 'Insulae Canariae', which means 'Island of the Dogs'.

182. 'Idaho' is one of the states in the United States of America. Unfortunately, the name doesn't mean anything in any language.

183. William Shakespeare by writing plays used to earn an average annual income of less than £20. That means he used to get approximately about £8 per play.

184 Agatha Christie wrote in total 78 mystery novels that have sold an estimated two billion copies.

185. The Guinness Book of World Records in 1974 had set a record of itself by becom-

ing the fastest-selling book in the world.

186. After Julius Caesar won over Pompey, he gave a banquet at which 150,000 guests were seated at 22,000 tables. He also declared a rent-free year for every poor family in his Empire.

187. Prince Henry the Navigator never navigated the seas on exploring expeditions. Henry was given this title because he ran an exploration institute at Sagres, Portugal, where astronomers, geographers, admirals and shipbuilders pooled their expertise for voyages along the African coast that culminated, long after Henry's death, when Vasco de Gama rounded the Cape of Good Hope and went on to reach India, in 1497.

188. Christopher Columbus' first transatlantic voyage was accomplished at a speed of about 2.8 miles per hour.

189. In the era of Hammurabi, King of Babylonia, the penalty for medical malpractice was to cut off the doctor's hands.

190. It is against law to eat ice cream on Bank Street in Ottawa, Ontario, Canada, on a Sunday.

191. India is the only country, which has *a bill of rights* for cows.

192. Currently around 5,000 languages are spoken in the world.

193. Japan has the shortest national anthem, which is only four lines long. Greece has the longest national anthem, which is 158 verses long.

194. Singapore is the largest country in the world, which has no farms. And the world's three smallest countries, which are without farms are Vatican City, Monaco and Nauru.

195. Indonesia comprises of more than 17,000 islands.

196. Albert Einstein might have said some relevant words at his deathbed but those words will never be known because he spoke them in German and the attending nurse didn't know Ger-

man and so she couldn't recall what he had said.

197. There is an interesting story about Sir Francis Bacon, one of the most influential minds of the 16th century. In 1625, while watching a snowstorm, he was struck by the notion that snow could be used to preserve meat. To prove his notion, he purchased a chicken, killed it and then, standing outside in the snow, attempted to stuff the chicken full of snow to freeze it. The chicken never froze, but Bacon caught a cold that turned into pneumonia and died a few weeks later.

198. There are more than 34,000 species of spiders and all are technically venomous. Only 20-30, however, poses a danger to humans and it's usually only the female who causes serious harm. Of the 2,700 species of snakes worldwide, only about 500 are venomous. Venomous animals are immune to their own venom. If two rattlesnakes of the same species fight, the venom they inject will harm neither. Rattlesnakes do not always rattle before they strike. Baby rattlesnakes can be particularly dangerous because they have not shed their skin enough to develop a warning rattle. An adult rattlesnake can rattle at a rate of 50 times per second.

They produce venom before they are one full day old. In the U.S., venomous snakes bite about 8,000 people each year. Most recorded bites are from the Western diamondback rattlesnake.

The taipan of Australia is considered the most dangerous venomous snake in the world. Australia is the only continent where venomous snake species outnumber the non-venomous ones.

Most venomous snakes replace their fangs every few weeks. Fangs wear out quickly, so up to six replacements are continually growing in each jaw.

A cobra can make itself appear larger by erecting a set of extra-long ribs into a 'hood', thereby warding off enemies. Wearing boots that cover the ankle could prevent Sixty percent of all snakebites.

199. Aishwarya's first ever commercial was for Camlin pencils while in 9th grade. Aishwarya Rai's pet name at home is 'Gullu'. In his youth, actor Dharmendra was such a big fan of actress Suraiya that he walked miles to watch her film Dillagi, over 40 times. Sushmita

Sen keeps a python as a pet. Many years ago, Mahesh Bhatt and daughter Pooja Bhatt had created a sensation by posing for a picture, kissing lip to lip. Pooja was in her teens then. When Mithun and Sridevi were involved, Mithun had given Sri a pet name. He used to call her Pepsi. This was before the soft drink came to India. Actor Amjad Khan was almost denied from Sholay because scriptwriter Javed Akhtar found his voice weak for Gabbar Singh's role. Raveena Tandon had adopted two girls from an orphanage a few years ago. The girls live with her and are, at present, schooling. Aamir Khan was supposed to play the role of Max in Josh, which was being played by Shahrukh. In the early stages of her career, Karisma Kapoor was mortally terrified of photo-sessions. Bikram Saluja is a tennis Champion. While shooting for the underwater scene in Kaho Na Pyar Hai, Hrithik Roshan's foot got stuck in a rocky crevice and he nearly drowned. Shamita Shetty is deeply into Sports and Body training and she also holds a Diploma in Fashion Designing. Akshay Kumar is superstitious. He will never write anything on a page unless he first heads it with an 'Om'. Amitabh is a great fan of Brazilian soccer players; his favourite however is Rudd Gullit. Vibrant Talent Manoj Bajpai of the 'Bhiku Mhatre' fame failed several screen tests before finally getting into filmdom. Salman Khan likes to collect soaps; in his bathroom, there is a collection of all kinds of handmade and herbal soaps; his favourite are soaps made from natural fruit and vegetable extracts. Salman's pet name at home is 'Sallu'. Hrithik Roshan loves collecting photographs; he would never travel anywhere without his personal camera even as a child. He has a vast collection photographs and special scrapbooks marking each occasion.

200. The first star on the Walk of Fame, located on Hollywood Boulevard and Highland, was dedicated to actress Joanne Woodward on February 9, 1960.

The 'gateway' to Hollywood Boulevard at LaBrea features a 30-ft.

high stainless steel gazebo designed by movie industry production designer, Catherine Hardwicke. The four actresses that elegantly adorn this gateway are Dolores del Rio, Anna May Wong, Mae West and Dorothy Dandridge. The Hollywood Sign, a symbol of the excitement and heartbreak of the movie industry, originally read 'Hollywoodland'. Constructed to attract attention to the home sites over looking the business area of Hollywood, one of the builders put up the $21,000 sign with 50 feet high letters. It took 4000 20-watt light bulbs to illuminate the sign.

The Chinese Theatre, constructed in 1927, is the third most visited tourist attraction in Los Angeles and the most famous movie theatre in the world.

The legendary footprints in the forecourt of the Chinese Theatre began as a silent screen star, Norma Talmadge, visited the newly built theatre and accidentally stepped into a sidewalk of wet cement. Only about 25% of the best-known living actors reside on the streets covered in the 'Maps to the Stars' Homes'. Celebrities reside all over the greater Los Angeles Area. Founded in 1888 by Harvey Henderson Wilcox and his wife Daeida, Hollywood was named after a summer home in Chicago. In the year 1909, the population of Hollywood reached 4,000, while today it registers around 280,000. Angelina Jolie has a tatoo on her stomach that spells out the Latin words meaning 'What Nourishes Me Also Destroys Me'. Actress Demi Moore is totally blind in her left eye after undergoing an operation to correct a squint when she was a child. Denise Richards' first kiss was with a boy who had his front teeth taken out the day before. Musician Eric Clapton grew up thinking his mum was his sister. Singer Mick Jagger was once a porter at a mental hospital.

201. Hairs in the nose help to clean the air we breathe as well as warming it. The highest recorded 'sneeze speed' is 165 km per hour. At rest, the body takes in and breathes out about 10 litres of air each minute. A person at rest usually breathes between 12 and 15 times a minute. The breathing rate is faster in children and women than in men.

The right lung is slightly larger than the left. The surface area of the lungs is roughly the same size as a tennis court. The capillaries in the lungs would extend 1,600 kilometres if placed end to end.

We lose half a litre of water a day through breathing. This is the water vapour we see when we breathe onto glass.

202. 1.7 litres of saliva is produced each day. We eat about 500kg of food per year. An adult's stomach can hold approximately 1.5 litres of material. The oesophagus is approximately 25cm long. Muscles contract in waves to move the food down the oesophagus. This means that food would get to a person's stomach, even if they were standing on their head. Every day 11.5 litres of digested food, liquids and digestive juices flow through the digestive system, but only 100mls is lost in faeces.

203. The skin secretes antibacterial substances. These substances explain why you don't wake up in the morning with a layer of mold growing on your skin - most bacteria and spores that land on the skin die quickly. Tears and mucus contain an enzyme (lysozyme) that breaks down the cell wall of many bacteria.

Lymph nodes contain filtering tissue and a large number of lymph cells. When fighting certain bacterial infections, the lymph nodes swell with bacteria and the cells fighting the bacteria, to the point where you can actually feel them. Swollen lymph nodes are therefore a good indication that you have an infection of some sort.

204. If Marco Polo had not been captured by the Genoese and imprisoned for a year, the tales of his historic twenty-two-year adventure

in the Far and Middle East (at the end of the thirteenth century) might never have been collected and written down. When he returned to Venice after his odyssey, he became a 'gentleman commander' of a war vessel striving to hold of Genoese traders. In a battle of Curzold Island, his galley was captured and Marco was hauled off to Genoa and gaoled. There he met a writer named Rustichello, who, after hearing Marco's yarns, insisted that they be written down.

205. Unlike other body cells, brain cells cannot regenerate. Once brain cells are damaged they are not replaced. The brain and spinal cord are surrounded and protected by cerebrospinal fluid.

206. There are about 60 muscles in the face. Smiling takes 20 muscles to smile and over 40 to frown. The longest muscle in the body is the sartorius, from the outside of the hip, down and across to the inside of the knee. It twists and pulls the thigh outwards. The smallest muscle in the body is the stapedius, deep in the ear. It is only 5mm long and thinner than cotton thread. It is involved in hearing.

The biggest muscle in the body is the gluteus maximus, in the buttock. It pulls the leg backwards powerfully for walking and running.

207. The heart beats around 3 billion times in the average person's life span.

About 8 million blood cells die in the human body every second and the same number are born each second. Within a tiny droplet of blood, there are some 5 million red blood cells, 300 000 platelets and 10 000 white cells. It takes about 20 seconds for a red blood cell to circle the whole body. Red blood cells make approximately 250,000 round trips of the body before returning to the bone marrow, where they were born, to die. Red blood cells may live for about 4 months circulating throughout the body, feeding the 60 trillion other body cells.

208. The record for the longest period without sleep is 18 days, 21 hours, 40 minutes during a rocking chair marathon. The record holder reported hallucinations, paranoia, blurred vision, slurred speech and memory and concentration lapses. It's impossible to tell

whether someone is really awake without close medical supervision. People can take catnaps with their eyes open without even being aware of it.

Dreams, once thought to occur only during REM (rapid eye movement) sleep, also occur (but to a lesser extent) in non-REM sleep phases. It's possible there may not be a single moment of our sleep when we are actually dreamless.

REM dreams are characterised by bizarre plots, but non-REM dreams are repetitive and thought-like, with little imagery - obsessively returning to a suspicion you left your mobile phone somewhere, for example.

Certain types of eye movements during REM sleep correspond to specific movements in dreams, suggesting at least part of the dreaming process is analogous to watching a film

Elephants sleep standing up during non-REM sleep, but lie down for REM sleep.

Some scientists believe we dream to fix experiences in long-term memory that is, we dream about things worth remembering. Others reckon we dream about things worth forgetting - to eliminate overlapping memories that would otherwise clog up our brains.

Dreams may not serve any purpose at all but be merely a meaningless byproduct of two evolutionary adaptations - sleep and consciousness.

REM sleep may help developing brains mature. Premature babies have 75 per cent REM sleep, 10 per cent more than full-term bubs. Similarly, a newborn kitten puppy rat or hampster experiences only REM sleep, while a newborn guinea pig (which is much more developed at birth) has almost no REM sleep at all.

Scientists have not been able to explain a 1998 study showing a bright light shone on the backs of human knees can reset the brain's sleep-wake clock.

British Ministry of Defence researchers have been able to reset soldiers' body clocks so they can go without sleep for up to 36 hrs. Tiny optical fibres embedded in special spectacles project a ring of bright white light (with a spectrum identical to a sunrise) around the edge of soldiers' retinas, fooling them into thinking they have just woken up. The system was first used on US pilots during the bombing of Kosovo.

In insomnia following bereavement, sleeping pills can disrupt grieving. Tiny luminous rays from a digital alarm clock can be enough to disrupt the sleep cycle even if you do not fully wake. The light turns off a 'neural switch' in the brain, causing levels of a key sleep chemical to decline within minutes.

Body temperature and the brain's sleep-wake cycle are closely linked. That's why hot summer nights can cause a restless sleep. The blood flow mechanism that transfers core body heat to the skin works best between 18 and 30 degrees. But later in life, the comfort zone shrinks to between 23 and 25 degrees - one reason why older people have more sleep disorders.

A night on the grog will help you get to sleep but it will be a light slumber and you won't dream much. After five nights of partial sleep deprivation, three drinks will have the same effect on your body as six would when you've slept enough.

Humans sleep on average around three hours less than other primates like chimps, rhesus monkeys, squirrel monkeys and baboons, all of whom sleep for 10 hours. Ducks at risk of attack by predators are able to balance the need for sleep and survival, keeping one half of the brain awake while the other slips into sleep mode.

Ten per cent of snorers have sleep apnoea; a disorder, which causes sufferers to stop breathing up to 300 times a night and significantly, increases the risk of suffering a heart attack or stroke.

Teenagers need as much sleep as small children (about 10 hrs) while those over 65 needs the least of all (about six hours). For the average adult aged 25-55, eight hours is considered optimal.

209. In the summer, a single beehive has

- 1 queen
- 250 drones
- 20,000 female foragers
- 40,000 female house-bees
- 5,000 to 7,000 eggs
- 7,000 to 11,000 larvae being fed

• 16,000 to 24,000 larvae developing into adults in sealed cells

The average worker bee makes 1 1/2 teaspoons of honey in her lifetime.

Bees are fully grown when they are born. For centuries, bees have been used to guard valuables. In India bandits used the large Asian honeybee Apis Dorsata to guard loot near mountain caves. Without bees, about one-third of the food we eat would not be available!

Bees maintain a temperature of 92-93 degrees Fahrenheit in their central brood nest regardless of whether the outside temperature is 110 or -40 degrees.

When a bee stings, it dies.

210. There was no grass during the time of the dinosaurs. Grass evolved from bamboo-like plants only 24 million years ago.

211. On August 8, 1969, novelist Jerzy Kosinski was flying to Los Angeles from Paris, with a short stopover in New York. His entire luggage was accidentally unloaded in New York and he had to get

off the plane to go through customs. That night because of the luggage mix-up, he missed his visit with the actress Sharon Tate and other friends and thus was absent when Charles Manson and his disciples paid their murderous visit to the Tate house. Kosinski later wrote about this close call in the novel *Blind Date*.

212. Chimpanzee DNA and human DNA is about 98.4% identical.

213. A healthy person farts 16 times a day on the average. Many animals Cats, dogs and cows fart too. Elephants fart the most. People fart the most in their sleep. Farts that contain a large amount of methane and hydrogen can be flammable.

214. The fastest restaurant in the world serves the client's food within 13 seconds after the order is made (in tables of 4.) The name of the restaurant is Karne Garibaldi and it is located in Guadalajara, Mexico.

215. Napoleon took 14,000 French decrees and simplified them into a unified set of 7 laws. This was the first time in modern history

that a nation's laws applied equally to all citizens. Napoleon's 7 laws are so impressive that by 1960 more than 70 governments had patterned their own laws after them or used them verbatim.

216. Of the 262 men who have held the title of pope, 33 have died by violence.

217. The United States dropped atom bomb on August sixth, 1945,

during World War Two, on Hiroshima, Japan, killing an estimated 140,000 people.

218. Cheng Ho, court eunuch and great admiral of the Ming Dynasty, led Chinese fleets on seven voyages of conquest and diplomacy, between 1405 and 1433. As a result of Cheng Ho's voyages, which ranged as far as West Africa, 36 countries sent tribute to China. However, in 1433, the eunuchs' opponents gained the upper hand in a power struggle in the Chinese court and the fleets stopped, shipyards were dismantled and outbound shipping was forbidden. Had these voyages continued, it is possible that the Chinese would have 'discovered' America before Columbus.

219. Seven of the eight US Presidents who have died in office, either through illness or assassination, were elected at precisely 20-year intervals.

220. The 'Spruce Goose', built by Howard Hughes, is the largest aircraft ever built. It has a wingspan of 320 feet, 140-ton eight-engine seaplane, made of birch. It was built as a prototype troop trans-

port. Rejected by the Pentagon, Hughes put the plane into storage, never to be flown again.

221. The ancient Egyptians slept on pillows made of stone.

222. The first country to abolish capital punishment was Austria in 1787.

223. The first-known contraceptive was crocodile dung. It was used by Egyptians in 2000 BC.

224. The Hundred-Year War actually lasted 116 years (1337 to 1453).

225. The longest reigning monarch in history was Pepi II, who ruled Egypt for 90 years; 2566 to 2476 BC. The second longest was France's Louis XIV, who ruled for 72 years, 1643 to 1715.

226. The name of the first airplane flown at Kitty Hawk by the Wright Brothers, on December 17, 1903, was Bird of Prey.

227. The shortest war on record was fought between Zanzibar and England in 1896. Zanzibar surrendered after 38 minutes.

228. The Titanic was the first ship to use the SOS signal. It was adopted as the international signal for distress in 1912 and the Titanic struck the iceberg in April of that year.

229. The total number of Americans killed in the Civil War is greater than the combined total of Americans killed in all other wars.

230. The USSR set off the largest nuclear explosion in history, detonating a 50 megaton bomb (2600 times the Hiroshima bomb) in an atmospheric test over the Novaya Zemla Islands, October 30 1961.

231. The very first bomb dropped by the Allies on Berlin during World War II killed the only elephant in the Berlin Zoo.

232. The White House, in Washington DC, was originally *gray*.

It was the colour of the sandstone of which it was built of. After the War of 1812, during which it had been burned by Canadian troops, the outside walls were painted white to hide the smoke stains.

233. The worldwide 'Spanish Flu' epidemic, which broke out in 1918, killed more than 30 million people in less than a year's time.

234. Until 1965, driving was done on the left-hand side on roads in Sweden. The conversion to right-hand was done on a weekday at 5 p.m. All traffic stopped as people switched sides.

235. Yellowstone is the world's 1st national park. It was dedicated in 1872.

236. A foetus acquires fingerprints at the age of three months.

237. A fingernail or toenail takes about 6 months to grow from base to tip.

238. A human being loses an average of 40 to 100 strands of hair a day.

239. A person will die from total lack of sleep sooner than from starvation. Death will occur about 10 days without sleep, while starvation takes a few weeks.

240. After spending hours working at a computer display, look at a blank piece of white paper. It will probably appear pink.

241. Beards are the fastest growing hairs on the human body. If the average man never trimmed his beard, it would grow to nearly 30 feet long in his lifetime.

Blondes have more hair than dark-haired people.

242. By age sixty, most people have lost half of their taste buds.

243. Each square inch of human skin consists of twenty feet of blood vessels.

Every human spent about half an hour as a single cell.

244. Every person has a unique tongue print.

245. Every square inch of the human body has an average of 32 million bacteria on it. Humans shed about 600,000 particles of skin every hour - about 1.5 pounds a year. By 70 years of age, an average person will have lost 105 pounds of skin. Humans shed and re-grow outer skin cells about every 27 days - almost 1,000 new skins in a lifetime.

246. If you are locked in a completely sealed room, you will die of carbon dioxide poisoning first before you will die of oxygen deprivation.

247. In the late 19th century, millions of human mummies were used as fuel for locomotives in Egypt where wood and coal was scarce, but mummies were plentiful.

248. Jaw muscles can provide about 200 pounds of force to bring the back teeth together for chewing.

249. Laughing lowers levels of stress hormones and strengthens the im-

mune system. Six-year-olds laugh an average of 300 times a day. Adults only laugh 15 to 100 times a day.

250. The average human body contains enough iron to make a 3 inch nail, sulphur to kill all fleas on an average dog, carbon to make 900 pencils, potassium to fire a toy cannon, fat to make 7 bars of soap, phosphorous to make 2,200 match heads and water to fill a ten-gallon tank. The human body has enough fat to produce 7 bars of soap.

251. The average human produces 25,000 quarts of spit in a lifetime, enough to fill two swimming pools.

252. The average person releases nearly a pint of intestinal gas by flatulence every day. Most is due to swallowed air. The rest is from fermentation of undigested food. The body's largest internal organ is the small intestine at an average length of 20 feet. The feet account for one quarter of all the human bodies bones.

253. The human brain is about 85% water.

254. The largest cell in the human body is the female reproductive cell, the ovum or egg cell. It is about 1/180 inch in diametre. The smallest cell in the human body is the male sperm. It takes about 175,000 sperm cells to weigh as much as a single egg cell.

255. The largest human organ is the skin, with a surface area of about 25 square feet.

256. The most common blood type in the world is Type O. The rarest, Type A-H, has been found in less than a dozen people since the type was discovered.

257. The only bone in the human body not connected to another is the hyoid, a V-shaped bone located at the base of the tongue between the mandible and the voice box. Its function is to support the tongue and its muscles.

The permanent teeth that erupt to replace their primary predecessors (baby teeth) are called succedaneous teeth.

258. There are 45 miles of nerves in the skin of a human being.

259. Three-hundred-million cells die in the human body every minute.

260. Women burn fat more slowly than men, by a rate of about 50

calories a day.

Women's hearts beat faster than men's.

261. Approximately 2,300 children are reported missing each day.

262. Sweat glands can produce up to three gallons of sweat each day.

263. One in ten Americans have spent at least one night in jail.

264. An ostrich's eye is bigger then its brain.

265. Peanuts are one of the ingredients in dynamite.

266. In England, the Speaker of the House is not allowed to speak.

267. Humming Birds cannot walk.

268. A rat can last longer without water than a camel.

269. There are more nutrients in the cornflake package itself than there are in the actual cornflakes.

270. Earth is the only planet not named after a god.

271. Snails can sleep for three years without eating.

272. Acupuncture was first used as a medical treatment in 2700 BC by Chinese emperor Shen-Nung.

273. At the height of its power, in 400 BC, the Greek city of Sparta had 25,000 citizens and 500,000 slaves.

274. Britain's present royal family was originally named Saxe-Coburg and Goth. The name was changed in 1917, during WW1 because of German connotations. The name Windsor was suggested by one of the staff. At the same time, the Battenberg family name of the cousins to the Windsors was changed into Mountbatten.

275. Captain Cook lost 41 of his 98 crew to scurvy (a lack of vitamin C) on his first voyage to the South Pacific in 1768. By 1795, the importance of eating citrus was realised and lemon juice was issued on all British Navy ships.

276. Fourteenth century physicians didn't know what caused the plague, but they knew it was contagious. As a result they wore an early kind of bio-protective suit, which included a large beaked headpiece. The beak of the headpiece, which made them look like large birds, was filled with vinegar, sweet oils and other strong smelling compounds to counteract the stench of the dead and dying plague victims.

277. From the Middle Ages up until the end of the 19th century, barbers performed a number of medical duties including bloodletting, wound treatment, dentistry, minor operations and bone setting. The barber's striped red pole originated in the Middle Ages, when it was a staff the patient would grip while the barber bled the patient.

278. A typical lightning bolt is two to four inches wide and two miles long.

279. If the sun stopped shining suddenly, it would take eight minutes for people on earth to be aware of the fact.

280. More than 99.9% of all the animal species that have ever lived on earth were extinct before the coming of man.

281. Nearly 50% of all bank robberies take place on Friday.

282. The base of the Great Pyramid of Egypt is large enough to cover 10 football fields.

283. The greatest snowfall ever in a single storm was 189 inches at the Mount Shasta Ski Bowl in February 1959.

284. The Gregorian calendar was introduced by Pope Gregory in 1582 AD and was adopted by Great Britain and the English colonies in 1752.

285. The linen bandages that were used to wrap Egyptian mummies averaged 1,000 yards in length.

286. The lowest temperature ever recorded in the world was 129 degrees below 0° at Vostok, Antarctica, on July 21, 1983.

287. Though it goes to 10, 9 is estimated to be the point of total tectonic destruction from an earthquake (2 is the smallest that can be felt unaided.)

288. Polar bears don't drink water

289. Apparently Shakespeare (or Bacon), at the age of 46, was head of a group of 46 people who created the Authorised version of the Bible. By a little manipulation of the word order, Shakespeare managed to get his name in the book!

290. Americans and Europeans spend $17 billion a year on pet food — $4 billion more than the estimated annual additional total needed to provide basic and nutrition for everyone in the world.

291. On average, 100 people choke to death on ballpoint pens every year.

292. On average people fear spiders more than they do death.

293. Only one person in two billion will live to be 116 or older.

294. It's possible to lead a cow upstairs...but not downstairs.

295. Over 2500 left handed people a year are killed from using products made for right-handed people

296. Bulls are colour-blind, therefore will usually charge at a matador's waving cape no matter what colour it is — be it red or neon yellow.

297. Apples are more efficient than caffeine in keeping people awake in the mornings

298. Men are 6 times more likely to be struck by lightning than women

299. In Bangladesh, kids as young as 15 can be jailed for cheating on their finals.

300. The two-foot long bird called a Kea that lives in New Zealand likes to eat the strips of rubber around car windows.

301. It is estimated that squirrels that bury nuts and then forget where they hid them accidentally plant millions of trees in the world

302. Louis XIV owned 413 beds

303. By the time the king of Siam died in 1910, he had fathered 370 children.

304. One in ten children sleepwalk.

305. If you're an average sleeper, you'll roll over 12 times in bed tonight.

306. According to research the three things pregnant women dream about most during their first trimester are 1) frogs 2) worms 3) potted plants.

307. On average 13% of the letters in writing are the letter 'e'.

308. It takes 720 peanuts to make a pound of peanut butter.

309. The Earth is turning in to desert at a rate of 40 square miles per day.

310. It costs more to buy a new car today in the United States than it cost Christopher Columbus to equip and undertake three voyages to and from the New World.

311. One-fourth of the world's population lives on less than $200 a year. Ninety million people survive on less than $75 a year.

312. The word race-car and kayak are the same whether they are read left to right or right to left.

313. More people are killed by donkeys annually than are killed in plane crashes.

314. According to tests made at the Institute for the Study of Animal Problems in Washington, D.C., dogs and cats, like people, are either right-handed or left-handed — that is, they favour either their right or left paws.

315. A giraffe can go without water longer than a camel can.

316. Mosquitoes are attracted to the colour blue twice as much as to any other colour.

317. If one places a tiny amount of liquor on a scorpion, it will instantly go mad and sting itself to death.

318. Every night, wasps bite into the stem of a plant, lock their mandibles (jaws) into position, stretch out at right angles to the stem and, with legs dangling, fall asleep.

319. Los Angeles's full name is 'El Pueblo de Nuestra Senora la Reina de los Angeles de Porciuncula' and can be abbreviated to 3.63% of its size, 'L.A'.

320. Alfred Hitchcock didn't have a belly button. It was eliminated when he was sewn up after surgery.

321. The Mongol emperor Genghis Khan's original name was Temujin.

322. No two lions have the same pattern of whiskers.

323. Grapes explode when you put them in the microwave.

324. 111,111,111 x 111,111,111 = 12,345,678,987,654,321. See the

increasing pattern of numeral in the product. The peak number is 9, which is same as the number of digits of one of the multiplicands.

325. The giant squid has the largest eyes in the world.

326. St. Paul, Minnesota was originally called Pigs Eye after a man who ran a saloon there.

327. When a female horse and male donkey mate, the offspring is called a mule, but when a male horse and female donkey mate, the offspring is called a hinny.

The way to get more mules is to mate a male donkey with a female horse.

A donkey will sink in quicksand but a mule won't.

328. Stalin was only five feet, four inches tall. Stalin's left foot had webbed toes and his left arm is noticeably shorter than his right.

329. Tomb robbers believed that knocking Egyptian sarcophagi's noses off would and therefore forestall curses.

330. Medieval knights put sharkskin on their sword handles to give them a more secure grip; they would dig the sharp scales into their palms.

331. Jellyfish have no brains, yet they can tell light from dark and sense movement.

332. The term 'flying on cloud 9' originates from military flights. Cloud types are classified as numbers... with 'cloud 9' being a very tall thunderstorm. Jets have to climb to an extremely high altitude in order to fly over 'cloud 9.

333. Dentists have recommended that a toothbrush be kept at least 6 feet away from a toilet to avoid airborne particles resulting from the flush.

334. Oak trees do not produce acorns until they are fifty years of age or older.

335. The first owner of the Marlboro Company died of lung cancer. So did the first 'Marlboro Man'.

336. Michael Jordan makes more money from Nike annually than all of the Nike factory workers in Malaysia combined.

337. A cough releases an explosive charge of air that moves at speeds up to 60 mph.

338. The Bible does not say there were three wise men; it only says there were three gifts.

339. If a statue in the park of a person on a horse has both front legs in the air, the person died in battle. If the horse has one front leg in the air the person died as a result of wounds received in battle. If the horse has all four legs on the ground, the person died of natural causes.

340. Dolphins sleep with one eye open!

341. The world's oldest piece of chewing gum is over 9000 years old!

342. In space, astronauts cannot cry properly because there is no gravity, so the tears can't flow down their faces!

343. About 3000 years ago, most Egyptians died by the time they were 30!

344. More people use blue toothbrushes, than red ones!

345. A sneeze travels out your mouth at over 100 m.p.h.!

346. Your ribs move about 5 million times a year, every time you breathe!

347. In the White House, there are 13,092 knives, forks and spoons!

348. Slugs have 4 noses!

349. Recycling one glass jar saves enough energy to watch T.V for 3 hours!

350. Lightning strikes about 6,000 times per minute on this planet.

351. The average American/Canadian drinks about 600 sodas a year!

352. It was once against the law to slam your car door in a city in Switzerland!

353. Humans blink over 10,000,000 times a year!

354. In the year 2000, Pope John Paul II was named a 'Honorary Harlem Globetrotter'.

355. Every second, Americans collectively eat one hundred pounds of chocolate.

356. The fear of vegetables is called Lachanophobia!

357. There are approximately fifty Bibles sold each minute across the world!

358. Every year, kids in North America spend close to half a billion dollars on chewing gum!

359. An earthquake on Dec. 16, 1811 caused parts of the Mississippi River to flow backwards!

360. Honolulu is the only place in the United States that has a royal palace!

361. One gallon of used motor oil can ruin approximately one million gallons of fresh water!

362. More money is spent on gardening than on any other hobby!

363. Rice paper does not have any rice in it!

364. In England, in the 1880's, 'Pants' was considered a dirty word!

365. The blesbok, a South African antelope, is almost the same colour as grape juice!

366. The average person laughs 13 times a day!

367. Ernest Vincent Wright wrote a novel, 'Gadsby', which contains over 50,000 words — none of them with the letter E!

368. The sun is 330,330 times larger than the earth!

369. It's Impossible to lick your eyebrow. 3 out of 4 people will try and lick their eyebrow

370. Ten years ago, it was estimated, there were around 65 million hives worldwide producing nearly 1 million tonnes of honey each year. In the UK, there are currently between 20,000 and 30,000 beekeepers producing approximately 2,000 tonnes of honey each year.

371. Elephant's teeth can weigh as much as nine pounds each?

372. If Zebra or a tiger were in your backyard, you would know it. However, if you were in their neighbourhood, you might miss them. Striped coats are hard to see in the light and dark shadows of forests and grasslands. This helps to keep them safe from predators and help tiger to get its prey easily.

373. The vibration of shell-like rings on the end of its tail makes the rattling sound. The rattle is made up of dry, hard pieces of unshed

skin. As the snake grows, the number of rings increases. So the louder the rattle, bigger the snake. The snake will shake its rattle to fright away the intruder.

374. When it rains, the frog absorbs water through its skin. Then it burrows into the sand, where it can stay for over two years until the next rainfall. Frogs have strong back legs for jumping. The biggest frog in the world, the Goliath frog, is also the best high jumper. It can leap 3 metres into the air. In America, competitions are held to find the best long-jumping frogs. The fire-bellied toad turns on its back when it is alarmed to display its bright belly. This sudden show of colour is often enough to startle its enemy. It is also a warning that the toad's skin is poisonous. Some South American frogs have poison in their skin, although the poison is not always deadly. They are known as arrow-poison frogs because Indian hunters use the poison to tip their arrows.

375. Several animals that live in the far north, like stoat, become white in the winter to blend in with the snow. They moult and grow a thicker coat. Some Arctic birds change colour and grow white feathers.

376. Kangaroos hop across the grassy plains of Australia at high speed. They cruise at 40 kmph. and reach 60 kmph. for short bursts, using their long tail to help them balance. One red kangaroo made a record breaking long-jump of almost 13 metres.

377. The tuatara is just like a reptile that lived millions of years ago, even before the dinosaurs. Today it only lives in New Zealand, where it often shares a petrel's burrow. In the day, the tuatara may

even be left with a baby chick while the mother hunts for food.

378. Pronghorn antelopes live on the open plains of the Western United States. Their lungs and heart are large which enables them to run at a fast, steady speed for long distance. They can keep going at 56 kmph for 6 kilometres.

379. The stickleback is one of the few fishes that builds a nest. The male, in his red breeding colours, makes a nest of weeds where the female lays her eggs. Then the male stays by the nest to guard the eggs until they hatch.

380. Beavers build their home or lodge, with wood and mud in lakes and rivers. They cut down trees by gnawing their trunks with their teeth. First the beavers cut the trees into pieces. Then they drag or roll them into the water and build a dam to make a deep pool. They build their lodge in the pool, using sticks and mud. It has entrance underwater and twigs and bark are stored nearby for food.

381. Pumas are very agile. They bound from rock to rock, pounce on their prey and spring up into trees. They can cover 18 metres in a single leap. Most Pumas now live in the western part of America.

382. Scrub hen uses the heat from volcanoes to keep its eggs warm. It buries its eggs in the side of a volcano on the pacific island where it lives.

383. Many caribou live in Arctic Canada. In winter, the ground is covered in ice so the caribou move south in search of moss and lichen to feed on. They return to the north in the spring.

384. A column of army ants may consist of 150,000 insects and take several hours to march past one spot. They prey on almost any animal that cannot escape from them.

385. The Beaded lizard and the Gila lizard are the only two poisonous lizards in the world. They wander over the prairies and deserts of North America. The Gila monster is one of the two poisonous lizards in the world. When it bites its prey, such as mice and rabbits, it squirts poison down through grooves in its teeth.

386. When the puss moth caterpillar is disturbed, it lifts up its red face and two long red 'whips' flick out of its tail. It also produces a smelly fluid, which it can even spray at its attacker.

387. The cheetah races across the grassy plains of Africa at 100 km/hr, maybe more, arching and stretching its body to run faster. It is the fastest runner in the world, but it can only stay at top speed for a few hundred metres.

388. The Egyptian Plovers pick off tiny animals that live on the crocodile's body. They can even climb into its mouth without being harmed.

389. Dragonflies are fast-flying insects, especially the darter dragonflies, which are named after the way, they dart about.

390. Bumblebees live high up in the mountains in Europe, where they feed on the pollen and nectar of the flowers that grow there. Some insects even fly over the snowy peaks of the Himalayas as they migrate.

391. Ants carry the caterpillars of the large blue butterfly into their nest. There, the ants feed on the sweet honeydew produced by the caterpillars, which in return feed on the tiny ant larvae.

392. Some monarch butterflies fly from Canada to Mexico, where they mass together on trees to hibernate for the winter.

393. The African ostrich makes up for not being able to fly by running faster than any other bird. Its strong thighs and long legs enable it to run at 50 km/hr for as long as half an hour and it can reach 70 km/hr for a short burst. When danger threatens, it makes itself look as large and fierce as possible, by fluffing out its feathers, spreading its wings and opening its eyes wide.

394. The giant panda lives only in bamboo forest in a remote, mountainous corner of China. It spends most of the day on the ground, feeding on bamboo, but it can climb trees. In winter, it shelters from the snow in caves and hollow trees.

395. The crested porcupine, which lives in Africa and parts of Europe, has often been hunted for its tasty meat. Now it is becoming rare. When the Porcupine meets an enemy it turns its back towards its foe and rattles its long black and white spines.

396. The Sumatran rhinoceros is smaller than other rhino and has two horns. Only about 150 remain, but even these are in serious danger from hunters.

397. Locusts fly in huge swarms to find food. They may travel 5,000 kilometres, eating thousands of tonnes of green plants on the way. Desert locusts in Africa destroy vast areas of crops every year.

398. Scorpions use their poison for attack and defence. Some kinds of scorpion have a sting that is so powerful that can kill people.

399. A spider's web is not its home but a food trap. Orb webs, like this one, have sticky threads that trap the spider's insect prey. Some spider in tropical forests build huge orb webs nearly 6 metres across.

400. The Australian frilled lizard can frighten off an intruder by suddenly spreading out its huge neck frill. It opens its mouth wide, too, to look more fierce.

401. The chameleon snatches up its insect prey in a fraction of a second. It waits for an insect to land within range and then it shoots out its long tongue. The insect is caught on the sticky tip of the tongue.

402. A tiger's stripes help to break up the outline of its body and make it hard to see. They also look like shadows as the tiger stalks through long grass in the moonlight. Tigers live in Asia. Those that live in hot countries often sit in shallow water to keep cool. Tigers in very cold countries have thick shaggy coats to keep them warm.

403. Coconuts are plentiful on the pacific islands where the giant robber crabs live. The crabs feed on dead animals, but they also like eating coconut up a palm tree and then drop it to crack it open. They scoop out the flesh with a claw.

404. The North American harvester ants can give people a nasty sting. They live in deserts, where they build volcano-shaped nests in the sand. The ants feed on grass seeds.

405. The most poisonous spider of all is probably the American black widow. The female is more dangerous than the male. Its bite is extremely painful and sometimes causes death.

406. Pythons and boas are large snakes that feed on animals as big as goats and deer. The snake holds its prey in its mouth and then coils itself tightly round the animal so that it cannot breathe. The snake may take several hours to swallow its meal.

407. Emperor penguins spend much of their time in the waters of the Antarctic, but they move on to the ice to breed. They cannot fly so they have to jump up out of the water.

408. Most meat-eating animals only feed on freshly-killed prey and avoid animals that may have been dead for some time.

409. The common flea, a tiny wingless insect, can jump 20 centimetres into the air. This means it jumps more than 130 times it's own height. Flea jumps on to animals to feed on their blood.

410. A few animals, like the flying squirrel, have a flap of skin between their front and back legs, which help them, glide from tree to tree. The colugo has a bigger cloak of skin and it can glide twice as far-up to 100 metres.

411. Social weaverbirds live in Africa. In the breeding season, many

pairs come together to build their nests. They build one huge domed roof of grass and straw. Then each pair builds its own nest under the roof, each with its own entrance.

412. The prairie dog makes burrows, which is called Town. The town may contain 1,000 animals and it can stretch under the ground for miles.

413. In Australia, termites build towers 6 metres high and 30 metres wide. Ten tonnes of mud are collected bit by bit by millions of insects. Solider termite guard the mud castle, where the queen lays her eggs and is fed by worker termites.

414. Today only a few hundred snow leopards are left because human hunters have killed them all for their beautiful fur. Snow leopards live in the Himalayas, where they are now a protected species.

415. The rusty numbat is rare Australian mammal. Its other name is banded anteater, although its favourite food is termites. At night, it shelters in a hollow log. It is not clear why these animals are dying out. Perhaps they are eaten by foxes or perhaps they die in bush fires.

416. Huge footprints have been found in the snow of the Himalayas and some people claim to have seen a monster, half person, half monkey, but no-one has ever captured such creature. The most likely explanation is that the prints were made by the huge Moon bear.

417. In Japan, where macaque monkey live, the winters are very cold. The Japanese macaques have shaggy coats to keep them warm and some keep out the cold by sitting in the hot water from volcanic springs.

418. Crocodiles are the largest reptiles and the estuarine crocodile over 8 metres, is the largest of them all. It is also one of the most dangerous, since it often adds people to its diet of fish and animals.

419. The pygmy marmoset, the smallest monkey in the world,

whose body is only 10 centimetres long, lives in the forests along the Amazon River, in South America. Unlike other monkeys, marmosets have claws for gripping on to the bark as they climb trees. They curl their long tail round branches to help them balance. They eat insects and nuts.

420. The royal antelopes live in thick forests of West Africa. They are the smallest of the antelopes, only 25 or 30 centimetres high at the shoulder. They are agile, alert animals and will dart into the undergrowth at the slightest sound or smell of danger.

421. Camel can go for several days without food or water. They carry a supply of fat in their humps. A camel with a sagging hump is a hungry camel! They lose no water from their bodies. They do not sweat and their urine is solid crystal.

422. The yak (Bos grunniens) of Tibet and the Sichuanese Alps, China occasionally climbs to altitudes of 6100m 20000ft when foraging.

423. In terms of weight, the smallest marine mammal is probably Commerson's dolphin (Cephalorhynchus commersonii), also known as Le Jacobite, which is found off the tip of South America. The weights of group of six specimens ranged from 23 kg 51 lb to 35 kg 77 lb. The sea otter (Enhydra Lutris) of north Pacific is of comparable size (25-38.5 kg 55-81 lb), but this species sometimes comes ashore during storms.

424. The smallest land mammal in terms of length is Savi's White-toothed pygmy shrew, also called the Etruscan shrew (Suncus etruscus), which has a head and body length of 36-52 mm a tail length of 24-29 mm and weighs 1.5-2.5g. It is found along the Mediterranean coast and southwards to Cape Province, South Africa.

425. The European pygmy shrew (Sorex minutus) has a head and body length of 43-64 mm a tail length of 31-46 mm and weighs 2.4-6.1g.

426. The largest toothed mammal ever recorded is the sperm whale or cachalot (Physeter catodon). In the summer of 1950 a recorded sized bull measuring 20.7 m 67 ft 11 inch. was captured off the kurile islands in the Pacific, but much larger bulls were reported in the early days of whaling.

427. Stags are normally about 1.11m (3 ft 8") in tall at the shoulder weigh 104-113 kg. The heaviest ever recorded was a stag killed at Glenfiddich, Grampian in 1831, which weighed 238 kg. The heaviest park red deer on record was a stag weighing 215 kg (1.37m 4 ft 6 in tall at the shoulder), killed at Woburn, Beds in 1836. The so-called wild pony (Equus Caballus) may weigh up to 320 kg, but there are no truly feral populations living today.

428. The greatest number of young born to a wild mammal at a single birth is 31 (30 of which survived) in the case of tail-less tenrec (tenrec ecaudatus), found in Madagascar and the Comoro islands.

429. The tallest elephants are those of the endangered desert species from Damaraland, Namibia (reduced to 84 individuals in August 1981) because they have proportionately longer legs than other elephants.

430. The slowest growth rate in the Animal Kingdom is that of the deep-sea clam Tindaria callistisormis, which takes about 100 years to reach a length of 8-mm 1/3 inch. It is found in the North Atlantic.

431. Although many differences exist in the animal world between the male and female of any species, the most striking difference in size can be seen in the marine worm Bonellia viridis. The females of this species are 10-100 cm 4-40 inch. long compared with just 1-3 mm 0.04-0.12 inch for the male, thus also making the females millions of times heavier than males.

432. The most valuable animals in cash terms are thoroughbred race-horses. The most paid for yearling is $13.1 million.

433. The larva of the Polyphemus moth (Antheraea Polyphemus) of North America consumes an amount equal to 86000 times its own birth weight in the first 56 days of its life. In human terms, this would be equivalent to a 3-17 kg baby taking in 273 tonnes of nourishment.

434. During a 7 month lactation period, a 120-tonne female blue whale (Balaenoptera Musculus) can lose up to 25 percent of her body weight nursing her calf.

435. The low - frequency pulses made by Blue Whales when communicating with each other have been measured up to 188 decibels, making it the loudest sound emitted by any living source. They have been detected 850 km/ 530 miles away.

436. Experiments carried out with a Snodgrass gnathodynamometre (shark-bite metre) at the Lerner Marine Laboratory in Bimini, Bahamas revealed that a 2m 6 ft 6 ¾ in long dusky shark (Carcharhinus obscurus) could exert a force of 60 kg/132 lb between its jaws. This is equivalent to a pressure of 3-tonnes/ cm^2 or 19.6 tons/in^2 at the tips of the teeth.

437. The world's most dangerous animal (excluding man) are malarial parasites of the genus *plasmodium* carried by mosquitoes of the genus *anopheles*, which, if we exclude wars and accidents, have probably been responsible directly or indirectly for 50% of all human deaths since the Stone Age. Even today, despite major campaigns to eradicate malaria, at least 200 million people are ailing by the disease each year and more than one million babies and children die annually from it in Africa alone.

438. The most active known poison is the *batrachotoxin* derived from the skin secretions of the golden poison-dart frog (*phyllobates terribilis*), which was not discovered until 1973 in western Colombia. Its skin secretions are at least 20 times more toxic than those of any other known poison-dart frog (human handlers have to wear thick gloves) and an average specimen contains enough poison (1900 micrograms) to kill nearly 1500 people. Rather surprisingly, this species is preyed upon by the frog-eating snake (*leimadohis epinephelus*), which is obviously immune to its poison.

439. Jenny Wood-Allen from Dundee, Scotland, was 87 years old when

she completed the 1999 London Marathon with a time of 7 hrs 14 min. 46 sec. She has completed more than 30 marathons, raising over $44,600 for charity in the process. The World's oldest male marathon finisher was Dimitrion Yordanidis of Greece, who set the record aged 98 on October. 10, 1976, in Athens, Greece. His time was 7 hrs. 33 min.

440. Fu Mingxia (China) was 12 years. 141 days old when she won the women's world platform driving title at Perth, Western Australia, on January 4, 1991.

The youngest golfer to have achieved a hole-in-one is Matthew Draper (UK). He was 5 years, 212 days old when he set this record at the 122-yd, fourth Cherwell Edge Golf Club, Oxfordshire, England, on June 17, 1997.

441. Llewellyn Owen from King's Cross, London, England, also known as DJ Welly, headlined at the London club The Wrap on May 1, 2000, when he was 8 years, 70 days old. He was paid $180 per hour, the standard rate for headlining DJs. As of June 2000, he was scheduled to play a number of sites in both the UK and Paris, France.

442. On April 15, 2000. Supermarket chain Tesco announced that it had hired seven-year-old Laurie Sleator from Hertfordshire, England, to advise senior executives on the Pokemon craze currently sweeping the globe. Laurie receives Pokemon products in return for his services.

443. Dr. A. Koteswar Rao of Mare Haven Stud Farm Jind made a 5.24 km long, 2.75 cm wide chain from 51,618 empty cigarette packets of 53 different brands without using any glue. The multi-coloured chain which was started in 1992 with packets from all over the country has 4,12,944 links each measuring 3 cm in length, 0.937 cm in width. The chain is wound on a 3.33 ft diametre iron sheet spool, which is 2.75 ft wide.

444. The bag division of Sane Sportswear at Vadodara made a skybag 13.3 ft long, 4.16 ft wide and 8.75 ft tall. The brainchild of Thomas Verghese, it took eight people 105 hours to make the suitcase at a cost of Rs. 85,000. The bag was exhibited at the Vadodara Chamber of Commerce and Industry Fair at the Navlakha Palace grounds in January 1999.

445. The subway system with the most stations in the world is the Metropolitan Transportation Authority / New York City Transportation Authority subway (first section opened on October 27, 1904). The network covers 238 route miles, comprising 469 subway stations. In 1994, it served an average of 3.5 million passengers per day, plus an additional 3,611,000 in student population.

446. The 'Mona Lisa' by Leonardo da Vinci (1452-1519) in the Louvre, Paris, was assessed for insurance purposes at $100 million for its move to Washington, D.C. and New York City for exhibition from December 14, 1962 to March 12, 1963. However, insurance was not purchased because the cost of the closest security precautions was less than that of the premiums. It was painted c. 1503-07 and measures 30.5 by 20.9 inches.

447. The highest ever personal majority for any politician was 4,726,112 for Boris Yeltsin, the people's deputy candidate for Moscow, in the parliamentary elections held in the former Soviet Union on March 26, 1989. Yeltsin received 5,118,745 votes out of the 5,722,937 that were cast in the Moscow constituency, his closet rival obtaining 392,633 votes.

448. Benazir Bhutto achieved 98.48 percent of the votes in the Larkana-III constituency in the 1990 general elections in Pakistan, with 94,462 votes. The next-highest candidate obtained just 718 votes.

449. The world's largest radio telescope is the partially steerable iono-

spheric assembly built over the natural bowl at Arecibo, Puerto Rico, completed in November 1963. The reflector dish is 1,000 feet in diametre and covers 18 1/2 acres suspended 426 feet under a 600-ton triangular platform.

450. A Galapagos tortoise (Geochelone elephantopus) named Goliath, who has lived at the Life Fellowship Bird Sanctuary in Seffner, FL, since 1960, measures 53 5/8 inches long, 40 1/2 inches wide and 27 inches high and weighs 849 pounds.

451. India is the world's leading cattle farming nation in 1993, with an estimated 271.3 million head out of the worldwide total of 1.05 billion head.

452. The leading producer of milk in 1994 was United States, with 154 billion pounds. As of January 1, 1995, there were 103.3 million head of cattle farmed in the United States. The leading cattle producer was Texas, with 15.1 million head.

453. Fingernails grow at a rate of about 0.02 inches a week - four times faster than toenails. As of February 25, 1995, the aggregate measurement of Shridhar Chillal's fingernails (b. 1937, Pune, Maharashtra, India) was 226 inches for the five nails on his left hand (thumb 52 inches, index finger 40 inches, middle finger 43 inches, ring finger 46 inches and pinkie 45 inches). He last cut his nails in 1952.

454. Madge Bester (b. April 26, 1963) of Johannesburg, South Africa is

the 25½ inches tall. She suffers from Osteogenesis imperfecta, a disease characterised by brittle bones and skeletal deformities and she is confined to a wheelchair. Her mother, Winnie, is not much taller, measuring 27½ inches.

455. On June 17, 1984, identical twin sisters Mildred Widman Philippi and Mary Widman Franzini of St. Louis, celebrated their 104th birthday. Mildred died on May 4, 1985, 44 days short of the twins' 105th birthday.

456. The longest wooden ship ever constructed was the 115 m 377 ft 4 in Rochambeau formerly the Dunderderg, built in New York (1867-72). By comparison, the biblical length of Noah's Ark was 300 cubits or, at 45.7 cm 18 in to a cubit, 137 m 450 ft. The 8662 tonnes, 101.7 m 333 2/3 ft long Richelieu was launched in Toulon, France on 3 December 1873. HM battleship Lord Warden, completed in 1869, displaced 8060 tonnes.

457. The Turbinia was designed by the Hon. Sir Charles Parsons (1854-1931) and built in 1894 at Wallsend-on-tyne by Tyne & Wear. She was 30 m 100 ft long, had a displacement of 45.2 tonnes and was powered by three steam turbines totalling about 2000 ship. First publicly demonstrated in 1897, when a speed of 34.5 knots 64 km/h was achieved, the ship is now preserved at Newcastle-upon-tyne.

458. Marine propulsion by steam engine was first achieved in 1783 when the Marquis Jouffroy d'Abbans (1751-1832) ascended a reach of the river saone near Lyon, France, in the 180-tonne paddle steamer Pyroscaphe.

459. The first successful power-driven vessel was the tug Chariotte Dundas, a stern paddle-wheel steamer built for the Forth and Clyde Canal in 1801-2 by William Symington (1763-1831), using a double acting condensing engine constructed by James Watt (1736-1819).

460. The greatest number on an aircraft carrier in one day was 602, achieved by Marine Air Group 6 of the United States Pacific Fleet Air Force aboard the USS Matanikau on 25 May 1945 between 8 am and 5 pm.

461. The giant ship Tessarakonteres, a three-banked catamaran galley

built for Ptolemy IV 210 BC in Alexandria, Egypt, measured 128 m 420 ft. The ship was built for 4000 rowers, with up to eight men to an oar of 38 cubits (17.4 m 57 ft) length.

462. The largest propeller ever is the 11 m 36 ft in diametre triple-bladed screw made by Kawasaki Heavy Industries of Japan and Delivered on 17 Mar 1982 for the 208739-dwt-bulk carrier Hoei Maru, now known as New Harvest.

463. The body of late Stone Age man who is thought to have died in 3300 BC was found almost perfectly preserved in an Austrian glacier in September 1991.

464. Mummification from Persian word means wax. Mummification dates from 2600 BC or the 4th dynasty of the Egyptian pharaohs. The oldest known mummy is that of a high-ranking young woman who was buried in 2600 BC on a plateau near the Great Pyramid of Cheops at Giza or Al-Gizeh, Egypt. Her remains, which appear to represent an early attempt at mummification, were discovered in an excavation on 17 March 1989, but only her skull was intact. She is believed to have lived in the lost kingdom of Ankh Ptah. The oldest complete mummy is of Wati, a court musician of 2400 BC from the tomb of Neferin Saqqara, Egypt, found in 1944.

465. The oldest steam Engine in working order is the Smethwick Engine dating from 1779. It was designed by James Watt in 1736-1819 and built by the Birmingham Canal Company at a cost of £ 2000, the pump originally a 60 cm 24" in bore with a stroke of 2.4 m 8 ft-worked on the canal locks at Smethwick, W Mids until 1891. The engine was presented to Birmingham Museum of Science and Industry in 1960

and is regularly steamed for public. One of the most complete (almost 40% complete) skeletons of 'Lucy' was found by Dr. Donald C. Johansson and T. Gray at locality 162 by the Awash River, Hadar, in the Afar region of Ethiopia on November 30;1974. She was estimated to be 106 cm 3ft 6" in tall and was 40 years old at the time of death i.e. 3 million years ago.

466. The Sahara is the world's largest desert, over 3,500,000 sq mi (9,065,000 sq km), located in northern Africa and is 2.5 million years old. The whole land area of United States of America fits inside it. Its name Sahara is the Arabic translation of the Tuareg word Tenere meaning desert. The boundaries of the Sahara are the Atlantic Ocean on the west, the Atlas Mountains and the Mediterranean Sea on the north, the Red Sea and Egypt on the east and the Sudan and the valley of the Niger River on the south. Sahara is divided into Western Sahara, the central Ahaggar Mountains, the Tibesti massif the Ayr Mountains (a region of desert mountains

and high plateaus), Tenere desert and the Libyan desert (the most arid region). The highest peak in the Sahara is the Emi Koussi Mount in Tibesti massif in northern Chad. The Sahara divides the continent into North and Sub-Saharan Africa. These two regions are culturally and climatically distinct. The southern border of the Sahara is marked by a band of semiarid savannah called the Sahel, south of the Sahel lies the lusher Sudan.

467. Located within the Lambert Graben, the Lambert Glacier is the largest valley glacier in the world, measuring up to 80 km in width

and more than 500 km in length. As such, it drains one-fifth of the East Antarctic Ice Sheet and contributes over 35 km^2 of ice to Prydz Bay, via the Amery Ice Shelf, each year. The Lambert Glacier - Amery Ice Shelf system is fed by a number of ice sheet outlet glaciers, which pass through the Prince Charles Mountains from the polar plateau to the west. These include the Fisher Glacier in the southern Prince Charles Mountains and the Charybdis and Scylla Glaciers in the northern Prince Charles Mountains. These, as well as a number of smaller outlet and alpine-type valley or cirque glaciers, often serve as prominent physical barriers, separating mountain ranges and other rocky exposures within this region. As a result, the Lambert Glacier and its tributaries tend to dominate both the topography and scenery of the Prince Charles Mountains.

468. Studies of the Lambert Glacier and its tributaries provide crucial information regarding the movement of the East Antarctic Ice Sheet and its response to climate change during the Last Glacial Maximum.

469. Greenland is an internally self-governing part of Denmark, situated between the North Atlantic and Arctic oceans. Greenland lies mostly north of the Arctic Circle and is separated from the Canadian Arctic Archipelago, on the west, primarily by Davis Strait and Baffin Bay and from Iceland, on the east, by the Denmark Strait. The largest island in the world, Greenland has a maximum extent, from its northernmost point on Cape Morris Jessup to Cape Farewell in the extreme south, of 2,660 km (1,650 mi). The maximum distance from east to west is 1,300 km (800 mi). The entire coast, which is deeply indented with fjords, is roughly estimated at 44,000 km (27,000 mi). The total area of Greenland is 2,170,000 sq km (836,330 sq mi), of which 1,834,000 sq km (708,000 sq mi) is ice cap. The capital and largest city is Nuuk.

470. The Caspian Sea, the largest lake in the world, is located in the northern Iran. The Caspian Coast including the three littoral provinces of Gilan (centre Rasht), Golestan (centre Gorgan) and Mazanderan (centre Sâri), with its thick forests and intensive rice cultivation presents a striking contrast to the dry inner plateau of Iran. The picturesque provinces of Golestan, Mazanderan and Gilan

bound by the Caspian Sea in the north and, Alborz (Elborz) Range in the south, are divided into a multitude of valleys whose rivers drain into the sea.

471. A lake any body of water surrounded by land and very large lakes are sometimes called seas. The world's largest lake is the salty Caspian Sea at 143,200 square miles (370,886 km^2). The Caspian Sea is surrounded by Russia, Azerbaijan, Iran, Turkmenistan and Kazakhstan.

472. The world's second largest lake and the world's largest freshwater lake is North America's Lake Superior at 31,700 mi^2 (82,103 km^2).

473. The Pacific Ocean (from the Spanish *Pacífico*, meaning *peaceful*) is the world's largest body of water. It encompasses a third of the Earth's surface, having an area of 179.7 million km^2 (69.4 million sq mi). Extending approximately 15,500 km (9,600 mi) from the Bering Sea in the Arctic to the icy margins of Antarctica's Ross Sea in the south, the Pacific reaches its greatest east-west width at about 5 deg N. latitude, where it stretches approximately 19,800 km (12,300 mi) from Indonesia to the coast of Colombia. The western limit of the ocean is often placed at the Strait of Malacca. The lowest point on the earth's surface—the Mariana Trench—lies within the Pacific.

474. The Pacific contains about 25,000 islands (more than the total number in the rest of the world's oceans combined), the majority of which are found south of the equator.

475. Fraser Island is the largest sand island in the world. It is situated just north of Noosa. Named after shipwreck victim Eliza Fraser, the World Heritage listed sub-tropical Fraser Island has a truly amazing array of natural wonders including beautiful rainforests, pristine lakes, endless surf beaches, immense sand blows, cliffs of coloured sands, crystal clear streams and vast stretches of mangroves.

476. Fraser Island is 125 km long and over 160,000 hectares in area. It was formed during the ice age when the prevailing winds transported vast quantities of sand from New South Wales and deposited it along the coast of Queensland forming Fraser Island, as we know it today.

477. In this fragile eco-system, the rainforest consists of huge satinay and brush box, kauri pines, piccabeen palms and the rare angiopteris fern which is one of the largest ferns in the world. All this growing in pure sand! There are some wonderful walking tracks through these areas to enable visitors to appreciate the unique beauty of Fraser Island.

478. The world's largest swamp is called the Pantanal, Mato Grosso in Brazil. It is 42,000 sq miles long. The animals that live around it are jaguars, anacondas and cattle. There are two protected areas: Taiama Ecological station and National park of Pantanal Mato Grossense.

Pantanal is a 'large swamp or marsh'. In reality, the definition is not precise. The term Pantanal is applied to a large land mass, which becomes partially submersed during the raining season, covering an area of about 210,000 square kilometres in Central-Western Brazil, Eastern Bolivia and part of Paraguay. The largest portion of Pantanal, about 140,000 square kilometres lies, in Brazil, stretching over two states— Mato Grosso and Mato Grosso do Sul. By comparison, Florida Everglades has only 10,000 square kilometres.

If you compare this to region of the Amazon tropical forest with area of 2,300,000 square miles (6,000,000 square km), Pantanal seems to be small and not as significant. In reality, Pantanal is more important than its territory might imply. With great area and rich fauna, Amazon is difficult to explore and appreciate. While you will encounter some animal life, you will definitely see more in Pantanal, where unlike Amazon, great areas are not tropical forest, but rather like an African Savannah. This allows unrestricted view of animal life. Hundreds of species of more or less likable animals, birds and insects, jaguar and snakes. Two distinctive seasons: Rainy and dry and the Pantanal topography, is the reason for the richness of the region's fauna and flora. Here you can find almost any plant that is typical of the South American continent. Because of this region's topography, water that falls during rainy season is drained very slowly and gradually, throughout the dry season. Nutrients are not carried away with the swift water current because water flow is very slow. This gives the plants opportunity to establish themselves.

Any outside influence that would change drainage speed, can cause an ecological disaster much greater that even Florida Everglades problem.

479. The world's longest fjord is the Nordvest Fjord arm of Scoresby Sund in eastern Greenland, which extends inland at 195 miles (313 kilometres) from the sea.

480. Kazumura Cave is a very recent discovery. In the mid 1990s, several known lavatubes and some new discoveries were connected to one big cave. So today, Kazumura Cave is the longest lava tube of the world, more than 60 km long. It is the deepest cave of the USA and the eighth longest. The second deepest cave of the USA is still a lava tube of Hawaii, Huehue Cave. This statistic is rather impressive, although a comparison with karst caves is not very useful.

481. A through trip from the Progress of Man entrance near Volcano National Park to the lowest entrance in Paradise Park near Hilo takes two days. Such a trip includes 17 rope drops and 50 km of traverse. On the tours provided by Harry Shick, the visitors see three kilometres of the cave without any drops. Still such an adventure takes five hours.

This cave is rather young, the lava flow and the forming of the caves happened only about 350 to 700 years ago. The tube contains all kinds of lava formations, like lava Falls, lava blades, tubular lava stalagtites, stretched lava and lava plunge pools.

482. The Andes Mountains are located in South America, running north to south along the western coast of the continent. The latitude is 10° N. to 57° S. The longitude is 70° W. to 80° E. The Andes Mountains are the longest and one of the highest mountain ranges in the world. They are located in South America and stretch 4,500 miles from north to south, along the west coast of the continent. The climate is not the same throughout the biome because there are places nearer to the equator than others. The Andes are separated into three natural regions: the southern, central and northern regions. In the northern region, it is hotter because it is closest to the equator. There are rain forests in this region, due to the more humid, rainy climate. In the southern region, the mountains are nearer to the Antarctic and it is much colder. It is not very popu-

lated in the southern area.

In the central region of this biome, the weather is milder because it is not near either the equator or the cold Antarctic. The largest herb in the world, Puya raimondii, grows in this region and can survive at high elevations up to 13,000 feet. The herb can also live for 100 years. The herb's leaves all grow from one big stem, which allows for moisture to run down the leaves to the base of the plant. Therefore, during times of drought, the plant can survive. Many of the plants, which grow in the Andes Mountains, are small to conserve energy. Their leaves can be stiff and strong to protect them from frost and cold weather if they are high in the mountains. The Andes Mountains supply many birds with homes like the Flamingo andean Flicker, the Condor and the Hillstar Hummingbird. Types of land animals include the Mountain Lion, the Red Perll and Llamas to name a few. The Spectacled Bear also lives in this biome. The Giant Toad and Andean Iguana are some examples of reptiles. This iguana is one of the few lizards found in that cold climate. The Andes Mountains are hurt by humans because they cut down trees which shelter many unique Andean animals. Man also mines for gold, silver and copper, which then erodes the soil and hurts the plants of the Andes.

483. The Nile River is the longest river in the world, stretching for 4,187 miles. The Nile flows from south to north and is formed by three major tributaries: the White Nile, the Blue Nile and the Atbara. The Blue Nile has its source in the highlands of the African country of Ethiopia, by Lake Tana. The runoff from spring rain and melting snow caused the annual summer flood of the Nile that the

Egyptians depended on for water to irrigate their crops and deposit fertile top soil.

Just north of of Khartoum the combined White and Blue Nile meet their final major tributary, the Atbara which also has its source in the Ethiopian highlands. The Nile then plunges into a canyon. Before the construction of the Aswan High Dam, the Nile rolled through a series of six rapids, called cataracts, between northern Sudan and southern Egypt. Since construction of the dam, the river has gradually changed its course. North of Cairo, the Nile splits into two branches (or distributaries), the Rosetta Branch to the west and the Damietta to the east.

484. Lake Nasser is a man-made lake created by the construction of the Aswan High Dam, opened in 1971. The dam was built to regulate the flow of the Nile River and thus benefit the region's inhabitants. However, technology often also disrupts a local ecosystem, the life and nature it affects.

The canyon that was once behind where the dam is now was flooded after the dam was built. Before the region was flooded for the dam, some Ancient sites were carefully moved. Others were permanently covered and destroyed by the water. Lake Nasser stretches over a distance of 312 miles. Gone are the days when Egyptians worried that the Nile will flood too high, destroying their crops or fall too low, not providing proper irrigation. To enjoy the benefits of a steady river flow, thousands of peoples homes were submerged when the dam went into operation and Lake Nasser was formed.

The Aswan High Dam has caused other changes. The water surface of the lake has reduced the average temperature in the region. The dam has also harnessed the water for the production of electricity and navigation has been improved.

Farmers are forced to use chemical fertilisers because the rich topsoil is now deposited in Lake Nasser instead of along the banks of the Nile. Furthermore, the Nile is no longer flowing strongly enough to keep salt water from the Mediterranean Sea from forcing its way up the Nile. The salt water disrupts the animal habitat and sterilizes the soil in the northern delta region where the banks of the Nile are becoming badly eroded.

485. Kilauea is the youngest and south-eastern most active volcanoes on the Big Island of Hawaii. Topographically, Kilauea appears as only a bulge on the southeastern flank of Mauna Loa and so for many years Kilauea was thought to be a mere satellite of its giant neighbour, not a separate volcano. However, research over the past few decades shows clearly that Kilauea has its own magma-plumbing system, extending to the surface from more than 60 km deep in the earth.

In fact, the summit of Kilauea lies on a curving line of volcanoes that includes Mauna Kea and Kohala and excludes Mauna Loa. In other words, Kilauea is to Mauna Kea as Loʻihi is to Mauna Loa. Hawaiians used the word Kilauea only for the summit caldera, but earth scientists and, over time, popular usage have extended the name to include the entire volcano.

486. Don Juan Pond is not spooky so much as it is surreal. The pond and surrounding area contain rocks carved into fantastical shapes by wind-blown particles of ice or stone. These rocks, which are known as ventifacts, give the place the curious look of a sculpture garden. Salts left behind by evaporated water create oddly beautiful patterns on the ground.

Perhaps the strangest feature of Don Juan Pond, though, is the small waves that ripple across its entire surface. The other water bodies we would see there are covered with ice except for relatively small moat areas that developed along the edges as the summer progressed. Don Juan Pond, in contrast, was pure liquid. The fact that the pond is much smaller and shallower than the lakes we had been visiting could have something to do with that.

However, even during the height of the Antarctic winter when air temperatures drop to -50 degrees Celsius, the pond remains at least partially unfrozen. This is because the pond is quite salty and dissolved salts lower the freezing point of water by interfering with the bonding among water molecules.

The pond contains so much salt in fact - some 10 to 15 times that of normal seawater - that it is thought by many to be the saltiest body of water on earth.

Don Juan Pond was discovered in the South Fork of the Wright Valley in 1961 during field reconnaissance by a U.S. Navy helicopter. The pond was named after Lieutenants Donald Roe and John Hickey, both of whom were members of the first field party to study the pond.

487. Arctic Ocean is the smallest ocean in the world. This, the smallest of the four oceans, lies almost entirely above the Arctic Circle (66.5° N). Nearly surrounded by land, its only outlets are the Bering Strait between Alaska and Russia, Davis Strait between Greenland and Canada and Denmark Strait and the Norwegian Sea between Greenland and Europe. The Arctic Ocean has an area of 14,090,000 sq km and an average depth of 3,658 m off the continental shelf. The lowest point is Fram Basin, which is 4,665 m deep. The Artic Ocean has the widest continental shelf of all the oceans.

The Lomonosov Ridge divides the Arctic Ocean into two basins, the Eurasian Basin and the North American Basin. There are also submarine ridges between the Arctic and Atlantic Oceans. This results in a large stagnant pool of cold water at the bottom of the Arctic Ocean, since land and submarine ridges block water from flowing out. The main current in the Arctic Ocean is the East Greenland current. This current is strong due to the number of rivers that flow into the Arctic Sea, the low rate of evaporation and the land and submarine ridges surrounding the ocean. Two other weak currents flow out of the Arctic Ocean, the Labrador Current, which runs through Smith Sound and Baffin Bay and one that runs out of the Bering Straight. There is also a circular current in the Arctic Basin, which is created by water deflecting off of Northern Greenland.

The central part of the ocean is permanently covered in about ten feet of ice. Pressure ridges in the ice can sometimes reach three times that height. In the summer months, the icepack is surrounded by water and free-floating. During the winter, the icepack expands to nearly twice its summer area, reaching the land on all sides. Due to the extreme temperatures people thought that non-oceanic life didn't exist in the Arctic. However, marine life abounds in the open seas and hares, polar bears, seals, gulls and guillemots have been found as far north as 88°.

488. Lake Titicaca in Peru is the highest navigable lake in the world. It is about 12,500 feet (3,810 metres) above sea level. This lake is also South America's second largest freshwater lake.

It covers some 3,200 square miles (8,300 square km) and extends in a northwest-to-southeast direction for a distance of 120 miles (190 km). It is 50 miles (80 km) across at its widest point. A narrow strait, Tiquina, separates the lake into two bodies of water.

489. The lowest lake is the Dead Sea (it's considered a lake but called a sea), which is in the Jordan Valley of Israel. The surface of the water is 1,302 feet below sea level. The Dead Sea is also the saltiest lake in the world. Almost nothing can survive in it besides some special green algae. Bounded on the west by Israel and the West Bank and on the east by Jordan, the Dead Sea forms part of the Israeli-Jordanian border. The surface of the Dead Sea, 408 m (1,340 ft) below sea level as of 1996, is the lowest water surface on earth. The lake is 80 km (50 mi) long and has a maximum width of 18 km (11 mi), its area is 1,020 sq km (394 sq mi). The Dead Sea occupies a north portion of the Great Rift Valley. On the east, the high plateau of Moab rises about 1,340 m (about 4,400 ft) above the sea, on the west the plateau of Judea rises to half that height. From the eastern shore, a peninsula juts out into the lake. To the south of this peninsula the lake is shallow, less than 6 m (less than 20 ft) deep, in the north it reaches its greatest depth of 399 m (about 1,309 ft) below surface level and 799 m (about 2,621 ft) below sea level.

The Dead Sea is fed mainly by the Jordan River, which enters the lake from the north. Several smaller streams also enter the sea, chiefly from the east. The lake has no outlet and the heavy inflow of fresh water is carried off solely by evaporation, which is rapid in the hot desert climate. Due to large-scale projects by Israel and Jordan to divert water from the Jordan River for irrigation and other water needs, the surface of the Dead Sea has been dropping for at least the past 50 years.

Nearly seven times as salty as the ocean, the Dead Sea contains at a depth of 305 m (1,000 ft) some 27 percent solid substances: sodium chloride (common salt), magnesium chloride, calcium chloride, potassium chloride, magnesium bromide and many other substances. Because of the density of solids in the water, the human body easily floats on the surface. The lake contains no life of any sort except for a few kinds of microbes, sea fish put into its waters soon die.

The Dead Sea is economically important as a source of potash, bromine, gypsum, salt and other chemical products, which are extracted inexpensively. The shores of the Dead Sea are of growing importance as a winter health resort. The lake is closely associated with biblical history, the sites of the cities of Sodom and Gomorrah are believed to lie beneath the lake.

490. Lake Superior is the largest of North America's Great Lakes. It is the largest freshwater lake in the world by surface area. (The Caspian Sea is larger, but contains salt water.) Lake Superior has a surface area of 82,000 km^2 (32,000 sq. mi.), larger than the Czech Republic. It has a maximum length of 350 mi (563 km) and maximum width of 160 mi (257 km). Its average depth is 489 ft (149 m) with a maximum depth of 1,333 ft (406 m). Lake Superior contains 2,935 cubic mi (12,232 cubic km) of water. The shoreline of the lake stretches 2,730 miles (4393 km) (including islands).

It borders Ontario in Canada and Minnesota, Wisconsin and Michigan in the United States of America. It is an important shipment route for iron ore and is part of the Great Lakes Waterway.

491. The world's shortest river is the Roe River. It is only 200 feet (61 metres) long and flows between Giant Springs and the Missouri River near Great Falls, Montana. There has been debate, though, about which river is really the shortest. The D River in Oregon has been measured as being only 120 feet (37 metres) long. It connects Devil's Lake directly to the Pacific Ocean near Lincoln City.

492. Talc is softest mineral. Talc is an important industrial mineral. Its resistance to heat, electricity and acids make it an ideal surface for lab counter tops and electrical switchboards. It is also an important filler material for paints, rubber and insecticides. Even with all these uses, most people only know talc as the primary ingredient in talcum powder. Mineral specimens are not very common, as it does not form very large crystals. However, it often replaces other

minerals on an atom-by-atom basis and forms what are called pseudomorphs (false shape). The talc takes the form of the mineral it replaces. A specimen of what looks like milky quartz is quite a surprise when it not only has a soapy feel but also can be scratched by a fingernail.

493. Tightrope Walkers Jean Francois Gravelet, the great Blondin, was the first of many tightrope walkers to appear at Niagara Falls. He was a professional artist and showman trained in the great tradition of the European circus. At age 31 he came to America and made the announcement that he would cross the gorge of the Niagara River on a tightrope.

494. On June 30, 1859, the rope was in position and at five o'clock in the afternoon. Blondin started the trip that was to make history. Incredulous watchers saw him lower a rope to the Maid of the Mist, pull up a bottle and sit down while he refreshed himself. He began his ascent toward the Canadian shore, paused, steadied the balancing pole and suddenly executed a back somersault. Never content merely to repeat his last performance, Blondin crossed his rope on a bicycle walked blindfolded, pushed a wheelbarrow, cooked an omelette in the centre and made the trip with his hands and feet manacled.

495. In October 1829, Sam Patch jumped twice from a platform on Goat Island, 33.50 metres (110 feet). He survived both but killed himself the following year at the Genesee Falls, Rochester, New York, in a similar but slightly higher attempt.

496. Annie Telson Taylor a woman is the first person who went over the tumultuous Canadian Falls and survived it, on October 24th 1901 in a wooden barrel.

497. Of the 16 known attempts in a barrel or contraption, 6 have died and 10 have survived, not such a bad record considering the exploit.

Paddy Doyle has succeeded in his latest endurance endeavour to earn the title the World's Fittest Man. Paddy attempted his 125th endurance record in the form of the World Physical Fitness Challenge at the Virgin Active gym in Blythe Valley on Wednesday. Former Paratrooper Doyle, now living in Balsall Common, had to complete a series of tough tests in a record-breaking time and spent months preparing for the challenge. On the list of test were: 1,250 press ups, a two-mile swim, a 12 mile march, 3,250 sit ups, 1,250 hip flexors, a 110 mile cycle and a 20 mile row. Added to that was a 20 mile elliptical walk, 1,250 star jumps, weight lifting, a 12 mile run, 5 km on the stepper machine and as many burpees and squat thrusts as possible in five minutes. Paddy completed it in around 20 hours 35 minutes, comfortably smashing the previous record by more than three hours.

He also completed a one-mile treadmill run, carrying a 44 lb backpack. In preparation, Doyle trained in New York, at the famous Glesason's boxing gym, where he was pushed to the limit by professional boxer Troy Blackmore. He also received coaching from instructors at Virgin Active.

498. Arulanantham Suresh Joachim after setting a record by walking and trotting up and down escalators in a shopping mall for seven straight days without a break.

499. The Sri Lankan completed 14,000 laps on a set of escalators for a total of 155 miles (250 kilometres), while adding to his reputation as a man for whom no challenge is too bizarre. His escapade on the escalators, which was also a fund-raiser to help children, is his sixth record. His other feats include standing on one foot for 76 hours and 40 minutes and running non-stop for six days, during which he covered 638.18 miles (1,027.02 kilometres). Joachim broke the existing world record for escalator walking at 4:55 am. Sunday, but kept going until 11:20 am to put plenty of distance between himself and the millions — no, billions — who have no interest whatsoever in challenging his record. Moreover, the one or two who might.

500. The Star of India is the world's oldest seafaring ship. Built in 1863 at Ramsey Shipyard in the Isle of Man, it was an experimental design utilising iron instead of wood. Launched as Euterpe, a full-rigged ship named after the Greek goddess of music, the ship's initial voyages involved some rough sailing. Her first trip included a collision and mutiny. She came face to face with a cyclone in the Bay of Bengal on her second journey. Her topmasts cut away, she

barely made port. Following that, the first captain died on board and was buried at sea.

The waters finally quieted and it was smooth sailing during numerous uneventful voyages and several 'change of owner' transactions. She served as a cargo ship to India, a passenger vessel hauling emigrants to New Zealand and a commercial salmon fishing and packing facility. Her name was changed to Star of India in 1906 and after 60 years of solid performance in 1923, she was towed to the San Diego bay. Saved from the axe or torch by concerned historians, she sat in port for over 50 years until funding helped renovate the tired old lady, which was once a star. In 1976, the fully restored Star of India put to sea for the first time in fifty years, under the command of Captain Carl Bowman. She sailed beautifully that day, to the applause of half a million fans, ashore and afloat. Since then, the Star of India has sailed on numerous special occasions. Now part of a maritime museum tour, you can visit the Star of India.

501. The Papal Swiss Guard, founded in 1506, is the oldest army. It is today largely ceremonial, but like the Guards in London, they are an operational modern military force. When in ceremonial 16th century uniform, they keep their firearms in guard boxes nearby. The Papal Guard are the only mercenary unit permitted under Swiss law since 1859 and are the last of a long tradition of a million mercenaries in the world's armies. The Guard today consists of 5 officers, 25 NCOs and 70 halberdiers.

502. At the age of fifty-nine, Satchel Paige became the oldest player in the major leagues. He may also have been the best pitcher in baseball ever. Leroy Robert 'Satchel' Paige was born on July 7, 1906. He earned his nickname, Satchel, when he was a young boy carrying bags (and satchels) at railroad stations for passengers. Initially barred from the major leagues because he was African American, Paige played in what was referred to as 'the Negro Leagues'. Paige's pitching took the Kansas City Monarchs to five Negro American League pennants. He also showcased his skills by barnstorming across the country.

503. The Oldest male astronaut is John Herschel Glenn Jr. Born July 18,

1921, Cambridge, Ohio. Glenn was the first American to orbit the Earth. The 'Clean Marine' flew missions in W.W.II and Korea, selected in 1959 to be one of the Original Seven astronauts. Third American in Space. Resigned from space programme in 1964 and the Marine Corps in '65. Elected to the Senate from Ohio as a Democrat in 1974. Re-elected in '80 and '86. Made unsuccessful bid for Democratic Presidential Nomination in 1984. One of five senators investigated by Senate Ethics Committee for improper intervention on behalf of Charles Keating. He was exonerated.

He entered the Naval Aviation Cadet Programme in March 1942 and was graduated from this programme and commissioned in the Marine Corps in 1943. After advanced training, he joined Marine Fighter Squadron 155 and spent a year flying F4U fighters in the Marshall Islands.

During his World War II service, he flew 59 combat missions. After the war, he was a member of Marine Fighter Squadron 218 on the North China patrol and served on Guam. From June 1948 to December 1950, Glenn was an instructor in advanced flight training at Corpus Christi, Texas. He then attended Amphibious Warfare Training at Quantico, Virginia. In Korea he flew 63 missions with Marine Fighter Squadrons 311 and 27 while an exchange pilot with the Air Force in F-86 Sabrejets. In the last nine days of fighting in Korea Glenn downed three MIG's in combat along the Yalu River.

After Korea, Glenn attended Test Pilot School at the Naval Air Test Centre, Patuxent River, Maryland. After graduation, he was project officer on a number of aircraft. He was assigned to the Fighter Design Branch of the Navy Bureau of Aeronautics (now Bureau of Naval Weapons) in Washington from November 1956 to April 1959, during which time he also attended the University of Maryland.

In July 1957, while project officer of the F8U Crusader, he set a transcontinental speed record from Los Angeles to New York, spanning the country in 3 hours and 23 minutes. This was the first transcontinental flight to average supersonic speed. Glenn has nearly 9,000 hours of flying time, with approximately 3,000 hours in jet aircraft.

504. Yuichiro Miura is the oldest person ever to reach the summit of Mount Everest. He was 70 years and 222 days old when he got to the summit on May 22, 2003. Yuichiro Miura was born in 1932. He is in the Book of Records.

505. The Boston Marathon is the world's oldest marathon. The 2000 Boston Marathon was the closest in the race's 104-year history. Kenya's Elijah Lagat and Ethiopian star Gezahenge Abera sprinted to the finish, with Lagat prevailing. The two actually recorded the same exact time (2:09:47) while Kenyan Moses Tanui followed just three seconds behind.

In 1988, Ibrahim Hussein became the first black male to win at Boston.

506. Desai, Morarji Ranchhodji, 1896–1995, Indian political leader became the oldest person to become prime minister. He joined the government in 1956, becoming minister of finance (1958–63). He returned to government in 1967 as deputy prime minister and minister of finance, but in 1969 was manoeuvred from office by Indira Gandhi and became leader of the conservative opposition. Leading an opposition coalition, he prevailed in the 1977 elections, ending Gandhi's emergency rule. He served as prime minister until 1979, when the coalition broke apart.

507. A 71-year-old cancer survivor who performed feats of strength pulled off another one Monday, hauling a 60,000-pound car carrier all by himself.

508. The World Team '99, a large multinational group of skydivers who assemble occasionally to break world skydiving records, completed a freefall formation of 282 skydivers, on December 16, 1999, above Ubon Ratchathani, Thailand, when they held a link for 7.11 seconds. The World Team formed part of the Royal Sky Celebration, an aerial party for Thailand's King Bhumibol Adulyadey's 72nd birthday. At the request of the Thai organisers, the colour pattern of the formation was chosen to match the colours of the Thailand national flag. The skydivers were dispatched from four Hercules C-130 transport aircraft at 7,010 m. (23,000 ft.).

509. Vesna Vulovic, a flight attendant from Yugoslavia, survived a fall

from 10,160 m. (33,330 ft.) when the DC-9 in which she was travelling blew up over Czechoslovakia (now Czech Republic), on January 26, 1972. No other passengers survived. It is believed that the plane crashed after the detonation of a bomb planted by Croatian terrorists in the forward cargo hold. Vesna Vulovic fell 10,160 m. (33,330 ft.) - breaking both legs and becoming paralysed from the waist down.

510. The longest delayed skydive was made by Capt. Joseph W. Kittinger, who dropped 25,820 m. (84,700 ft.) from a balloon at Tularosa, New Mexico, USA, on August 16, 1960. He fell for 4 min. 37 sec. before his parachute was deployed automatically.

511. Dolni Vestonice is located in the modern Czech Republic. This Palaeolithic cite was inhabited from ca. 27,00 to 23,000 BC. This drawing is an artist's recreation. To give some sense of scale, the round structure in the lower centre, which perhaps was a wind screen, measured about 27 and 45 feet. The settle had perhaps 100 people who inhabited the cite the year round. In this period, Europe was in the midst of the Ice Age so the average daily temperature was probably around freezing.

512. Adeline Ablitt (b. 1903), from Coventry, England, was the oldest woman to loop the loop. It was 95 when she took to the skies in a glider and looped the loop. At the age of 90, someone told her that age is a state of degeneration, now she is a woman who does not believe in old age anymore and her zest for life certainly proves it. The loop-the-loop flight with the Wellesbourne Gliding Club was an amazing occasion for Adeline. She was not nervous, but enjoyed the peace and tranquillity - she believes heaven will be something like that! Not one to rest on her laurels, Adeline has taken up swimming again and one day hopes to take a ride in a hot-air balloon.

513. The oldest fully authenticated age to which any human has ever lived is 122 years and 164 days, by Jeanne Louise Calment. She was born in France on February 21, 1875 and died at a nursing home in Arles, southern France on August 4, 1997.

514. Cal Ripken, Jr. set the Major League record for most consecutive seasons playing all of a team's games with fifteen and they were in

consecutive (1983-1997) order.

Cal Ripken, Jr. was born on Wednesday, August 24, 1960 and began his Major League baseball career on August 10, 1981, with the Baltimore Orioles. The 21 year-old played for 21 seasons on one team and ended his big league playing career in 2001.

515. Pete Rose set two other games played Major League records: most seasons playing in more than one-hundred games with twenty-three and most consecutive seasons playing more than one-hundred games with twenty-three.

516. Pete Rose was born on Monday, April 14, 1941 and began his Major League baseball career on April 8, 1963, with the Cincinnati Reds. The 22 year-old played for 24 seasons on 3 different teams and ended his big league playing career in 1986.

517. During the 1979 season Frank Taveras split one-hundred sixty-four games with the Pittsburgh Pirates and the New York Mets which is the Major League record for most games played with two teams during the same season.

518. Frank Taveras was born on Saturday, December 24, 1949 and be-

gan his Major League baseball career on September 25, 1971, with the Pittsburgh Pirates. The 22 year-old played for 11 seasons on 3 different teams and ended his big league playing career in 1982.

519. Valentina Tereshkova was the youngest astronaut. Valentina Tereshkova, born in 1937, was the first woman in space. In 1963, she spent 3 days in space and orbited the earth 48 times. Valentina was the youngest of three children. Her father was a tractor driver. He fought with the Soviet Army in World War II and was killed before she was three years old. Her mother struggled to raise three children alone. As a child, she had to help her mother with farm chores and she did not attend school until she was ten years old. Eventually they left the farm and went to live in the city, where her mother worked in a cotton mill. At 17, she started working in factories. First, she worked in a tire factory and then she joined her mother and sister in the cotton mill. She finished her schooling by correspondence course and graduated from the Light Industry Technical School. This was by no means the end of her education, though.

Valentina was a great believer in the communist system and joined the young communists leagues at the factory. She later became a full member of the communist party. She also joined an amateur parachuting club and became an expert parachutist.

Valentina was at work with her mother and sister when Yuri Gagarin, the first ever astronaut, went into space. Her mother commented that next time it should be a woman that went. Valentina was inspired. Every person in the Soviet Union was entitled to apply to the space programme. Valentina applied and was accepted. Her parachuting experience was one of the reasons she got in, along with three other women. The Soviets wanted to send a woman to space, just once, to see if they could endure the hardships as well as men. In order to become a cosmonaut (a Soviet astronaut) she had to join the Air Force as an Officer. She began her training in 1961 and it took 18 months. It was not easy. She had to spend hours studying technical manuals, rocket science and spaceship design. She also underwent strenuous physical training.

On June 16, 1963, as a Junior Lieutenant and chief pilot of the Vostok VI, she became the first ever woman to go into space. She orbited Earth 48 times and parachuted out of the spacecraft following its re-entry into Earth's atmosphere. She had proven that women could withstand the physical and emotional stresses of space flight as well as any man. She was awarded a medal at the Kremlin three days later and proclaimed as a Hero of the Soviet Union. She never returned to space, but worked in the Space Programme and married another Cosmonaut in 1963. One year later their daughter, Elena, was born. She was the first child to be born to parents who had both been to space. Doctors were a little worried that she would not be normal, but Elena, now a doctor, proved them wrong.

520. Michael Kearney was the world's youngest graduate. Michael Kearney slept very little as a baby. He would be frustrated at not being able to speak. At the age of six months, he said his first sentence 'I have a left ear infection' and showed signs of understanding what was going on when he was being treated. People thought his mother was a ventriloquist, as he would speak while he was being carried around.

He was characterised by a 'rage to learn'. When they could, he was schooled at home by his parents specially his mother and accelerated in his academic career since he was unable to display interest in the slow pace of conventional schooling. For a while, he was the world's youngest postgraduate until Tathagat Avatar Tulsi. He also listed as the world's youngest graduate at the age of 6 years and 7 months with an Associate of Science degree also at Santa Rosa Junior College.

521. Balamurali Ambati of Hollis Hills, New York, USA, became the youngest graduate doctor on May 19, 1995, graduating from the Mount Sinai School of medicine in New York City, USA, aged 17. Balamurali Ambati, graduated from New York University at the age of 13 and Mt. Sinai School of Medicine at age 17, becoming the world's youngest doctor. A National Merit Scholar and a winner in the Westinghouse Science Talent Search and the International Science & Engineering Fair, he is currently in ophthalmology at Harvard, where he is developing strategies to reverse corneal angiogenesis.

522. John Payton was 18 years, 11 months old when he took office as a

justice of the peace in Plano, Texas, USA, in January 1991. He is the youngest judge in the world.

523. Laura Sweeting from Watford, Herfordshire, England, became the UN's youngest goodwill Ambassador on June 9, 2000, age 16. Her role is to help raise awareness and funds for the 'Water for life' appeal/children helping children campaign. Sweeting was officially appointed on June 9 at a ceremony in London during the UK launch of the UN's 'Water for Life' appeal, which aims to raise $40 million to reduce water-borne diseases and to treat contaminated water. She will be part of the UN's promotional activities in helping to raise awareness of challenges facing developing nations, where one child dies every eight seconds because of the lack of clean water.

524. The youngest golfer to have achieved a hole in one is Matthew Draper (UK). He was 5 years, 212 days old when he set this record at the 122-yards. Fourth at Cherwell Edge Golf Club, Oxfordshire, England, on June 17,1997.

525. The 1973 thriller 'Lex the Wonderdog' was written, produced and directed by Sydney Ling when he was just 13 years old, making him the youngest director of a professionally made, feature-length movie.

526. Shirley Temple (1929-) was the youngest millionaire. She was the most famous child actor of all time. She single handily save a studio and provided a little cheer in the dark days of the Depression. Her mother was her guiding light. She was with her every minute, helped her learn her lines (especially before she could read) and coached her during the shootings. Whenever Shirley had to be bubbly, her mother would whisper, 'Sparkle, Shirley Sparkle'. She was always well prepared for her parts and in the process of learning her lines would know the lines of the actors appearing with them. During rehearsals, she would sometimes correct them if they made a mistake—but in an innocent sort of way. Shirley was a box office sensation and for several years during the 1930s, her films had larger earnings than the major adult film stars, with men and women. The famous child actor appeared in a large number of movies. Several of the films are pertinent to HBC because boys also appeared to them. As Shirley was often cast as an orphan, there were smartly dressed boys in her film but they provide some insights as to how children dressed in the 1930s. She often wore very short dresses.

527. Lil' Bow Wow at age three told his mother he wanted to start rapping. Three years later, he began performing his raps and six years after that he was a bonafide rap star! Bow Wow has rhymed since he was five years old. Bow Wow's big break came when he jumped up on stage and started rapping in between acts on the Chronic Tour rap concert when he was only six. Lucky for Bow Wow, the top dizzowg himself, Snoop Dogg was impressed and gave him the nickname Lil Bow Wow. Now that Bow Wow's growing up, he has dropped the 'Lil' to prove that he can role the big dogs.

By the time the lil' rapper was 13 he had worked on the soundtracks for Wild Wild West and Big Momma's House. In 2000, Lil Bow Wow released his first CD called *Beware of Dog*, which included the hits *Bow Wow (That's My Name)* and *Bounce With Me*. The cool thing about Lil Bow Wow is that he does not sing profanity-filled lyrics like so many other rap acts do. Another reason to look up to Bow Wow is that he gets good grades in school - even with his crazy schedule. Aside from his own stuff Bow Wow's also been featured on songs by Snoop, Will Smith and joined other artists on Destiny's Child's Jumpin' Jumpin' remix. Bow Wow starred in the movie Like *Mike* in 2002 and his third album *Unleashed* hit record stores in August 2003.

528. The youngest person ever to have travelled to all seven continents is South African Tanya Daniella Donkin (b. January 2, 1997). On November 16, 2000. Tanya landed in Dubai (Asia) at the age of 3 years 10 months 14 days, thereby visiting her seventh continent. All her travels were with her parents Dave and Irene Donkin.

529. The UK's Robert Schumann (born March 7, 1982) went to the North Pole on April 6, 1992, at the age of 10 and the South Pole on December 29, 1993, at the age of 11. He arrived at the South Pole by mountain bike after having flown in nearby. Robert visited both Poles with his father. He is the youngest person who reached both the poles.

530. Jerry Yang (USA), the co-founder of Internet search engine, Yahoo! Inc., became the youngest billionaire in 1998, aged 29. He is now worth an estimated $4 billion. In 1994, bored with writing their doctoral theses in electrical engineering, he and college-friend David Filo began compiling a list classifying their favourite websites,

leading to 'Jerry and David's Guide to the World Wide Web'. In summer 1994, they came up with the name Yahoo! an acronym for 'Yet Another Hierarchical Officious Oracle!', a play on the Unix programme YACC, 'Yet Another Compiler Compiler'.

531. Dorothy Straight [USA] was the youngest author. When she wrote *How the World Began* in 1962 she was only four years old. It was published in Aug 1964 by Pantheon Books.

532. Capetonian Susan Fraenkel is the oldest woman to have swum the English Channel - at the age of 46 years 103 days, in 12 hr 5 min. Fraenkel, who calls herself an 'average' swimmer, says that it is 90% mental. 'I've done the Comrades - and that was much harder'. Then there is the Longest Drumming Marathon by an individual. It lasted for 50 hours 30 minutes and was achieved by Michael MacPherson in KwaZulu-Natal.

533. Andre Ludwick lives in Parys in the Free State and has the largest number of nail clippers in the world. He's got every sort of nail clipper - articulated, decorated, in silver, steel, gold plate and titanium and brushed stainless steel.

534. Rahul Samant is in the Book of World Records created a new category for his collection - coins from the maximum number of countries.

Samant did his schooling at the Abhinav Vidyalaya and graduated from the Government College of Engineering Pune. While his collection grew rapidly ever since he moved to the U.S.A., thanks to the easy contact established with other numismatists over the Internet, the roots of his hobby are entrenched in his childhood here. And the initial collection was just like that of any child - a random non-specific one. 'I would collect whatever I got. My father's colleague, Mr. Shirodkar, has a huge collection of coins - basically British age coins of India - and that really inspired me', he remembered.

At the beginning of 1995, Samant had around 45 countries. Some visits to Juna Bazaar and a couple of coin shows later, it had reached 100. Then the pace escalated and by July the next year, Samant approached the Limca Book of Records with a collection from 134 countries. 'By the time I arrived in U.S.A. around mid-1997,

I boasted of 165 countries. In India, it was difficult to get coins from some 'tough' countries like Niue and Palau. However, access to dealers is not the problem here with the easy communication systems. Today, my collection stands at 223 countries".

535. Grand Coulee Dam, one of the largest concrete structures in the world, is an awesome sight. After decades of planning, it was built over an 8-year period, starting in 1933, as a depression relief project.

Grand Coulee is a hydroelectric dam and part of the Columbia River Hydro System, a series of 14 dams harnessing the energy of the mighty Columbia River. Interestingly, the System is an example of the close ties between Canada and the US in this Pacific Northwest region, as it includes 3 dams above the border. Grand Coulee Dam is the largest U.S. producer of hydroelectric energy, generating 6,800 of the 35,000 megawatts of electricity generated by the System. That translates to about $500 million worth of power that is supplied to British Columbia and hundreds of towns and cities in the western states.

Grand Coulee Dam also provides water that irrigates over 500,000 acres of eastern Washington and without which much of the farming you see would not be possible. In addition to Franklin D Roosevelt Lake, water is actually pumped out of the dam to create Banks Lake above, which functions as a stabilising reservoir and stores irrigation water. This was quite a controversial design decision at the time and took advantage of an existing containment area in the form of the upper Grand Coulee Canyon.

536. The Suntec City is the latest among Singapore's mega-structures. Documented in the 1998, its total floor area 7 million square feet, 888,000 sq. ft. shopping space, 3,200 units of parking lots. 1,000,000 sq. ft. of conference area and outdoors fountain occupying 18,018 sq. ft. This is the world's largest outdoors fountain-the spring of wealth. It spans over 18018 sq. ft. of the basement, of 46 feet height, with a diametre of 66 feet. Constructed of pure copper weighing 85 tones, its manufacture cost was $6 Million.

This one of a kind fountain designed is allocated the pivotal position. From its formation, four outer main roads embrace it providing influx of water whilst the form inner lanes interlinked represents the reverting of four flows towards its depository. The four inner lanes are respectively situated on Qian, Sun, Kun, Ken round a circle. This circulation of water enables the utmost perfect display of pivotal water. Qian, Kun, Ken, Sun water is termed 'Official water' which according to a classic book-Tian YU Classic depicts the visiting of officials. No wonder the numerous international conferences held with lots of international organisations taking up space for its offices.

The Suntec City is a combination of five blocks of offices, three malls and a conference cum exhibition hall. Each of these buildings is unique, with the aggregation of every two office blocks forming the Tui Gua, - the caving in at the top with the base protruded. (The I-ching states: Tui is the exclusion of the apex).

This is utterly agreeable during the 7th Age Tui Gua, which span from 1984 to 2003. Metal cannot prosper without earth thus the location of a square building by its side. (Square depicts earth).

The roof of the conference hall makes up by the assembly of numerous pyramids. Western mystics believe in the power of pyramids for energy storage, the sealing in of freshness of food and the ground for meditation. Thus the adoption of pyramids as tombs in ancient Egypt was built in the hope of resurrection and the continuation of power. The ensemble of these pyramids offers immense motivation and optimism.

537. In the second half of the 6th century BC, the Ionian island of Samos developed into a major naval power under its ruler, Polykrates. He built city walls and a 360 m-long jetty, which is still in use today, 2,500 years later. He also commissioned a 2.5 m x 2.5 m aqueduct to bring water from the north of the acropolis to the south, near the city. Eupalinos of Megara carried out the work, using teams from both ends of the 1,046 m alignment. They met roughly in the middle, with only marginal error, creating a lasting monument. To this day, the tunnel of Eupalinos is viewed as an outstanding technical feat and is well worth a visit.

538. Avebury is the largest stone circle in the world. It is 427m (1401ft) in diametre covers an area of some 28 acres (11.5 ha). Although not so immediately impressive as Stonehenge, it is an extraordi-

nary site formed by a huge circular bank (a mile round), a massive ditch now only a half its original depth and a great ring of 98 sarsen slabs enclosing two smaller circles of 30 stones each and other settings and arrangements of stones.

539. The outer bank, still very impressive, was originally 17m (55 ft) high from ditch bottom to bank top. The stones, each weighing about 40 tons or more, were left rough and not dressed, as were the Stonehenge blocks. They were obtained from the same place, the nearby Marlborough Downs. Now there are only 27 in place because a few hundred years ago lighting fires beneath them and pouring cold water over them broke many of the stones up. They were then used to construct the present village, which grew up within the earthwork.

540. In the 14th century, some of the stones were buried. In that period, a man was killed by one of the stones falling over unexpectedly in the pit, which was being prepared for its burial. No attempt was made to extract his body. A pair of scissors, a lancet and three silver coins were found next the poor skeleton and the stone is now called the Barber's Stone. Other remarkable stones are the Swindon Stone, the largest (it weighs about 60 tons), the Devil's Chair (local legends attribute mystic powers to the stone such as the ability to summon the devil if you run round it 100 times anti-clockwise) and the Repaired Stone, which has been reconstructed in an odd shape.

541. The two smaller circles within the great ring were probably the heart of the ritual or ceremony. Of the northern one, only few stones are visible. Two of the central ones are called The Cove and may have been erected first, even before the great circle. Shortly before mid-summer 1996, they were daubed with graffiti, but a sculpture restoration team promptly cleaned them, as the megalithic monument is in care of the National Trust.

542. Mt Baker Ridge is the world's largest diametre soil tunnel. This 25.2 m outside diametre, 19.4 m inside diametre, 406 m-long tunnel was constructed in 1986 to carry five lanes of traffic and a bicycle/pedestrian lane through an 80 m high ridge along the east side of Seattle, WA, USA. The tunnel was constructed by Guy F.

Atkinson Construction Company, using an innovative-stacked drift method developed by HNTB and Shannon & Wilson, Inc.

The 24 horseshoe-shaped drifts forming the final structural lining of the tunnel were designed as a semi-flexible, un-reinforced compression ring with a minimum thickness of 1.5 m. The 3 m-diametre drifts were excavated with a horseshoe-shaped digger shield through hard glacial clay. Total settlement after removal of the soil core was generally less than 5 cm. Three decks were constructed within the structural lining for carrying traffic.

543. Paijanne is the world's longest water supply tunnel. The 120 km-long x 13.5-18.0 sq m aqueduct from Lake Paijanne to Helsinki was constructed in seven separate contracts commencing in 1975 using pneumatic drill rigs. It has a volume of 2 million cu m and capacity 10 cu m/sec without pumping and 20 cu m/sec with pumping. The change in elevation end to end is just 36 m and the depth in bedrock varies from 30 to 80 m. The flow runs an 830 kW turbine.

544. Laerdal is the world's longest road tunnel. The 24.5 km-long Laerdal was opened to traffic on 27th November 2000 as part of the E16 Bergen-Oslo highway. It was constructed during the period 1995-2000 by Statens Vegvesen Sogn og Fjordane (SV), who built 11 km from the Aurland portal and 0.8 km from the Laerdal side. They subcontracted the 2 km-long Tynjadalen access adit, together with 7 km of the main alignment towards Aurland and 5.7 km towards Laerdal, to NCC Anlegg AS. A combination of Atlas Copco drillrigs, Dyno explosives and loaders equipped with Gjerstad side-dumping buckets produced the extremely tight work cycles necessary to the success of this project. The tunnel is in Precambrian gneiss, with cover of up to 1,400 m and suffered rock burst over much of its route. A 1,000 cu m fall of rock 10 km from the Aurland portal was grouted in place and reminded. Some 200,000 galvanised rock bolts and 45,000 cu m of shot Crete were placed as support within the tunnel. Ventilation air is extracted from the entire tunnel at Tynjadalen by a pair of 3 m-diametre Howden Sirocco fans. To reduce the volume of fresh air required and hence the air speed, the longer Aurland leg is filtered of dust and nitrogen

dioxide in a Howden treatment plant housed in a 100 m-long gallery some 9.5 km from the portal. There are 32 x 1.6 m-diametre ABB impulse fans ranged along this 18 km-long section of the tunnel.

545. Seikan is the world's longest rail tunnel. Marine railway tunnel 53.9 km long joining Japanese home islands of Hokkaido and Honshu. Extended construction period 1972-1985 was bedevilled by flooding and differing ground conditions. It is said that this tunnel was redundant before completion because of the proliferation of 600-seat jumbo jets flying between the two islands.

546. Channel Tunnel is world's largest construction project. Opened for traffic in March 1994 having cost $14 billion for 50 km tunnel and two terminals with all rolling stock. Employed 11 TBMs on two large-section running tunnels and smaller service tunnel driving from shafts at Sangatte in France and Shakespeare Cliff in England. One of the French landward running tunnel TBMs was turned for a second run. Two major crossover chambers under the Channel.

547. CERN is the most successful collider. 26.7 km, 3.8 m internal diametre Large Electron Positron collider situated near Geneva. One of the series of particle physics laboratories built since the War (known as atom smashers), CERN achieved its design objective within three weeks of commissioning in 1992. Currently under extension to accommodate larger experiments. Two rivals of CERN, the 20.7 km x 5.1 m internal diametre Protvino collider near Moscow and the 86 km x 4.3 m internal diametre Supercollider at Waxahachie, TX were cancelled during their construction phase.

548. Viikimaki is the largest underground treatment plant. Built in Helsinki over the period 1988-1991, to serve a population of 650,000 together with associated industry, the Viiki sewage plant involved excavation of 997,000 m^3 of rock using drill/blast techniques to form 28 caverns. At peak production, 3,500 m3/day was broken and trucked away. Lemminkainen was the contractor.

549. London Water Ring Main is the largest circulating aqueduct. Completed in 1993 and commissioned in 1995, the 80 km main supplies 6 million people with 1,300 million litres of drinking water

each day. Much of the tunnel was excavated by 3.3 m and 2.5 m diametre Lovat EPBs installing a wedgeblock concrete segmental lining at up to 100 m/day.

550. The largest windows in the world are those in the Palace of Industry and Technology at Rondpoint de la Défense, Paris, France. The three matching windows, made up of a vast number of panes of glass, have an extreme width of 218m (715 ft) and a maximum height of 50m (164 ft). The whopping windows are each bigger than your average house and this building boasts three of them.

551. The world's largest dam is currently being built across the Yangtze in China's Hubei region. Its permanent wall is nearly 183m (600 ft) high and, when complete, the dam will be capable of pumping out 18,200 megawatts of electricity from 26 generators, each equal to a medium-sized nuclear reactor. Two million people will be displaced due to the lake created by the dam. The Yangtze River in China is the World's third longest river. In 1997 that country began work on what will eventually be the world's largest dam and largest concrete structure, when it is finished in 2009. The Three Gorges Dam, in Hubei province, is a massive undertaking.

552. The highest bungee jump from a building was by New Zealander AJ Hackett who leaped off the Sky Tower Casino, the highest building in Auckland, New Zealand, plunging 180.1m (590 ft 10 in). His fall ended just 12m (40 ft) above the concrete pavement before he rebounded.

553. The largest church in the world is the Basilica of Our Lady of Peace (Notre Dame de la Paix) in Yamoussoukro, Ivory Coast. It has an area of 30, 000 sq metres (322,917 sq ft) and is 158m (518 ft) high.

The Basilica of Our Lady of Peace of Yamoussoukro, also known as Basilique de Notre Dame de la Paix de Yamoussoukro, is the largest and tallest place of worship in Africa. Situated in Yamoussoukro, the administrative capital of Côte d'Ivoire, the basilica was constructed between 1985 and 1989 for a cost of USD $300 million and intentionally modelled after the Basilica of Saint Peter in Rome. The cornerstone was laid on August 10, 1985 and was consecrated on September 10, 1990 by Pope John Paul II.

554. The world's longest bridge is the Second Lake Pontchartrain Cause-

way, which joins Mandeville and Metairie, Louisiana in the US. It is 38.422 km (Just under 24 miles) long. The Lake Pontchartrain Causeway...the World's Longest Bridge. The Causeway is the longest over-water highway bridge in the world.

The northbound span extends 23.87 miles and the southbound 23.86 miles.

Components of the Causeway were pre-cast and pre-stressed in steel forms at the Louisiana Bridge Company's prefabricated and assembling plant near Mandeville. They were then assembled, loaded on barges and towed to construction points on the lake.

The first span was built in 1955 - 1956 and opened August 30, 1956. The bridge took 14 months to complete and cost $30,677,000. The second span was built in 1967 - 1969 and opened May 10, 1969. This bridge took 20 months to complete and cost $29,887,174. The twin spans are 80 feet apart and connected by seven crossovers which function as pullover bays for motoring emergencies. Eight million vehicles travelled the Causeway in 1992. Lake Pontchartrain is 610 square miles and was named for the Count de Pontchartrain, minister of the marine during the regime of France's 'Sun King' for whom Louisiana was named. The bottom of the lake is thick with clamshells and its brackish water with shellfish, oysters and many species of skillet fish. Lake Pontchartrain and its Causeway comprise one of America's most scenic attractions.

555. The largest wooden structure in the world is the Woolloomooloo Bay Wharf in Sydney, Australia. The wharf is 400m (1,312 ft) long and 63m (206 ft) wide. It was built in 1912 and holds a hotel complex and a marina.

556. The Galleria Vittorio Emanuele in Milan, Italy, built between 1865 and 1877, is the world's oldest shopping mall. It was designed by Giuseppe Mengoni and named after the first king of Italy. The design is neo-classical and was inspired by London's Crystal Palace exhibition centre.

557. The shortest escalator is the moving walkway at Okadaya More's Shopping Mall in Kawasaki-shi, Japan. It has a vertical height of 83.4 cm (2 ft 8 in), making it some 20 times smaller than the

average escalator.

558. The world's largest palace complex is the Forbidden City (1407-1420) in Beijing. The seat of imperial power in China until 1911, it covers 74 hectares (183 acres) and includes 9,999 buildings.

559. The tallest indoor waterfall measures 34.75m (114 ft). It is situated in the lobby of the International Centre, Detroit.

560. The widest long-span bridge is the 503m (1,650 ft) long Sydney Harbour Bridge in Australia. It carries two railway tracks, eight lanes of roadway and a cycle track and footpath. It was officially opened on March 19, 1932.

561. The Akashi-Kaikyo Bridge is a bridge in Japan that employs the longest central section of any suspension bridge in the world to cross the Akashi Strait (Akashi-Kaikyo) linking Maiko in Kobe and Matsuho, on Awaji Island as part of the Honshu-Shikoku Highway. It was planned one of three Honshu-Shikoku connecting bridges. The original plan was for a mixed railway-road bridge but when the bridge was begun in April 1986, it was restricted to road only, with six lanes. Actual construction did not begin until May 1988 and the bridge was opened for traffic on April 5, 1998. The Akashi Strait is an international waterway and required a 1500 metre wide lane. The bridge has three spans. The central span is 1991 metres, with the two other sections each 960 metres and the bridge is 3911 metres overall. The central span was originally only 1990 metres but was stretched by a further metre in the Kobe earthquake on January 17, 1995.

562. At 5.46 am on January 17th 1995, whilst many of its citizens were still asleep, the Japanese city of Kobe was hit by largest earthquake in Japan since 1923. The Hyogo-ken Nanbu earthquake was not only powerful (magnitude 6.9), but with the epicentre only 20 km southwest of the city, it resulted in massive damage to property and loss of life. The worst effected area was in the central part of Kobe, a region about 5 km by 20 km alongside the main docks and port area. This area is built on soft and easily moved rocks, especially the port itself which is built on reclaimed ground. Here the ground actually liquefied and acted like thick soup, allowing buildings to topple sideways, resulting in the huge cranes in the harbour toppling over into the sea.

Large earthquakes in remote, uninhabited areas can do relatively little damage to the human population, but when they strike in places like the Kobe / Osaka region with a population of 10 million people, the damage levels will always be significant. More than 102,000 buildings were destroyed in Kobe, leaving over a fifth of the city population, some 300, 000 people, homeless. The local government's estimate of the cost to restore the basic infrastructure of the city was about $150 billion dollars and that was just for the state owned buildings and services. When all the costs are added up, it makes the Hyogo-ken Nanbu earthquake probably the most expensive natural disaster in modern history. All this damage was the result of just 20 seconds of earthquake.

563. Lebanese villagers have turned a traditional recipe into what could become the longest sandwich. It was measured a 720-metre long sandwich.

564. The 'Labneh' or strained yoghurt, sandwich was made by more than 700 people from Kfar Qatra, a village 25 km southeast of Beirut. The villagers used 3500 loaves of Lebanese village bread, 140 kg of Labneh, 21,000 olives, 280 kilograms of tomatoes and cucumbers to make the giant sandwich. The sandwich was cut into 14,260 pieces and distributed among ceremony attendees, including the Lebanese officials.

565. World War II was the most extensive and costly armed conflict in the history of the world, involving the great majority of the world's

nations, being fought simultaneously in several major theatres and costing approximately 55.5 million lives. It is estimated that over fifty-four million people died in World War II, which was the bloodiest war in history. The war was fought between two groups of powers: the alliance of the British Commonwealth, United States, Soviet Union, China and the governments-in-exile of France, Poland and other occupied European countries—collectively known as the Allies and the alliance of Germany, Italy and Japan—collectively known as the Axis.

566. A CVR (T) Scorpion Tank, Upgraded to the latest Repair craft PLC S 2000 Peacekeeper specifications, is the world's fastest tank. Peacekeeper took the world record at an average speed of 82.23 kph / 51.10 mph.

567. During World War II, Britain's heaviest bombs were designed by Sir Barnes Wallis (1887-1979), an engineer who had also designed aircraft. In 1943, Dr. Wallis designed an 8,600-pound bomb for use against German dams. He then outdid himself by building the 'Tall Boy' bomb, which weighed 12,000 pounds. This heavy bomb was used against targets on both land and sea.

Finally, Wallis enlarged Tall Boy to make the 22,000-pound Grand Slam bomb. The Grand Slam was so big that it could only be carried once at a time by strong four-engine bomber planes — which had to be specially refitted for the purpose.

568. The largest and heaviest bomb ever deployed by the US is The Mk 17/24 (as the deployed versions were eventually designated) was 24 ft. 8 in. long, with a 61.4 in. diametre and a weight of 41,400-42,000 lb (30,000 lb of this was the 3.5 in. steel casing).

569. Rawalpindi Express and Pakistan's star pacer Shoaib Akhtar was officially declared the fastest bowler in the world after breaking the 100 mph mark. Although Shoaib finished wicketless as his

side defeated New Zealand by 66 runs in the third one-day international on Saturday, he clocked 100.04 mph (161 kph) with the sixth ball of his second over to Craig McMillan.

570. The highest Test batting average is Australia's Sir Donald Bradman, with 99.94. Given that a career batting average over 50 is generally regarded as qualifying the player as of legendary status and that only four other players have averages (just barely) over 60, this is an outstanding statistic. Sir Donald Bradman is an Australian sporting legend. No other sportsperson in Australian history has captured the respect and admiration of the sporting public the way 'The Don', the cricketer from Bowral in the State of New South Wales (NSW), has done. During his 21 years of first-class cricket, Bradman achieved everything that was possible in the sport - he captained his South Australian Sheffield Shield team, was a State selector, Test selector and captain of the Australian Team for almost a decade, including of the 1948 Australian Test team known as The Invincible. Bradman averaged a century - 100 runs - once in every three innings he played. His batting averages are revered. In his first international tour (1930) Bradman made 2960 runs (with a batting average of 98.66), including 10 centuries. In his final tour 18 years later, he made 2428 runs with an 89.92 batting average, including 11 centuries. When he retired in 1948, Bradman's legacy to the cricketing world was a remarkable Test batting average of 99.94.

571. Because of Iceland's geographical isolation from mainland Europe, no human beings ever set foot on Iceland until medieval times. The first humans to arrive on Iceland were Irish explorers, who arrived no later than 795 A.D. They established a colony, but it didn't last. By the time the Vikings arrived eighty years later and established a permanent settlement, only a few hermits remained.

572. Tendulkar and Dravid's partnership of 331 against New Zealand in the 2nd ODI was a New world record for any wicket beating Dravid and Ganguly's partnership of 318. Indian captain Sachin Tendulkar and Rahul Dravid have broken the world record for a one-day international partnership. The pair put on a massive 331 runs against New Zealand in Hyderabad with both batsman mak-

ing their highest scores in limited overs internationals. Tendulkar was unbeaten after a 186 containing 19 fours and four sixes against erratic Kiwi bowling. Dravid hit 15 fours and 2 sixes on his way to 153 in the second wicket partnership. The final 376 for two was the highest score by India in a one-day international.

573. The record for the highest score in a test innings is 952 by Sri Lanka against India at Colombo on 6th August 1997 at the R. Premadasa Stadium. Sanath Jayasuriya and Roshan Mahanama added 576 for the second wicket, as the Indians were condemned to spending close to 20 hours on the field.

574. Gavaskar still holds the record for the most number of test centuries (34) and is the only player to score centuries in each innings three times. Gavaskar was also the first batsman to reach 10,000 test runs and held the record for the most number of runs till broken by Alan Border. Sunil Gavaskar was a cricket player during the 1970s and 1980s for Bombay and India. He is considered one of the greatest opening batsmen in the sport's history. He made a spectacular test debut scoring 774 runs in his first series against the West Indies helping India win for the first time in the Caribbean. From then until his retirement in 1987 he was a mainstay of the Indian batting line-up. In 1983, Gavaskar broke one of the oldest and most prestigious records in the game: Donald Bradman's 29 test centuries. Gavaskar was captain of the Indian team on several occasions in the late 70's and early 80's though here his record is more mixed. Often equipped with weak bowling attacks

he tended to use conservative tactics that resulted in a large number of draws. Still he had several successes as captain especially a 2-0 victory over Pakistan in 1979 and a victory in the World Championship of Cricket held in Australia in 1985. On the downside, there was a heavy defeat against Pakistan in 1982, which cost him the captaincy for a while. Overall, he played 125 test matches and scored 10,122 runs at an average of 51.12. He scored 34 centuries and 45 half-centuries with a highest score of 236.

LONGEST MUSIC VIDEO

575. Michael Jackson holds the record for the longest music video, 'Ghosts' released in 1996 is 35 minutes long and is based on a Steven King horror.

Michael Jackson is unquestionably the biggest pop star of the '80s and certainly one of the most popular recording artists of all time. In his prime, Jackson was an unstoppable juggernaut, possessed of all the tools to dominate the charts seemingly at will: an instantly identifiable voice, eye-popping dance moves, stunning musical versatility and loads of sheer star power. His 1982 blockbuster 'Thriller' became the biggest-selling album of all time (probably his best-known accomplishment) and he was the first black artist to find stardom on MTV, breaking down innumerable boundaries both for his race and for music video as an art form. Yet as Jackson's career began, very gradually, to descend from the dizzying heights of his peak years, most of the media's attention focused on his increasingly bizarre eccentricities, he was often depicted as an arrested man-child, completely sheltered from adult reality by a life spent in show business. The snickering turned to scandal in 1993, when Jackson was accused of molesting a 13-year-old boy, although he categorically denied the charges, his out-of-court settlement failed to restore his tarnished image. He never quite escaped the stigma of those allegations and while he continued to sell records at superstar-like levels, he did not release them with enough frequency (or, many critics thought, inspiration) to once again become better known for his music than his private life. Whether as a pop icon or a tabloid caricature, Jackson always remained bigger than life.

576. The fastest server in the women's game is Venus Williams (USA), who recorded a serve of 127.4 M.P.H. during the European Indoor Championships at Zurich, Switzerland, on October 16, 1998. Venus burst into women's tennis in the early '90s and sent fans home amazed by her speed and incredible strength. The pure talent she possesses has led her to four Grand Slam victories and a seat alongside sister Serena atop her sport, as the No. 2 female tennis player in the world.

577. Andy Roddick, who clocked a massive 149 mph serve at the Stella Artois Championships, recorded the fastest serve in tennis history. Previously Greg Rusedski was the man who holds the world record for the fastest serve .

578. Jean Borotra (b. 13 August 1898) of France did not easily give up, he entered in the men's singles competition 35 times between 1922 and 1964 his last title coming at the age of 41. In 1977, he appeared in the Veterans' Doubles at the ripe age of 78. That's a 55 years span Wimbledon love affair.

579. The Youngest Champion in Australian Open for men's is Ken Rosewall (Aus). He won the title in 1953 when he was 18 years and 2 months. Rosewall won the first of his singles titles at the 1953 Australian. He also holds the record of the Oldest Men's Champion in Australian Open at the age of 37 years and 2 months in 1972. Ken Robert Rosewall, born November 2, 1934 in Sydney, Australia, was a champion tennis player. Born into a family that played tennis and owned tennis courts. A natural left-hander,

Rosewall's father taught him to play right-handed and as a result, he developed a powerful and effective backhand. He was only 18 years old when he won the Australian and French Open men's singles title. In 1956, partnered with Lew Hoad, he won the doubles Grand Slam in tennis, taking all four major championships that year.

During an outstanding playing career, he remained virtually injury free, something that helped him to still win championships at the age of 43 and remain ranked in the top 15 in the world. Although he was a finalist 4 times at the Wimbledon championships, the one major tournament eluded him. In 1980, Ken Rosewall was inducted into the International Tennis Hall of Fame.

580. Martina Hingis (Swz) won the title in 1997 when she was 16 years and 3 months, claiming the youngest Champion for women's category. Martina Hingis of Switzerland wins the Australian Open trophy after she defeated France's Mary Pierce during their final match at the Australian Open January 25. Sixteen-year-old Hingis beat Pierce 6-2, 6-2 to become the youngest player to win a professional grand slam title.

581. Charlotte (Lottie) Dod became the youngest player ever to win a Wimbledon singles event when, in 1887, she won at the age of 15 years, 285 days. In 1996, Martina Hingis became a Wimbledon doubles champion at 15 years, 282 days. Dod was also a silver medallist in archery at the 1908 Olympics, a member of the British national field hockey team in 1899 and the British Amateur golf champion in 1904.

582. The youngest male champion was Boris Becker (West Germany)(b.22 November 1967) who won the men's singles title in 1985 at 17 yr 227 days.

At the same time, he became the only un-seeded player and the only German ever to win the title, as well as the youngest person ever to win any Grand Slam title in men's singles.

583. The youngest women to win Wimbledon was Jennifer Capriatti (USA) (b. 29 March 1976) at 14 yr 89 days at the time of her first match on 26 June 1990. She won this match making her the youngest ever winner at Wimbledon. Youngest Grand Slam semi-finalist ever (age 14 in 1990 French Open), surprise gold medal winner at 1992 Olympics, left tour from 1994 to 96 due to personal problems including an arrest for marijuana possession, surprised many with comeback, winning French Open (2001) and 2 Australian Opens (2001,02).

584. William Renshaw holds the crown for most men's singles titles. He won a total of seven Wimbledon men's crowns (1881-86, 1889).

585. Sampras, Pete (1971-), American professional tennis player holds the record for most career grand slam singles titles with 14 times. Born Peter Sampras in Washington, D.C., he was raised in Rancho Palos Verdes, California. In 1988, he left high school to become a professional tennis player. In 1990, he won the United States Open and the inaugural Grand Slam Cup tournament.

586. Sampras, modelling his style of play on that of Australian tennis player Rod Laver, developed an extremely fast serve and powerful ground strokes. He also became known for his proficient volleying. In 1993, Sampras won Wimbledon and then his second U.S. Open. That year he also became the first professional player to record more than 1,000 *aces* (serves beyond the reach of the opponent) in a single year. During the mid- and late 1990s, Sampras dominated the grand slam tournaments, which in tennis are Wimbledon, the U.S. Open, the French Open and the Australian Open. He twice won the Australian Open (1994, 1997) and the U.S. Open (1995, 1996) and captured six more Wimbledon titles (1994, 1995, 1997-2000). With his seventh Wimbledon singles championship, Sampras tied a record set more than 100 years earlier. Sampras won at least one grand slam title every year from 1993 to 2000. In 2002, he won his fifth U.S. Open title, his 14th overall singles title in a grand slam event.

587. Most women's singles titles was hold by Martina Navratilova, 9 times. Martina Navratilova is the leader among women. She won nine women's singles titles.

588. Youngest men's singles seed record was hold by Bjorn Borg (17 years, 19 days) His seed ranking was 6 in 1973. Borg's brilliant baseline play and the athletic ability that often enabled him to retrieve seemingly impossible shots made him the dominant male player in international tennis during the late 1970s and into the 1980s. Even though he never played in the Australian Open and never won the U. S. Open, Borg won 11 singles championships in grand slam events, third on the all-time list behind Pete Sampras and Roy Emerson. He won the Wimbledon title five years in a row, 1976 through 1980 and reached the finals again in 1981 but lost to John McEnroe. Borg also won the French Open a record 6 times, in 1974 and 1975 and from 1978 through 1981. He lost in the U. S. Open finals four times. Borg was an unusual champion in that he never followed the entire worldwide tour. He insisted on taking a four-month vacation, which embroiled him in a dispute with the men's tennis council in 1982. Borg was told he would have to enter the qualifying round for every major event that year because he refused to commit himself to playing the required number of tournaments. As a result, he took the year off and then announced his retirement in 1983, when he was only twenty-seven. A major celebrity in Europe, Borg married Rumanian tennis pro Mariana Simionescu in Bucharest on July 24, 1980. It was the major social

event of the year; a company paid about $200,000 for the right to photograph the ceremony and reception. That was just a fraction of Borg's non-tennis income, which reached about $4 million a year in commercial endorsements. When he retired, he had a choice of homes, a penthouse in Monte Carlo, not far from his successful pro shop and a small island off the Swedish coast. Borg attempted a comeback in 1991, still using his old wooden racket, but because of his long layoff and the fact that other players had begun using high-tension graphite rackets, he had little success and retired for good.

589. The tallest NBA player was the Romanian born 7 ft. 7 in. Gheorgehe Mureasan. He made his debut in 1994. Gheorghe Muresan is most well known for being an NBA player. He, along with Manute Bol, were the tallest players ever to play in the NBA. They both measured 7 feet 7 inches. Gheorghe was able to show flashes of unusual dexterity for a man his height. He quickly became a fan favourite and a friend of the highlight reel. Muresan was able to turn this fame into a small acting career, appearing in a few commercials and a major motion picture.

His best season in the NBA was the 1995/96 season. He was named the NBA's Most Improved Player after posting 14.5 points per game, 2.26 blocks per game and 9.6 rebounds per game. He wears a size

19 shoe.

590. A will drafted by Choudhary Hiranand of New Delhi for his client Rishi on April 1, 1994 had 489 pages (1,04,567 words) was the longest will.

591. Bimla Rishi of Delhi Signed a lease in the first floor of building for 9,99,99,999 years and 364 days (one less than a billion years) charging only one paise per year on July 13, 1999. She has already received for one million years in advance. It was longest lease ever made by a person.

592. Reagan Jones of Kerala wrote the longest letter in the world. He took four years to complete a letter addressed to pope John Paul II, using more than 10 crore words on the 2.4 km (7,872 ft) long, 61 cm (2 ft) wide paper, which weighed over 100 kg.

593. The fastest needle-threading record is hold by Om Prakash Singh of Allahabad. He threaded a strand of cotton through a No. 13 needle 20,675 in 2 hours on July 25,1993.

594. In 1997, as part of the 50 years of Independence celebrations, Prithvi Silk Creations of Banglore wove a pure crepe silk sari 121 m long and 45 in wide. It was the longest sari.

595. Eight people of the bag division of Sane Sportswear at Vadodara made a skybag 13.3 ft long. 4.16 ft wide and 8.75 ft tall in 105 hours at a cost of Rs 85,000. It was the largest sky bag.

596. The largest sky lantern was 38 ft tall, 22 ft wide lantern using 2000 sheets of 3 x 3 sq inch thermocol and 25 kg nails. The lamp built in 15 days (225 man-hours) was lit by ten 250 watt bulbs for a month from October 15, 1998 at Ganesh kala Krida, Pune.

597. Dr A. Koteswar Rao of Jind made a 6.1466 km (20,166 ft) long, 2.75 cm wide chain from 60,498 empty cigarette packets of 57 different brands without any glue.

598. On June 3, 1990, three riders, Harprakash Rishi, Amarjeet Singh and Navjyot Chaddha road a 100 cc Kinetic Honda non-stop for 1,001 hours in 42 days covering 30,965 km using 621 litres of petrol and 21 litres of oil.

599. Ramzan ali of Pitampura, Delhi, dressed, styles and cut the hair of 1,200 clients from 4 pm on April 23,1999 to 10 pm on April 27

non-stop.

600. V. Jayaraman of Tamil Nadu clapped for 58 hr and 9 min at Chennai from 6:35 pm on Feb. 12 to 1:40 pm on Feb. 15, 1988. The claps being audible from a distance of 109.7 m.

601. Yougesh Sharma of Gwalior shook hands non-stop with 31,118 people in 8 hours on Jan. 14, 1996 at the Gwalior Trade Fair, breaking his previous record of shaking hands with 28,233 people in 8 hours.

602. Inder Pal Komal of Delhi sent a 100 m long greeting on fax to Mark Cohen on Feb. 22, 1993 starting at 19:01.48 sec. It took 2 hr 54 min 47 sec.

603. Jonathan is a human spoon rest! The 11-year-old from Oregon set a record by balancing seven spoons on his face for five seconds. The spoons weighed between .69 ounces (21.5 grams) and 1.4 ounces (43.5 grams). Maybe he celebrated with seven bowls of ice cream!

604. The digital Gollum from *The Lord of the Rings: The Two Towers* had 250 facial expressions and 300 muscles, making him the most complex digital character on film. The actor who provided Gollum's voice and movements was filmed wearing a skin-tight suit with dots. A computer captured the dots' movement, then digital Gollum was created.

605. Helios 2 is a spacecraft that approached closest to the sun. Helios 2 was launched into a solar orbit on 15 January 1976. It had a perihelion of 0.29 AU and an aphelion of 1 AU. Its orbit made it an ideal platform for making long baseline time-of-arrival measurements to obtain source direction. The satellite rotated with a ~ 1-s spin period. The mission ended in 1981. HELIOS 1 was launched on 10 December 1974 and HELIOS 2 on 15 January 1976. Both were placed in elliptical orbits about the Sun with their perihelion well within the orbit of Mercury, aphelion at the orbit of Earth, with orbital periods of about 190 days.

What made the two Helios missions so unusual was that the two spacecraft made incredibly close passes to the Sun resulting in very high orbital speeds. These high speeds resulted from the fact that both probes were placed into very elliptical orbits around the Sun. When a probe is placed into a circular orbit, its speed remains a constant. When in a highly elliptical orbit, however, a vehicle will reach very high speeds when it is close to the body it is orbiting but slow down considerably when it is far away.

The Helios missions both orbited in this manner, with a furthest distance (or aphelion) of nearly 1 Astronomical Unit (AU), which is the distance at which the Earth orbits the Sun. Meanwhile, the closest approach (or perihelion) of the Helios probes was about 0.3 AU, closer than any spacecraft had been at the time. The eccentricity of such an orbit is about 0.54 with a period of about 190 days.

606. A Scottish man Campbell Aird is being fitted with the world's first fully mobile 'bionic' arm. The major advance in prosthetic limbs will come when Campbell Aird will be given the electronic arm developed by the Prosthetics Research and Development team at Edinburgh's Princess Margaret Rose Orthopaedic Hospital. The new limb allows Campbell Aird, a hotelier from Moffat, to carry out functions that he would normally find impossible. It is powered by complex electronics, which permit the wearer to control movement through micro switches and pressure points. Dr. David Gow, who has led the research project for 10 years, said: 'It's bionic because it's restoring a biological function in terms of prosthetic upper limb and it's using electronics to control and power it. 'The arm is obviously not a match for the real arm but it has more functions than has been possible with electrical power previously'. Mr Aird had his real arm removed to stop a cancer spreading to the rest of his body. Whereas many prosthetic limbs currently have some limited use of wrist or elbow, the new limb, powered by motors and gearboxes, will give Mr Aird use of his shoulder for the first time

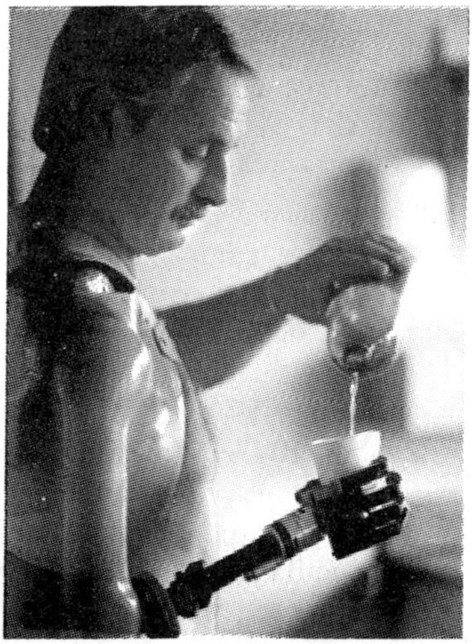

since his amputation 16 years ago. It requires high electrical power to operate as prosthetic limb at shoulder level and it is only the development of advanced new motors in recent year that has allowed the researchers to make the step forward.

Campbell Aird is keen to see how the new arm will cope with the work he does around the hotel. Already, he has expressed some concern that the project has not received more backing in Britain.

'Funding is a bit tight. The thing that is very frustrating is that other countries are showing a bigger interest in it than Britain', the hotelier said. The limb, which has four basic functions, will also have a degree of realism thanks to a skin-like covering with wrinkles and fingerprints. The researchers said the limb would cost round £10,000 ($16,200) if produced commercially.

607. Dinesh Kumar Pathak typed non-stop for 210 hours at the Hindustan Mitra Mandal School, Jamshedpur starting at 12 noon on Jan .4, 1999 and ending at 4 pm on Jan. 14.

608. Mahesh Kumar (25) of Chandigarh typed non-stop on a PC for 31 hours from 203 printed pages from the Selected on may 7, 1998 at 11:15 am he finished the following day at 6:15 pm.

609. The seven-and-a-half-foot-tall American actor Matthew McGrory has a mild-mannered speaking voice and a composed screen presence. Growing up in suburban Pennsylvania, McGrory played drums and studied at Widener University. His proportions earned him media exposure when he was named as having the largest feet in the world (size 29 1/2).

610. Sam Stacey, an 18-year-old from Stainforth, England, is reputedly the female with the longest pair of legs. Her legs measured from 49.75 inches from hip to heal in January 2001. This is the height of an average 10-year-old English child.

611. When Fabien Pretou and Natalie Lucius (both France) walked down the aisle on April 14, 1990, they became the married couple with the greatest difference in height. He is 6 ft. 2 in. (188.5 cm) tall, while she is only 3 ft. 1 in. (94 cm)—a difference of 3 ft. 1.2 in. (94.5 cm).

612. Jon Brower Minnoch weighed 1,400 lb. (635 kg) when he married

his 110-lb. (50-kg) wife, Jeannette, (both USA) in March 1978. At 1,289.7 lb. (585 kg), this is the greatest recorded difference in weight for a married couple. Jon was also the heaviest person in medical history. He suffered from obesity as a child and by 1963, when he was 22 years old and 6 ft. 1 in. (1.85 m) tall, he weighed a huge 392 lb. (178 kg). By September 1976, he weighed 974 lb. (442 kg). He died in 1983, still weighing more than 798 lb. (362 kg).

613. The record of the most weight gained by a woman is hold by Doris James (USA). She is alleged to have gained 324 lb. (147 kg) in the 12 months before her death in August 1965. At this time, she was aged 38, weighed 675 lb. (306 kg) and measured 5 ft. 2 in. (1.57 m) in height.

614. The record of the most weight gained by a man Arthur Knorr (USA), who was born in 1916 and died in 1960. He gained a record 293 lb. (133 kg) in the last six months of his life.

615. Rosalie Bradford (USA) is claimed to have registered a peak weight of 1,199 lb. (544 kg) in January 1987, age 43. After following a controlled diet, she weighed 282 lb. (128 kg) in February 1994.

616. The record of the lightest person in the world is hold by Lucia Xarate (1863-89, Mexico), an emaciated ateleiotic dwarf of 26.8 in. (67 cm) who weighed 2.8 lb. (1.1 kg) at birth, weighed only 4.7 lb. (2.13 kg) at the age of 17. She had fattened up to 13 lb. (5.9 kg) by her 20th birthday. The lightest recorded adults of normal height are those suffering from Simmond's Disease (hypophyseal cachexia). Losses of up to 65% of the original body weight have been recorded in females, with a 'low' of 44 lb. (20 kg) in the case of Emma Shaller (USA) who stood 5 ft. 2 in. (1.57 m). Edward C. Hagner, alias Eddie Masher (USA), is alleged to have weighed only 48 lb. (22 kg) at a height of 5 ft. 7 in. (1.7 m). He was also known as the 'Skeleton Dude'.

617. Billy Leon and Benny Loyd McCrary, alias McGuire (both USA), were normal in size until the age of six. In November 1978, just before their 32nd birthday, Billy and Benny weighed 743 lb. (337 kg) and 723 lb. (328 kg) respectively and both had waists measuring 84 in. (2.13 m). They became professional tag wrestling per-

formers. When weighed before competitions, they clocked weights of up to 769 lb. (349 kg).

618. The record of the lightest twins is hold by Roshan Maralyn (17.28 oz. or 490 g) and Melanie Louise (13.05 oz. or 370 g). Two sets of twins have been born with a combined weight of 30.33 oz. (860 g). Roshan Maralyn (17.28 oz. or 490 g) and Melanie Louise (13.05 oz. or 370 g) were born to Katrina Gray (Australia) at the Royal Women's Hospital, Brisbane, Queensland, Australia, on November 19, 1993. Wendy Morrison (Canada) gave birth to Anne (14.81 oz. or 420 g) and John (15.52 oz. or 440 g) at Ottawa General Hospital, Ontario, Canada, on January 14, 1994.

619. The shortest living twins are John and Greg Rice (USA), born on December 3, 1951. They are identical twins and both measure 2 ft. 10 in. (86.3 cm).

620. The shortest twins on record were Matyus and Bela Matina (Hungary, later USA, 1903—c. 1935), who were both 2 ft. 6 in. (76 cm) tall.

621. Younis Edwan (Jordan) is believed to be 2 ft. 1.5 in. (65 cm) tall. He was born c. 1971 and is the sixth sibling in a family of seven sisters and brothers.

622. The shortest mature man for whose height there is independent evidence was Gul Mohammed (India). When examined at Ram Manohar Hospital, New Delhi, in 1990, he was found to be just 1 ft. 10.5 in. (57 cm) tall. He died at the age of 39 in 1997, after a long struggle with asthma and bronchitis.

623. The tallest living man is Radhouane Charbib (Tunisia), who measures 7 ft. 8.9 in. (2.35 m). He is one of 11 brothers and sisters, who all measure a normal 5 ft. 6 in. (1.7 m).

624. The tallest man in medical history was Robert Wadlow (USA). When measured in June 1940, shortly before his death, he was 8 ft. 11.1 in. (2.72 m) tall. His greatest recorded weight was 491 lb. (222.71 kg) on his 21st birthday. He weighed 438 lb. (199 kg) at the time of his death. His shoe size was (18.5 in. or 47 cm long) and his hands measured 12.75 in. (32.4 cm) from the wrist to the tip of the middle finger. His arm span was 9 ft. 5.75 in. (2.88 m)

and his peak daily food consumption was 8,000 calories. At the age of nine, he was able to carry his father, Harold F. Wadlow, who stood 5 ft. 11 in. (1.8 m) and weighed 170 lb. (77 kg), up the stairs of the family home.

625. Sandy Allen (USA) is 7 ft. 7.25 in. (2.31 m) tall, making her the tallest living woman. As a 2.95-kg baby, her abnormal growth began soon after birth. She stood 6 ft. 3 in. (1.90 m) by the age of 10 and was 7 ft. 1 in. (2.16 m) by 16.

626. The tallest woman ever for whose height there is reliable evidence. was Zeng Jinlian (China). She was 8 ft. 1.75 in. (2.48 m) tall when she died on February 13, 1982, aged 17.

627. The largest waist was that of Walter Hudson (USA), which measured 9 ft. 11 in. (3.02 m) at his peak weight of 1,201 lb. (545 kg) body parts.

628. The two-toed syndrome exhibited by some members of the Wadomo tribe of the Zambezi Valley, Zimbabwe and the Kalanga tribe of the eastern Kalahari Desert, Botswana, is hereditary, via a single mutated gene.

629. An inquest held on a baby boy on September 16, 1921 in London, UK, reported that he had 14 fingers and 15 toes. This condition, known as polydactylism, can be caused by any one of over 30 rare

congenital medical syndromes (syndromes that are present at birth). The condition is relatively common, with as many as two in 1,000 births affected. These extra digits are most commonly fleshy bumps without any bones, but can be complete fingers or toes.

630. Jose Lopez (originally Mexico, now USA) has a third foot, consisting of an ankle and four toes, growing out from the ankle of his left leg.

631. The heaviest brain ever recorded weighed 5 lb. 1.1 oz. (2.3 kg). It belonged to a 30-year-old male and was reported by Dr. T. Mandybur of the Department of Pathology and Laboratory Medicine at the University of Cincinnati, Ohio, in December 1992. An average-size brain for an adult would weigh 2.8 to 3 lb. (1.3 to 1.4 kg).

632. There are historical accounts that Thomas Wedders, who lived in the UK during the 1770s and was a member of a travelling freak circus, had a nose measuring 7.5 in. (19 cm) long.

633. The world's lightest normal (non-atrophied) brain weighed just 1 lb. 8 oz. (680 g). It belonged to Daniel Lyon (Ireland), who died in New York, in 1907 at the age of 46. He was just over 5 ft. (1.5 m) tall and weighed 145 lb. (66 kg).

634. In 1816, a tooth belonging to scientist Sir Isaac Newton (UK, 1642-1727) was sold in London for £730 ($3,633). This is approximately £25,000 ($35,700) in today's terms. It was purchased by an aristocrat who had it set in a ring.

635. The moustache of Kalyan Ramji Sain (India) spanned 133.4 in. (3.39 m). In July 1993, the right side measured 67.7 in. (1.72 m) and the left measured 65.7 in. (1.67 m). The moustache had been growing since 1976.

636. The world's longest documented hair belongs to Ho Sateow, a tribal medicine man from Chiang Mai, Thailand. On November 21, 1997, his hair was unravelled and it was officially measured at 16 ft. 11 in. (5.15 m) long. He had not had a haircut in over 70 years. He fell sick after cutting his hair when he was 18 years and vowed never to cut it again. The hair is washed annually with detergent and worn wound up in a fashionable beehive.

637. The beard of Hans Langseth (Norway) measured 17 ft. 6 in. (5.33

m) at the time of his burial in Kensett, Iowa, in 1927. He started growing his beard at the age of 30 and it took 51 years to grow to this length. It grew at an average rate of 0.007 in. (2 mm) per week and was presented to the Smithsonian Institution, Washington D.C., in 1967.

638. The beard of the 'Bearded Lady', Janice Deveree (USA), was measured at 14 in. (36 cm) long in 1884.

639. The world's longest fingernails are those of Shridhar Chillal (India), who last cut his fingernails in 1952. On July 8, 1998, the nails on his left hand had a total length of 20 ft. 2.25 in. (6.15 m).

640. The woman with the world's longest fingernails is Lee Redmond (USA). Her nails measure a total length of 21 ft. 9 in. (6.63 m). Lee has been growing her nails for 19 years. The longest nail is on her left thumb and measures 27 in. (68.58 cm).

641. On March 15, 1989 at the National Naval Medical Centre in Bethesda, Maryland, Prof. Bimal C. Ghosh removed a gall bladder weighing a record-breaking 23 lb. (10.4 kg) from a 69-year-old woman. This is more than three times the weight of an average newborn baby. The patient made a full recovery after the operation.

642. The right bicep of Denis Sester (USA) measures 30 in. (77.8 cm) when cold. He built up his amazing muscles by performing arm curls with a 150-lb. (68-kg) bucket of sand. As a youngster, he wrestled hogs weighing 400 lb. (180 kg) on his parents' farm to get fit.

643. The greatest fully authenticated age to which any human has ever lived is 122 years 164 days by Jeanne Louise Calment (France). She was born on February 21, 1875 and died on August 4, 1997. Centenarians surviving beyond their 113th year are extremely rare. It is thought that only one 115-year life can be expected in 2.1 billion lives.

644. Rosanna Dalla Corte (Italy), born in 1931, gave birth to a baby boy on July 18, 1994 when she was 63. The baby was conceived through artificial insemination of donor eggs. On November 7, 1996, 63-year-old Arceli Keh (USA) gave birth to daughter Cynthia having

undergone IVF treatment.

645. The oldest mother to have quadruplets is Merryl Thelma Fudel (Australia) who gave birth to three girls and one boy on April 18, 1998, at the age of 55 years 286 days, at Sharp Memorial Hospital, San Diego, California. One baby died at birth due to respiratory failure.

646. The oldest twins ever documented are Eli Shadrack and John Meshak Phipps (USA), born on February 14, 1803 in Affington, Virginia. Eli died on February 23, 1911 at the age of 108 years, his brother John died on December 10, 1916 at the age of 113. The chance of identical twins both reaching and surpassing the age of 100 is about one in 700 million.

647. Born in 1952, Ronnie and Donnie Galyon (both USA) are the oldest living conjoined male twins. For 36 years they travelled in sideshows, carnivals and circuses. In 1991, they retired and now live in Ohio.

648. Giacomo and Giovanni Battista Tocci (Italy) were born on October 4, 1877 and lived to be 63 years old. They were separate above the waist, but shared an abdomen, pelvis and two legs.

649. The record of the greatest number of descendants is hold by Samuel S. Mast. At the time of his death on October 15, 1992, age 96, Samuel S. Mast (USA), had 824 living descendants. The roll call consisted of 11 children, 97 grandchildren, 634 great-grandchildren and 82 great great grandchildren.

650. The longest toenails record belongs to Californian Louise Hollis who has managed to grow and maintain toenails that are approximately six inches long. This is facilitated by wearing nothing but open toed shoes, something that would be possible with the mild climate in her hometown of Compton, CA. Maintenance for her toes takes a total of two days each week when all the time for filing and painting them is combined.

651. One world record for most body piercing was set by Canadian Brent Moffat who had 700 piercing all done with 18g surgical needles in one session of just over seven hours. This form of pierc-

ing is 'play piercing' where the skin is pierced for the effect and not for permanently healing to wear jewellery. In the UK, a record for most body piercing in one session was achieved by piercer Charlie Wilson and subject Kam Ma, who endured 600 permanent piercing in just over eight and a half hours. The titanium rings were set in long rows up and down his arms and torso, with the rings being pierced about one per minute. Overall, the entire weight of the new jewellery came to about nine ounces.

652. Currently two men are nearly tied for the Most Tattoo Man record. One is a retired military man who lives in Scotland named Tom Leppard, who just happens to have 99.9% of his *body covered in leopard spots. He has no other tattoo designs other than this all-covering pattern, which is, only absent from the insides of his ears and between his toes. The other tattoo fan vying for the record is an Australian named Lucky Rich who has covered nearly all his body in a tribal-style patterning.*

653. The record for the longest tattoo session endured goes to Britain. Tattooist Chris Goodwill tattooed Kevin Budden for 33 hours straight in April, 2003. Designs executed during this time-included peacocks, a Union Jack and flames.

654. For women, Canadian stripper/dancer Krystyne Kolorful has been known as the Most Tattoo Woman for many years. Her full body suit took nearly a decade to complete and was started to give her a difference in her dance work. More recently, American Julie Gnuse has tied the title. Julie has a complex floral-influenced patterning all over her body, including her entire face. Her motivation for tattooing is that she suffers from porphyria, a rare disease whose symptoms include an extreme sun sensitivity. The tattooed designs give her some protection and cover the scarring that results from the heavy blistering and burning she had suffered before being inked.

655. The blind land speed record was broken by Alistair Weaver, a journalist who is sighted but used a blindfold. Alistair Weaver broke the blind land speed record in Yorkshire in April, by driving his Audi S8 at speeds of over 140 mph. He was guided by a friend in a chasing car with a radio link.

There was only one problem. Weaver does not have sight impairment. He simply wore a blindfold to 'level the playing field' between fully sighted and visually impaired drivers.

656. Madeline Mann was born in 1989 with the lowest birth weight of any surviving premature birth. She was born by Caesarean section, 13 weeks premature, when her mother developed pre-eclampsia. She was 9.9 ounces and 10 inches at birth. Despite her humble beginnings, she has developed normally and now lives in Chicago

657. The youngest person ever to give birth is Lina Medina, a Peruvian girl from the Andean village of Ticrapo. She gave birth to a boy by caesarean section on May 14, 1939 at the age of five years, seven months and 21 days.

The girl's father was initially suspected of being the father but authorities were never able to determine who fathered Lina's child. Medical examination at the time of birth revealed that Lina had the ovaries of a fully mature woman. Her medical history also claimed that she had been having menstrual cycles for years before giving birth. She had also developed breasts. Doctors theorised that her abnormal sexual maturity was a result of an extraordinary hormonal disorder of pituitary origin.

658. The largest single-ticket jackpot winner in history is Jack Whittaker Jr. of West Virginia. In December 2002, he had the sole winning ticket for a $314.9 million jackpot in the U.S. Powerball lottery.

659. In 2003, Author Michael Hawley, a scientist at the Massachusetts Institute of Technology, published 'Bhutan: A Visual Odyssey across the Kingdom' the largest book ever published. Each book is 5-by-7 feet, 112 pages and 133-pounds. The book, which costs $2000 to produce, is being sold along with its easel-like stand for $10,000. All proceeds are being donated to a charity.

660. The world record distance for hurling a pumpkin (called pumpkin chunking) was set again by an air cannon called Allodium Q-36 Pumpkin Modulator in 2001 at the Morton Pumpkin Festival, Illinois. The 36,000-pound cannon constructed by Brad Livek has a barrel 80 feet long and fired a 10 pound pumpkin 4,860 feet.

661. The Fresh Kills landfill site on the western shore of Staten Island, New York accepted its last barge of garbage on March 22, 2001. The site opened in 1948 and originally occupied 2,900 acres but was downsized to 2,200 acres. At its peak in 1986-87 the landfill accepted 29,000 tons of garbage a day.

662. FIA World Rally Championship (WRC) driver Carlos Sainz (41) of Spain became the most successful in the history of the WRC on July 18, 2004 when he won the Rally Argentina. The win was his 26th WRC victory, more than any other WRC driver.

663. On Valentine's Day (February 14, 2002) the four foot tall humanoid robot Asimo became the first non-human to open the New York Stock Exchange by pushing a white hand into a button to ring the famed bell.

Asimo, an acronym for Advanced Step in Innovative Mobility, was designed by Honda Motor Co. Ltd. and is a demonstration of technology that will hopefully be used for minesweeping dangerous regions.

664. The X-15 rocket plane is the fastest ever aircraft. In 1967, the X-15

experimental rocket-powered aircraft reached a record speed of Mach 6.72 at an altitude of 108 km. The X-15 programme was a joint effort between NASA and USAF between 1959 and 1968.

665. The Lockheed SR-71 Blackbird, first flown in 1963, is the fastest operational aircraft to fly within earth's atmosphere. At an operational altitude of 80,000 feet the SR-71 can achieve speeds over 2,200 MPH or above. The airframe is built almost exclusively of titanium to withstand the extreme heat generated and two Pratt and Whitney J-58 axial flow turbojets producing a total of 68,000 pounds of thrust.

The SR-71 officially set the air speed record on July 28, 1976 when it set a two way average speed of 2193 mph around a closed course in California.

Only the experimental X-15 surpasses the SR-71 for the outright records at Mach 6.72.

666. On October 15th, 1997 a British team lead by Richard Knoble broke both the land speed record and the sound barrier when, British fighter pilot Andy Green set a two way average speed of 762.721 MPH. The twin jet powered car, Thrust SSC, set the record in the Black Rock desert of Nevada just one day after the 50th anniversary of Gen. Chuck Yeager's flight through the sound barrier on October 14th, 1947 and beat Richard Knoble's previous record of 633.47 MPH set on October 4, 1983 in the Thrust 2.

667. In the dying months of the Second World War in Europe, German refugees were struggling to flee Western Europe ahead of the advancing Russian army. Tales of atrocities, rape and death made the need for escape desperate. In an effort to escape refugees crowded onto the former, cruise ship (turned troop transport and hospital ship), Wilhelm Gustloff. The ship had a capacity of 1,850 passengers and crew, but was massively overcrowded with several times that number.

After leaving the port in Gotenhafen, East Prussia, the Gustloff made it 20 miles out into the Baltic Sea on January 30, 1945, before it was struck by three Russian torpedoes at 9:00 pm on the port side of the ship. The ship sank in only 50 minutes. Only 996 people survived the sinking.

Official military sources pegged the numbers on board at just over 6,000 people at the time, but because so many people had crammed onto the ship before it departed, the official passenger list was well short of the numbers actually on board. Though the actual number will never be known, estimates based on eye witness accounts and computer modelling place the actual number of passengers at just over 10,600 people. This puts the death toll at just over 9,600 men, women and children.

The disaster is not well documented or remembered by the world because it came at the end of a war where Germany had been guilty of horrific atrocities. At the time, many felt the Germans got what they deserved. Even most Germans did not want to talk about the disaster, instead hoping to put the war behind them.

668. On July 25, 1978, the first test tube baby was born in England. Louise Brown was the product of the first successful in vetro fertilisation (IVF). Initially, IVF had a 3 to 6 percent success rate, but medical technology has raised that to 24 percent. Since 1978, more than 114,000 babies have been born in the US alone.

669. The first civilian tourist in space is Dennis Tito. Amid controversy, California businessman Dennis Tito became the first civilian and paying tourist in space when he took off from Baikonur Cosmodrome in Kazakhstan aboard a Russian Soyuz rocket on April 28, 2001. Tito paid an estimated $20 million for the eight-day trip to the International Space Station. NASA officials believed that the timing was not right for a civilian to visit the station due to safety concerns and a potential work slowdown during the installation of the Canadian robotic arm.

670. The Russian Sputnik 1 spacecraft was the first man made object placed into orbit. It was launched from Baikonur Cosmodrome at Tyuratam in Kazakhstan on October 4, 1957. The word 'Sputnik' means 'companion' in Russian. Sputnik 1 was a 58.0 cm-diametre aluminium sphere that carried four whip-like antennas. The satellite transmitters operated for three weeks, until the on-board chemical batteries failed. The achievement sparked a heated space race between the U.S.S.R. and the United States.

671. First woman to sail single-handed and non-stop around the world is Lisa Clayton. On September 17th, 1994, Lisa Clayton set out from England on a journey to become the first woman to sail non-stop and unaided around the world. She set sail in a strong steel hulled 35-foot vessel she had purchased from the University of Birmingham and named it 'Spirit of Birmingham'. After 285 days at sea, she returned to England on June 29th, 1995, having covered almost 31,000 miles.

672. The only woman to fly across the Atlantic solo is Amelia Earhart. On May 20th, 1932, Amelia Earhart lifted off from Harbour Grace in a Lockheed Vega and flew to Londonderry, Northern Ireland, becoming the first woman to fly across the Atlantic alone. Earhart remains the only woman to have flown across the Atlantic solo.

673. The highest jump and longest free fall ever recorded was done by Joseph W. Kittinger Jr. on August 16th, 1960, as a part of the Air Force research programme (Project Excelsior), Air Force Capt. Joseph W. Kittinger Jr. stepped off a platform raised to 102,800 feet over Tularosa, New Mexico by a high-altitude balloon. The Air Force programme was designed to investigate the use of a parachute for escape from a space capsule or high-altitude aircraft. To survive the altitude Kittinger wore a pressure suit like those for astronauts.

After 4 minutes, 36 seconds of free fall Kittinger reached a speed of 714 mph (becoming the only human to break the sound barrier without being enclosed in a machine of any kind) and falling 84,700 feet before opening his parachute. He landed safely after 13 minutes, 45 seconds after jumping.

674. The world's longest motorcycle jump was made by Ryan Capes. After a day of every increasing jumps to build up his world record attempt, Ryan Capes jumped his 250 cc motorcycle from a ramp to a dirt landing ramp covering a total distance of 260 feet on September 19, 2003 at the Las Vegas Speedway, Las Vegas, Nevada. Capes hopes to continue to extend the record eventually surpassing 300 feet.

675. Daniel Baraniuk, an out-of-work 27-year-old from Gdansk, Poland set the world record for pole sitting by sitting at the top of an 8-

foot, 2 1/2 inch pole for 196 days and nights. In doing so, he won the World Pole-Sitting Championship and nearly $23,000 prize money. All the competitors mounted their poles on May 15, 2002 and were only allowed to leave their 16 by 24 inch platform for 10 minutes every two hours. While his nearest competitor fell off the pole in October, Baraniuk finally gave up on November 26, 2002.

676. Strongman, John Evans hold the world's record for the heaviest weight balanced only on his head by balancing 101 bricks with a total weight of 416 pounds. The stunt was broadcast live on television on December 24, 1997. John, who weighs in at just under 350 pounds himself, currently holds 29 World Records. Head balancing is a skill John developed when he worked as a brick layer, climbing ladders with stacks of bricks balanced on his head.

677. The v0 first disabled person to climb Mount Everest is Tom Whittaker. On May 27, 1998, Tom Whittaker made history as the leader of his own expedition to climb Mount Everest, the tallest mountain on earth. Tom lost his right leg below the knee in an auto accident in 1979. Tom climbed using a prosthetic leg.

678. Erik Weihenmayer from Denver, Colorado became the first blind person to climb to the summit of the tallest mountain on earth on May 25, 2001 at the age of 32. Erik went blind at the age of 13 due to a rare genetic disease of the retina called retinoschisis. Even after loosing his sight he has lead an active life rock climbing, diving, wrestling and dirt bikes.

679. With faces standing 60 feet tall and 500 feet up, the Mount Rushmore National Monument is the largest art object in the world. The four faces of American presidents: George Washington, Thomas Jefferson, Theodore Roosevelt and Abraham Lincoln are carved into the face of Mount Rushmore (named for Charles E. Rushmore) in the Black Hills of South Dakota.

Sculptor Gutzon Borglum began carving the mountain on August 10, 1927 and, along with 400 workers, would work on the monument until his death in 1941. Borglum's original plan called for all four presidents to be carved in detail down to the waist, but after his death it was never completed.

680. The first to cross the Atlantic on a jet-ski is Alvaro de Marichalar. Four months after leaving Rome (February 23) Alvaro de Marichalar, a Spanish count arrived in Miami on June 22, 2002 becoming the first man to cross the Atlantic on a personal watercraft. Escorted by a support ship with six crew, Count Marichalar rode his 9 foot jet-ski for twelve hours per day, mostly standing to prevent back injury.

681. The world's longest non-stop commercial flight is made by Singapore Airlines. Singapore Airlines opened a non-stop service from Singapore to Los Angeles with a flight time of more than 18 hours. The flight beats out Continental Airlines' flight from Newark NJ to Hong Kong at just under 16 hours. Singapore Airlines, Asia's biggest airline, flies once-a-day using 5 new Airbus A340-500 aircraft. The flight is expected to cost 5 or 10 percent over the usual single stop flights, but will shave hours off the trip.

682. The West Edmonton Mall, located in Edmonton, Alberta, Canada is the world's largest shopping mall. The mall includes 5.3 million square feet of space. There are over 800 stores, over 110 eating establishments, 26 movie theatres and seven attractions, including an amusement park, waterpark, mini-golf, ice rink, the world's largest indoor lake and varied sea life. The mall occupies 121 acres and the parking can accommodate 20,000 cars. The total cost for the four phases of construction for the mall topped $2.8 billion.

683. United Airlines, the world's second largest airline, filed for bankruptcy protection on December 9, 2002 after suffering $1.7 billion in losses for the first three quarters of 2002. With $25.2 billion in assets, United Airlines is the largest bankruptcy in aviation history.

684. The world's fastest helicopter is a slightly modified version of the ZB500 G-Lynx. At a European air show on August 6, 1986, a slightly modified version of the ZB500 G-Lynx, manufactured by GKN Westland Helicopters (UK), set the world speed record for a conventional helicopter at 217.5 Kts (400.80 km/h or 249.10 mph). The theoretical top speed for a rotary winged aircraft is about 250 mph (402 km/h).

685. The Caterpillar 797B dump truck is currently the largest in the world. Used primarily in open pit mining, the 797B has a load

capacity of 380 tonnes. It is powered by a 117.1 Litre turbocharged diesel engine making 3,550 horsepower. The 797B is 21.5 feet tall, 28 feet wide and 47.7 feet long. It has an empty operating weight of approximately 278 tonnes. Each tire is thirteen feet tall and weighs four tonnes each. They need to be replaced after approximately 35,000 miles, at a cost of $25,000.00 a piece.

686. On December 22, 2003, Cunard officially launched its first new cruse ship built in 34 years. The $800 million Queen Mary 2 is the longest, tallest, widest and heaviest passenger ship ever constructed. The ship measures 1138.5 feet (345 metres) long, 135.3 feet (41 metres) wide, 237.6 metres (72 metres) tall and weighing some 150,000 tonnes. The ship accommodates 2,630 passengers and features five swimming pools, 14 restaurants, 24 massage parlours and an art gallery.

687. The Taipei 101 office tower in Taipei, Taiwan became the tallest building in the world when a huge 60-metre metal spire was placed on the top of the 101-floor structure on October 17, 2003. The final height of the building is 1,674 feet (508 metres), surpasses the 452-metre high Petronis twin towers in the Malaysian capital, Kuala Lumpur.

688. CargoLifter hangar, located in Brand, Germany (60 kilometres south of Berlin) on a former Soviet military airport, is the largest self-supporting hangar in the world. With 360-metres in length, 210-metres in width and 107-metres in height the hanger was designed to accommodate the planned CargoLifter CL 160, a 260-metre long airship.

689. The Royal Caribbean ship Voyager of the Seas holds the record for the largest cruise ship in the world. The ship is 1020 feet long, 157.5 feet wide and has 17 decks rising more than 200 feet above the waterline. The ship has a gross tonnage of 138,000 tonnes and a cruising speed of 23.7 knots. Since the ship's maiden voyage on November 21, 1999 it has cruised the Caribbean continuously with a capacity of 3,114 passengers and more than 1,000 crew members. Amenities include a 1,350-seat Broadway style theatre, an ice rink, the largest casino afloat, rock climbing wall, in-line skating track, full court basketball and the Royal Promenade running two

football field lengths long and four decks high. The Voyager of the Seas is only the first of a five ship Voyager-class of ships.

690. Built in 1997, the Demag CC 12600 is the strongest lattice-boom crawler crane in the world. It has a total lifting capacity of 1600 tonnes.

691. The largest warship and first nuclear-powered carrier is the USS Enterprise (CVN 65). In Newport VA, on September 24, 1960 the USS Enterprise (CVN 65) was christened by Mrs. William B. Franke, wife of the former Secretary of the Navy, is the largest warship ever built and the first nuclear-powered aircraft carrier. The ship is the eighth ship and the second aircraft carrier to be called Enterprise. At 1,123 feet long and 250 feet high the ship is both the longest and tallest warship ever built. With a top speed over 30 knots it is also the fastest carrier in the US fleet. Weighing in at 90,000 tonnes the Big E (as the ship is known) is home to over 5,000 officers and crewmembers. Since being commissioned in 1961 and its maiden voyage on January 12, 1962 the Enterprise has been involved almost every major US Navy operation since.

692. The Russian built Tupolev Tu-144 became the first supersonic passenger aircraft to fly when it had its first flight on December 31, 1968, two months ahead of the first flight for the Concorde SST. Nicknamed the 'Konkordski' by the western press, due to its strong resemblance to the Concorde, the Tu-144 was based largely from stolen Concorde plans. The Soviets had worked feverishly to win the race to produce a supersonic jetliner and had cut corners in the design and production of the aircraft and improvised when details of the Concorde plans were missing or could not be deciphered. The aircraft was plagued by deficiencies and had to be radically re-engineered before being shown to the world in 1973. The debut at the Paris Airshow was marked by the in-flight break-up and crash of the Tu-144. The crash was the result mishandling, not a design or manufacture defect but the damage was done. The Tu-144 entered service in 1977 but due to mechanical problems it was unable to maintain even its modest one due to mechanical problems it was not able to maintain even a modest schedule.

A programme beginning in 1993 saw the Tu-144 pulled out of

storage for use by Boeing and NASA for high speed research. The aircraft were modified in 1996 to create what NASA called the Tu-144LL Flying Laboratory. Between November 1996 and February 1998 the Tu-144LL flew 19 research flights.

693. The oldest living tree known is a Bristlecone Pine known as 'Methuselah' located at an elevation of 10,400 feet in the White Mountains on the California-Nevada border. The tree is estimated to be 4,767 years old. It stands about 55 feet tall, with a misshapen oval-shaped trunk measuring about 4 1/2 feet wide.

694. The Giant Sequoia (Sequoiadendron giganteum) is generally considered the largest living organism on earth. The Sequoia is native primarily to the Sierra Nevada Mountains of eastern California. The largest Sequoia is the General Sherman tree with a height of 250 feet and a diametre near the base of 24.75 feet. The trunk of the tree weighs almost 1400 tons or equivalent to 15 adult blue whales. It can be argued, however that the tree is not the largest living organism since most of the tree consists of dead, not living tissues.

695. On August 4, 1988 Rajinder Singh of Theog, Himachal Pradesh typed at an average speed of 484 strokes a minute (96.8 words) and completed 2,90,392 strokes over a continuous stretch of 10 hours at Shimla. His accuracy figure stood at 99.97%. It was the fastest accurate typing.

696. On May 3, 1999 as tornadoes ravaged Oklahoma scientist measured the highest recorded wind speed at about 7:00 pm near Moore, Oklahoma. A wind speed of 318 mph was recorded where a tornado killed four people and destroyed 250 homes. It was the fastest wind speed ever recorded. The fastest wind measured prior was 286 mph on April 26, 1991 in a tornado near Red Rock, Oklahoma. The 318 mph speed placed the tornado 1 mph below an F6 on the 0 to 6 Fujita scale. No tornado has ever been classified as an F6.

697. Katharine Hepburn won the highest number of Oscar for best actor/actress. Katharine Hepburn has won four Oscars for best Actress from twelve nominations. She won for her roles in: Morning Glory (1933), Guess Who's Coming to Dinner (1967), The

Lion in The Winter (1968), On Golden Pond (1981).

698. The longest-running theatrical show in the world is 'The Mousetrap'. The murder mystery 'The Mousetrap', originally called 'Three Blind Mice', was written by Agatha Christie in 1947 as a 30-minute radio play to celebrate the then Queen Mary's 80th birthday. The play has become a fixture in London, England and performance number 20,807 on November 25, 2002, marks its 50th anniversary as the world's longest-running play. The performance was attended by the Queen, also celebrating her 50th year on the throne. The play has been seen by over 10 million people and performed in 44 different countries.

699. The longest snake ever found is a reticulated python that was found in Sulawesi Island, Indonesia in 1912. It was 33 feet long. While it is believed that the American water boa (known as the anaconda) may grow larger or heavier, the largest snakes found both in the wild and in captivity are reticulated pythons.

The largest snake ever held in captivity was a python named Colossus. She lived at the Pittsburgh Zoo in Pennsylvania and at the time of her death she was 28.5 feet long, had a girth of 37.5 inches and weighed an estimated 320 pounds.

700. African Gambian Pouch rats, also known as the African giant pouch rats are the largest rats in the world. They grow to 13-17 inches from tip of nose to the base of the tail and the tail is about the same length or longer. They can be more than six pounds. They live in forests and thickets from Senegal to Central Sudan and down to South Africa.

701. The Whooping Cranes is the tallest bird in North America, standing at five feet tall. They are named for their loud and penetrating mating call, live and breed in wetland areas where they feed on crabs, clams, frogs and other aquatic creatures. They are pure white with black wing tips and a red crown. The Whooping crane is an endangered species with 400 of the birds in the wild. In 1941 there were as few as 20 left.

702. The California condor is the largest flying land bird in North America. The Condor (Gymnogyps Californianus) can have a wingspan of 9 ½ feet and weigh up to 23 pounds. Similar to a Vulture, the Condor is mostly black and has a bare head and neck. The California condor is an endangered species with only 199 left in the world and only 73 living in the wild. Condors are often killed when they met power lines.

703. Republican, Michael Bloomberg spent a reported $73 million on his 2001 winning campaign to become the mayor of New York City, making it the most expensive non-presidential campaign in history. Bloomberg won the mayor's seat previously occupied by Rudolph Giuliani.

704. Senator Strom Thurmond from South Carolina was the longest-serving member of the upper house of Congress. He retired from the Senate at the end of 2002, just one month after his 100th birthday, after 47 years and 5 months in the Senate. Thurmond died six months later on June 26th, 2003.

705. At the end of his presidency in 1988, Ronald Reagan (born February 6, 1911) was the oldest man ever to hold the office of the President of the United States. He was the oldest man elected, at the age of 69 when he was elected to his first term and ended his presidency a few months before his 78th birthday.

Ronald Reagan is also the only divorced person to have been elected.

706. Surgeons in Italy have carried out the world's first ever whole jaw transplant. In an 11-hour operation at Rome's Regina Elena Hospital, an 80-year-old man suffering from a cancerous tumour of the mouth received the new bone from a donor half his age. Membrane was taken from the patient's own arm to envelope the new jaw bone and to substitute the gums of the mouth.

707. There are as many as 3,000 cases of cancer of the mouth in Italy each year - the majority of which are caused by smoking - and in 15% of cases the tumour is too diffuse to be removed by traditional invasive surgery. Usually such cases require amputation of the jaw, with problematic reconstructive surgery utilising metal plaques. However, these are often susceptible to rejection by the recipient.

708. Another reconstruction method involves transferring bone from the patient's own limbs. However, these bone transfers can often prove unsuitable for replicating the specific movements of the jaw, especially when it involves rebuilding the curved frontal section of the bone.

The team at the Regina Elena hospital, led by surgeon Professor Giuseppe Spriano, was for the past six months been pioneering a procedure for removing tumourous jaw bones, treating them with liquid nitrogen to rid them of the tumorous cells, sterilising them and then re-inserting the jaw into the patient.

In this case, Professor Spriano, internationally renowned in his field, judged the tumour to be so diffused as to make reconstruction of the jaw impossible.

Instead, they opted for the groundbreaking whole-transplant surgery.

The donor was a 39-year-old man who died of a brain haemorrhage two weeks before Christmas at Cesena on Italy's east coast.

The bone was transported to the national 'bone bank' at the Rizzoli Orthopaedic Institute in Bologna where it underwent radiotherapy and was conserved at -196 degrees C to render it sterile and reduce the chances of rejection. A regional transplant co-ordination network matched the jaw to the shape of the face of the patient in Rome.

709. The longest coma was gone through by Elaine Esposito who was in her coma for 77 years and 111 days. The years for this were from 1941-1978.

710. Longest attack of hiccups goes to Charlie Osborne, 98 hiccupped over 435 million times before it stops, He dies 11 months after it stops.

711. Donna Griffiths made allergy history when she was 12 years old. Starting in 1981, the British girl sneezed every few minutes for 977 consecutive days. Doctors estimate Griffiths sneezed 1 million times the first year, she eventually slowed to a sneeze every 5 minutes. Fortunately for most of us, battling allergies is a mercifully short springtime affair. Still, there are few things as frustrating as finally getting on the trail only to have your vistas blurred by watery eyes and the smell of evergreens lost in your sniffles. And there's plenty of it going around. Researchers at the American Academy of Allergies, Asthma and Immunology estimate that allergic rhinitis or hay fever, affects at least 36 million Americans each year. However, do not despair. Doctors agree there is no reason seasonal allergies should keep you from enjoying your favourite backcountry haunts. With the right mix of preparation, knowledge of when plants pollinate and treatment options, you'll be able to stop and smell the grasses without giving Griffiths a run for her record.

712. Jayne Bleackley is the mother who holds the record for the shortest interval between two children born in separate confinements. She gave birth to Joseph Robert on September 3, 1999 and Annie Jessica Joyce on March 30, 2000. The babies were born 208 days apart.

713. Elizabeth Ann Buttle is the mother who holds the record for the longest interval between the births of two children. She gave birth to Belinda on May 19,1956 and Joseph on November 20, 1997.

The babies were born 41 years 185 days apart. The mother was 60 years old when her son Joseph was born.

714. Bobbie McCaughey is the mother who holds the record for the most surviving children from a single birth. She gave birth to the first set of surviving septuplets - four boys and three girls -on November 19, 1997, at the University Hospital, Iowa, US. Conceived by in vitro fertilisation, the babies were delivered after 31 weeks by caesarean in the space of 16 minutes. The babies are named Kenneth, Nathaniel, Brandon, Joel, Kelsey, Natalie and Alexis.

715. Her future brightened by a medical miracle, Sarah Marshall is ready for some serious sampling of birthday cake. Sarah, a bouncy infant with a heart-stopping smile, will celebrate her first birthday on Valentine's Day, thanks to ground-breaking transplant surgery in August in which doctors at London Health Sciences Centre replaced her liver, bowel, stomach and pancreas. Sarah became the youngest patient in the world to undergo this kind of surgery, performed only at the hospital in London.

After a difficult couple of months following surgery, the tot has recovered rapidly and doctors believe she can now look forward to a normal lifestyle and lifespan.

Sarah, the daughter of Dave and Cindy Marshall of Cobourg, was back at the hospital for an early birthday celebration— and so hospital staff could share her story at a combination news conference and party. Hospital staff and reporters joined in singing Happy Birthday. Then Sarah happily sampled a taste of the icing from a large white, pink and red cake inscribed with the words 'Happy Birthday Sarah, Our Special Valentine'.

Sarah was born with a rare and dangerous condition called megacystis microcolon hypoperistalis syndrome. This meant that her bowel did not function and her bladder worked only poorly, said Dr. Paul Atkison, director of paediatric transplants at the hospital.

716. Abhishek Jain of Goraya, Punjab is the first and youngest typist in the country to win a gold at the INTERSTENO World Championship held at Brussels in 1991. In June 1995, he was again declared fastest typist in the world with a speed of 135 wpm.

717. Clint Hallam of New Zealand has had his right hand amputated three times. He first lost his hand in 1984 after an accident with a circular saw. Surgeons re-attached the limb, but an infection developed and it was removed again in 1988. In September 1998, doctors performed a pioneering hand transplant on Clint at a hospital in Lyons, France. However, he later requested it be amputated again and the operation was carried out at a London hospital on February 2, 2001.

718. Ken Edwards of Derbyshire ate 36 cockroaches in one minute on the set of *The Big Breakfast*, London, on March 5, 2001.

719. Paul Hunn, from London, registered a burp at 118.1 decibels on the set of World Records, London, on April 5, 2000.

720. On June 13, 1998, Kim Goodman of Chicago popped her eyeballs to 11 mm beyond her eye sockets.

721. A 58-year-old woman from Shizuoka, Japan, was admitted to Isogaki Gastro-Entero-Surgical clinic in May 1990. She complained of severe gastric pain and nausea brought on by eating raw fish. Doctors discovered 56 white, thread-like worms in her stomach and later removed them during a 90-minute operation. The worms were identified as the larvae of Anisakis simplex and measured up to 17.27 mm in length.

722. The Jailu Restaurant in Canton, China, serves approximately 9,300 rats every year to its customers. Self-proclaimed rat king and restaurateur Quang Li-Do has been catching and eating rats for 30 years.

723. The most live scorpions eaten in a lifetime by a human is approximately Alvarenga of El Salvador. He catches them with his bare hands and eats between 20 and 30 of them every day.

724. Radhakant Bajpai of India has hair sprouting from the centre of his outer ears that measures 13.2 cm at its longest point.

725. In July 1997, a foetus was discovered in the abdomen of 16-year-old Hisham Ragab of Egypt, who had been complaining of stomach pains. A swollen sac found pressing against his kidneys turned out to be Hisham's 18cm-long identical twin. The foetus, which had been growing inside had lived to be 32 or 33 weeks old.

726. The world's longest courgette measured 1.34m on October 1, 2002. It was grown by Sher Singh Kanwal in Niagara Falls, New York.

727. Kevin Cole of New Mexico holds the record for the longest spaghetti strand ejected from a nostril in a single blow. On December 16, 1998, he successfully achieved a distance of 19 cm.

728. Donald Gorske of the USA holds the record for the most Big Macs consumed. By March 7, 2002, Donald had consumed 18,250 - eating 708 in 2000 alone. He began his quest in 1972 with nine Big Macs a day.

729. The indistinguishable eggs of the hookworms Ancylostoma duodenale and Necator americanus are found in the faeces of 1.3 billion people worldwide. In cases of heavy infestation, the lining of the gut is so thickly covered with worms that they look like the pile of a carpet. The bleeding that results from their feeding adds up to 10 million litres of blood worldwide every day.

730. In August 1999, Gary Bashaw of West Virginia mixed milk and chocolate powder in his mouth and dispensed the chocolate milk mixture - measuring 54 ml - from his nostril.

731. Garry Turner of Lincolnshire stretched the skin of his stomach to a measured length of 15.8 cm on October 29, 1999.

732. A hair grown just below the knee of the right leg of Brit Julian Rowe reached a length of 10.1 cm when measured in West Yorkshire on July 2, 2002.

733. An appendix removed from Spencer Bayles on November 2, 2002, at Lister Hospital, Stevenage, measured 21 cm in length.

734. Danny Capps of Wisconsin, USA, spat a dead cricket from his mouth a distance of 9.17m on June 26, 1998.

735. The farthest a marshmallow has been blown out of one nostril and caught in the mouth of a catcher is 4.96m. Scott Jeckel of Illinois, USA, launched a marshmallow into the mouth of Ray Perisin on the set of American World Records, on August 13, 1999.

736. Gallo of the UK had 37 concrete blocks with a total weight of 519.8 lbs (235.8 kg) placed on his chest and broken with a 14 lb sledgehammer while he lay on a bed of nails at Hemel Hempstead, Herts on August 24, 2002.

737. Shakuntala Dev of Bangalore took only 50 seconds to compute the 23 th root of a 201-digit number in 1977 while it took a computer over a minute, on June 18, 1980.

738. Lou Ferrigno the tallest Mr Olympia. As a teenager, Ferrigno trained in his home basement in Brooklyn, New York. Ear infections as a youngster caused Ferrigno to suffer permanent hearing loss, but he continued to hear the call of iron and entered his first contest, the 1970 Mr. New Jersey Open Hercules, which was staged in Trenton. Twenty-one men placed ahead of him, but last place would not last long on Ferrigno's agenda.

After several more minor contests, Ferrigno switched to the IFBB in 1973, winning the Mr. America and the tall class of the Mr. Universe in Geneva. The next year, he won the Mr. Universe in Verona, Italy. Then, in the 1975 Mr. Olympia in South Africa, Ferrigno faced Arnold Schwarzenegger, whose physique he had tried to emulate. Ferrigno came in third and he was done with physique competitions for 17 years, until 1992, when he appeared in Helsinki, finishing 12th in the Olympia. In 1993, a final try for the Olympia yielded 10th place, so he switched to the Masters Olympia in 1994, but was edged out by Robby Robinson for that inaugural crown. It would be Ferrigno's last contest.

Ferrigno played the Incredible Hulk on television from 1978-1982, where fits of rage would hurl him from quiet to chaotic when his 6'5' body would explode with green-tinted muscularity. Other acting appearances have been TV's *Trauma Centre* in 1983 and several movies including *Hercules*, *Sinbad* and *Cage*. Currently, he occasionally appears on the TV show *The King of Queens*. Ferrigno married Carla Green on May 30, 1980. They have three children: Shanna, Lou Jr. and Brent.

739. Not only is the Orion Nebula one of the most spectacular of nebulae, but it is also one of the easiest to locate, lying in the middle of the conspicuous Sword of Orion. It is in fact the brightest nebula in the sky. Though not apparent to the naked eye, Orion contains a gigantic dark cloud of matter, the largest such cloud known in

the Milky Way Galaxy. Within the Orion Molecular Cloud, new stars are forming, a process that creates a pocket or 'bubble' around the newly emerged stars. The quadruple star known as the Trapezium is one of these young systems, thought to be little more than 100,000 years old. It started to form just within the edge of the cloud and its bubble has burst through that edge, leaving us with an illuminated view of the cloud's interior: the Orion Nebula. The nebula's reddish colouration betrays the predominance of ionised hydrogen in the parent cloud, but more complex molecules such as carbon monoxide have also been detected. Stellar formation in this region of space is still in progress and infrared observation suggests that at least two new stars will shortly come into existence.

740. Full of excitement and thoughts, *The Diary of Anne Frank*, is one of the best selling books of all time and has been translated into several different languages. Anne's diary was published in 1947, about 2 years after Anne's death and the liberation of the people from the

concentration camps. The Diary of Anne Frank has sold over 25 million copies!

741. Agatha Christie is the author of best selling fiction. With over one hundred novels and 103 translations into foreign languages, Agatha Christie was by the time of her death the best-selling English novelist of all time. Agatha Christie (1890-1976), prolific British author of mystery novels and short stories, is especially famous as the creator of Hercule Poirot, the Belgian detective and Miss Jane Marple.

Agatha Christie was born in Torquay, in the county of Devon, as the daughter of Frederick Alvah Miller and Clarissa Miller. Her father died when she was a child. Christie was educated at home, where her mother encouraged her to write from a very early age. At sixteen, she was sent to school in Paris where she studied singing and piano. In 1914, Christie married Archibald Christie, an officer in the Flying Royal Corps, their daughter, Rosalind, was born in 1919.

Christie's first detective novel, *The Mysterious Affair at Styles,* introduced Hercules Poirot, the Belgian detective, who appeared in more than 40 books, the last of which was *Curtain* (1975). Christie's other famous detective, Miss Marple, an elderly spinster, was a typical English character, but while Poirot used logic and rational methods, Marple relied on her feminine sensitivity and empathy to solve crimes. Marple was featured in 17 novels, the first being *Murder At The Vicarage* (1930) and the last *Sleeping Murder* (1977). Both Poirot and Marple have been adapted for film and television.

In 56 years, Christie wrote 66 detective novels, among the best of which are *The Murder of Roger Acroyd, Murder On the Orient Express (1934), Death on the Nile* (1937) and *Ten Little Niggers* (1939). In addition to these works, Christie wrote her autobiography (1977) and several plays, including *The Mousetrap,* which ran more than 30 years continuously in London.

Christie's marriage broke up in 1926. Archie Christie, who worked in the City, announced that he had fallen in love with a younger woman, Nancy Neele. In the same year Christie's beloved mother died. The story of Christie's real life adventure in the 1926, when she disappeared for a time and lived in a Harrowgate hotel under the name Mrs. Neele, was the basis for the film Agatha.

During WW II Christie worked in the dispensary of University College Hospital in London. After the war, she continued to write prolifically, also gaining success on the stage and in the cinema. *Witness for the Prosecution,* for example, was chosen the best foreign play of the 1954-55 season by the New York Drama Critics Circle. Christie was most innovative when she revealed the guilty party in her detective stories, it has been the narrator, a group of people, a serial killer who tries to hide an obvious motive for his killing one of the victims and so forth.

In 1967, Christie became president of the British Detection Club and in 1971, she was made a Dame of the British Empire. Christie died on January 12, 1976. With over one hundred novels and 103 translations into foreign languages, Christie by the time of her death was the best-selling English novelist of all time.

742. Best-selling children's author JK Rowling has become Britain's highest-earning woman. The 35-year-old writer, who began her literary career just four years ago, netted more than £20.5m over the last year, according to the Mail on Sunday's annual list of top female earners. The Harry Potter series, about a schoolboy wizard, started life when Rowling was day-dreaming on a train journey to London. Her fourth book, Harry Potter and the Goblet of Fire, was launched in July and shot into the record books by selling more than a million copies on its first day. JK Rowling is among 64 women on the newspaper's top 100 list who earned more than £1m in the past year. The second-highest earner was Nikki Beckett, who made £14.03m by selling shares in her computer business, NSB Retail Systems. Eight out of the top 10 earners on the list are businesswomen but those in show business also featured strongly. Singer Sarah Brightman came in at number 10 with £4m, while ex-Spice Girl Geri Halliwell earned £3.7m, placing her at number 12. Golfer Laura Davies was the only sportswoman to make the list, earning £1.3m. Moreover, the youngest person on the list is 14-year-old Welsh classical singer Charlotte Church, whose £3.5m income last year puts her in 14th place. Despite a collective income

of £212m, Britain's top 100 female earners still have a long way to go before they rival their American counterparts.

743. Japan's ***The Yomiuri Shimbun*** is the world's largest-selling newspaper. The Yomiuri Shimbun will mark its 130th anniversary in November this year as a leading newspaper in Japan with the world's largest daily circulation of 10 million copies in the morning and 4 million in the evening.

With an extensive network of more than 300 bureaus in Japan and more than 30 bureaus abroad, The Yomiuri Shimbun delivers accurate and insightful news, features, commentary and analysis pieces.

Furthermore, the newspaper is widely respected as a pioneer for offering its own policy proposals on key issues, such as the 1994 proposal for the revision of the Constitution of Japan. There is now a consensus among lawmakers that the Diet (parliament) ought to work hard on the constitutional revision issue, which had been regarded as a political taboo for nearly half a century.

The Yomiuri Shimbun publishes *The Daily Yomiuri,* an English-language newspaper with a publicly audited daily circulation of 43,000. In terms of home delivery, The Daily Yomiuri is the number one English-language daily.

The Yomiuri Shimbun Holdings, which owns The Yomiuri Shimbun, also owns Chuokoron-Shinsha Inc., a highly respected publisher and the Yomiuri Giants, Japan's number one pro baseball team.

744. Barnes & Noble began as a college book emporium. Now, this huge company sells virtually every new book you can think of. There are more than a dozen Barnes & Noble stores in Manhattan alone, including this 'superstore'. Textbooks are still a strong point at the Union Square location, as are volumes from the great literature of the world, paperbacks and children's books. Seating is available and authors frequently put in an appearance to sign their latest creations. Most branches have a cafe as well as an extensive magazine section.

745. The world's biggest book publisher is German based conglomerate

Bertlesmann AG. Bertelsmann AG is one of the largest media corporations in the world (third as of 1995). Headquartered in Gutersloh, Germany, Bertelsmann is an international media conglomerate with major investments in book and magazine publishing, records and music publishing, broadcasting, on-line services and other allied entertainment and information products. A privately owned corporation dating back to 1835, Bertelsmann was revived after World War II by Reinhard Mohn, a fifth generation member of the founding family. In the 1950s, Bertelsmann established itself as a major publisher through its book clubs. To this day, publishing remains the centre of Bertelsmann's profitability (and accounts for 55% of total sales). That profitability was enhanced in the 1970s with the purchase of a 74.9 percent interest in Gruner + Jahr, the German newspaper and magazine publisher of such titles as *Stern and Geo* and the 1986 purchase of Bantam Doubleday Dell, the second largest trade publisher in the United States. Book clubs continue to be an important growth area for Bertelsmann, as the corporation recently expanded into Eastern Europe, China and Latin America.

746. 'Frank Richards' was just one pseudonym of Charles Harold St. John Hamilton (CH from hereon), born in Ealing, Middlesex, England on August 8, 1876. The most prolific boys' fiction author of all time Charles attended a local private school, Thorne House. His first story is said to have been penned in 1885, possibly for one of the Trapps Holmes boys' story papers. Using in excess of 20 pen names, he wrote school stories but, adventure, travel, crime - every genre imaginable.

747. Sidney Sheldon was also honoured as the most translated author in the world. His publisher estimates that there are more than 275 million copies of his books in print worldwide. Sidney Sheldon began his tremendous career-writing award winning works for television, film and the stage during the middle of the twentieth century. Well know for shows such as 'I Dream of Jeannie' and 'Hart to Hart', Sheldon went on to focus on novels, many of which became instant bestsellers. 'Bloodline', (1977) and 'Windmill of the Gods' (1987), among others, went on to become television

miniseries. He once admitted '[Novels] never occurred to me' and yet he is now considered the best-selling novelist in the world, with his books in print in some thirty-nine countries and was a recipient of a star on the prestigious Hollywood Walk of Fame.

748. The Narasingannavars of Lokur, Karnataka have 170 members living as a single unit Farmers by profession, they grow almost everything they need on their 200-acre farm. As one shift of the 178-strong Narsinganna family finishes eating, another hungry batch replaces them. Feeding the family takes up most of the day and the family women cook in two-hour shifts, squatting before the wood fires in the smoky kitchen to prepare 1,600 millet rotis and vast quantities of vegetables and lentils. 'Cooking and housework is all that we know', Saraswati, the family's oldest woman, said resignedly. The men eat first, served by the girls under 11 years old who do not yet cook. Dozens of infants crawl in and out of the laps of their elders, helping themselves. Five generations - about 130 people - live in the ancestral home, with the remaining 50-odd family members accommodated nearby. "It is compulsory to eat together twice a day in the main house", said Bhimanna, the 71-year-old patriarch. He explains that the family that eats together stays together, bringing happiness and security. This is why they continued to live together when the traditional Indian joint family is swiftly disintegrating. They believe that the womenfolk had kept them together, preferring brides of around 15 years old who had not studied beyond the sixth grade. A senior Narsinganna pointed out

that keeping the women under control ensured harmony — undue freedom could spell ruination. "We consume what we produce and share everything", said Thiranandra, 37, in charge of the family's rather full diary. 'There is no room for individual wants'. The annual budget is about 1.2 million rupees (£14,000) while a further £3,500 goes on clothing, medicines and farm labour. Annually they consume about 132,000 lb of millet and 33,000 lb of wheat in addition to homegrown vegetables. The family is clothed with about 20 bales of varied cloth bought during the Hindu festival of Dusherra. Weddings are celebrated on a grand scale, sometimes several couples at once. A lone television set has pride of place at the top of the family house and is switched on sparingly for popular soap operas. 'It's like watching television on a busy railway platform'.

749. *The Observer*, founded in 1791, is the world's oldest Sunday newspaper. Its correspondents covered the execution of Marie Antoinette and Nelson's triumph at Trafalgar. In recent times, The Observer was the first to break the news of talks between the IRA and the British government and to raise awareness of the suffering of the Algerian people in the current unrest there.

750. Anant memorised a 400-digit binary number and recalled all the digits in the forward and reverse orders with an amazing 100 % accuracy. First person in the world to recall binary number in the reverse order. He is the youngster who flooded his way into the Limca Book of Records by remembering an overwhelming 73 telephone numbers and the names of their owners on the spot and recalled the info with 100% accuracy on May 4, 1997. Undertaking to memorise, retain and recall telephone numbers is first of its kind feat in the entire country. Even in the Book of World Records, there is no such entry. Anant is now all set to make his way into the Book of World Records in the events of remembering telephone numbers and remembering names and faces of people. He is all set to take part in the World Memory Championship 2003 to be held at London.

751. Dhruva Arya and Waiga Arya, both three years and nine months old, memorised Astadhyayi of Panini containing 4,000 rules of

Sanskrit grammar.

752. The Dattajirao Kadam Textile Institute has weaved a 4-km long red carpet for the Oman Sultan, which extends from the Airport to Sultan's Palace. The carpet was not produced by instant magical utterances, instead it took eight months of hard labour by the textile men of Ichalkaranji, the Manchester of Maharastra. The work of weaving the carpet was finished on time and the Sultan was accorded a red carpet welcome on November 19, the national day of Oman. The experts from the institute had flown to Muscat, redesigned the looms and worked day and night for the Sultan's magic carpet. They had also designed a special carpet-laying device.

753. The world's largest art gallery is the State Hermitage Museum in St. Petersburg, Russia. Visitors would have to walk 15 miles to see the 322 galleries which house nearly 3 million works of art. The Hermitage Museum is Russia's best gallery of world art, one of the most prominent art museums in the world and definitely the main tourist attraction of St. Petersburg. The museum was founded in 1764 when Catherine the Great purchased a collection of 255 paintings from Berlin. Nowadays, the Hermitage has about 2.7 million exhibits and displays a full range of world art from Ancient Egypt to early 20th century Europe. It includes works by Leonardo da Vinci, Michelangelo, Raphael, Titian, unique collections of Rembrandt, Rubens, French Impressionists (Renoir, Cezanne, Manet, Monet, Pissarro), plus Van Gogh, Matisse, Gaugin and sculptures by Rodin. The collection is huge and very exciting. They say that 'you can be absorbed for days in its treasures and still come out wishing for more'. The main building of the Hermitage Museum is the Winter Palace which was once the main residence of the Russian Tzars. Magnificently located on the bank of the Neva River, this green-and-white Baroque-style three-storey palace is truly impressive. It has 1786 doors, 1945 windows and 1057 halls and rooms, many of which are open to the public. The Baroque Winter Palace was built in 1754-62 and Catherine the Great was the first monarch to live there. Many of the impressive interiors have been remodelled after the huge fire of 1837. Some of the best Russian and foreign architects worked hard to make this residence of the

Russian tzars one of the world's most luxurious palaces. Hermitage collections are displayed in four buildings which together make a huge museum complex: Winter Palace, Small Hermitage, Old Hermitage and New Hermitage. Hermitage Theatre is used both for lectures and concerts. It had been calculated that if you decide to spend only one minute in front of each exhibit, you will have to stay in the Hermitage for 11 years.

754. 12-year-old child-wonder Kruti Parekh is 'the world's youngest magician and India's first test-tube baby'.

755. Major Ashok Kumar Singh, a permanent member of the Trishna crew and winner of the National Adventure Award in 1994 was the first disabled sailor in the world to sail around the globe

756. Not many people in this world dare to defy the boundaries of physics the way Narinder Singh does. Singh, a native of India, holds the World Record for pulling the heaviest vehicle — with his teeth.

It all began when Singh, a sturdy 6-foot tall, 40-year-old, 100 kilograms, was 15, growing up in the village of Killa Rai Pur, in India's Ludhiana District. Singh says he was inspired when he saw one man in his village compete in a competition with the talent of pulling a very heavy piece of machinery a few metres — with his teeth. Singh was so impressed that he went home and began testing his own strength, pulling things with his own teeth.

Singh started with sugar cane processing machines and then slowly moved up to tractors. In his twenties, he took on bigger challenges. He began pulling heavier objects such as railroad engines and railroad cars, buses, barges and ships. In 1992, he set his first World Record by pulling a 219-ton set of railroad cars in Armenia. He went on to set yet another World Record in Kaoshiung, Taiwan, by pulling a 320-ton ship six metres on January 4, 1997.

Singh's real job is in India, where he works as a member of the Punjab Police Department. His home is in Nawabind Akalgarh, Vhagwara, Katurthala, Punjab. He and his wife Charanjeebgour have recently spent much time travelling in-between Taiwan and India so that he can make his performances at Taichung's World of Records Museum.

Singh is currently a guest performer at the Museum in Taichung through December 28. While visiting the island this time, he has pulled a 16-ton bus packed with 82 students and also shocked a Taipei crowd by pulling a similar bus packed with people at the Chiang Kai-shek Memorial square. Last year, he pulled a 190-ton railroad car in Taipei. Upon his return this year, he doubled this weight by pulling two of these, both times just for practice.

Singh's active lifestyle stretches beyond time spent breaking world records. In his lifetime, he has run 20 marathons, always finishing in the lead or close to it. For six years starting in 1983, he ran 42 kilometres, taking first place every time. One of his best times was two hours and twenty-nine minutes.

757. About 20% Indians are practising vegetarians. There are 744 vegetarian communities comprising 16% of the population, prominent among them being, Jains and Vaishnavas.

758. India accounts for 42% of the world's total cashew nut production (9.25 lakh tonnes) and consume about one third of global consumption or 2.10 lakh tonnes per annum.

759. India has 268-lakh sq. km land under oilseed cultivation, accounting for 21% of the world's area under this crop.

760. Abdul Masfoor of Hunsur, Mysore, has a 20 feet tall brinjal plant in his garden with three different varieties growing on it. The plant, which began fruiting in April 1998, had produced around 80 Kg. of brinjal by April 1999.

761. In July 1993, Abdulla Alireza of Europe produced one kg. of Castleton tea for Rs. 14,250, the highest selling price so far. Castleton Tea Ltd. in the Darjeeling area of West Bengal accounts for 23.5% of the world's tea production.

762. The Jammu and Kashmir State Road Transport Corporation operated the first vehicle across Khardung La Pass at 18,380 ft. in 1962.

763. Jeevan Rekha or Lifeline Express, the first full-fledged hospital on wheels, was flagged off from Mumbai on July 16, 1991. The train has three specially designed air-conditioned coaches that house an operation theatre, sterilising room and wards apart from accommodation for the mobile medical team.

764. Leh Airport in Ladakh at a height of 3,256 m(10,680 ft) is the highest non-military airport.

765. The corridor in the Ramanathswamy temple at Rameshwaram, Tamil Nadu, is 1,220m (4,002 ft) long. It has 983 pillars, though popularly known as 'corridor with thousand pillars'.

766. Indira Gandhi Nahar Pariyojana (IGNP) canal at Rajasthan is 649 km. long. The Rs. 4,600-crore project, meant for the irrigation of 13.58 lakh ha in six districts of Rajasthan, took 35 years to complete.

767. The world's first fingerprint bureau was set up in Calcutta in June 1897. A murder case in 1898 in Jalpaiguri was among the first in the world where the culprit was caught based on dactyloscopy, the science of fingerprint identification.

768. Lt Col. S. Naicker and Manoj Taranvir Singh of Corps of Signals organised a motorcycle raid starting at Delhi on October 5, 1994 and ending at Khardung-la on October 10.

769. On Dec. 16, 1997, 4,459 interservice musicians formed a mass band as a part of a 50-minute Vijay Diwas show. A total of 251 pipe and drum bands, 30 military, four Air Force and two Naval bands came together under the baton to play Amazing Grace as a single unit of 227 pipes, 902 drums, 258 buglers, 937 brass band personnel and 135 band majors.

770. Plt. Offrs Namrita and Supreet Chandi trained in the same course and both opted to for helicopters. Posted to different Air Force stations, Namrita files a Chetak while Supreet files a Cheetah.

771. A set of four stamps with first-day-cover on Himalayan Ecology depicting the flora and fauna of the first day cover region was carried by a team from the Indo-Tibetan Border Police which scaled stamps Mt. Everest on May, 10, 1996. The stamps were released at the base camp at a height of 21,400 ft.

772. Ravi Shastri made 200 not out in 113 minutes for Bombay against Baroda at Mumbai in 1984-85. He holds the fastest double century record.

773. Aarti Pradhan was the first woman to swim the straits of Gibraltar. Aarti Pradhan (then 17) swam the 30 km Straits on August 29, 1988 in 7 hr 17 min.

774. The records of rice 'domestication' have been found at Neolithic sites (pre-7000 BC) at Koldhiwa, Mahagara in Allahabad district, Manigara and Baraunha in Mirzapur district, Sohgaura in gorakhpur district and Lahura Deva in Basti district.

775. The World's first dwarf wheat variety DDK 1001 (yield potential 4 tons/ha) was developed at the Directorate of Wheat Research, Karnal in 1995.

776. India produced 161 lakh tonne pulses in 1999, accounting for 27.2% of the global production (593 lakh tonnes).

777. India produced 80.96 lakh tonnes of millet in 1999 sharing 30.7% of the global figure (263.5 lakh tonnes). Nigeria came second with 54.57 lakh tonnes.

778. India produced 45.5 lakh tonnes of dry beans in 1999 out of the global output of 193.93 lakh tonnes. Brazil came second with 28.89 lakh tonnes.

779. India produced 67 lakh tonnes of chickpea in 1999 out of the global output of 92.44 lakh tonnes. Pakistan was next with 6.99 lakh tonnes.

780. India produced 52,00,000 tonnes of cauliflower in 1999 sharing 37.6% of the global output (138.42 lakh tonnes).China came second with 46,13,959 tonnes.

781. V. Balasubramanyam of Jayanagar, Bangalore grew an Amaranthus hypochondriacs (a leafy vegetable) in his garden which reached a height of 11 ft 7 in before it started withering during the first week of Dec. 1998.

782. India ranked first in the production of mangoes in 1999 with 120 lakh tonnes accounting for more than 50% of global output, Mango trees occupy 10.78 lakh land. India grows over 1,000 out of 1,100 verities of mangoes in the world.

783. India accounts for one-fourth of the global trade in spices and herbs, estimated at 5,00,000 tonnes worth US $150 crore.

784. The world's hottest chilli grows in India. Tezpur chilli, named after the place annually. Indian export in terms of quantity touched an all-time high 2,31,398 tonnes in 1998-99 earning Rs. 1,758 crore.

785. With an output of 57,000 tonnes of pepper, India accounted for 24.7% of global production in 1999. India also has the largest area (1,79,590 ha) under the crop in the world.

786. Saffron is the most expensive spice in the world. Domestic market price for saffron, a spice commonly found in Jammu and Kashmir, touched Rs. 34,500 per kg in October 1999 while in the international market it was priced at US $ 365 per pound.

787. India is the largest ginger producer in the world. With an annul output of 2.35 lakhs tonnes of ginger and an area of 70,910 ha under the crop, India shared 34.3% of global production (6.86 lakh tonnes) in 1999. In India, Kerala accounts for nearly 70% of the national output.

788. India is the largest mint oil producer. India produced 12,000 tonnes of mint oil and exported 8,000 tonnes. Mint oil is derived from the aromatic herb menthol mint (Mentha arvensis) grown in parts of Punjab, H.P., U.P. and Bihar.

789. India is the largest sugar producer in the world. India registered an output of about 180 lakh tonnes of sugar in 1999-2000 season against 152.38 lakh tonnes the previous year.

790. India is the largest tea producer in the world. With an output of 8,16,060 tonnes in 1999-2000, India became the world leader sharing over 26% of the global production.

791. India is the largest production of jute & allied fibres. With an output of 20.9 lakh tonnes India contributed 62.8% of global output (33.27 lakh tonnes) and exported 13.28 lakh tonnes. India also accounts for 11.1 lakh ha under the cultivation out of 18.3 lakh ha worldwide.

792. India is the only producer of the golden coloured muga silk of Assam. With an output of 15,500 tonnes in 1999, India is the largest producer of silk after China

793. India developed the first non-narcotic poppy. Sujata, a new opium variety developed in 1998 at the Central Institute of Medicinal and Aromatical plants, Lucknow is non-narcotic, very free from both opium and alkaloids.

794. Khardung-la road in the Leh-Manali sector is the highest motorable road in the world. It was constructed by the Border Roads organisation at an altitude of 5,682 m (18,383 ft).

795. Indian Railway employs 15.78 lakh people, the largest by any single organisation in India.

796. The Mumbai suburban railway system carries 59 lakh passengers a day, the highest in the world when compared to track length. About 1,077 suburban trains run every day on a track length of just 288 km.

797. The railway platform at Kharagpur in West Bengal is the longest platform in the world. It is measured 833 m (2,733 ft) long.

798. The Man-of-War jetty in Calcutta is the first floating maritime museum. The steamer River Ganga floating at the Man-of-War jetty in Calcutta was converted to maritime museum and training centre of the Calcutta Port Trust in July 1993.

799. Leh Airport in Ladakh at a height of 3,256m(10,680 ft) is the highest non-military airport.

800. In 1962, Air India became the world's first all-jet carrier when it replaced Super Constellation with a fleet of Boeing 707s.

801. Devinder Kumar Mehta, a flight purser with Indian Airlines, was hijacked thrice on three IA flights, the first time being in 1982. He was also on a plane that crash-landed in 1965.

802. India has 1,54,149 post offices of which 89% are in the rural areas serving 6,04,341 villages in the country. Letters are collected from 5,64,701 letter boxes, processed by a network of 573 Railway mail service (RMS).

803. Hikkim branch post office in Lahaul and Sprite district, Himachal Pradesh is at an approximate height of 15,000 feet and was opened of November 5, 1983.

804. The maximum numbers of stamps honouring an Indian are of Mahatma Gandhi. More than 80 stamps of Gandhiji have been issued from 81 countries, including the Republic of South Africa.

805. The ISD booth at the Siachen base camp at a height of 18,000 ft is the highest ISD booth. It was set up by the Army's Crop of Signals n October 1997.

806. The City Montessori School (CMS) Lucknow, founded in 1959 by Jagdish Gandhi and Bharti Gandhi, M.Ed. (Child psychologist) with five students on roll is now the world's largest private school in a single city.

807. Soupati Divya Tej of Guntur, born on June 8, 1990 secured an aggregate of 323 marks in SSC public exams held in March 1999 at the age of nine years two days.

808. Born on September 9, 1987 Tathagat Avatar Tulsi of Bihar passed the B.Sc. examination with honours in Physics from Science College, Patna at 11 years, 2 months to go on to pass M.Sc. on November 28, 1999 at the age of 12 years, 2 months.

809. Navyug Military and General Stores at Bangalore is the largest wholesale and retail military accessory store. Apart from being manufacturers, they are suppliers, contractors, traders, advisors, exporters and importers in virtually every item that the armed forces require.

810. Translated, Siachen means 'rose garden', a wildly romantic name given to the 76.8 km river of ice abutted by knife-edged, fluted, serrated ridgelines exceeding 7,100 m at some places. It is the highest and coldest battlefield with posts at altitudes varying from 15,000 to 21,000 ft.

811. When Mauritian Coast Guard vessel Vigilante needed repairs on its shafting systems within a year of commissioning, CGS Sarang towed her for 14 days over 2,650 nautical miles to Naval Dockyard, Mumbai. It was repaired in a record four months.

812. Sqn. Ldr. C. S. Raje (later Air Mshl.) was the first to land and take off from the makeshift airstrip at Daulatabeg Oldi. He landed with 32 fully equipped jawans at Daulatbeg Oldi (17,000 ft), the highest airstrip in the world, on July 22, 1962 in Ac-119 Packet aircraft.

813. The MI-26 is the heaviest helicopter. It has a cross between a heavy transport aircraft and a versatile helicopter. The twin-engine MI-26 with a payload of 20 tonnes carries 82 fully-equipped, combat-ready troops.

814. Brahmagupta (598-660) was the first mathematician to treat zero as a number and show its mathematical operations. Bhaskaracharya (1114) was the first to understand mathematical implications by stating 'any non-zero value divided by zero is infinite'.

815. Shirin and Deepak Gadhia devised a giant solar cooker which can cater to 10,000 people at a time. The cooker has 84 solar dishes and a surface of 840 sq m.

816. Varahamihira, a sixth century astronomer and scientist, was the first to mention seismological zones and the most earthquake prone regions in his treatise Brihatsamhita.

817. An artefact (No. 4189) containing 6.04% zinc was found at the Harappan site at Lothal (2200-1500 BC), in Gujarat. It was the earliest zinc artefact.

818. Dr. Murugappa Chennaveerappa Modi affectionately called 'Kannu Kotta Anna' meaning 'brother who gives sight' has performed more than 5,95,019 eye operations and examined 10,094,632 patients since 1943.

819. A Novel combination of twin machines, the ultra fast spiral CT

with smart score and the Cardiac MRI to increase sensitivity and specificity of packing up early coronary artery disease was inaugurated on May 15, 2000 at the Escort's Heart Institute and Research Centre, New Delhi.

820. The Lunar meteorite crater in the Vidarbha region of Maharashtra measures 1,800 m across. It is 170 m deep, with the rim rising to 20 m 65.6 ft above the surrounding area.

821. Sundarbans- the combined Ganga and Brahmaputra delta basin in West Bengal and Bangladesh covers 75,000 sq km (30,000 sq m.) is the largest delta.

822. To commemorate the World Environment Day on June 5, 1998, Sahara India Housing Ltd, planted 1,25,256 salins of 63 different species in 6 hr 35 min at their project site at Amby Valley near Lonavala, Maharashtra. The entire exercise was completed between 9 am and 3.35 pm.

823. In 1951, a 680-year-old teak tree with a girth of 7.6 m (25 ft) was felled in kakankote forest of Mysore. The lowest branches were 20 m (66 ft) above ground and it yielded 659 cu ft of timber.

824. A Banyan tree discovered in 1988 by photographers Regret Iyer and K.S. Ramakrishana of Bangalore in the Thimmamma Marrimanu village in the Anantpur district of Andra Pradesh has a canopy that covers an area of 2.1 hectares and over 1,100-odd prop roots

825. Fruits of the Jackfruit tree Artocarpus integrifolia weigh on an average 10 kg. It is the largest fruit.

826. Pilea microphylla, an artillery plant has blooms whose diametre is only 1/72 of an inch. It is the smallest bloom.

827. The scarlet rhododendron arboretum found on Mount Japfu of Nagaland reaches heights of over 20 m 65 ft.

828. Normally monkeys give birth to one or at the outside, two offspring. However, in March 2000 a Hanuman Langur in Jodhpur gave birth to quadruplets, something that has never happened before.

829. The quills of the Indian porcupine Hysterix Indica are over 35 cm

in length.

830. On July 4, 2000, Nandan Kanan near Bhubaneswar, Orissa, one of India's premier zoological institutions and home to the world's largest population of white tigers woke to find ten tigers seven white and three Royal Bengal -grievously ill or dead. It was the most tiger death seen at one time.

831. Dr. Hugh Falconer discovered 2 m long fossils of the chelonian Collossochelys atlas (c. 7-12 million years) in the Shivalik Hills in 1837. In 1923, Dr. Barnum Brown, curator of the Fossil Reptiles at the American Museum of Natural History, New York discovered the first complete skull in the same locality that measured 2.23 m long over the curve and 1.52 m wide.

832. Gahirmatha beach in Orissa is one of the largest rookies that witnesses an arribaba (Spanish for 'The Coming') of an estimated 1,30,000 Olive Ridley turtles to mate and nest.

833. Of the 2500 species in the order Cypriniformes, the Himalayan Msahaseer Tor tor, which grows to a length of six feet, is the largest.

834. Mud Shrimps Thalassinoidea can move large quantities of mud to form mounds about 2 m high and over 20 m wide in or near mangrove forests.

835. Megapodes, of which one species is found in India, can fly within hours of hatching from the egg!

836. Tragopans, of which four species are found in the Himalayas and N.E. India, are the only pheasants that nest in trees.

837. The Great crested Grebe podiceps cristatus of N. India measures 50 cm. It is also found in Europe, Africa, Australia and New Zealand. The Dabchick or Little Grebe podiceps ruficollis measures 23 cm.

838. The Raven Corvus corax that measures about 70 cm is the largest passerine or songbird in the world.

839. The Goldcrest Regulus, which occurs in the Himalayas and Europe, measures 3 inches and weighs 0.2 ounces or 5.7 gm.

840. There are about 15 species of crane in the world and of these six

are found in India. The Sarus Crane Grus antigone is the tallest at 1.52 m (4.99 ft).

841. Conducting General Elections to the Lok Sabha involves over 61-crore electorate voting in about 8,50,000 polling stations spread across varying geographic and climatic zones. The paper used only for the printing of ballot papers in 1999 general elections exceeded 7,700 metric tonnes.

842. In a landmark trial Special Judge V. Navaneetham, hearing the Rajiv Gandhi's assassination case sentenced all 26 accused (including 16 Sri Lankans) to death on January 28, 1998 at the end of the six-and-a -half year-long investigation and judicial process carried out by the Special Investing Team.

843. India imported gold worth $ 6.7 bin in 1998-99, making gold the second highest value commodity after fuel.

844. India has 4,20,000 ration shops under its public distribution system (PDS). Uttar Pradesh with 80,000 outlets tops the list.

845. Sanskrit, the Indo-Aryan language is perhaps the oldest recorded language of the world, Rig Veda being the first Sanskrit prevalent during 2000-500 BC. 1000 AD and later into modern Sanskrit.

846. Of the 7,000 languages and dialects spoken in the world, 845 are Indian.

847. The Mahabharata, composed by Veda Vyasa around 1000 BC chronicles the battle between the children of two brothers, Pandu and Dhritarashtra, in more than 1,00,000 slokas. It is the longeat epic in the world.

848. Vikram Seth's *A Suitable Boy* (1993) exceeds 5,00,000 words and comprises 1,349 pages and is said to be the longest novel in of the century, in English.

849. The late Osho Rajneesh is credited with over 650 books translated into 32 languages making 1, 150 published titles.

850. Dinesh Shadilya of Agra, U.P. has made and plays a flute, over 5 ft long and 3.5 inches in diametre. He also plays the smallest flute which is 4.5 inches long

851. Western music maestro Zubin Mehta spent over 13 years with the

New York. The 1990-91 season was his last with the 150- members orchestra.

852. The free open -air classical music concert conducted by Zubin Mehta at the Great Lawn in Central Park, New York City, U.S.A. on July 5, 1986 had an estimated audience of about 80,000 people.

853. Shrushtee Thakkar, a ten-year-old student from Baroda, Gujarat played the harmonium non-stop for 14 hours. The performance took place in Mumbai on December 30,1999.

854. Jamnagar Municipal Corporation organised the largest Raas Garba called Lakhota Raas Garba Mahotsav on September 27, 2000 in the sylvan srroundings of Lakhota Lake.

855. 'Chutti', used in Kathakali, is a three dimensional mask-like attachment made up of rice paste and paper that often extends up to 15 cm (6 in) from the face. It was the thickest make-up.

856. S.L.N. Swami's Kannada play *Anu* was performed at Banglore on August 15, 1999 in 24:13 seconds. A chorus of 22 artistes came on stage at 11.45 am and finished 25 seconds later! It was the shortest play.

857. Journalist-turned-director Swagat Thorat and the 88 students from the Pune School for the Blind staged a one-act play, *Swatantryachi Yashogatha*, on August 2, 1997 at Pune. The play portrayed the nation's struggle for Independence. Swagat Thorat again directed 44 visually impaired adults to act P.L. Deshpade's Teen Paisyacha Tamasha, an adaptation of Bertolt Bercht's *Three-Penny Opera*. It was unique because it was performed by visually challenged persons.

858. Sanat Chatterjee of Lucknow has done a 100ft x 11ft silk scroll painting, titled.

859. The 80-tonne single piece granite Shikhara atop the Brihadeshwara temple at Thanjavur, Tamil Nadu is the heaviest single-stone shikhara. It was a marvel of engineering technique. It is the first temple in the world built with granite.

860. According to Jane's World Armies, China's 'People's Liberation' Army had 2.2 million service personnel as of May 2000.

861. The longest-running UN peacekeeping mission is UNTSO (United Nation Truce Supervision Organisation), which has been in place since June 1948. UNTSO's headquarters are in Jerusalem, Israel, but it maintains military observation posts throughout the Middle East. It was the longest-running peacekeeping operation.

862. 'God's Army', a renegade ethnic group from Burma (Myanmar) led by 12-year-old twins Johnny and Luther Htoo, who are said to posses mystical powers, took 700 people hostage for 24 hours at a hospital in Ratchaburi, Thailand, on January 24, 2000. They were the youngest guerrilla leaders ever known. The guerrilla faction was formed when a splinter group left the Karen National Union (KNU) insurgent army.

863. Franklin Chang-Diaz (Costa Rica) has flown on a record six missions (1986-1998), as have Americans Story Musgrave (1983-1996), Shannon Lucid (1985-1996) and John Young (1965-1983).

864. On April 21, 1997, the ashes of 24 Space pioneers and enthusiasts, including Star Trek creator Gene Roddenberry and counter-culture guru Timothy Leary, were sent into orbit on board Spain's Pegasus rocket at a cost of $4,920 each. It was the first space funeral.

865. Eileen Collins (USA) has made a record two shuttle-flight landings. In February 1995, she became the first woman to land a space shuttle as a pilot, on the STS-63 mission and in July 1999, on the STS-93 mission, she became the first ever-female shuttle com-

mander.

866. The most populous city in the world is Tokyo, Japan. According to the United Nations, it had an estimated population of 26.4 million in March 2000.

867. Monaco is the country with the most telephones per capita, with 1,994 for every 1,000 people.

868. The country with the greatest number of pharmacists is China, with 418,000 in 1995. The Chinese have relied on traditional herbal cures dispensed by pharmacists for over 2,000 years.

869. The independent countries with the least income tax are Bahrain and Qatar, where the rate, regardless of income, is zero. For both nations, oil is the backbone of the economy, providing over half of government revenues.

870. In the Economist Intelligence Unit's biannual survey, Indian cities New Delhi and Mumbai (Bombay) finished with the lowest and cheapest ranking in a survey of the cost of living in 126 cities. With New York City, used as a median (ranked at 100), Mumbai and New Delhi rated only 42 and 41 respectively.

871. According to a 1998 World Bank survey, agriculture contributed to 62.8% of Guinea-Bissau's GDP. One of the 20 poorest countries in the world, it depends mainly on farming and fishing.

872. Graca Machel was married to Samora Machel, the president of Mozambique, from 1975 to October 19, 1986, till he was killed in a plane crash. On July 18, 1998, she married Nelson Mandela, president of South Africa, making her the first woman to be 'first lady' of two different countries.

873. The current world's youngest monarch is King Mswati III of Swaziland. He was crowned on April 25, 1986, aged 18 years, 6 days.

874. Jaspal Bhatt's Punjabi satire *Mahaul Theek Hai* (The Atmosphere is Right) premiered at New Delhi's Tihar Jail No. 3, in February 1999. As it was about police, terrorists and corruption. It was the first film premiered in a jail in India.

875. On December 9, 1999, 80 days after an earthquake struck Taiwan, killing an estimated 2,400 people, a cat was discovered alive in a collapsed building in Taichung, Taiwan. It was taken to veterinary hospital, where it made a full recovery.

876. The Australian Royal Flying Doctor Service was set up in 1928. In 1998, the service's 53 doctors, 103 nurses and 95 pilots treated 181,621 patients, performed 21,604 aerial evacuations and flew a total of 8.3 million miles. It is the most successful flying doctor service.

877. In January 2000, Flight Lieutenant Jeanine Godfrey, an officer with the British Royal Air Force, fell 1,299 ft. down a Scottish mountain, landing on snow-covered rocks. She sustained severe head and spinal injuries, but made a full recovery.

878. A total of 520 people were killed when a JAL Boeing 747, flight 123, crashed between Tokyo and Osaka, Japan, on August 12, 1985. It is the worst single-aircraft disaster.

879. On January 28, 1986, all seven people on board Challenger 51L were killed when the craft exploded 73 seconds after lift off from the Kennedy Space Centre, Florida, USA. It is the worst space disaster.

880. 105 people were killed when an elevator operating at the Vaal Reefs gold mine, South Africa, fell 1,608 ft. on May 11, 1995. It is the worst elevator disaster

881. Playback singer Kumar Sanu recorded 28 songs in a single day in 1993 at the Musicians Studio at Mumbai for Sterling Records and Cassettes. It is the most songs recorded in a day in India.

882. Director and screenwriter Manoj Night Shyamalan signed a $ 10 million deal in 2000 with Disney to write and direct *Unbreakable* his second film, *The Sixth Sense.* The $ 5 million for the script is the highest paid for an unsolicited non-commissioned screenplay. It is the highest paid screenwriter in India.

883. Saeed Jaffrey made his debut in 1977 in the Indian film *Shatranj Ke Khiladi* and has since acted in 100 Hindi films and 1 Punjabi film. In 1998, he opted to act in international cinema and British television and has appeared in 18 international films, including *A Passage to India* and *Gandhi* (both UK 1982). He also features in UK's longest-running soap opera, Coronation Street. It is the most appearances in international films by an indian.

884. A record of 39 films with South Indian star Prem Nazir as hero

was released in a single year - 1979. Fourteen films starring Mithun Chakraborty were released in 1999 while 20 other films in different stages of completion. It is the maximum films in India by an actor in a year.

885. Christian Adam beat his own record as he was sitting backwards on his bike and covered a distance of 60,45 km in 5:08 h with playing his violin.

886. In 1996, Kenichi Horie (Japan) made the fastest ever crossing of the Pacific in a solar-powered boat when he travelled 10,000 miles from Salinas, Ecuador, to Tokyo, Japan, in 148 days.

887. Caroline Hamilton, Ann Daniels, Pan Oliver, Rosie Stancer and Zoe Hudson (all UK) completed a trek to the South Pole on January 24, 2000, having reached the North Pole in 1997. They were raising funds for the charity Special Olympics, UK. It was the first female team to reach both poles.

888. Nicholas Bourne (UK) set off from Cape Town, South Africa on January 21, 1998, arriving at the Great Pyramids, Cairo, Egypt, on December 5, 1998. He ran over 7,500 miles. It is the fastest cape-to-cairo run.

889. Ivan Andre Trifonov (Austria) has been under, on and over the North Pole in the space of a day. He dived 47.7 ft under, stood upon and flew for 21.8 miles over the pole in an OE-KZT balloon, at an altitude of 4,921 ft., on April 27, 1999. The record was set as a part of 16-nation expedition to the North Pole in which six balloons took part.

890. Brad Hauter of Lake in the Hills, Illinois, USA, rode a lawn mover 4,039 miles through 16 states in 51 days. Hauter began the journey on April 7, 1999, in Atlanta, Georgia and finished, despite sustaining a fractured arm, at Santa Monica, California, USA, on May 19, 1999. It is the longest lawn mover ride.

891. The world's largest ever aerobics display was Capital Aerobica, which was organised by the University of Guadalajara, Mexico and took place at Metropolitan Park, Mexico, on June 6, 1998. A record 38,633 people took part.

892. On February 19, 2000, a record 3,333-yd.-long Chinese dancing

dragon was brought to life by 3,200 people at the Great Wall of China, near Beijing. The record was set to celebrate the Chinese Year of the Dragon.

893. On December 18, 1998, a total of 462 people, including students, teachers, parents and guests of Brock Corydon School, Winnipeg, Monitoba, Canada, took part in the World's biggest hug. The event was staged as part of citizenship programme being run at the school and was intended to teach the children respect and tolerance for other people.

894. On July 24, 1999, 34,309 people gathered at the National Stadium of Jamor, Lisbon, Portugal, to create the Portuguese Euro 2004 logo as part of the country's successful bid to host the soccer tournament. It was organised by Realisar Eventos Especias.

895. On May 16, 1999, before a soccer match at West Ham United's Boleyn Ground, London, England, a total of 23,680 people blew bubbles for one minute. West Ham's anthem is 'I'm Forever Blowing Bubbles. It is the most people blowing bubbles.

896. Gordon Cates of Alachua, Florida, USA kissed 10 monocle cobras and a 15-ft. king cobra consecutively on September 25, 1999.

897. Danny Higginbottom of Metairie, Louisiana, USA dived from a height of 29-ft. 0 water on August 23, 1999. He dedicated his dive to his late father.

898. The 2000 Dubai World Cup, held at Nad Al Sheba, Dubai United Arab Emirates, on March 25, 2000, had a total prize fund of $6 million, with the winner receiving 3.6 million. The race was won by Godolphin Stable's Dubai Millennium ridden by Frankie Dettori. His time was 2 minutes, giving him a record-winning rate of $30,000 per second.

899. The career earnings record for a racehorse is $10 million, by US champion Cigar (foaled in 1990) from

1993 to 1996. This includes a single-year record of $4.9 million in 1996. The top-earning filly or mare is Hokuto Vega (foaled in 1990), who had winnings of $8.3 million in Japan between 1993 and 1997.

900. Les Stewart of Mudjimba Beach, Queensland, Australia, spent 16 years typing the numbers 1 to 1,000,000 on 19,990 sheets of paper. Starting in 1982, he made the final keystroke on December 7, 1998.

901. Arulanantham Suresh Joachim (Sri Lanka) balanced on one foot for a record 76 hrs, 40 min, at Uihara Maha Devi Park Open Air Stadium, from May 22 to 25, 1997.

902. Stephan Kovaltchuk spent 57 years in his attic in Montchintsi, Ukraine, before emerging at the age of 75 in September 1999 because his sister, who had looked after him, had died. Having originally gone into hiding from Nazis, who occupied Ukraine in 1942, he remained in isolation to avoid the draft by the Russians after the Red Army's victory over the Germans.

903. On April 5, 1999, Karmit Tsubera and Dror Orpaz kissed for a record 30 hrs. 45 min. to win a kissing contest held in Rabin Square, Tel Aviv, Israel. 107 couples took part in the event.

904. On January 19, 2000, Fakhruddin Takulla (India) travelled from Mumbai (Bombay) to New Delhi, both India, using a ticket he had purchased on July 15, 1973 - 26 years, 6 months earlier. Takulla used the unlimited reservation service offered by the Indian Railways Authority so that he could attend the celebrations marking the 50th anniversary of Indian Independence.

905. Leo Clouser (USA) shot a rubber band a record-breaking distance of 99 ft. at the Wyomissing Area High School Gym. Wyomissing, Pennsylvania, USA, on June 18, 1999.

906. Between May 15 and 27, 1999, Bryan Berg of Spirit Lake, Iowa, USA, built a 24-ft. 4-in., 127-story freestanding house of cards from 1,200 packs of standard playing cards, without using adhesives. The record was set at the College of Design, Iowa State University, Ames, Iowa, USA.

907. The greatest distance travelled in a Zorb ball in a single roll is 353

yds. by Rich Eley (UK, centre) near Glynde, E. Sussex, England, on May 10, 1999. The ball reached a record speed of 31 m.p.h.

908. Jeremy Barrell (UK) climbed up an 80-ft.-high pole in 10.75 seconds during the 1999 World Pole climbing Championship, held at the Hampshire County Show, England, on July 28, 1999. He broke his own record of 11.36 seconds, set on July 28, 1998, at the same show.

909. Kevin Thackwell of Stock-on-Trent. Staffordshire, England, attached 116 clothespins to his face and neck in five minutes at the Horseshoe Inn, Church Lawton, Cheshire, England, on September 27, 1999.

910. Dani Abergel (professionally known as Dani Figaro) of Dimona, Israel, can style hair using seven pairs of scissors in one hand, controlling each pair independently. Abergel started to use multiple pairs of scissors and now regularly uses seven at a time in his Dimona salon. He claims that the technique allow him to create a 'more interesting' look.

911. The most hula hoops spun simultaneously between the shoulders and the hips is 82, by Lori Lynn Lomeli (USA) at the Atlantis Casino Resort, Reno, Nevada, USA, on August 5, 1999. Each of the hoops completed three full revolutions.

912. On December 17, 1998, Li Jian Hua of Jiangshan, China, lifted a 110.1 lb (50 Kg). a column of bricks hanging from a clamp joined to his ear. He held the weight for 9.3 seconds.

913. On June 9, 1996, Walter Arfeuille (Belgium) pulled eight railways passenger coaches with a combined weight of 493,563 lbs. a distance of 10ft. 6in. along a track, with his teeth. The record was set at Diksmuide, Belgium.

914. On March 5, 2000, Paddy Doyle (UK) completed a record 660 push-ups on the backs of his hand in one hour.

915. A disco ball at the Mayan Club, Los Angeles, California, USA has a diametre of 7ft. 11.25in and weighs 304lbs. Made by Big Millennium Balls of Santa Clarita, California, it consists of 6,900 mirrored squares, each measuring 2in. X 2in. It is the biggest ball.

916. The Ireland Millennium Drum, designed by Brian Fleming and Paraic Breathnac and constructed by Bill Wright and Seamus Purcell, has a diametre of 15 ft. 6 in. and a depth of 6 ft. 3 in. Made from birch plywood and sailcloth, it was first played at the St. Patrick's Festival in Dublin, Ireland's Millennium Festivals.

917. US actor Paul Newman was 75 years old when he took part in the Rolex 24 at Daytona International Speedway. Florida, USA, from February 6 to 7, 2000. His team, which included 17-year-old co-driver Gunnar Jeannette, completed in a Champion Racing Porsche 996-GT3. He was the oldest racing driver.

918. Jack Mackenzie (Canada) was the oldest person to ski to North Pole. He joined a ski expedition to the geographic North Pole at the age of 77 years, 10 months and 13 days, reaching the pole on April 28, 1999. Jack was born in New Richmond, Quebec, on June 15, 1921. He joined the Royal Canadian Air Force in 1940, flying to England and the Middle East and from Gibraltar and North Africa to Italy, until 1945. After World War II he worked for the Bank of Nova Scotia, Ottawa, before joining the Federal Public Service. Retiring in 1976, Jack spent the following 19 years travelling extensively with his wife on six continents, never repeating a destination. After his wife died in 1995, he continued adventure

travel by joining various expeditions - to the west coast of Greenland, across the Drake Passage to Antarctica, the seventh and final continent for him to visit and 4,000 km. (2,485 miles) across China. During his North Pole expedition, as part of a nine-member team led by explorers Richard Weber (Canada) and Dr. Mikhail Malakhov (Russia), Jack reached the pole after covering 100 km. (62 miles) in five and a half days, skiing five to seven hours each day. In July 2000, the Government of the Province of Ontario, Canada, made him Senior Citizen of the Year for the Township of Goulbourn, for charitable works. He now continues to travel. In April 1999, Jack MacKenzie (Canada), then aged 77, joined a ski expedition to the North Pole as part of celebrations to mark the International Year of Older Persons. He and the other eight members of his team skied 62 miles in five and a half days, reaching the pole on April 28, 1999.

919. The characteristics typical of the Hominidae include a large brain and bipedal locomotion. The earliest hominid relic is an Australopithecine Jaw-bone, with two molars 5 cm 2 in long, found by Kiptam Chepboi near Lake Baringo, Kenya in February 1984. It has been dated to 4 million years ago by associated fossils and to 5.4-5.6 million years ago through rock correlation by potassium argon dating.

920. Earliest primates appeared in the late Cretaceous epoch about 65 million years ago. The earliest members of the sub-order Anthropoid are known from both Africa and South America in the early Oligocene, 30 - 34 million years ago, when the two infra-orders, playrrhini and Catarrhini, from the New and Old worlds respectively, were already distinct. Finds from Faiyum, Egypt, are being studied and may represent primates from the early Oligocene period, 37 million years.

921. The oldest steam Engine in working order is the Smethwick Engine dating from 1779. It was designed by James Watt in 1736-1819 and built by the Birmingham Canal Company at a cost of £ 2000, the pump originally a 60 cm 24 in bore with a stroke of 2.4 m 8 ft-worked on the canal locks at Smethwick, W Mids until 1891. The engine was presented to Birmingham Museum of Science and Industry in 1960 and is regularly steamed for public.

922. The oldest engine working as such and on original place is the 1812 Boulton & Watt 26-hp, 1066 mm 42 in bore beam engine on the Kennet and Avon Canal at Great Bedwyn, Wilts. The Crofton Society restored it in 1971 and it still runs periodically.

923. The largest ever-single cylinder steam engine was designed by Mathew Loam of Cornwall and built by the Hayle Foundry Co. in 1849 for land draining at Haarlem, Netherlands. The cylinder was 3.6 m 12 ft in diametre and each stroke also of 3.65 m 12 ft, lifted 61.096 litres 13440 gal of water.

924. The most efficient steam engine was Taylor's engine built by Michael loam for United Mines of Gwennap, Cornwall in 1840. It registered only 0.8kg 1.7 ib of coal per horse power per hour.

925. The most powerful installed power station is the Itaipu Hydroelectric plant on the Parana River near the Brazil-Paraguay border. Opened in 1984, the station's 18th turbine was put into operation in May 1991, giving a total capacity of 12600 MW from a projected 13320 MW. A 20,000 MW power station on the Tunguska River, Russia was announced in February 1982.

926. The earliest programmable electronic computer was the 1500-valve colossus formulated by Prof. Max H.A. Newman (1897-1985) and built by T.H. Flowers. It was run in December 1943 at Bletchley Park, bucks to break the German coding machine Enigma. It arose from a concept published in 1936 by Dr. Alan Mathison Turing 1912-54 in his paper on Computable numbers with an application to the Entscheidungs problems. Colossus was declassified on October 25, 1975.

927. The world's first stored-programme computer was the Manchester University Mark I, which incorporated the Williams storage cathode ray tube. It ran its first programme by Prof. Tom Kilburn, on June 21, 1948.

928. Computers were greatly advanced by the invention of the point-contact transistor by John Bardeen and Walter Britain and the junction transistor by R.L Wallace, Morgan Sparks and Dr. William Bradford Shockley (1910-89) in early 1951.

929. The invention of Microprocessor Chip '4004' of Microcomputer

was invented by the team led by M.E. Holf Jr, of Intel Corporation in 1969-71. However, the priority was accorded to Gilbert Hyatt who devised a single chip microcomputer at Micro Computer Inc. of Van Nuys, Los Angeles in 1969-71 with the award of US patent No. 4942516 in July 17, 1990.

930. The highest accepted named number in the system of successive powers of ten is the centillion, first recorded in 1852. It is the hundredth power of a million or 1 followed by 600 noughts. The number 10100 is designated a googol. The term was suggested by the 9-year-old nephew of Dr. Edward Kasner (USA). Ten raised to the power of a googol is described as a googolplex. Some conception of the magnitude of such numbers can be gained when it is said that the number of electrons in some models of the observable Universe is of the order of 1087.

The highest named number outside the decimal notation is the Buddhist *asankhyeya*, which is equal to 10140 and mentioned in Jain works of 100 BC.

The highest number ever used in a mathematical proof is a bounding value published in 1977 and is known as Graham's number. It contains bi-chromatic hypercubes and is beyond description without the special arrow notation, devised by Knuth in 1976 and then extended to 64 layers.

A prime number is any positive integer (excluding 1) having no integral factors other than itself and unity, for example 2, 3, 5, 7 or 11. The lowest prime number is thus 2.

The highest known prime number is 2756839 –1, founded in February 1992 by analysts at AEA Technology's Harwell Laboratory, Oxon. The number contains 227832 digits and was found by means of a CRAY-2 supercomputer.

The largest known twin primes are 1706595x 211235 –1 and 1706595x2 11235 +1, discovered on August 6, 1989 by a team in Santa Clara, California, USA using an Amdahl 1200 supercomputer. A number is said to be perfect if it is equal to the sum of all divisors of the number other than itself, for example 1+2+4+7+14=28. The lowest perfect number is therefore 6, as in 1+2+3.

The highest known perfect number, is the 32nd so far discovered, is 2756839 –1 x 2756838. It is derived from the largest known Mersenne prime also the largest prime known namely 2756839 –1, discovered in February 1992. 'As I was going to St. Ives, I met a man with seven wives. Every wife had seven sacks and every sack had seven cats. Every cat had seven kits. Kits, cats, sacks and wives, how many were going to St. Ives?' Apart from slight differences in wording, this is identical to a puzzle found in the Rhind papyrus, an Egyptian scroll bearing mathematical tables and problems, copied by the scribe Ahmes 1650 BC.

931. The most most accurate version of 'pi' has been calculated is 1073740000 by Yasumasa Kanada and Yoshiaki Tamura of The University of Tokyo, Japan on 19 Nov 1989 using a Hitac S-820/80E computer.

932. The prolific output of Swiss mathematician Leonard Euler (1707-83) was such that his papers were still being published for the first time more than 50 years after his death. His collected works have been printed bit by bit since 1910 and will eventually occupy more than 75 large quarto volumes. He is the most prolific mathematician.

933. The floating flowering aquatic duckweed (Wolffia angusta) of Australia, depicted in 1980, is only 0.6 mm, 0.024 in long and 0.33 mm, 0.013 in wide. It weighs about 0.00015 g and its fruit, which resembles a minuscule fig, weighs 0.00007 g.

934. The greatest certain altitude at which any flowering plants have been seen is 6400 m (21000ft) on Mt. Kamet (7756 m 25447 ft) in the Himalayas by N.D.Jayal in 1955. They were Ermania Himalayensis and Ranunculus lobatus.

935. The most massive organism was a network of quaking aspen trees (Populus tremuloides) reported in December 1992, rowing in Wasatch Mountains, Utah, USA from a single root system, covering 43 ha 106 acres and weighing around 6000 tonnes. This particular network was first described in 1975.

936. Oldest 'King Clone', the oldest known clone of the creosote plant (Larrea tridentata), California, USA, was estimated in February 1980 by Prof. Frank C. Vasek to be 11700 years old. It is possible

that crustose lichens in excess of 500 mm 20 in diametre may be as old and in 1981 it was estimated that Antarctic lichens larger than 100 mm 4in in diametre are at least 10,000 years old.

937. The deepest plant found is marooned coloured algae found in Bahamas in October 1984 by Mark and Diane Littler of San Salvadore Island. This plant-survived although 99.9995 percent of sunlight was filtered out. This plant was found at the depth of 269 m 884 ft.

938. Some species of 45 genera of bamboo have been found to grow at a rate of up to 91 cm 3 ft per day. It is the fastest growing plant.

939. The flower angiosperm is believed to be 120 million years old, it was discovered in 1989 by Drs. Leo hickey and David Taylor of Yale University, Connecticut, USA from the fossil found in Melbourne, Victoria, Australia. The flower resembles the modern black pepper plant, has two leaves and one flower and is known as the Koonwarra Plant.

940. Largest flower of all are the Parasite stinking corpse lily (Rafflesia arnoldii), which can grow to 91 cm 3ft wide, 1.9 cm ¾ in thick and weigh up to 7 kg 15 lb. The plants attach themselves to cissus vines in the jungles of Southeast Asia and, true to name have an extremely offensive scent.

941. Largest bloom of any native British plant is the wild white water lily (Nymphaea alba), at 15 cm 6 in across.

942. The largest known inflorescence is of the Puya raimondii, which is a rare Bolivian monocarpic member of the Bromeliaceae family. Its erect panicle (diametre 2.4 m 8 ft) emerges to a height of 10.7 m 35 ft and each of these bears up to 8000 white blooms.

943. The flower-spike of an agave measured in Berkeley, California, USA in 1974 was found to be 15.8 m 52ft long.

944. The Giant Chinese Wisteria (Wisteria sinensis) at Sierra Madre, California, USA was planted in 1892 and now has branches 152 m 500 ft long. It covers nearly 0.4 ha 1 acre, weighs 22 tonnes and has estimated 1.5 million blossoms during its blossoming period of five weeks, when up to 30000 people pay admission to visit it.

945. The male litigon (a hybrid of an Indian lion and a tiger - itself the offspring of tiger and a lioness)-named Cubanacan at Alipur Zoo-

logical Gardens, Calcutta, India was believed to weigh at least 363 kg 800 lb. This unique animal stood 1.32 m at the shoulder and measured a record 3.5 m (11½ ft) in total length. He died on 12 April 1991.

946. The smallest member of the order Carnivora is the least weasel (Mustela rixosa), also called the dwarf weasel, which is circumpolar in distribution. The smallest of the four recognised races is Mustela r. pygmaea, which has an overall length of 177-207mm 6.96-8.14 in and weighs 35-70g 1¼-2½oz. It is native to Siberia, Russia.

947. The largest member of the cat family (Felidae) is the protected long-furred Siberian Tiger. It is also called Amur or Manchurian tiger. Males average 3.15m 10ft 4in length from the nose to the tip of the extended tail, stands 99-107cm 39-42in at the shoulder. It weighs about 265kg 585lb. In 1950, a male weighing 384kg 846½lb was shot in the Sikhote Alin Mountains, Maritime Territory, Russia. This weight was exceeded by an Indian tiger (Panthera t. tigris) shot in northern Uttar Pradesh in November 1967 which measured 3.22 m 10 ft 7 in between pegs (3.37 m 11ft over the curves) and weighed 389 kg 857 lb. It is now on display at the Smithsonian Institution, Washington DC, USA.

948. The largest tiger ever held in captivity and the heaviest 'big cat' on record, is a nine-year-old male Siberian named 'Jaipur', owned by animal trainer Joan Byron-Marasek of Clarksburg, New Jersey, USA. This tiger measured 3.32 m 10 ft 11in in total length and weiged 423 kg 932 lb in October 1986.

949. The little brown bat (Myotis Lucifugus) has been recorded at a depth of 1160m 3805ft in a Zinc mine in New York, USA. The mine serves as winter home for 1000 members of this species, which normally roosts at a depth of 200 m 650 ft.

950. The largest concentration of bats found living anywhere in the world today is that of the Mexican free-tailed bat (tadarida brasiliensis) in Bracken Cave, San Antonio, Texas, USA, where up to 20 million animals assemble after migration.

A bat colony in Greywell Canal Tunnel, Hants contains about 2000 individuals made up of six different species.

951. The average African lion (Panthera leo) measures 2.7 m 9 ft total length. It stands 91-97 cm 36-38 in at the shoulder and weighs 181-185 kg 400-410 lb. The heaviest wild specimen on record weighed 313 kg 690 lb and was shot near Hectorspruit, Transvaal, South Africa in 1936.

952. The smallest member of the cat family is the rusty spotted cat (Felis Rubiginosa) of Southern India and Sri Lanka. Average height of males is 64-71 cm 25-28 in the tail measures 23-25 cm 9-10 in and weigh about 1.35 kg 3 lb.

953. The male eastern lowland gorilla (Gorilla gorilla graueri) of eastern Zaire and South-western Uganda is 175 cm 5 ft 9 in tall and weighs 165 kg 360 lb. The mountain gorilla of the volcanic mountain ranges of western Rwanda, south-west-Uganda and eastern Zaire is of comparable size, i.e. 173 cm 5ft 8in tall and 155 kg 343 lb and most of the exceptionally large gorillas taken in the field have been of this race. It was the largest gorilla.

The tallest recorded for a gorilla in the wild is 1.88m 6ft 2in for a mountain bull shot in the eastern Congo (Zaire) 1920. The tallest gorilla ever kept in captivity is reportedly an eastern lowland male named 'Colossus' (1966). Who is currently on display at a zoo in Gulf Breeze, Florida, USA. The estimate of his height and weight is 1.88 m 6 ft 2 in tall and 260.8 kg 575 lb respectively.

The heaviest gorilla ever kept in captivity was a male of the mountain race names 'N' gagi, who died in San Diego Zoo, California, USA on 12 January 1944 at the age of 18. He weighed 310 kg 638 lb at his heaviest 1943. He was 1.72 m 5ft 7¾ in tall and boasted a record chest measurement of 198 cm 78 in.

Britain's largest captive gorilla is probably 'Djoum' of Howletts Zoo, Kent, whose weight is stable at 213 kg 470 lb. Another male example of the western lowland gorilla named 'Bukhama' at Dudley Zoo, W Mids was reportedly 227 kg 500 lb in 1969.

954. The greatest age recorded for a non-human primate is 59 years 5 months for a Chimpanzee (Pan troglodytes) named gamma, who died at the yerkes primate research Centre in Atlanta, Georgia, USA on 19 February 1992. 'Gamma' was born at the Florida branch of the Yerkes Centre in September 1932. A similar age was reached by a male Orang-utan (Pongo Pygmaeus) named 'Guas' who died in Philadelphia Zoological garden, Pennsylvania, USA on February 9, 1977. He was at least 13 years old on his arrival at the zoo on 1st May 1931.

955. The world's oldest monkey was a male white-throated capuchin (Cebus capucinus) called 'Bobo'. He died on July 10, 1988 at the age of 53 years following complications related to a stroke.

956. The streaked tenrec (Hemicentetes semispinosus) of Madagascar is the youngest breeder. It is weaned after only five days and females can breed 3-4 weeks after their birth. The tenrec (Tenrec ecaudatus) is a small mammal. One of the largest of the insectivores, it uses its snout to dig for worms and insects.

957. The Asiatic elephant (Elephas maximus) has the longest gestation period. It has an average gestation period of 609 days (over 20 months) and a maximum of 760 days, more than two and a half times that of humans.

958. The American opossum has the shortest gestation period. The gestation periods of the American opossum (Didelphis marsupialis), also called the Virginian Opossum, the rare water opossum or yapok (Chironnectes minimus) of central and northern South America and the eastern native cat (Dasyurus viverrinus) of Australia are all normally 12-13 days but can be as short as eight days.

959. The largest herds on record were those of the Springbok (Antidorcas maesupialis) during migration across the plains of western part of

Southern Africa in the 19th century. In 1849 John (Later Sir John) Fraser observed a trekbokken that took three days to pass through the settlement of Beaufort West, Cape Province. Another herd seen moving near Nels Poortje, Cape Province in 1888 was estimated to contain 100 million heads, although 10 million is probably a more realistic figure. Another herd estimated to be 24 km 15 miles wide and more than 160 km 100 miles long was reported from Karree Kloof, Orange River, South Africa in July 1896.

960. The Bowie Knife, the Knife with a guard between the long, heavy blade and the handle to protect the user, though associated with and credited to the famous defender of the Alamo, James Bowie, was actually invented by his lesser-known brother, Rezin Pleasant Bowie. James was more adept at using the Knife, carried it everywhere and soon became identified with it.

According to U.S. Patent Office records, Thomas Jefferson was the inventor of the first Hideaway Bed ever patented in the United States. Though the original plans for the Bed have disappeared, we know from contemporary descriptions that when the bed was not in use it was hoisted to the ceiling and secured by a complicated system of pulleys and ropes.

961. Adult frogs breathe with lungs, but also absorb oxygen through their skin. They can see and breathe while the rest of the body is under water because frogs have eyes and nostrils that are on the tops of their heads.

962. Frogs have smooth skin and long legs to help them leap. Toads have drier warty skin and short legs and they move by crawling or hopping rather than by leaping. Technically, though, toads are just a type of frog. Some frogs lay as many as 25000 eggs while others may lay as few as 4. Some tree frogs live their whole lives in the trees and never come down. They even lay their eggs in the tree branches or on leaves. The red-eyed tree frog from Central America lays its eggs on leaves that are over the water. When the eggs hatch, the tadpoles fall into the water below. The smallest frog in the world is from Cuba and is only 1/2' long. The largest frog in the world is from West Africa (Conraua goliath) and is about 12 inches long. There are over 4000 species of frogs in the world, though only 88

species in the US and Canada. They are all over the world, except for Antarctica and Iceland.

963. The name 'gorilla' means hairy person and was coined by an explorer from ancient Carthage almost 2,500 years ago. A baby gorilla may weigh only 4.5 pounds at birth but grow to become a 400-pound adult. A male gorilla can weigh twice as much as a female. Although its head is larger, a gorilla's brain is smaller than a human's. An estimated 10,500 Eastern lowland gorillas are located slightly east of the Congo Basin in Central African Republic and Zaire. The extremely rare Mountain gorilla numbers only 500 and is concentrated in the volcanic regions of Rwanda, Uganda and Zaire. Gorilla groups can be composed of different social forms.

Family troops are lead by an adult male, commonly identified as a 'silverback'. Although some groups may be all male, one adult will be the lead or the 'silverback'. The troop spends most of its time in search of the 40 pounds of leaves, stems and roots each adult needs. At night they build nests for sleeping, sometimes in trees, sometimes on the ground. Gorillas are gentle animals. They treat each other with kindness and consideration. Gorillas are the largest of the primates. An adult male can weigh 350-600 pounds. They have thick, springy hair covering most of their bodies. However, adults do not have hair on the face, chest, palms or the soles of their feet. They can live more than 50 years. Gorillas can stand on their legs but they walk using their legs and 'hands' in a four-footed manner, which is an easier way to balance the heavy weight of their head and upper body. They use the hand like a foot and walk on the knuckles. The biggest threat to gorillas is the loss of land due to human development. Gorillas need large areas of dense forest. Lumbering and farming compete for space and war refugees create additional demands on limited resources. Poaching for bush meat or trophies is yet another threat. The bones and muscles of gorillas and humans are similar but the body shape is different. The gorilla's stomach is much larger than the chest, permitting the gorilla to eat and store bulky, vegetative food. The faces of gorillas are different from one another, just like humans. The physical parts and mechanics of a gorilla's hand are similar to a human's but it is twice as big. The Western lowland gorillas are also the most plentiful and relatively widespread subspecies in the wild with a population of 110,500 animals. They are located across the political borders of six countries in west Equatorial Africa. Almost 80 percent are in the Congo and Gabon, with a few troops also in Central African Republic, Equatorial Guinea, Cameroon and Nigeria. There are an estimated 125,000 gorillas among the four subspecies. The Louisville Zoo gorilla troop will be captive-born Western lowland gorillas - the subspecies found in almost all the world's zoos. They are methodical in search of food and they are smart enough to remember when and where the most desirable food ripens. They savor their meals, smacking lips together and grumbling with contentment. While people have arms equal in length to their legs, gorillas' arms are proportionately different. An average male gorilla is six inches shorter than an average man but its arms are about a foot longer. A gorilla can use its feet to grab.

964. An adult woman's heart weighs about 8 ounces, a man's about 10 ounces. An average heart weighs 300g (10.7 ozs.) and is about the size of a fist. A well-trained endurance athlete has a resting heart rate of 40 bpm. A well-trained heart can be 30 to 40% larger than a normal heart and pump 50% more blood with each beat. In a 70-year lifetime, the average human heart beats more than 2.5 billion times. The heart beats about 100,000 times each day. In a lifetime, it has been calculated that the heart pumps enough blood to fill the Albert Hall! The adult heart pumps about 5 quarts of blood each

minute – approximately 2,000 gallons of blood each day – throughout the body. The average resting heart rate is 66 - 72 beats per minute (bpm).

When attempting to locate their heart, most people place their hand on their left chest. Actually, your heart is located in the centre of your chest between your lungs. The bottom of the heart is tipped to the left, so you feel more of your heart on your left side of your chest. Your system of blood vessels – arteries, veins and capillaries – is over 60,000 miles long. That's long enough to go around the world more than twice!

965. Blood is about 78 percent water. Blood is circulated around the body every 45 seconds. Blood takes about 20 seconds to circulate throughout the entire vascular system. If the blood vessels were put end to end, they would circle the world twice!

966. A captive tiger can live up to twenty years, while a wild tiger can expect to live ten to fifteen years. A cub will begin eating solid food at around 12-13 weeks and should be completely weaned around seventeen weeks. A female tiger will usually give birth to 2-3 cubs in the wild, unfortunately the fatality rate for cubs can be quite high. A group of tigers is called a Streak. A male tiger can copulate up to six times an hour. A male's territory can overlap several females' territories. A single brewery in Taiwan imported 2,000 kg of tiger bone annually during the 1980's, the equivalent of 100-200 tiger carcasses, to produce 100,000 bottles of tiger wine. A tiger can go two to three days without eating. A tiger can only usually expect a one in twenty success rate when bringing down prey. A tiger can spend up to eighteen hours sleeping. A tiger cub can gain 100 grams in weight per day. A tiger cub will make its first kill around 18 months of age. A tiger eats around six kilos of meat per day, but can go as long as a week without a meal.

A tiger is Diurnal, which means its peak times of activity are dawn and dusk.

An adult wild tiger is a solitary animal and will establish its own territory, which can cover over 100 square miles. A tiger marks its territory by spraying surrounding trees and bushes with urine, dropping prominently placed scat and leaving deep scratch marks on tree trunks. A tiger will circumnavigate its territory every few days. A tiger's canine teeth can grow up to three inches long and would be capable of crunching through the vertebrae of any creature on this earth. A tiger's night vision is six times greater than a human's. A white tiger is not an albino, all white tigers are believed to have descended from a single white Bengal male called Mohan. Adult tigers have thirty teeth. After a feed, a tiger will usually bury the remaining animal carcass in an attempt to hide it from scavengers and then exhume it for its next meal. All tigers have a similar marking on their forehead, which resembles the Chinese symbol Wang, meaning King. All tigers typically show a 1:1 sex ratio at birth. Tigers kill approximately fifty humans each year. Between 1960 and 1984 3000 South China tiger pelts were officially recorded. Due to the cold winters of Southern Russia and Northern China the Siberian tiger is the largest of the subspecies with an average length of 9 ft 8' and an average weight of 540 pounds, it has the thickest fur and roams the largest territories. Every single part of the tiger is used in traditional Chinese medicine. If you were to shave the fur from a tiger it would still have stripes. In 1959, the Siberian tiger was declared an endangered species and awarded protection. In 1959, the South China tiger was declared a pest and a bounty was placed on its head. In a part of India called Sunderban, tigers have been known to eat man. In Asia, illegal tiger farms operate to supply tigers for the traditional Chinese medicine market. It is also believed in Chinese mythology that the tiger can take human form. It is believed that the two white dots on the back of a tiger's ears are designed to act as a visual beacon to enable the cubs to follow their parent. It is believed that when a tiger dies its spirit enters the ground and becomes amber. It is impossible to count how many tigers are left in the wild but experts estimate there to be less than 6000. It is said that the South China tiger is impossible to train; many Chinese circuses gave up after trying to implement them into their acts. Tiger's roar can be heard from two miles away. Like the domestic cat the tiger's claws are retractable. Male tigers have been known to kill and sometimes eat cubs of other males before taking the tigress as its own mate.

967. Hair is the fastest growing tissue in the body, second only to bone marrow. A hair grows by 0.3 to 0.5 mm per day - about 1 to 1.5 cm a month and 12 to 15 cm a year. A single hair can support up to 100 grams in weight and a whole head of hair could support up to 12 tonnes - the equivalent of two African elephants! African and European people are more prone to balding than Asian people. African hair grows more slowly and is more fragile than European hair. Asian hair grows the fastest and has the greatest elasticity. Children lose an average of 90 hairs each day, which increases to 120 by old age. Early hair remedies read like witches' potions. One sixteenth-century doctor claimed to restore hair by applying a mixture of boiled slugs, olive oil, honey, saffron, soap and cumin to the head. But nobody knows if it worked. Hair is the second fastest growing tissue in the body. Only bone marrow is quicker. It is possible for your hair to turn white from shock... but not overnight! Hair pigment is produced in the hair shaft beneath the skin, so it would take about 13 days for any white hairs to show. Many drugs can cause hair loss. One centimetre of hair can reveal much about your behaviour in the past month - what you ate, drank and the environments you encountered. The average person's head has 100,000 to 150,000 hairs. The word shampoo comes from the Hindi 'champna', meaning to massage or knead. Thyroid imbalance and iron deficiency are reversible causes for hair loss. Women often experience major, but reversible, loss of hair two or three months after giving birth. The massive production of the hormone oestrogen during pregnancy puts hair follicles into their 'growth phase'. After the birth, the hormonal balance is restored and the hair follicles go into the 'loss phase', causing a large number of hairs to fall out at once. You must lose over 50% of your scalp hairs before it is apparent to anyone.

968. Dolphins have to be conscious to breath. This means that they cannot go into a full deep sleep because then they would suffocate. Bottlenose dolphins eat several kinds of fish (including mullet, mackerel, herring, cod) and squid. The composition of the diet depends very much on what is available in the area they live in and also on the season. The amount of fish they eat depends on the fish species they are feeding on mackerel and herring have a very high

fat content and consequently have a high caloric value, whereas squid has a very low caloric value, so to get the same energy intake (calories) they will need to eat much more if they feed on squid than if they feed on mackerel or herring. On average an adult dolphin will eat 4-9% of its body weight in fish, so a 250 kg (550 lb) dolphin will eat 10-22.5 kg (22-50 lb) fish per day. The maximum age for bottlenose dolphins is between 40 and 50 years. The average age a dolphin can get (the life expectancy) can be calculated from the ASR Annual Survival Rate (the percentage of animals alive at a certain point that is still alive one year later). For the dolphin population in Sarasota Bay, the ASR has been measured to be about 0.961. This yields a life expectancy of about 25 years. For the population in the Indian/Banana River area, the ASR is between 0.908 and 0.931. This yields a life expectance between 10.3 and 14 years. So the actual life expectancy differs per region. The deepest dive ever recorded for a bottlenose dolphin was a 300 metres (990 feet). Most likely dolphins do not dive very deep, though. Many bottlenose dolphins live in fairly shallow water. Other whale and dolphin species are able to dive to much greater depths even. The pilot whale (Globicephala melaena) can dive to at least 600 metres (2000 feet) and a sperm whale (Physeter macrocephalus) has been found entangled in a cable at more that 900 metres (500 fathoms) depth. Most dolphins live in the ocean and the ocean water is too salty for them to drink. If they would drink seawater, they would actually use more water trying to get rid of the salt than they drank in the first place. Most of their water comes from their food (fish and squid). Also, when they metabolise (burn) their fat, water is released in the process. Their kidneys are also adapted to retaining as much water as possible. Although they live in water, they live as desert animals with no direct source of drinkable water.

969. Some crabs near Danno-ura in Japan have patterns on their shells bearing an uncanny resemblance to a face of a samurai. When caught, these crabs are thrown back in commemoration of the Heike samurai clan, who lost a naval battle there in 1185. The patterns on the crabs"shells are inherited and it is believed that the patterns evolved because fishermen tended to throw back crabs with patterns resembling faces. So, crabs with patterns that most

resembled a face had a better chance of survival. Eventually, the pattern of the face of a fierce, scowling samurai evolved.

970. King Alexandros I of Greece (1917-1920) died from blood poisoning after being bitten by his pet monkey.

971. The Falkland Islands have a human population of around 2,000 but a sheep population of 700,000, making 350 sheep for each person.

972. Winnie-the-Pooh, the cartoon character is based on a real bear. On August 24th, 1914, a Canadian soldier and veterinarian named Harry Colebourn, en route to a training camp in Valcartier, Quebec, purchased an orphaned black bear cub for $20 in White River, Ontario, which he named Winnipeg or Winnie for short. When his unit was sent over to France during World War I, Colebourn loaned her to the London Zoo, intending to take her back to Canada after the war. However, Winnie's gentle disposition made her the zoo's top attraction and on December 1, 1919, he donated her to the zoo. In the mid 1920's, writer A. A. Milne often took his young son, Christopher Robin, to the zoo and Christopher named his teddy bear 'Winnie-the-Pooh' after Winnie. A. A. Milne went on to write several best-selling children's books about Christopher Robin and Winnie-the-Pooh. Lord Byron had a pet bear. He kept one at Cambridge University because dogs weren't allowed. Polar bears are left-handed.

973. The first successful corneal transplant was performed as early as 1835 by a British army surgeon in India. His pet antelope had only one eye and it had a badly scarred cornea. He removed a cornea from a newly killed antelope and transplanted it into his pet's eye. The operation was a success.

974. The only purple animal in the world is the Blesbok, a small antelope exclusive to South Africa.

975. The Wake Island rail was only discovered in 1903 and was extinct by 1946. It was wiped out when the island was occupied during World War II by Japanese soldiers, who found it a tasty delicacy.

976. During the hundred days of the opening games at the Colosseum in Rome, in 80 A.D., more than 5,000 animals were killed. They included elephants, tigers, lions, elks, hyenas, hippopotamuses and

giraffes.

977. The Canary Islands got their name not from Canaries but from the wild dogs that the Romans found when they landed there. They called the island *Insulae Canariae*, which means 'Island of the Dogs'.

978. The fourth Mogul Emperor, Jahangir, who ruled from 1605 to 1627, had a harem of 300 royal wives, 5,000 more women and 1,000 young men for alternate pleasures. Outside the palace, he stabled other kinds of pet 12,000 elephants, 10,000 oxen, 2,000 camels, 3,000 deer, 4,000 dogs, 100 tame lions, 500 buffalo and 10,000 carrier pigeons.

979. Mineral water bottles are meant for one time use only for packing drinking water and old ones can cause poisoning. PET (Polyethylene Terephthalate) bottles have diethylhydroxylamine, which can cause cancer. After opening them, don't use them more than a few days, a week at most. Also, keep them away from heat. Repeated washing and rinsing can cause the plastic to breakdown and the carcinogens can leach into the water that you are drinking.

980. Even mild dehydration will slow down one's metabolism as much as 3%. One glass of water shuts down midnight hunger pangs for almost 100% of the dieters. Preliminary research indicates that 8-10 glasses of water a day could significantly ease back and joint pain for up to 80% of sufferers. A mere 2% drop in body water can trigger fuzzy short-term memory, trouble with basic math and difficulty focusing on the computer screen or on a printed page. Drinking 5 glasses of water daily decreases the risk of colon cancer by 45%, plus it can slash the risk of breast cancer by 79% and one is 50% less likely to develop bladder cancer.

981. Dueling is legal in Paraguay as long as both parties are registered blood donors. Donald Duck comics were banned in Finland because he doesn't wear pants.

982. Shakespeare invented the words 'assassination' and 'bump'.

983. Marilyn Monroe had six toes.

984. Right handed people live, on average, nine years longer than left handed people do.

985. The sentence 'the quick brown fox jumps over the lazy dog' uses every letter in the English language.

986. The name of the entire continents end with the same letter that they start with.

987. Typewriter is the longest word that can be made using the letters on only one row of the keyboard.

988. A snail can sleep for 3 years.

989. The longest word in the English language is 1909 letters long and it refers to a distinct part of DNA.

990. Cats have over one hundred vocal sounds; dogs only have about ten.

991. Our eyes are always the same size from birth, but our nose and ears never stop growing.

992. Feb 1865 is the only month in recorded history not to have a full moon.

993. Cat's urine glows under a black light.

994. Leonardo Da Vinci invented the scissors.

995. Babies are born without knee caps. They don't appear until the child reaches 2-6 years of age.

996. If you fart consistently for 6 years and 9 months, enough gas is produced to create the energy of an atomic bomb. Banging your head against a wall uses 150 calories an hour.

997. Humans and dolphins are the only species that have sex for pleasure.

998. A cockroach will live nine days without its head, before it starves to death.

999. Some lions mate over 50 times a day.

1000. Butterflies taste with their feet.

1001. A pig's orgasm lasts for 30 minutes.

1002. In Tokyo, a bicycle is faster than a car for most trips of less than 50 minutes!

1003. Your body is creating and killing 15 million red blood cells per second!

1004. The Mona Lisa has no eyebrows. It was the fashion in Renaissance Florence to shave them off!

1005. Starfish haven't got brains.

1006. In Iceland, tipping at a restaurant is considered an insult!

1007. The Nobel Peace Prize medal depicts three naked men with their hands on each other's shoulders!

1008. A Boeing 747 airliner holds 57,285 gallons of fuel!

1009. A lightning bolt generates temperatures five times hotter than those found at the sun's surface!

1010. A violin contains about 70 separate pieces of wood!

1011. Almost half the newspapers in the world are published in the United States and Canada!

1012. The range of a leopard's hearing is twice that of a human's and, in dim light its sight is six times better. The leopard likes to drink daily but can go for as long as a month without water. Leopards have a highly developed homing instinct. A group found wandering in a suburb of Nairobi was captured and released in the Tsavo National Park, 200 miles away. Within a few weeks, the leopards found their way back to Nairobi. Black leopards, called black panthers, were once regarded as a separate species, but they are now considered true leopards. Although they are black, their rosettes of spots are still faintly visible and sometimes they re even born into the same litters as common leopards.

1013. The 'koala' never drinks because it gets all the liquid it needs from eucalyptus leaves. 'Koala' is the aborigine word for 'no water'. The koala is an excellent swimmer, crossing rivers in order to survive heavy flooding. Ironically, many koalas are killed in sanctuaries by being run over by cars belonging to visitors. A newborn koala is only the size of a lima bean. Its hind legs are barely formed, but its forelimbs and claws are relatively well developed. It drags itself to the pouch following a trail of saliva laid down by its mother.

1014. The beaver is a skilled swimmer and has scales on its tail, so the Catholic church once regarded it as a fish. This meant Catholics could eat beaver meat during Lent. A beaver slaps the surface of the water loudly with its tail to warn others of danger. A beaver dam in Russia was 400 feet long, 3 feet high and up to 3 feet wide. Dams up to 1,650 feet long have been found in North America.

1015. The little finger of the beaver functions like a human thumb and is used to grip branches and stones.

1016. Donkeys are very social animals. They are most active in the evening and in the wild they travel in herds of up to one hundred individuals. At one or two years of age, a male donkey is sexually mature and leaves the group to search for a mate when the group disbands during mating season. By the time he reaches three or four years of age, he achieves an adult position within his group. Donkeys are very observant and cautious animals. They will refuse to do anything that seems dangerous to them.

1017. Donkeys can hear several octaves higher and lower than a human. It has been documented that donkeys 'rumble' to each other in tones too low for the human ear to detect.

1018. In 10 minutes, a hurricane releases more energy than all the world's nuclear weapons combined.

1019. The Main Library at Indiana University sinks over an inch every year because when it was built, engineers failed to take into account the weight of all the books that would occupy the building.

1020. A shrimp's heart is in its head.

1021. It is physically impossible for pigs to look up into the sky.

1022. Horses can't vomit.

1023. The 'sixth sick sheik's sixth sheep's sick' is said to be the toughest tongue twister in the English language.

1024. If you sneeze too hard, you can fracture a rib. If you try to suppress a sneeze, you can rupture a blood vessel in your head or neck and die.

1025. If you keep your eyes open by force, they can pop out.

1026. Rats multiply so quickly that in 18 months, two rats could have over a million descendants.

1027. Wearing headphones for just an hour will increase the bacteria in your ear by 700 times.

1028. When astronauts remain weightless in space for prolonged periods, scientists have discovered, their bones lose a measurable amount of weight and thickness. This means that weightlessness actually causes human beings to shrink.

1029. Butterfly commonly have 12,000 eyes.

1030. A Crocodile weighing 120 pounds exerts a force of about 1,540 pounds between its jaws. A human's jaw exerts a force of about only 40 to 80 pounds.

1031. The Chow is the only dog that has a black tongue. The tongues of all other dogs are pink.

1032. More than 99.9 percent of all animal species that have ever lived on earth were extinct before the coming of man.

1033. The giraffe's tongue is 18 inches long.

1034. At birth, baby kangaroos are only about an inch long, no bigger than a large water bug or a queen bee.

1035. A full-grown moose may be 8 feet high at the shoulder and weigh almost a ton.

1036. A newborn polar bear cub weighs only twice as much as a newborn human, about 15 pounds. Yet when fully-grown, polar bears reach weights of up to 1,600 pounds.

1037. A rat can fall from a five-story building without injury.

1038. Lanolin, an essential ingredient of many expensive cosmetics, in its natural form, a foul smelling, waxy, tarlike substance, is extracted from the fleece of sheep.

1039. Most varieties of snakes can go an entire year without eating a single morsel of food.

1040. The Blue Whale weighs as much as thirty elephants and is as long as three Greyhound buses.

1041. Alligators, dolphins, crocodiles, frogs, porpoises, turtles, water snakes, whales and several other water going creatures will drown if kept underwater too long. Unlike fish, these animals require a certain amount of air in order to survive.

1042. The Incas considered bridges to be so sacred that anyone who tampered with one was put to death. Among the most impressive Inca bridges were the chacas or rope bridges that spanned great distances over gorges and rivers. They were made of plaited grasses woven together into a single cable as thick as a man's body and they sometimes extended for 175 feet. It took as many as a thousand people to build such a bridge and many of these remarkable structures lasted more than five hundred years.

1043. A bridge built in Lima, Peru around 1610 was made of mortar that was mixed not with water but with the whites of 10,000 eggs. The bridge, appropriately called the Bridge of Eggs, is still standing today.

1044. The Column of Trajan, built in 113 A.D. to commemorate the Roman emperor Trajan's victories against the Dacian tribes of the lower Danube, contains a continuous frieze a yard wide and 218 feet long in which more than 2,500 human figures as well as hundreds of boats, horses, vehicles and pieces of military equipment are depicted. This great column, still standing today, rises 128 feet from the ground, is 12 feet thick at the base and is made entirely of gilded bronze. Inside is a circular staircase where the ashes of Trajan were sprinkled.

1045. There are 10 million bricks in the Empire State Building.

1046. Japanese farmers, after removing the hulls from their rice crop and sorting out the white kernels, take the hulls from the leftover rice, mix them into a kind of paste, mould the substance into brick-shaped blocks and build houses with them. Such buildings are known in Japan as 'houses of rice skin'

1047. The Escorial, the famous palace located outside Madrid, was built in the shape of a gridiron because Saint Lawrence, to whom the palace was dedicated, was roasted on one.

1048. It takes a person fifteen to twenty minutes to walk around the Pentagon once.

1049. In the mid-sixteenth century Hicleyoshi, the so-called peasant ruler of Japan, ordered that all the swords in the nation be collected and melted down. The metal was then used, in 1586, to construct an enormous statue of Buddha. It took 50,000 artisans more than six years to build the statue and exactly ten years after it was completed an earthquake razed it. Not a trace of this giant figure remains today.

1050. The sixty-storey John Hancock Tower in Boston is haunted by one of most mysterious problems in skyscraper history. It's windows, huge 4 X 11 foot panes of glass, pop out unexpectedly and shatter on the street below. The building, completed in 1972, was less than a month old when suddenly dozens of its windows began popping for no discernible reason. Determined to remedy the situation, the John Hancock Mutual Life Insurance Company replaced all 10,334 windows with 400-pound sections of half-inch tempered glass. The windows kept popping out. Today the mystery remains unsolved and windows occasionally still pop. To protect passers John Hancock has hired two permanent guards who do nothing but peer up and spot the cracked panes before they tumble to the sidewalk.

1051. The only manmade structure visible from space is the Great Wall of China.

1052. Turtles can live for more than 100 years.

1053. An elephant trunk has no bone but 40,000 muscles.

1054. The cicada, a fly found in Africa, spends 17 years of its life sleeping; and only two weeks is awake during which mates and then dies.

1055. The ant can lift things 10 times its own weight.

1056. If your skin is laid flat it will cover an area of 18 square feet.

1057. A Giraffe has the same number of bones in its neck as a man.

1058. Ocean waves can travel as fast as a Jet Plane.

1059. The first drawings of a helicopter are nearly 500 years old.

1060. Yes, a butterfly warms up its body up to 81 degrees Fahrenheit before flying.

1061. A whale can swim for 3 months without eating.

1062. A human being drinks 16,000 tons of water in a lifetime.

1063. We blink 25 times a minute.

1064. To melt away 1 pound of fat, you will need to walk 34 miles.

1065. The starfish is actually not a fish, it's an animal.

1066. Male mosquitoes do not bite.

1067. The small intestine is 7-8 metres long, making it the largest organ inside the human body. The large intestine is only 1-1.5 metres long!

1068. Oysters can change from one gender to another and back again.

1069. The largest lizard in the world is the Komodo dragon which reaches up to 3 metres and sometimes longer was named because of its fiery tongue. It is often longer than a car.

1070. The great wealth of the Egyptians was due to the precious metals carried from Africa by donkeys. Most of the wagon trains that opened up the American West were pulled by mules. The wool that was exported from South Australia in the 19th century was carried to the railhead by teams of donkeys, sometimes up to 24 in a single hitch. China has the largest donkey population in the world estimated at 11 million.

1071. Sharks have been on the earth a little over 350 million years. Sharks skeletons are made of cartilage (Like the soft bone in your nose). A shark's skin is smooth if you stroke it in one direction, but stroke it in the opposite direction and you may get cut. Most sharks give birth to live sharks, which are called pups. Other sharks lay eggs, which are called Mermaid's Purse. A shark can live for months without a meal because its liver has stored fat in it. Sharks do not chew their food they swallow it whole. The biggest shark (and fish) living is the Whale Shark. It can grow to be 50 feet (15 metres) long and weigh 15 tons. The smallest living shark is the Tsuranagakobitozame (Dwarf Shark). It is 5 inches (12.5 centimetres) long. The shark that seems the friendliest to man is the Whale Shark, who is so gentle that divers often take rides on them. Most shark attacks occur when a person is mistaken for prey. The Swell

Shark, found in New Zealand, barks like a dog. Weird things have been found inside a shark, such as a nail, a bottle of wine, a treasure chest, coats, a suit of armour, a drum and a torpedo. A shark's skin is covered with denticles, which are small razor-sharp teeth. Denticles can be removed from a shark's body. After the small teeth are removed, the remaining skin can be made into very strong leather. A pair of shoes made from shark leather can last up to four times longer than shoes made with cowhide. Sharks have very good senses. Sometimes a shark is called 'a swimming nose', for its great sense of smell. Sharks can easily detect prey that is in the sand, as well as at night. A shark also has a remarkable sensitivity to vibrations in the water. It can feel the movements made by other animals that are hundreds of feet away. They can hear sounds from thousands of feet away. Sharks can tell the direction from where the sound is coming from, too. Sharks cannot eat Puffer Fish because the Puffer Fish inflates like a balloon and pokes the shark's mouth with its sharp needles. Most sharks give birth to their babies. Only a few sharks lay eggs. Most sharks have six to twelve babies at a time, but the Hammerhead and Tiger Shark can have as many as 40 babies at a time. Most species of sharks can swim up to 20-40 miles per hour. A Mako Shark has been recorded at more than 60 miles per hour. A shark has three types of fins. They have two dorsal fins on their back, one fin beneath their body, called the pectoral fin (not all species have it) and the caudal fin is the tail. A Whale Shark has more than 4,000 teeth, but each is less than 1/8 inch long. A shark may go through 1,000 sets of teeth during its lifetime. When a shark loses a tooth, one replaces it.

1072. A Whale Shark weighs about 90,000 pounds. The second largest shark is the Basking Shark. It can be as much as 40 feet long.

1073. Dogs have about 220 million olfactory receptors to help them smell-roughly 40 times the number humans have.

1074. The only wild Dromedary (one-hump) camels in the world are now found in Australia. These animals were first brought to Australia in 1840 for exploration and for carrying cargo in the vast desert outback.

1075. Lions, one of the speediest land animals, spend about 20 hours a day resting.

1076. An ant can survive for up to two days underwater. The animal with the largest brain in proportion to its size is the ant. Ants don't sleep. Ants taste like sweet tarts. The ant always falls over on its right side when intoxicated.

1077. The closest relative to the Manatee is the Elephant; scientists think the elephant crawled back into the sea to become a Manatee.

1078. If Benjamin Franklin had had his way, the symbol of the United States would not have been the Eagle. In 1789, he proposed that it be replaced by the Turkey.

1079. The Great Pyramid at Giza in Egypt, constructed around 2500 B.C., was the tallest structure in the world until the Eiffel Tower was erected in 1889.

1080. Between A.D. 1400 and 1520 the Inca emperors of South America built more than 15,000 miles of roads from sea level to high into the Andes Mountains.

1081. A bowl of wheat contains twice as much sodium as a bowl of potato chips.

1082. One of the preposterous cures for the Black Plague in the 14th century was to place a pig next to the dying person.

1083. The famous battle of Bunker Hill in the American Revolutionary War was not fought on Bunker Hill but actually on nearby Breed's Hill instead.

1084. The world's worst earthquake occurred in 1556 in China killing approximately 830,000 people.

1085. In the 3rd to 2nd century B.C, Eratosthenes measured the radius of the earth without the use of precision instruments and came within one-percent of the actual value determined by today's space craft technology.

1086. Each day some forty-five thousand thunderstorms occur worldwide, resulting in as many as one hundred lightning strikes every second. Lightning strikes the earth somewhere more than seventeen million times every day or about two hundred times every second. A bolt of lightning travels at speeds of up to one hundred million feet per second or seventy-two million miles per hour. A lightning bolt generates temperatures five times hotter than those found at the sun's surface.

1087. A skunk will not bite and throw its scent at the same time.

1088. The woolly mammoth, extinct since the Ice Age, had tusks almost 16 feet long. The name Coca-Cola in China was first rendered as Ke-kou-ke-la. Unfortunately, the Coke company did not discover until after thousands of signs had been printed that the phrase means 'bite the wax tadpole' or 'female horse stuffed with wax' depending on the dialect. Coke then researched 40,000 Chinese characters and found a close phonetic equivalent, 'ko-kou-ko-le', which can be loosely translated as 'happiness in the mouth'.

1089. Americans on average eat 18 acres of pizza every day.

1090. The weight of air in a milk glass is about the same as the weight of one aspirin. The gases emitted from a banana or an apple can help an orange ripen.

1091. Adolph Hitler was a vegetarian and had only 1 testicle.

1092. Al Gore and Tommy Lee Jones were once roommates.

1093. Australia is a major exporter of camels. Australia has no native monkeys. Australia's box jellyfish has toxins more potent than the venom in cobras and is one of the most dangerous jellyfish in the world.

1094. Hans Christian Anderson, creator of fairy tales, was born-blind.

He never learned to spell correctly and his publishers always had errors.

1095. On average, Americans spend about 6 months of their lives waiting at red traffic lights.

1096. The human heart creates enough pressure when it pumps out to the body to squirt blood 30 feet.

1097. The strongest muscle in the body is the *tongue*.

1098. It's impossible to sneeze with your eyes open.

1099. A crocodile cannot stick its tongue out.

1100. The catfish has over 27,000 taste buds that makes the catfish no.1 for animal having the most taste buds.

1101. The Statue of Liberty's tablet is two feet thick.

1102. There are two credit cards for every person in the United States.

1103. The slogan on New Hampshire licence plates is 'Live Free or Die'. Prisoners in the state prison in Concord manufacture these licence plates.

1104. David Prowse was the guy in the Darth Vader suit in Star Wars. He spoke all of Vader's lines and didn't know that he was going to be dubbed over by James Earl Jones until he saw the screening of the movie.

1105. There are only thirteen blimps in the world. Nine of the thirteen blimps are in the United States. The existing biggest blimp is the Fuji Film blimp.

1106. The Swiss flag is square.

1107. The word 'pound' is abbreviated 'lb' after the constellation 'libra' because it means 'pound' in Latin and also 'scales'. The abbreviation for the British Pound Sterling comes from the same source: it is an 'L' for Libra/Lb. with a stroke through it to indicate abbreviation. Sames goes for the Italian lira, which uses the same abbreviation ('lira' coming from 'libra'). So British currency (before it went metric) was always quoted as 'pounds/shillings/pence', abbreviated 'L/s/d' (libra/ solidus/ denarius).

1108. The three largest landowners in England are the Queen, the Church of England and Trinity College, Cambridge.

1109. The monastic hours are matins, lauds, prime, tierce, sext, nones, vespers and compline.

1110. No animal, once frozen solid (i.e., water solidifies and turns to ice) survives when thawed because the ice crystals formed inside cells would break open the cell membranes. However there are certain frogs that can survive the experience of being frozen. These frogs make special proteins, which prevent the formation of ice (or at least keep the crystals from becoming very large), so that they actually never freeze even though their body temperature is below zero Celsius. The water in them remains liquid: a phenomenon known as 'super cooling'. If you disturb one of these frogs (just touching them even), the water in them quickly freezes solid and they die.

1111. Madrid is the only European capital city not situated on a river.

1112. The Boston University Bridge (on Commonwealth Avenue, Boston, Massachusetts) is the only place in the world where a boat can sail under a train driving under a car driving under an airplane.

1113. Emus cannot walk backwards.

1114. It is believed that Shakespeare was 46 around the time that the King James Version of the Bible was written. In Psalms 46, the 46th word from the first word is shake and the 46th word from the last word is spear.

1115. The shopping mall in Abbotsford, British Columbia, Canada has the largest water clock in North America.

1116. The word posh, which denotes luxurious rooms or accommodations, originated when ticket agents in England marked the tickets of travellers going by ship to the Orient. Since there was no air conditioning in those days, it was always better to have a cabin on the shady side of the ship as it passed through the Mediterranean and Suez area. Since the sun is in the south, those with money paid extra to get cabin's on the left or port, travelling to the Asia and on the right or starboard, when returning to Europe. Hence their tickets were marked with the initials for Port Outbound Starboard Homebound or POSH.

1117. The top layer of a wedding cake, known as the groom's cake, traditionally is a fruitcake. That way it will save until the first anniversary.

1118. Both writer Edgar Allen Poe and LSD advocate Timothy Leary were kicked out of West Point.

1119. The German Kaiser Wilhelm II had a withered arm and often hid the fact by posing with his hand resting on a sword or by holding gloves.

1120. In every show that Tom Jones and Harvey Schmidt (The Fantasticks) wrote, there is at least one song about rain.

1121. A kind of tortoise in the Galapagos Islands has an upturned shell at its neck so it can reach its head up to eat cactus branches.

1122. The only city whose name can be spelled completely with vowels is Aiea, Hawaii, located approximately twelve miles west of Honolulu.

1123. Parthenogenesis is the term used to describe the process by which certain animals are able to reproduce themselves in successive female generations without intervention of a male of the species. At least one species of lizard is known to do so.

1124. Cats have over one hundred vocal sounds, while dogs only have about ten.

1125. The word 'Checkmate' in chess comes from the Persian phrase 'Shah Mat', which means 'the king is dead'.

1126. The ship, the Queen Elizabeth II, should always be written as QE2. QEII is the actual queen.

1127. 'Quisling' is the only word in the English language to start with 'quis'.

1128. All of the cobblestones that used to line the streets in New York were originally weighting stones put in the hulls of Belgian ships to keep an even keel.

1129. Nepal is the only country without a rectangular flag (it looks like two pennants glued on top of the other)

1130. Libya has the only flag, which is all one colour with no writing or decoration on it.

1131. The tune for the 'A-B-C' song is the same as 'Twinkle, Twinkle Little Star'.

1132. When a coffee seed is planted, it takes five years to yield its first consumable fruit.

1133. The common goldfish is the only animal that can see both infra-red and ultra-violet light.

1134. Linn's Stamp News is the world's largest weekly newspaper for stamp collectors.

1135. Tennessee is bordered by more states than any other. The eight states are Kentucky, Missouri, Arkansas, Mississippi, Alabama, Georgia, North Carolina and Virginia.

1136. There are only three animals with blue tongues, the Black Bear, the Chow Chow dog and the blue-tongued lizard.

1337. The first fossilised specimen of Austalopithecus afarenisis was named *Lucy* after the palentologists' favourite song, Lucy in the Sky With Diamonds, by the Beatles.

1138. There are six words in the English language with the letter combination 'uu'. Muumuu, vacuum, continuum, duumvirate and duumvir, residuum.

1139. The 'Calabash' pipe, most often associated with Sherlock Holmes, was not used by him until William Gillette (an American) portrayed Holmes onstage. Gillette needed a pipe he could keep in his mouth while he spoke his lines.

1140. The pupil of an octopus' eye is rectangular.

1141. The shortest French word with all five vowels is 'oiseau' meaning bird.

1142. Oliver Cromwell was hanged and decapitated two years after he had died.

1143. In the last 4000 years, no new animals have been domesticated.

1144. Iowa has more independent telephone companies than any other state.

1145. Many hamsters only blink one eye at a time. Hamsters love to eat crickets.

1146. The only 'real' food that U.S. Astronauts are allowed to take into space is pecan nuts.

1147. The word 'queueing' is the only English word with five consecutive vowels.

1148. All three major 1996 Presidential candidates, Clinton, Dole and Perot, are left-handed.

1149. The Madagascan Hissing Cockroach is one of the few insects who give birth to live young, rather than laying eggs.

1150. The book of Esther in the Bible is the only book, which does not mention the name of God.

1151. Dracula is the most filmed story of all time, Dr. Jekyll and Mr.

Hyde is second and Oliver Twist is third.

1152. The name Jeep came from the abbreviation used in the army for the 'General Purpose' vehicle, G.P.

1153. Goat's eyes have rectangular pupils.

1154. Walt Disney's autograph bears no resemblance to the famous Disney logo.

1155. Other than humans, black lemurs are the only primates that may have blue eyes.

1156. The United States has never lost a war in which mules were used.

1157. The two longest one-syllable words in the English language are 'screeched' and 'strengths'.

1158. Great Britain was the first county to issue postage stamps. Hence, the postage stamps of Britain are the only stamps in the world not to bear the name of the country of origin. However, every stamp carries a relief image or a silhouette of the monarch's head instead.

1159. Artist Constantino Brumidi fell from the done of the U.S. Capitol while painting a mural around the rim. He died four months later.

1160. Since 1896, the beginning of the modern Olympics, only Greece and Australia have participated in every Games.

1161. Blueberry Jelly Bellies were created especially for Ronald Reagan.

1162. Many Japanese golfers carry 'hole-in-one' insurance because it is traditional in Japan to share one's good luck by sending gifts to all your friends when you get an 'ace'. The price for what the Japanese term an 'albatross' can often reach $10,000.

1163. It takes a lobster approximately seven years to grow to be one pound.

1164. The ridges on the sides of coins are called reeding.

1165. The lot numbers for the cyanide-tainted Tylenol capsules scare back in 1982 were MC2880 and 1910MD.

1166. Montpelier, Vermont is the only U.S. state capital without a McDonalds.

1167. The Roman emperor Caligula made his horse a senator.

1168. At latitude 60 degrees south, you can sail all the way around the world.

1169. The hyoid bone, in your throat, is the only bone in the body not attached to another bone.

1170. Mice, whales, elephants, giraffes and man all have seven-neck vertebra.

1171. Giraffes have no vocal cords.

1172. All porcupines float in water.

1173. Many northern parishes (counties) of Louisiana did not agree with the Confederate movement. To show their disapproval, they changed their names. That's why there is a Union Parish, Jefferson Parish, etc.

1174. The Pentagon, in Arlington, Virginia, has twice as many bathrooms as is necessary. When it was built in the 1940s, the state of Virginia still had segregation laws requiring separate toilet facilities for blacks and whites.

1175. Residents of the island of Lesbos are Lesbosians, rather than Lesbians. (Of course, lesbians are called lesbians because Sappho was from Lesbos.)

1176. The Chinese ideogram for 'trouble' symbolises 'two women living under one roof'.

1177. German has a wood for the peace offerings brought to your mate when you've committed some conceived slight. This is 'drachenfutter' or dragon's food.

1178. In Chinese, the words for crisis and opportunity are the same.

1179. The poisonous copperhead smells like fresh cut cucumbers.

1180. In Disney's 'Fantasia', the Sorcerer's name is 'Yensid' (Disney backwards.)

1181. The smallest mushroom's name is 'Hop-low'.

1182. Mustard gas was invented in the McKinley Building on the American University campus. Additionally, preliminary work on the Manhattan Project was done in that building. The government used the McKinley Building because of its unusual architecture. If there would be any type of large explosion inside the building, the building would implode onto itself, containing any lethal gas or nuclear material. The building now houses the Physics Department.

1183. No modern language has a true concept of 'I am'. It is always used linked with are in reference of another verb.

1184. Little known Cathedral Caverns near Grant, Alabama has the world's largest cave opening, the largest stalagmite (Goliath) and the largest stalagmite forest in the World.

1185. The only person ever to decline a Pulitzer Prize for Fiction was Sinclair Lewis for his book Arrowsmith.

1186. Lesotho is the only country that borders on only one country.

1187. There are almost twice as many people in Rhode Island than there are in Alaska.

1188. Kudzu is not indigenous to the South, but in that climate it can grow up to six inches a day.

1189. The word 'byte' is a contraction of 'by eight'.

1190. The word 'pixel' is a contraction of either 'picture cell' or 'picture element'.

1191. Ralph Lauren's original name was Ralph Lifshitz.

1192. Bananas do not grow on trees, but on rhizomes.

1193. Astronauts in the Space Shuttle are weightless not because there is no gravity in space, but because they are in free fall around the Earth.

1194. St. Augustine was the first major proponent of the 'missionary' position.

1195. Roger Ebert is the only film critic to have ever won the Pulitzer prize.

1196. Columbia University is the second largest landowner in New York City, after the Catholic Church.

1197. Lorne Greene had one of his nipples bitten off by an alligator while he hosted 'Lorne Greene's Wild Kingdom'.

1198. Kerimski Church in Finland is world's biggest church made of wood.

1199. Vincent Van Gogh committed suicide while painting *Wheat Field with Crows.*

1200. The letter W is the only letter in the alphabet that doesn't have 1 syllable... it has three.

1201. All swans and all sturgeons in England are property of the Queen. Messing with them is a serious offence.

1202. The world's largest four-faced clock sits atop the Allen-Bradley plant in Milwaukee, Wisconsin.

1203. The first video ever played on MTV Europe was 'Money For Nothing' by Dire Straits.

1204. The term 'the whole 9 yards' came from WWII fighter pilots in the South Pacific. When arming their airplanes on the ground, the .50

calibre machine gun ammo belts measured exactly 27 feet, before being loaded into the fuselage. If the pilots fired all their ammo at a target, it got 'the whole 9 yards'.

1205. A bear has 42 teeth.

1206. The dot over the letter 'i' is called a *tittle*.

1207. Table tennis balls have been known to travel off the paddle at speeds up to 105.6 miles per hour.

1208. In Irian Jaya exists a tribe of tall, white people who use parrots as a warning sign against intruders.

1209. On Sesame Street, Bert's goldfish were named Lyle and Talbot, presumably after the actor Lyle Talbot.

1210. Louis IV of France had a stomach the size of two regular stomachs.

1211. Mark Twain smoked forty cigars a day for the last years of his life. Mark Twain was born on a day in 1835 when Haley's Comet came into view. When he died in 1910, Haley's Comet came into view again.

1212. The highest point in Pennsylvania is lower than the lowest point in Colorado.

1213. If you were born in Los Alamos, New Mexico during the Manhattan project (where they made the atomic bomb), your birthplace was listed as a post office box in Albequerque.

1214. Robert Kennedy was killed in the Ambassador Hotel, the same hotel that housed Marilyn Monroe's first modelling agency.

1215. The original story from *Tales of 1001 Arabian Nights* begins, 'Aladdin was a little Chinese boy'.

1216. When a film is in production, the last shot of the day is the 'martini shot', the next to last one is the 'Abby Singer'.

1217. The expression 'What in tarnation' comes from the original meaning: 'What in eternal damnation'.

1218. The volume of the Earth's moon is the same as the volume of the Pacific Ocean.

1219. Ingrown toenails are hereditary.

1220. The most common name in the world is Mohammed.

1221. Only humans and horses have hymens.

1222. In the great fire of London in 1666, half of London was burnt down but only 6 people were injured.

1223. There are more bald eagles in the province of British Columbia then there are in the whole United States.

1224. One of the reasons marijuana is illegal today because cotton growers in the 30s lobbied against hemp farmers — they saw it as competition. It is not chemically addictive as is nicotine, alcohol or caffeine.

1225. Olympic Badminton rules say that the bird has to have exactly fourteen feathers.

1226. The music group Simply Red is named because of its love for the football team, Manchester United, who have a red home strip.

1227. The earliest document in Latin is in a woman's handwriting (it is from the first century A.D.) is an invitation to a birthday party.

1228. Hydrogen gas is the least dense substance in the world, at 0.08988 g/cc. Hydrogen solid is the most dense substance in the world, at 70.6 g/cc.

1229. The international telphone dialing code for Antarctica is 672.

1230. A full seven percent of the entire Irish barley crop goes to the production of Guinness beer.

1231. The airport in La Paz, Bolivia is the world's highest airport.

1232. The glue on Israeli postage stamps is certified kosher.

1233. Chicago is closer to Moscow than to Rio de Janeiro.

1234. Original copy of the Declaration of Independence is lost. The copy in Washington D.C. is what is referred to as a holograph. That is a term for a handmade copy of a document and is not the same as a laser produced hologram.

1235. Singapore is the only country with one train station.

1236. The little bags of netting for gas lanterns (called 'mantles') are radioactive—so much so that they will set of an alarm at a nuclear reactor.

1237. The only capital letter in the Roman alphabet with exactly one endpoint is P.

1238. There are only four words in the English language, which end in '-dous': tremendous, horrendous, stupendous and hazardous.

1239. South Africa is the only country with three official capitals: Pretoria, Cape Town and Bloemfontein.

1240. Mickey Mouse is known as 'Topolino' in Italy.

1241. The red giant star Betelgeuse has a diametre larger than that of the Earth's orbit around the sun.

1242. If your eyes are six feet above the surface of the ocean, the horizon will be about three statute miles away.

1243. The one-hundred eleventh element is known as 'unnilenilenium'.

1244. The longest muscle name is the 'levator labii superioris alaeque nasi' and Elvis popularised it with his lip motions.

1245. A cat has 32 muscles in each ear.

1246. The oldest word in the English language is 'town'.

1247. The sea wasp is half an inch long at best and more poisonous than any other jellyfish known to man.

1248. After human death, post-mortem rigidity starts in the head and travels to the feet and leaves the same way it came — head to toe.

1249. Police dogs are trained to react to commands in a foreign language; commonly German but more recently Hungarian or some other Slavic tongue.

1250. Winston Churchill, Franklin Delano Roosevelt, Theodore Roosevelt and Eleanor Roosevelt were all cousins through one connection or another.

1251. A twelve-foot anaconda can catch, kill and eat a six-foot caiman, a close relative of crocodiles and alligators. While these snakes are not usually considered to be the 'longest' snake in the world, they are the heaviest, exceeding the reticulated python in girth.

1252. There is a word in the English language with only one vowel, which occurs six times: *Indivisibility*.

1253. The dome on Monticello, Thomas Jefferson's home, conceals a billiards room. In Jefferson's day, billiards were illegal in Virginia.

1254. According to Einstein's Special Theory of Relativity, it is possible to go slower than light and faster than light, but it is impossible to go at the speed of light.

1255. In most advertisements, including newspapers, the time displayed on a watch is 10:10 because then the arms frame the brand of the watch.

1256. Japan is the third most densely populated country in the world. First is the Netherlands, followed by Belgium.

1257. The strawberry is technically not a fruit at all. In botanical terms, fruits are seed-bearing structures, which grow from a flower's ovaries and a strawberry is merely the swollen base of the strawberry flower. The plant's true fruits are the small, hard, nut-like pips embedded on the outside of the flesh. The seeds are contained in the pips.

1258. Although the Pony Express was one of the most famous stories of American History, it lasted only nineteen months, from April 1860 to October 1861. It was a complete financial failure.

1259. The biggest Pyramid in the world is not in Egypt. It's actually about sixty miles southeast of Mexico City, Mexico. It covers more than forty acres and the largest Egyptian Pyramid, The Great Pyramid at Giza, covers about 13 acres.

1260. The YKK on the zipper of your Levis stands for Yoshida Kogyo Kabushibibaisha, the worlds largest zipper manufacturer.

1261. The horn of the Rhinoceros is not bone; it is hair.

1262. Artificial Christmas trees have outsold real ones every year since 1991.

1263. King George I of England could not speak English. He was born and raised in Germany and never learned to speak English even though he was King from 1714 to 1727. He left the running of the country to his ministers thereby creating the first government cabinet.

1264. The Inca tribe in Peru created the decimal system hundreds of years before it was introduced in Europe.

1265. Ancient Egyptian religion divided the human body into 36 parts and each part came under the protection of a god or goddess.

1266. 97% of all paper money in the US contains traces of cocaine.

1267. Before 1941, fingerprints were not accepted as evidence in court. Up to that time it was not an established fact that no two fingerprints are alike. Today, the only time in which fingerprints will not be allowed as evidence is if the defence can prove that there are in fact two identical sets of fingerprints.

1268. In 1875 the Director of the United States Patent Office sent in his resignation and advised the administration that his department be eliminated because he was convinced there was nothing left to invent.

1269. The first contact lens was actually conceived by Leonardo Da Vinci in the 15th century.

1270. In Venice in the 16th and 17th centuries prostitutes believed that the higher the heel on their shoe the more men would pay for their services. Consequently, a law was passed banning the wearing of high heels because they began to trip in the dark and fall into the canals and die.

1271. In ancient Egypt, women had more legal rights than those in some countries today. Even when a couple divorced, it was understood that the woman was entitled to up to one-half of the estate.

1272. There are more chickens than people in the world.

1273. 'Dreamt' is the only English word that ends in the letters 'mt'.

1274. The microwave was invented after a researcher walked by a radar tube and a chocolate bar melted in his pocket.

1275. The average person falls asleep in seven minutes.

1276. Napoleon's christening name was Italian: Napoleone Buonaparte (or Bonaparte). He was born on the island of Corsica one year after it became French property. As a boy, Napoleon hated the French.

1277. The brain of an average adult male weighs 1,375 gm (55 oz). The brain of Russian novelist Turgenev weighed 2021 gm (81 oz), Bismark's weighed 1807 gm (72 oz), while that of French statesman Gambetta was only 1294 gm (51 oz). Einstein's brain was of average size.

1278. The oldest living thing on earth is 12,000 years old. It is the flowering shrubs called creosote bushes in the Mojave Desert.

1279. Money notes are not made from paper, they are made mostly from a special blend of cotton and linen. In 1932, when a shortage of cash occurred in Tenino, Washington, USA, notes were made out of wood for a brief period.

1280. The Grammy Awards were introduced to counter the threat of rock music. In the late 1950s, a group of record executives were alarmed by the explosive success of rock 'n roll, considering it a threat to 'quality' music.

1281. Tea is said to have been discovered in 2737 BC by a Chinese emperor when some tealeaves accidentally blew into a pot of boiling water. The tea bag was introduced in 1908 by Thomas Sullivan of New York.

1282. Over the last 150 years, the average height of people in industrialised nations has increased 10 cm (about 4 inches). In the 19th century, American men were the tallest in the world, averaging 1,71m (5'6'). Today, the average height for American men is 1,75m (5'7'), compared to 1,77 (5'8') for Swedes and 1,78 (5'8. 5') for the Dutch. The tallest nation in the world is the Watusis of Burundi.

1283. The system of democracy was introduced 2,500 years ago in Athens, Greece. The oldest existing governing body operates in Althing in Iceland. It was established in 930 AD.

1284. According to a study by the Economic Research Service, 27% of all food production in Western nations ends up in garbage cans. Yet, 1,2 billion people are underfed - the same number of people who are overweight.

1285. The opposite sides of a dice cube always add up to seven!

1286. About 10% of the world's population is left-handed.

1287. The sun is 330,330 times larger than the earth!

1288. There is air in space, but very little of it. In fact, it is equivalent to a marble in a box 5 miles wide. Most of the gas is captured by the gravitational pull of other celestial bodies.

1289. Abdul Kassam Ismael, Grand Vizier of Persia in the tenth century, carried his library with him wherever he went. Four hundred camels carried the 117,000 volumes.

1290. Most Caucasian babies are born with dark blue eyes, although it normally changes colour after childbirth.

1291. One quarter of the *bones* in your body, are in your feet. Human thighbones are stronger than concrete. The only joint with less bone in your body is the hyoid bone in your throat.

1292. You can't kill yourself by holding your breath.

1293. Butterflies cannot fly if their body temperature is less than 86 degrees.

1294. Beetles taste like apples, wasps like pine nuts and white worms like fried pork rinds.

1295. Most people blink about 25 times a minute.

1296. According to National Geographic, scientists have settled the old dispute over which came first — the chicken or the egg. They say that reptiles were laying eggs thousands of years before chickens appeared and the first chicken came from an egg laid by a bird that was not quite a chicken. That seems to answer the question. The egg came first.

1297. Coca-Cola contains neither coca nor cola.

1298. Sunbeams that shine down through the clouds are called crespucular rays.

1299. A companion tomb was originally to have been built facing the Taj Mahal. The companion would have been identical to the Taj Mahal in every way but its black colour.

1300. If electrodes are inserted at opposite ends of a pickle and electricity is passed through, the pickle will glow.

1301. In Turkey, the colour of mourning is violet. In most Moslem countries and in China it is white.

1302. There is more bacteria in your mouth than the human population of U.S and Canada combined.

1303. The *Burramundy*, a fish, grows up as a male, but after 2 years or so, it turns into a female to breed.

1304. Birds are largely unaffected by spicy things, like chillies, as they not sensitive to capsaicin, the hot stuff in chillies.

1305. The paper nautilus has a detachable penis which swims off in search of a mate.

1306. The velocity of a male wombat's urine is twice that of a male human's.

1307. A gorilla can fart ten times louder than a human being.

1308. Men commit suicide three times more frequently than women do. But women attempt suicide two to three times more often than men.

1309. A raisin dropped in a glass of fresh champagne will bounce up and down continuously from the bottom of the glass to the top.

1310. A female ferret will die if it goes into heat and cannot find a mate.

1311. A duck's quack doesn't echo.

1312. During the chariot scene in the world fame movie 'Ben Hur', a small red car can be seen in the distance.

1313. Donald Duck comics were banned from Finland because he doesn't wear pants.

1314. Because metal was scarce, the Oscars given out during World War II were made of wood.

1315. The number of possible ways of playing the first four moves per side in a game of chess is 318,979,564,000.

1316. A bean has more DNA per cell than a human cell.

1317. Human babies are born 2 months prematurely for our size and lifespan, to accommodate for the fact that we have large brains during birth. Babies crawl an average of 200m a day.

1318. Barbie's full name is Barbara Millicent Roberts.

1319. If you put a piece of scotch tape on an inflated *balloon*, then stick it with a small pin or needle, it won't pop.

1320. Bruce Lee was the Hong Kong 'cha cha' dance champion in 1958. He was also an American born in San Francisco and had a German grandfather.

1321. The Beaver is America's largest rodent and can remain underwater for 20 minutes!

1322. Gutzon Borglum, the sculptor of the four Presidents on Mount Rushmore, died a few months before the project was completed. It took him 14 years.

1323. Eating breakfast will help you burn from 5-20% more calories throughout the day.

1324. Bamboo can grow up to 36 inches in a day.

1325. Colour-blind people are used to detect camouflaged units in previous warfare.

1326. Cats sweat through the pads of their feet (especially when they hear a dog barking) and cannot taste sweet things. Cats have over one hundred vocal sounds; dogs only have about ten.

1327. The cockroach has a high resistance to radiation and is the creature most likely to survive a nuclear war. Fried cockroach with garlic is used as medicine for the common cold. The cockroach is the fastest animal on 6 legs, covering a metre a second. Cockroaches can change course as many as 25 times in one second.

1328. A chicken that just lost its head can run the length of a football field before dropping dead. The longest recorded flight of a chicken is 13 seconds!

1329. Coffee beans can be mixed into B type blood, changing it into O type blood.

1330. Rubbing cocoa butter on your abdomen during pregnancy will prevent stretch marks.

1331. If you chew a cabbage/lettuce leaf properly, you'll lose more energy than you'll gain from actually eating it.

1332. The catfish has over 27,000 taste buds.

1333. Cicadas have their hearing organs in their stomachs, at the base of the abdomen.

1334. The caterpillar has more than 2,000 muscles.

1335. There are more than 40,000 characters in Chinese script.

1336. The first contraceptive diaphragms, centuries ago, were citrus rinds (i.e. half an orange rind). Casanova used half lemon rinds as a cervical cap and the acidic juice as a potent spermicidal stuff(something that kills sperms).

1337. Crocodiles have brains no larger than a cigar. Crocodiles can snap their jaws in 1/8th of a second and can use over 40 sets of teeth.

1338. Everyone is colour-blind at birth.

1339. Apple pips contain cyanide. Once, there was a man who really liked the taste of apple pips, so he saved up a cupful of them and ate them in one go and promptly died of cyanide poisoning.

1340. Sir Edmund Hillary, well known for climbing Mt. Everest, was also the first man to drive to the South Pole on a tractor.

1341. Brush fires are common around the Los Angeles area and often hundreds of acres are burnt. The amount of energy released by burning just 40 acres of brush is equal to that released by the atom bomb dropped over Hiroshima.

1342. The average size of a star is about 150,000 times bigger than the earth.

1343. Formula One is the fastest of all types of racing car.

1344. Of all the planets, only two, Venus and Mercury, have no known satellites.

1345. In 1963, two years into his Presidency, John F. Kennedy's popularity in the USA was rated in a Gallup Poll at 76 per cent. A few months later, he was assassinated.

1346. Eagles can live in captivity for up to 46 years.

1347. Forty-five different kinds of antelope can be found in Africa.

1348. Centipedes have between 28 and 354 legs.

1349. Cows release 50 million metric tonnes of methane gas a year. Cows sweat through their noses. An American cow called Fawn was not afraid of flying. In May 1963, she was swept up by a tornado and carried half a mile, only to land safely in another farmer's field. Five years later, another tornado carried her over a bus. She survived this too and lived to the ripe old age of 25. Cows do not have upper teeth.

1350. Chocolate is potentially lethal to a dog because cocoa beans contain theobromine which can poison the poor beast.

1351. Coral (pro osteon) has molecular architecture and chemistry similar to human bone and so it can be used to replace bone grafts, helping bones heal faster. 150-200 pounds of it can sustain hundreds of graphs.

1352. The liquid inside coconuts can be used as blood plasma substitutes!

1353. There are more coffee drug addicts in the US than drug addicts of any other kind.

1354. 80% of arrested criminals are male.

1355. Canada actually comes from the word 'Kanata', a Huron or Iroquois word for village and Canada is a 'big village'.

1356. Laika the dog was the first living thing, which was sent to space.

1357. Dominique Larrey, Napoleon's chief surgeon, could amputate a leg in 13 seconds.

1358. Donald Duck comics were once banned from Finland because he/ it doesn't wear pants.

1359. Dentistry has achieved the highest number suicidal deaths for a professional job.

1360. The average person has over 1,460 dreams a year.

1361. The placement of a donkey's eyes in its' heads enables it to see all four feet at all times.

1362. Dolphins sleep with one eye open.

1363. The dioxin 2,3,7,8-tetrachlorodibenzo-p-dioxin is 150,000 times deadlier than cyanide.

1364. Duelling is legal in Paraguay as long as both parties are registered blood donors.

1365. In the last 4000 years, no new animals have been domesticated.

1366. Calculating DNA length for each person, it would stretch across the diametre of the solar system. 6 000 000 000 000 basepairx 0.6 nm x 10^{13} cell = 3.6×10^{16} metres.

1367. If the information contained in the DNA could be written down, it would fill a 1000 volume encyclopaedia.

1368. Dragonfly larvae develop under the water and eject water from their anus to propel them for short distances. A dragonfly can fly 25 mph. A dragonfly is also known as 'devil's darning needle', 'horse stinger' and 'devil's steelyard'.

1369. The amount of drag or air resistance produced by putting your bicycle on top of your car is so great that on a trip from England to Scotland it would be cheaper to send it by train because of the fuel consumption.

1370. The 'Daddy long legs' spider has venom to be used as a defensive mechanism. It cannot puncture human skin and even if it did, it would probably only cause a allergic reaction.

1371. A human's scent membrane in the nose is about the size of a postage stamp. A dog's is about the size of a handkerchief. It's olfactory lobe is also 4 times that of a human.

1372. It has been reported that some dogs are able to sniff out skin cancer.

1373. Camels have three eyelids to protect themselves from blowing sand.

1374. Everest is not the tallest mountain. Mauna Kea Mountain in the Hawaiian Island is 230m taller. It is 4201m above water and 4877 underwater! Everest is only 8848m.

1375. There are approximately 10 million bricks in the Empire State Building.

1376. E-mails started in 1971 and the first e-mail was sent written entirely in upper-case.

1377. Baby elephants can drink over 80 litres of milk a day. An elephant has 4 knees.

1378. Pope Adrian VI choked to death after a fly got stuck in his throat as he was taking a drink from a fountain.

1379. Certain frogs can regurgitate their stomachs, in order to clean them.

1380. The phrase 'rule of thumb' is derived from and old English law, which stated that you couldn't beat your wife with anything wider than your thumb.

1381. The Eisenhower interstate system requires that one-mile in every five must be straight. These straight sections are usable as airstrips in times of war or other emergencies.

1382. The Boston University Bridge (on Commonwealth Avenue, Boston, Massachusetts) is the only place in the world where a boat can sail under a train driving under a car driving under an airplane.

1383. Back in the mid to late 80's, an IBM compatible computer wasn't considered a hundred percent compatible unless it could run Microsoft's Flight Simulator.

1384. A giraffe can clean its ears with its 21-inch tongue. *Giraffes* have the same number of vertebrae in their necks as humans. Their lips are prehensile, their tongues are 21 inches long and they cannot cough.

1385. Chewing gum while peeling onions will keep you from crying.

1386. Galileo became totally blind shortly before his death.

1387. If you rubbed garlic on the sole of your feet, it would be absorbed and eventually show up on your breath.

1388. If all the gold in the ocean were mined, every person on Earth would get about 20 kgs. of gold each. People drank gold powder mixed in with water in medieval Europe to relieve pain from sore limbs.

1389. Honeybees have a type of hair on their eyes.

1390. Astronauts grow taller (height) in space.

1391. The horse shoe crab has blue blood, which can be used to kill bacteria.

1392. A company, Warner Communications paid $28 million for the copyright to the song 'Happy Birthday'.

1393. A hippo can open its mouth wide enough to fit a 4-foot tall child inside. Hippos kill more people in Africa when compared to crocodiles. During warm weather, hippos secrete a reddish, oily fluid, called pink sweat, which acts as a skin conditioner to keep it moist.

1394. Hyenas can consume prey carrying anthrax without contracting the disease itself.

1395. The deepest hole ever made in the world is in Texas. It is as deep as 20 empire state buildings but only 3 inches wide.

1396. Hitler was voted 'Time Magazine's' man of the year in 1938.

1397. Food passes through the small intestine in just two hours, zipping along at 0.002 mph. inside the large intestine, it takes about 14 hours, travelling at a more leisurely rate of 0.00007 mph.

1398. An insect exerts so much energy in one hour of flying that it may lose as much as a third of its total body weight.

1399. In rural areas, there are more insects in 1 square mile than there are humans on earth.

1400. In Scotland, Irn-Bru is a soft drink that is more popular than Coca-Cola. When McDonalds opened in Glasgow and did not sell Irn-Bru, it was considered an insult and the restaurant was subsequently boycotted.

1401. A jellyfish is 95 percent water and humans around 70%.

1402. Joan of Arc was actually burned alive as a witch in 1431 and only considered a saint in the 20th century.

1403. The sound you hear when you macho people crack your knuckles is actually the sound of nitrogen gas bubbles bursting.

1404. Ketchup actually began in Thailand. There it was labelled 'Kachiap'.

1405. 4 tablespoons of ketchup has about the same amount of nutrition as a ripe tomato.

1406. Koalas have twin thumbs. Koala bears also have finger prints that are almost identical to ours. Koala sleeps 20 hours a day.

1407. If a person has two thirds of their liver removed through trauma or surgery, it will grow back to the original size in four weeks time.

1408. The right lung is slightly larger than the left.

1409. Chicken liver can be used to change A type blood to O type blood.

1410. Leonardo Da Vinci invented the scissors. He could also draw with one hand and write with the other.

1411. To prevent some numbers from occurring more frequently than others, dice used in crap games in Las Vegas are manufactured to a tolerance of 0.0002 inches, less than 1/17 the thickness of a human hair.

1412. A person who is lost in the woods and starving can obtain nourishment by chewing on his shoes. Leather has enough nutritional value to sustain life for a short time.

1413. You will have to walk 80 kilometres for your legs to equal the amount of exercise your eyes get daily.

1414. Los Angeles was formerly known as *El Pueblo de Nuestra Senora la Reina de los Angeles de Porciuncula* or The Town of Our Lady the Queen of Angels of the Little Portion although its official name was simply *El Pueblo de la Reina de Los Angeles.*

1415. Men are more likely to be left-handed (10%) than females (8%).

1416. Lightning bolts can sometimes be hotter than the sun.

1417. A Manatee (Dugong) has very slow-clotting blood and important in finding out about haemophilia.

1418. A male emperor moth can detect and find a female of his species a mile away.

1419. You can test for a two way mirror by putting your fingernail on the surface, if there's space between the tip and the image, then its a normal mirror, if not, its two way.

1420. A McDonald's straw will hold 7.7 ml or just over one-and-a-half teaspoons of whatever you are drinking.

1421. Marilyn Monroe's real name is Norma Jean.

1422. A day on the planet Mercury is twice as long as its year.

1423. Astronaut Neil Armstrong first stepped on the moon with his left foot.

1424. In December 1972 U.S. astronaut Eugene Cernan becomes the last person to set foot on the moon.

1425. The magnetic North Pole shifts by about 7 metres a day.

1426. Only female mosquitoes bite. Males only drink water and plant juice.

1427. Remember, when someone annoys you it takes 42 muscles in your face to frown.

1428. You can only tell the gender of a Macaw through an operation. They lack exterior genitals.

1429. As much as 80% of microwaves from mobile phones are absorbed by your head!

1430. A mole can dig about 92 metres in 1 night.

1431. Most marine fish can survive in a tank filled with human blood.

1432. A mosquito will become restless and start flying around if there is an increase of carbon dioxide in the surrounding air.

1433. Mosquito repellents do not really repel mozzies. They actually block the sensory pores and makes the mozzies think they are flying to a colder, dryer and more Carbon dioxide free area.

1434. Intelligent people have more zinc and copper in their hair.

1435. Coca-Cola was originally green.

1436. People sitting on them and photocopying their butts cause 23% of all photocopier faults worldwide.

1437. In every episode of Seinfeld, there is a Superman somewhere.

1438. Wearing headphones for just an hour will increase the bacteria in your ear by 700 times.

1439. More than 50% of the people in the world have never made or received a telephone call.

1440. In 1879, a mail service in Belgium employed 37 cats to carry bundles of letters to villages around the town of Liege, this experiment was shorted-lived as the cats proved thoroughly undisciplined.

1441. The greatest recorded number of children that have been born by one mother is 69! The lass gave birth to 16 pairs of twins, seven sets of triplets and a measly 4 sets of quadruplets.

1442. Males, on average, think about sex every 7 seconds.

1443. The favourite colour of mosquitoes is blue.

1444. The most common last name in the world is Wong.

1445. An oyster can change its sex once every seven days.

1446. The longest kebab was 324.9m.

1447. A polar bear's kidneys are poisonous.

1448. Pure carbon can exist in only three forms.

1449. The modern horse has evolved over 60 million years from a creature no bigger than a domestic cat.

1450. The highest ever amount paid out in a life insurance claim was $18,000,000 to Linda Mullendore.

1451. Adolf Hitler was addicted to speed.

1452. The dioxin 2,3,7,8-tetrachlorodibenzo-p-dioxin is 150,000 times deadlier than cyanide.

1453. It is said that when Black Beard the Pirate was beheaded his headless body danced around for eight minutes.

1454. The Western Deep Mine, Carlentonville, RSA, is the deepest gold mine in the world.

1455. The Phoenician navigator Hanno was likely the first to circumnavigate Africa, around 500 B.C. He observed that at the southern end of Africa the noonday sun shone in the north. This sounded ridiculous to Herodotus, the Greek historian, who reported the tale; but the very report shows us that Hanno likely did circumnavigate Africa or at least made a good attempt at it. He probably wouldn't have been able to imagine the sun shining in the 'wrong' part of the sky if he hadn't seen it.

1456. A camel does not sweat until its body is at 40 degrees C.

1457. An ounce of wild ginseng root has been sold for as high a price as $23,000.

1458. The most common name for a pub in England is 'The Red Lion'.

1459. If a tennis ball was bounced against a wall once a second and each time it hit its atomic structure changed randomly, once every five suns' lifetimes it would pass through the wall.

1460. The quickest boxing match in history was 10.5 seconds, this included the 10 second count.

1461. The longest banana split was 7.32 km.

1462. Every 5 seconds, a computer gets infected with a virus.

1463. The world's youngest parents were 8 and 9 and lived in China in 1910.

1464. Fish that live more than 800 metres below the ocean surface don't have eyes.

1465. Hydrogen is an explosive gas. Oxygen supports combustion. Yet when these are combined it is water, which is used to put out fires.

1466. The Ramses brand condom is named after the great phaoroh Ramses II who fathered over 160 children.

1467. Duelling is legal in Paraguay as long as both parties are registered blood donors.

1468. Each king in a deck of playing cards represents a great king from history.

1. Spades - King David
2. Hearts - Charlemagne
3. Clubs - Alexander the Great
4. Diamonds - Julius Caesar

1469. To 'testify' was based on men in the Roman court swearing to a statement made by swearing on their testicles.

1470. On average, 90% Dutch teenagers can speak fluent English whereas only 80% American teenagers can speak fluent English.

1471. In Texas, a recently passed anticrime law requires criminals to give their victims 24 hours notice, either orally or in writing and to explain the nature of the crime to be committed.

1472. No piece of square dry paper can be folded in half more than 7 times.

1473. 1 in every 200 people are a psychopath and they look just like everyone else.

1474. All the chemicals in the human body have a combined value of approximately £4.00 (6.25 Euro).

1475. In Alaska, it is legal to shoot bears. However, waking a sleeping bear for the purpose of taking a photograph is prohibited.

1476. The metric system was to blame for the loss of the Mars Climate orbiter.

1477. All mammals have tongues.

1478. Fingernails grow nearly 4 times faster than toenails.

1479. The Nile catfish swim upside down.

1480. A teaspoon of neutron star material weighs about 110 million tons.

1481. Neckties were first worn in Croatia.

1482. The entire worlds output of urine takes about 45 minutes to go over the Niagara Falls. The bridge across the Niagara Falls began with a kite carrying a line across it.

1483. It is impossible for anyone to verbally count up to the number 1 trillion.

1484. Your nose smells best when you are about 10 years old.

1485. The numbers 111, 222, 333, 444, 555, 666, 777, 888 and 999 are all multiples of 37.

1486. Owls are one of the only birds who can see the colour blue.

1487. The eggs from the ovaries of a pig, when shot into another animal, can sterilise it, making it impotent.

1488. Ostriches stick their heads into the sand to find underground drinking water.

1489. The Ostrich people in Africa are a group of people who have only 2 toes due to inbreeding.

1490. Pigeons can be killed by feeding them uncooked rice, because their stomach can't handle the carbohydrates or it swells in their throats and chokes them.

1491. In the 1960's, the US spent millions in developing a zero gravity pen for use in space.

1492. In ancient Egypt, priests plucked every hair from their bodies, including their eyebrows and eyelashes.

1493. The male praying mantis cannot copulate while its head is attached to its body. The female initiates sex by ripping the male's head off.

1494. In the early stages of development and pig's embryo is similar to that of a human's.

1495. Pears ripen from the inside out and according to a survey on the lifestyle channel, men prefer hard pears while women prefer soft pears.

1496. Penguins are not found in the North Pole.

1497. When potatoes were brought from South America over to Spain, it took about 200 years before it was recognised as a food.

1498. Prague consumes 3 times more beer than all the soft drinks combined.

1499. Magellan named the Pacific Ocean because it was calmer than the Atlantic.

1500. The hair on a polar bears not white, but clear. They reflect light, so they appear white. Pregnant female polar bears will not eat for several months while resting in her den under the snow. Polar bears can eat as many as 86 penguins in a single sitting. Pearls can melt/dissolve in vinegar.

1501. A pig's orgasm lasts for 30 minutes. Pigs cannot sweat because they don't have sweat glands. Instead, they roll around in mud to keep cool. In 1386, a pig was executed by public hanging for the murder of a child.

1502. The gender of Reptiles are determined not by the sex genes, but by the temperature in which the egg is incubated. A certain temperature will produce a male and vice versa for a female.

1503. A Red Giant (a kind of exploded star) has a lower density than any vacuum here on earth.

1504. Male feral rabbits urinate on the females to state their ownership.

1505. Female rabbits on the other hand, reabsorb their embryo for the proteins.

1506. Right-handed people live, on average, nine years longer than left-handed people do.

1507. Rubber bands last longer when refrigerated.

1508. Rice and some other grains contain chemicals that can enhance brain functions.

1509. The Ribbon worm will start eating itself to avoid starvation.

1510. Snakes have two sex organs.

1511. Scorpions can be killed by pouring vinegar over them. They'll 'snap' and sting themselves.

1512. No piece of dry square paper can be folded more than 7 times in half!

1513. The sloth (a mammal) moves so slowly that green algae can grow undisturbed on it is fur.

1514. The starfish is one of the only animals who can turn its stomach inside-out. They also don't have brains.

1515. In Britain, failed suicides were hanged in the 19th century.

1516. Skin is thickest, 1/5 inch, on the upper back. It is thinnest on the eyelids, which are only 1/50th inch thick.

1517. A strand of spider web may be stronger than an equal diametre of steel.

1518. All the coal, oil, gas and wood on Earth would only keep the Sun burning for a few days.

1519. An area of the Sun's surface the size of a postage stamp shines with the power of 1,500,000 candles.

1520. It is impossible for a solar eclipse to last for more than 7 minutes 58 seconds.

1521. The increased electricity used by modern appliances is causing a shift in the Earth's magnetic field. By the year 2327, the North

Pole will be located in mid-Kansas, while the South Pole will be just off the coast of East Africa.

1522. The idea for 'tribbles' in 'Star Trek' came from gerbils, since some gerbils are actually born pregnant.

1523. Male rhesus monkeys often hang from tree branches by their fascinating prehensile penises.

1524. Smearing a small amount of dog faeces on an insect bite will relieve the itching and swelling.

1525. The Boeing 747 is capable of flying upside-down if it weren't for the fact that the wings would shear off when trying to roll it over.

1526. The trucking company in which, Elvis Presley worked as a young man was owned by Frank Sinatra.

1527. The only golf course on the island of Tonga has 15 holes and there's no penalty if a monkey steals your golf ball.

1528. Manatees possess vocal chords, which give them the ability to speak like humans, but don't do so because they have no ears with which to hear the sound.

1529. Scuba divers cannot pass gas at depths of 33 feet or below.

1530. Catfish are the only animals that naturally have an odd number of whiskers.

1531. The Air Force's F-117 fighter uses aerodynamics.

1532. Silly Putty was 'discovered' as the residue left behind after the first latex condoms were produced. It's not widely publicised for obvious reasons.

1533. Approximately one-sixth of your life is spent on Wednesdays.

1534. The skin needed for elbow transplants must be taken from the scrotum of a cadaver.

1535. The sport of jai alai originated from a game played by Incan priests who held cats by their tails and swung at leather balls. The cats would instinctively grab at the ball with their claws, thus enabling players to catch them.

1536. A cat's purr has the same romance-enhancing frequency as the voice of singer Barry White.

1537. The volume of water that the Giant Sequoia tree consumes in a 24-hour period contains enough suspended minerals to pave 17.3 feet of a 4-lane concrete freeway.

1538. King Henry VIII slept with a gigantic axe.

1539. Human saliva has a boiling point three times that of regular water.

1540. Calvin, of the 'Calvin and Hobbes' comic strip, was patterned after President Calvin Coolidge, who had a pet tiger as a boy.

1541. Until 1978, Camel cigarettes contained minute particles of real camels.

1542. Seven out of every ten hockey-playing Canadians will lose a tooth during a game. For Canadians who don't play hockey that figure drops to five out of ten.

1543. A dog's naked behind leaves absolutely no bacteria when pressed against carpet.

1544. A team of University of Virginia researchers released a study promoting the practice of picking one's nose, claiming that the health benefits of keeping nasal passages free from infectious blockages far outweigh the negative social connotations.

1545. Among items left behind at Osama bin Laden's headquarters in Afghanistan were 27 issues of Mad Magazine. Al Qaeda members have admitted that bin Laden is reportedly an avid reader.

1546. Urine from male cape water buffaloes is so flammable that some tribes use it for lantern fuel.

1547. At the first World Cup championship in Uruguay, 1930, the soccer balls were actually monkey skulls wrapped in paper and leather.

1548. Every Labrador retriever dreams about bananas.

1549. If you put a bee in a film canister for two hours, it will go blind and leave behind its weight in honey.

1550. Due to the angle at which the optic nerve enters the brain, staring at a blue surface during sex greatly increases the intensity of orgasms.

1551. Never hold your nose and cover your mouth when sneezing, as it can blow out your eyeballs.

1552. Centuries ago, purchasing real estate often required having one or more limbs amputated in order to prevent the purchaser from running away to avoid repayment of the loan. Hence an expensive purchase was said to cost 'an arm and a leg'.

1553. Aardvarks are allergic to radishes, but only during summer months.

1554. If you part your hair on the right side, you were born to be carnivorous. If you part it on the left, your physical and psychological make-up is that of a vegetarian.

1555. In WWII, the US military planned to airdrop over France, propaganda in the form of Playboy magazine, with coded messages hidden in the models' turn-ons and turn-offs. The plan was scrapped because of a staple shortage due to rationing of metal.

1556. Although difficult, it's possible to start a fire by rapidly rubbing together two Cool Ranch Doritos.

1557. Napoleon's favourite type of wood was knotty chestnut.

1558. The world's smartest pig, owned by a mathematics teacher in Madison, WI, memorised the multiplication tables up to 12.

1559. Due to the natural 'momentum' of the ocean, saltwater fish cannot swim backwards.

1560. A piece of buttered toast contains about 315 kJ of energy. With that energy you could, jog for 6 minutes; cycle for 10 minutes; walk briskly for 15 minutes and sleep for 1.5 hours.

1561. When you run only 25% of the chemical energy in your muscles is converted into kinetic energy. The rest changes into heat energy.

1562. When you get goose pimples and your hair stand, the hair helps to trap air making you feel warmer by keeping in, your body heat.

1563. Over half the people in Iceland get their hot water from geothermal energy.

1564. A person who weighs 50 kg on earth will weigh 13,200 kg on Jupiter.

1565. The compressed air used by scuba divers in their cylinders can occupy the same volume if not compressed.

1566. On a clear day, a beam of sunlight can be reflected off a mirror and seen up to 40 km away.

1567. The sound energy of 200 pianos is equal to the electrical energy needed to light just one light bulb.

1568. Sound travels 15 times faster through steel and 4 times faster through water than through air.

1569. The world's largest and loudest musical instrument is in the Atlantic City, USA. It is an organ of 33,112 pipes that can make a sound as loud as 25 brass bands.

1570. Guitars often have to be tuned onstage because strong light heats them up, making them expand and out of tune.

1571. In ancient Greece, children of wealthy families were dipped in olive oil at birth to keep them hairless throughout their lives.

1572. It is nearly three miles farther to fly from Amarillo, Texas to Louisville, Kentucky than it is to return from Louisville to Amarillo.

1573. The 'nine lives' attributed to cats is probably due to their having nine primary whiskers.

1574. The original inspiration for Barbie dolls comes from dolls developed by German propagandists in the late 1930s to impress young girls with the ideal notions of Aryan features. The proportions for Barbie were actually based on those of Eva Braun.

1575. The Venezuelan brown bat can detect and dodge individual raindrops in mid-flight, arriving safely back at his cave completely dry.

1576. When you put a seashell to your ear, the sound you hear is not the waves, but actually the echo of the blood pulsing in your own ear.

1577. The salute of uniform bodies (e.g. army, police) originated from knights who lifted their visors to show their face to a royalty.

1578. When a person dies, hearing is the last sense to go.

1579. There is a member of the spider family called the demodex folliculorum that lives at the root of people's eye lashes. It's harmless and normal.

1580. Each day, there is over 120 million sexual intercourse taking place all over the world.

1581. Your body releases growth hormones when you sleep.

1582. Scarecrows frighten birds because of the human odour emitted from the clothes they wear.

1583. The sun's average period of rotation is 27 days.

1584. The Sea of tranquillity is found on the moon.

1585. Soybean actually has Diadzein and genistein that act like weak estrogen.

1586. Skin weighs about 3.2 kg.

1587. A giant squid has eyes that can grow up to 20 inches in diametre.

1588. Sweden is the largest spender on ketchup. $4 per capita. Australia is second at $2.50.

1589. The sea contains about 1/2 of the world's known animal groups.

1590. Male seagulls have red legs.

1591. A sneeze travels out your mouth at over 100 m.p.h. The highest recorded 'sneeze speed' is 165 km per hour.

1592. A snail can actually glide over the sharp edge of a knife or razor without harming itself. This has something to do with the mucus it produces.

1593. There is a flower called the Scarlet Pimpernel that can forecast the weather. If the flower is closed up, rain is coming and if it is opened up, the day will be sunny.

1594. In Shakespeare, Rosalind, the heroine of 'As You Like It', has more lines than any of Shakespeare's female characters. Cleopatra comes in second with 670 lines and third place belongs to Imogen ('Cymbeline'), with 591 lines.

1595. St. Teresa of Avila is the patron saint of chess-players!!

1596. The world's termites outweigh the world's humans 10 to 1.

1597. Like fingerprints, everyone's tongue print is different.

1598. Typewriter is one of the longest words that can be made using the letters only one row of the keyboard.

1599. When the German army invaded France in WWI, they actually followed the schedules of the local trains to invade (it was faster by rail and they wanted to surprise France), checking the timetable and abiding by it. And France, whose army was waiting at the border, sent taxis to pick up and transport the troops to counter the attack!

1600. The telescope on Mount Palomar, California, can see a distance of 7,038,835,200,000,000,000,000 miles.

1601. It is impossible to get water out of a rimless tyre.

1602. In most comic strips and magazine advertisments, the time on the clock is 10:10.

1603. In turtles, the colon (intestine) is also used for respiration, as it takes in oxygen.

1604. Tarantulas have retractable claws like cats and the hairs on their abdomen and back legs can stick into an enemy and itch. They also get bald on their thorax when they get old.

1605. Some reconstituted tobacco contains the same ingredients found in fart.

1606. When the temperature drops, the eyesight reaction time of insects (like the dragonfly and some animals like tortoises) decrease and that why they can be caught early in the morning or at night by predators like birds whose eyesight reaction times are unaffected by temperature.

1607. Turkeys can reproduce without having sex. It's called parthenogenesis.

1608. In Tibet, there is actually a practice called 'fraternal polyandry' where many men, usually brothers, marry a single woman. This takes place so that only one set of children will inherit the land.

1609. Uranus was originally called George, in honour of King George III of Britain. Uranus' axis is at 97 degrees which means that it orbits on its side.

1610. Laid end-to-end, the arteries, capillaries and veins would stretch for about 60,000 miles in the average child and would be about 100,000 miles in an adult - enough to wrap around the world nearly four times.

1611. Venus is the only planet in the solar system to spin backwards.

1612. A volcano can shoot its debris as high as 50 km into the sky.

1613. Over 10,000 birds a year die from smashing into windows.

1614. We lose half a litre of water a day through breathing. This is the water vapour we see when we breathe onto glass.

1615. The name Wendy was made up for the book 'Peter Pan'. It came from the author's friends, whom he called his 'fwendy' (friend).

1616. A whip makes a cracking sound because its tip moves faster than the speed of sound.

1617. Hot water weighs less than cold water for a given volume. If hot water is suddenly poured into a glass that glass is more apt to break if it is thick than if it is thin. This is why test tubes are made of thin glass.

1618. Windmills always turn counter-clockwise except in one country.

1619. Water based mammals like dolphins and whales swish their tails up and down. Only fish move them sideways.

1620. The words racecar, kayak, level and Navy Van are the same whether they are read left to right or right to left and these are called palindromes. The longest palindromes in the dictionary however are the words 'Malayalam' 'rotavator' 'redivider'.

1621. Xylophones were actually developed in South East Asia in the 14th century.

1622. If you yelled for 8 years, 7 months and 6 days, you would have produced enough sound energy to heat one cup of coffee.

1623. The term Y2K was invented by David Eddie in June 1995 through the email.

1624. Zero point energy is a source of energy, which is released when atoms stop moving, at -273 Celsius.

1625. Apples, not caffeine, are more efficient at waking you up in the morning.

1626. Alfred Hitchcock didn't have a belly button.

1627. A pack-a-day smoker will lose approximately 2 teeth every 10 years.

1628. When you sneeze, all bodily functions stop, even your heart!

1629. Forty people are sent to the hospital for dog bites every minute.

1630. Babies are born without kneecaps. They don't appear until they are 2-6 years old.

1631. A coat hanger is 44 inches long when straightened.

1632. The average computer user blinks 7 times a minute.

1633. Your feet are bigger in the afternoon than any other time of day.

1634. The only two animals that can see behind themselves without turning their heads are the rabbit and the parrot.

1635. Michael Jackson owns the rights to the South Carolina State anthem.

1636. In most television commercials advertising milk, a mixture of white paint and a little thinner is used in place of the milk.

1637. Prince Charles and Prince William never travel on the same airplane, just in case there is a crash.

1638. Most hospitals make money by selling the umbilical cords cut from women who give birth. They are used in vein transplant surgery.

1639. There are two kinds of pandas. There is the Long-tailed Himalayan. Carnivore that looks like a raccoon and there is the Giant panda bear that lives in Western China.

1640. There are two kinds of camels. One is the Arabian that lives in Western Asia and Northern Africa. It has one hump. And the second kind is called Bactrian, which has two humps and lives in Mongolia and Chinese Turkistan.

1641. The smallest bird in the world is the Hummingbird. It weighs 1 oz.

1642. Fishes talk to each other. Some of them communicate by making noises in their throats by rasping their teeth, others use their swim bladders to make sounds.

1643. The Grammy Awards were introduced to counter the threat of rock music. In the late 1950s, a group of record executives were alarmed by the explosive success of rock 'n roll, considering it a threat to 'quality' music.

1644. Tea is said to have been discovered in 2737 BC by a Chinese emperor when some tealeaves accidentally blew into a pot of boiling water. Thomas Sullivan of New York introduced the tea bag in 1908.

1645. Over the last 150 years, the average height of people in industrialised nations has increased 10 cm (about 4 inches). In the 19th century, American men were the tallest in the world, averaging 1,71m (5'6'). Today, the average height for American men is 1,75m (5'7'), compared to 1,77 (5'8') for Swedes and 1,78 (5'8. 5') for the Dutch. The tallest nation in the world is the Watusis of Burundi.

1646. If the amount of water in your body is reduced by just 1%, you'll feel thirsty. If it's reduced by 10%, you'll die.

1647. Look at the number four on a clock face that uses Roman numerals. If the clock is made correctly then the Roman numeral four is wrong. The standard and correct way to write the Roman numeral four is 'IV', but the traditional way to show it on a clock face is 'IIII'. Legend has it that a clock was made for a British king. When he saw the clock he misinformedly corrected the clock maker who re-did the clock face to show a 'IIII' instead of an 'IV' thus not risking offending the king. Other clock makers followed suit so as not to embarrass the king. Now it is the traditional way to make clocks.

1648. June Foray, the voice of Talking Tina from the classic Twilight Zone episode 'Living Doll', was also the voice of Rocky the talking squirrel from 'Rocky & Bullwinkle'.

1649. The dunce cap of schoolhouse fame originates from a paper cone that was placed on the heads of accused witches during the Middle Ages. When Joan of Arc was martyred, she was wearing one of them.

1650. Despite the hump, a camel's spine is straight.

1651. 'Rhythm' and 'syzygy' are the longest English words without vowels.

1652. There is no mention of Adam and Eve eating an apple in the Bible.

1653. Jacques Cousteau invented scuba gear while in the French resistance during World War II.

1654. More people are killed each year from bees than from snakes.

1655. 'Halloween' took place in the town of Haddonfield, Illinois but almost all the cars in the film had California licence plates.

1656. A rat can last longer without water than a camel.

1657. There are more nutrients in the cornflake package itself than there are in the actual cornflakes.

1658. Soda water does not contain soda.

1659. 'Smithee' is a pseudonym that filmmakers use when they don't want their names to appear in the credits.

1660. Crocodiles swallow stones to help them dive deeper.

1661. When opossums are playing opossum, they are not 'playing'. They actually pass out from sheer terror.

1662. The turkey was wrongly named after what was thought to be it's country of origin.

1663. There is a city called Rome on every continent.

1664. The screwdriver was invented before the screw.

1665. Flying from London to New York by Concord, due to the time zones crossed, you can arrive 2 hours before you leave.

1666. There are no rivers in Saudi Arabia.

1667. John Wilkes Booth shot Lincoln in a theatre and was found in a warehouse. Lee Harvey Oswald shot Kennedy from a warehouse and was found in a theatre.

1668. The spaceship 'Valley Forge' from 'Silent Running' (1971) actually got it's name from the location used to film some of its interiors; a decommissioned aircraft carrier named the U.S.S. Valley Forge.

1669. Anteaters prefer termites to ants.

1670. Every Swiss citizen is required by law to have a bomb shelter or access to a bomb shelter.

1671. Spain literally means 'the land of rabbits'.

1672. Jean-Claude Van Damme was the alien in the original 'Predator' in almost all the jumping and climbing scenes.

1673. The mask used by Michael Myers in the original 'Halloween' was actually a Captain Kirk mask painted white.

1674. Pamela Lee-Anderson is Canada's Centennial Baby, being the first baby born on the centennial anniversary of Canada's independence.

1675. Brazil got its name from the nut, not the other way around.

1676. The bat on the Bacardi symbol is there because the soil where the sugar cane grows is fertile from the excessive guano (bat droppings.)

1677. Kathleen Turner was the voice of Jessica Rabbit and Amy Irving was her singing voice.

1678. Catgut comes from sheep not cats.

1679. A lion's roar can be heard from five miles away.

1680. Due to gravitational effects, you weigh slightly less when the moon is directly overhead.

1681. If you can see a rainbow you must have your back to the sun. If you don't, you can't see it.

1682. St. Bernards, famous for their role as alpine rescue dogs, do *not* wear casks of brandy around their necks.

1683. Sharon Stone was the first 'Star Search' spokes model.

1684. Clark Gable used to shower more than 4 times a day.

1685. The launching mechanism of a carrier ship that helps planes to take off could throw a pickup truck over a mile.

1686. The placement of a donkey's eyes in its' heads enables it to see all four feet at all times.

1687. Walt Disney named Mickey Mouse after Mickey Rooney, whose mother he dated for some time.

1688. The name of the Vulcan's heaven is Sha Ka Ree, this is a play on the name Sean Connery who was considered for the part of Sarek, Spock's father.

1689. Blonde beards grow faster than darker beards.

1690. The first time the word 'hell' was spoken on TV was in an original 'STAR TREK' episode entitled 'City on the Edge of Forever'. The exact quote was "...let's get the hell out of here..." spoken by William Shatner.

1691. From the age of thirty, humans gradually begin to shrink in size.

1692. Roosters can't crow if they can't fully extend their necks.

1693. Ancient drinkers warded off the devil by clinking their cups.

1694. All of the officers in the Confederate army were given copies of Les Miserables, by Victor Hugo, to carry with them at all times.

1695. The fingerprints of koala bears are virtually indistinguishable from those of humans, so much so that they could be confused at a crime scene.

1696. The Nobel Prize resulted from a late change in the will of Alfred Nobel, who did not want to be remembered after his death as a propagator of violence. He invented dynamite.

1697. Months that begin on a Sunday will always have a 'Friday the 13th'.

1698. Pogonophobia is the fear of beards.

1699. Oak trees do not have acorns until they are fifty years old or older.

1700. In Ancient Peru, when a woman found an 'ugly' potato, it was the custom for her to push it into the face of the nearest man.

1701. The Eisenhower interstate system requires that one-mile in every five must be straight. These straight sections are usable as airstrips in times of war or other emergencies.

1702. The magic word 'Abracadabra' was originally intended for the specific purpose of curing hay fever.

1703. It is illegal to be a prostitute in Siena, Italy, if your name is Mary.

1704. Bruce Lee was so fast that they actually had to *slow* a film down so you could see his moves. That's the opposite of the norm.

1705. The car manufacturer Henry Ford was awarded Hitler's Supreme Order of the German Eagle.

1706. On 15 April 1912 the SS Titanic sunk on her maiden voyage and over 1,500 people died. Fourteen years earlier a novel was published by Morgan Robertson, which seemed to foretell the disaster. The book described a ship the same size as the Titanic, which crashes into an iceberg on its maiden voyage on a misty April night. The name of Robertson's fictional ship was the Titan.

1707. Other than humans, black lemurs are the only primates that have blue eyes.

1708. The Chinese ideogram for 'trouble' depicts two women living under one roof'.

1709. It is a criminal offence to drive around in a dirty car in Russia.

1710. The children's' nursery rhyme 'Ring-a-Round-The-Rosies' actually refers to the Black Death, which killed about 30 million people in the fourteenth-century.

1711. Woodward Avenue in Detroit, Michigan carries the designation

M-1, named so because it was the first paved road anywhere.

1712. Some Eskimos have been known to use refrigerators to keep their food from freezing.

1713. Lorne Greene had one of his nipples bitten off by an alligator while he was host of 'Lorne Greene's Wild Kingdom'.

1714. Chrysler built B-29's that bombed Japan. Mitsubishi built the Zeros that tried to shoot them down. Both companies now build cars in a joint plant call Diamond Star.

1715. The first product Motorola started to develop was a record player for automobiles. At that time the most known player on the market was the Victrola, so they called themselves Motorola.

1716. Napoleon Bonaparte designed the national flag of Italy.

1717. Ancient Egyptians shaved off their eyebrows to mourn the deaths of their cats.

1718. Hindu men believe it to be unluckily to marry a third time. They could avoid misfortune by marrying a tree first. The tree (his third wife) was then burnt, freeing him to marry again.

1719. The province of Alberta in Canada has been completely free of rats since 1905.

1720. Lady Astor once told Winston Churchill "If you were my husband, I would poison your coffee." His reply, "If you were my wife, I would drink it!"

1721. Most amazing to the troops of Ian Pharaoh Thutmose I around 1525 B.C., in their invasion of Syria and Carchemish on the upper Euphrates were the Nile 'falling from the sky' and the river that 'in flowing north flowed south'. The soldiers were sons of the cloudless land of the Nile and thus were fascinated when they encountered rain (the Nile from the sky) and amazed at the direction of the flow of the Euphrates. The Nile flows north, so 'north' meant 'downstream' to the Egyptians and they naturally saw the Euphrates as flowing 'backwards'.

1722. A dragonfly has a lifespan of twenty-four hours.

1723. A ten-gallon hat holds three-quarters of a gallon.

1724. On an American one-dollar bill, there is an owl in the upper left-hand corner of the '1' encased in the 'shield' and a spider hidden in the front upper right-hand corner.

1725. 'Evian' (the bottled water) spelled backwards is 'naive'.

1726. Armoured knights raised their visors to identify themselves when they rode past their king. This custom has become the modern military salute.

1727. It was illegal to sell ET dolls in France because there is a law against selling dolls without human faces.

1728. George Washington grew marijuana in his garden.

1729. Panama hats come from Ecuador not Panama.

1730. Human birth control pills work on gorillas.

1731. Cheryl Ladd (of Charlie's Angels fame) played the voice, both talking and singing, of Josie in the 70s Saturday morning cartoon 'Josie and the Pussycats'.

1732. Alexander the Great was an epileptic.

1733. When young and impoverished, Pablo Picasso kept warm by burning his own paintings.

1734. Heroin is the brand name of morphine once marketed by Bayer.

1735. The Declaration of Independence was written on hemp paper.

1736. 101 Dalmatians and Peter Pan are the only two Disney cartoon features with both parents that are present and don't die throughout the movie.

1737. According to Genesis 1:20-22 the chicken came before the egg.

1738. There are more beetles than any other kind of creature in the world.

1739. Tomb robbers believed that knocking Egyptian sarcophagi's noses off would forestall curses.

1740. Mozart was buried in an unmarked pauper's grave.

1741. Orcas (killer whales) kill sharks by torpedoing up into the shark's stomach from underneath, causing the shark to explode.

1742. Hershey's Kisses are called that because the machine that makes them looks like it's kissing the conveyor belt.

1743. Dr. Samuel A. Mudd was the physician who set the leg of Lincoln's assassin John Wilkes Booth and whose shame created the statement for ignominy, 'His name is Mudd'.

1744. Compact discs read from the inside to the outside edge, the reverse of how a record works.

1745. The term 'Mayday' is used for signalling for help. It comes from the French term 'M'aidez' which is pronounced 'MayDay' and means, 'Help Me'.

1746. Ninety eight per cent of the weight of water is made up from oxygen.

1747. A fully loaded super tanker travelling at normal speed takes at least twenty minutes to stop.

1748. No matter its size or thickness, no piece of paper can be folded in half more than 7 times.

1749. February 1865 is the only month in recorded history not to have a full moon.

1750. Astronauts are not allowed to eat beans before they go into space because passing wind in a spacesuit damages them.

1751. Former US President Ulysses S. Grant had the boyhood nickname 'Useless'.

1752. Boys who have unusual first names are more likely to have mental problems than boys with conventional names. Girls don't seem to have this problem.

1753. Russians generally answer the phone by saying, 'I'm listening'.

1754. Until 1967, LSD was legal in California.

1755. In the 40's, the Bich pen was changed to Bic for fear that Americans would pronounce it 'Bitch'.

1756. Termites eat wood twice as fast when listening to heavy metal music.

1757. The NY phone book had 22 Hitlers before WWII. The NY phone book had 0 Hitlers after WWII.

1758. John Wilkes Booth's brother once saved the life of Abraham Lincoln's son.

1759. The cigarette lighter was invented before the match.

1760. Men leave their hotel rooms cleaner than women do.

1761. While performing her duties as queen, Cleopatra sometimes wore a fake beard.

1762. The Egyptians believed in mummification because they thought if you wrapped the deceased body up it would preserve it and you could go into the afterlife. Ancient Egyptians decided to use mummification to preserve their dead when they discovered that the hot desert sands dehydrated corpses, shrivelling their skin onto their bones instead of turning the bodies to dust. Ancient Egyptians regarded the heart as the centre of intelligence and emotion. They believed the brain to have no significance whatsoever and in the process of mummification, the brain was removed through the nose and discarded. Many of the internal organs are removed from the body being mummified, as they are the first part of the body to decompose. The removed internal organs are dehydrated, wrapped in linen and returned to the body together with sawdust and leaves so that the body looks lifelike. The arms and legs of the mummy are tied together and a papyrus scroll with spells from the Book of the Dead is placed between the wrapped hands. Between the layers of wrapping, the ancient.

1763. Nearly 1,000 kinds of bats account for almost a quarter of all mammal species and most are highly beneficial. A single little brown bat can catch 600 mosquitoes in just one hour. A colony of 150 big brown bats can protect local farmers from up to 18 million or more rootworms each summer. Tropical bats are key elements in rain forest ecosystems, which rely on them to pollinate flowers and disperse seeds for countless trees and shrubs. In the wild, important agricultural plants, from bananas, bread-fruit and mangoes to cashew, dates and figs rely on bats for pollination and seed dispersal. Tequila is produced from agaves plants whose seed production drops to 1/3,000th of normal without bat pollinators. Desert ecosystems rely on nectar-feeding bats as primary pollinators of giant cacti, including the famous organ pipe and saguaro of Arizona. Bat droppings in caves support whole ecosystems of unique organisms, including bacteria useful in detoxifying wastes, in proving detergents and producing gasohol and antibiotics. An anticoagulant from vampire bat saliva may soon be used to treat human heart patients. Contrary to popular misconceptions, bats are not blind, do not become entangled in human hair and seldom transmit disease to other animals or humans. All mammals can contract rabies; however, even the less than half of 1% of bats that do, normally bite only in self-defence and pose little threat to people who do not handle them. Bats are exceptionally vulnerable to extinction, in part because they are the slowest reproducing mammals on earth for their size. Most produce only one young a year. The world's smallest mammal is the bumblebee bat of Thailand, which weighs less than a penny. Giant flying foxes that live in Indonesia have wingspans of nearly six feet. The common little brown bat of North America is the world's longest-lived mammal for its size with life spans exceeding 32 years. Mexican free-tailed bats sometimes fly up to two miles high to feed or to catch tailwinds that carry them over long distances at speeds of more than 60 miles per hour. The pallid bat of western North America is immune to the stings of scorpions and even the seven-inch centipedes upon which it feeds. Fishing bats have echolocation so sophisticated that they can detect a minnow's fin as fine as a human hair protruding only two millimetres above a pond's surface. African heart-nosed bats can hear the footsteps of a beetle walking on sand from a distance of more than six feet. Red bats, which live in tree foliage throughout most of North America, can withstand body temperatures as low as 23 degrees during winter hibernation. Tiny woolly bats of West Africa live in the large webs of colonial spiders. The Honduran white bat is snow white with a yellow nose and ears. It cuts large leaves to make 'tents' that protect its small colonies from jungle rains. Frog eating bats identify edible from poisonous frogs by listening to the mating calls of male frogs. Frogs counter by hiding and using short, difficult-to-locate calls. Vampire bats adopt orphans and have been known to risk their lives to share food with less fortunate roost-mates. Male bats have pouches in their shoulders that contain large, showy patches of white fur, which they flash during courtship to attract mates. Mother Mexican free-tailed bats find and nurse their own young, even in huge colonies where many millions of babies cluster at up to 500 per square foot.

1764. India is the world's largest, oldest, continuous civilisation. Varanasi, also known as Benares, was called 'the ancient city' when Lord Buddha visited it in 500 B.C. and is the oldest, continuously inhabited city in the world today. India is the world's largest democracy. India never invaded any country in her last 10000 years of history. India invented the Number System. The World's first university was established in Takshashila in 700BC. More than 10,500 students from all over the world studied more than 60 subjects. The University of Nalanda built in the 4th century BC was one of the greatest achievements of ancient India in the field of education. Sanskrit is the mother of all the European languages. Ayurveda is the earliest school of medicine known to humans. Charaka, the father of medicine consolidated Ayurveda 2500 years ago. Today, Ayurveda is fast regaining its rightful place in our civilisation. Although modern images of India often show poverty and lack of development, India was the richest country on earth until the time of British invasion in the early 17th Century. Christopher Columbus was attracted by India's wealth. The art of Navigation was born in the river Sindhu 6000 years ago. The very word navigation is derived from the Sanskrit word *navgatih*. The word navy is also derived from Sanskrit 'Nou'.

Bhaskaracharya calculated the time taken by the earth to orbit the sun hundreds of years before the astronomer Smart. Time taken by earth to orbit the sun: (5th century) 365.258756484 days. The value of *pi* was first calculated solved by Budhayana and he explained the concept of what is known as the Pythagorean theorem. He discovered this in the 6th century long before the European mathematicians. Algebra, trigonometry and calculus came from India. Quadratic equations were solved by Sridharacharya in the 11th century. The largest numbers the Greeks and the Romans used were 106 whereas Hindus used numbers as big as 1053(10 to the power of 53) with specific names as early as 5000 BC during the Vedic period. Even today, the largest used number is Tera 1012(10 to the power of 12). The pioneer of wireless communication was Prof. Jagdish Bose and not Marconi. The earliest reservoir and dam for irrigation was built in Saurashtra. According to Saka King Rudradaman I of 150 CE, a beautiful lake called Sudarshana was constructed on the hills of Raivataka during Chandragupta Maurya's time. Chess was invented in India.

Sushruta is the father of surgery. 2600 years ago he and health scientists of his time conducted complicated surgeries like cesareans, cataract, artificial limbs, fractures, urinary stones and even plastic surgery and brain surgery. Usage of anesthesia was well known in ancient India. Over 125 surgical equipment were used. Deep knowledge of anatomy, physiology, etiology, embryology, digestion, metabolism, genetics and immunity is also found in many texts. When many cultures were only nomadic forest dwellers over 5000 years ago, Indians established Harappan culture in Sindhu Valley (Indus Valley Civilisation).

The four religions born in India, Hinduism, Buddhism, Jainism and Sikhism, are followed by 25% of the world's population. The place value system, the decimal system was developed in India in 100 BC. India is one of the few countries in the World, which gained independence without violence. India has the second largest pool of Scientists and Engineers in the World. India is the largest English-speaking nation in the world. India is the only country other than US and Japan, to have built a super computer indigenously. 38% of doctors in America are Indians. 12% of scientists in America are Indians. 36% of NASA employees are Indians. 34% of microsoft employees are Indians. 28% of IBM employees are Indians. 17% of Intel employees are Indians. 13% of Xerox employees are Indians.

1765. There are more than 700 species of butterflies in North America, but only a handful feed on agricultural crops. Millions of shingle-like, overlapping scales give butterfly and moths wing their colours. The smallest Lepidoptera are moths of the family Nepticulidae, with a wingspan of less than 2 mm (their caterpillars are very tiny also). During the time from hatching to pupation, a caterpillar increases its body size more than 30,000 times. The largest Lepidoptera is the South American owlet moth Thysania agrippina, which has a wingspan of 32 mm (slightly over one foot). The chrysalises (pupae) of some gossamer-winged (lycaenid) butterflies are capable of producing weak sounds to scare off potential enemies. They do this by flexing and rubbing together body segment membranes. In some moths the wings are mostly transparent (scales only along the wing veins) and they are mimics of wasps. The fastest Lepidoptera are the sphinx moths. Some species have been clocked at 60 kph (37 mph). Many of these same moths are also capable of hovering in the air like a helicopter. The organs used to taste food are not located on a butterfly's head - they are located on the terminal segments of the leg (tarsi). The silkworm, Bombix mori, is the only truly domesticated insect. The adult moths are so tame that they can barely fly and they must be hand fed. The vampire moth of Asia has a stiff proboscis that enables them to suck juices from thick-skinned fruits, but occasionally they can be found sucking the blood from a water buffalo or deer. Many caterpillars are covered with stinging hairs, which carry a toxin that can be quite painful to humans if touched. It takes about ten pounds of mulberry leaves for silkworms to be able to manufacture 1 pound of cocoons, which can be spun into a silk thread over 100 miles long. The wings of some butterflies and moths are marked with patterns that look very much like letters of the alphabet, as well as numerals. Adult butterflies feed on the nectar of flowers, but may also be seen feeding on rotting fruit, tree sap, fluids from animal carcasses and mud puddles. The yucca plant and the yucca moth are totally dependent upon one another for their existence - a relationship known as mutualism. Monarch butterflies regularly migrate between southern Canada and central Mexico, a total distance in excess of 2500 miles. They only weigh 1/50 of an ounce yet travel at 20 mph and reach altitudes of 10,000 feet. Members of the silkworm moth family have been raised in China since 2697 BC, where the methods are silk production had been a closely guarded secret. Anyone caught removing these insects from China was executed! However, in 55 AD two monks managed to hide some silkworm moths in their walking canes and smuggle them to Constantinople. 'Puddle clubs' are groups of butterflies (usually males) that gather around mud puddles and other moist areas of soil to suck up salts and other minerals dissolved in water. Butterflies can see red, green and yellow. Some people say that when the black bands on the Woolybear caterpillar are wide, a cold winter is coming. The top butterfly flight speed is 12 miles per hour. Some moths can fly 25 miles per hour! Monarch butterflies journey from the Great Lakes to the Gulf of Mexico, a distance of about 2,000 miles and return to the north again in the spring. Butterflies cannot fly if their body temperature is less than 86 degrees. Representations of butterflies are seen in Egyptian frescoes at Thebes, which are 3,500 years old. Antarctica is the only continent on which no Lepidoptera have been found. The caterpillars of some Snout Moths (Pyralididae) live in or on water-plants. The females of some moth species lack wings, all they can do to move is crawl. The Morgan's Sphinx Moth from Madagascar has a proboscis (tube mouth) that is 12 to 14 inches long to get the nectar from the bottom of a 12-inch deep orchid discovered by Charles Darwin. Some moths never eat anything as adults because they don't have mouths. They must live on the energy they stored as caterpillars. Many butterflies can taste with their feet to find out whether the leaf they sit on is good to lay eggs on to be their caterpillars' food or not.

1766. People eat insects – called 'Entomophagy' it has been practiced for centuries throughout Africa, Australia, Asia, the Middle East and North, Central and South America. Many bugs are both protein-rich and good sources of vitamins, minerals and fats. Many insects can carry 50 times their own body weight. This would be like an adult person lifting two heavy cars full of people. There are over a million described species of insects. Some people estimate there are actually between 15 and 30 million species. Most insects are beneficial to people because they eat other insects, pollinate crops, are food for other animals, make products we use (like honey and silk) or have medical uses. Butterflies and insects have their skeletons on the outside of their bodies, called the exoskeleton. This protects the insect and keeps water inside their bodies so they don't dry out.

1767. Butter and margarine are similar in calories. Many people say 'No thanks' to butter in favour of margarine, which they think has fewer calories. In fact, unless they choose diet margarine, it probably has approximately the same number of calories per tablespoon as butter. The difference is that butter is higher in saturated fats, while margarine generally has more unsaturated fats. But calorie counts may be close.

1768. According to Acupuncturists, there is a point on the head that you can press to control your appetite. It is located in the hollow just in front of the flap of the ear.

1769. More Abortions than tonsillectomies are being performed in America. In Nepal, Cow Dung is used for medicinal purposes. The Nepalese, believing that Dung has antiseptic properties, often pack a woman's vagina with it after she has given birth. This practice is thought to be responsible for the high incidence of tetanus among new mothers in Nepal.

1770. Forty percent of the American population has never visited a Dentist.

1771. Dentists in medieval Japan extracted teeth by pulling them out with their fingers.

1772. In ancient China, doctors were forbidden in the name of propriety to see their female patients naked. To circumvent this prohibition, doctors on house calls brought with them a small ivory carving of a woman's naked body. This carving was passed into the curtained bedchamber of the ailing woman along with instructions on how to mark the troubled organs. The statue was then handed out through the curtains and the doctor made his diagnosis on the basis of the markings.

1773. The R sign used today on pharmaceutical prescriptions was originally an astrological sign for the planet Jupiter the use of this sign originated in the Middle Ages, when doctors believed that the planets influenced health. Jupiter was thought to be the most powerful of all the heavenly bodies in curing disease.

1774. According to the Centre for Health Administration, one out of every ten Americans spends one day a year in the Hospital.

1775. The theory of Immunisation and of smallpox Immunisation in particular, was known to Chinese doctors more than seven hundred years before its discovery in 1796 by the English physician Edward Jenner. To Immunize a child against smallpox, known euphemistically as 'the budding of blossoms', a doctor took a pustule from a smallpox patient, pulverized it and blew the powder into the child's nose through a specially molded tube. It was believed that since only the scabs were used, the mild case of smallpox caused by this injection would bestow natural immunity on the child without causing him to become too sick, Another method of immunisation was to wrap a child in a robe smeared with pus taken from someone with a mild case of smallpox so that the child's skin would be permeated by the secretions. This technique was also practiced by doctors in medieval India.

1776. The Insulin used to treat diabetes in human beings is taken from pigs and sheep. The substance produced in these animals is exactly the same as that found in the human body and has precisely the same sugar stabilising effect.

1777. Taliacotius, a sixteenth-century Italian Surgeon, devised an operation for rebuilding damaged tissue in the human nose. The patient's arm was raised to the face and held there, the inner part of the arm against the open flesh of the nose, by means of a special apparatus or system of bandages. The arm was kept adhered to the nose for several weeks, at the end of which time the two were supposed to have grown together. The Surgeon then cut the joint between arm and nose, leaving enough flesh for a new nose and the apparatus was removed.

1778. A typical surgical skin graft is done with a slice of skin eight thousandths of an inch thick.

1779. Runners in ancient Greece believed that the Spleen was a hindrance to endurance and long-distance running. Consequently they had a vast pharmacopoeia, of herbal concoctions especially designed to shrink this vital organ. One popular spleen-shrinker was a beverage made from a plant of the genus Equisetum. The drink was mixed with a variety of herbs and taken for three days before a race. According to contemporary witnesses, it proved enormously helpful in promoting endurance (whether it shrank the Spleen we do not know). Hippocrates, the famous Greek physician, mentioned a certain mushroom that, when burned over the area of the spleen, melted the organ completely.

1780. Before the sixth century B.C. Chinese coins were cast in the shapes of miniature shells, spades and knives. These objects had been the principal items of barter in China prior to the minting of Coins. The first paper money to appear in North America was printed on playing cards. In 1685 the French colonial government in Canada, suffering from a lack of francs, began issuing money printed on pasteboards frorn the standard playing deck of the time. These cards were signed by the colonial governor and were circulated throughout French Canada. Though this odd form of Currency was intended to be used only until the money arrived from France, it was so popular among the colonists that it was kept in circulation for the next hundred years. It is not known whether the first printed items of all time were used as money or in games. These ancient bits of printing, paper slips produced by the Chinese sometime during the Tangdynasty (618-906), seem to have been used interchangeably as currency and as a variety of playing cards. To this day no one has been able to determine what their primary purpose really was. Paper money developed in Europe in the following manner. During the Middle Ages, it was customary for wealthy families to store their gold, jewels and coins in vaults kept in the cellars of goldsmiths' shops. The goldsmiths gave written receipts for all valuables received and these articles could be redeemed with the receipts at any time. Eventually the receipts themselves were being used as currency by those who didn't want to take the trouble to go to the vault every time they needed money and businesses throughout Europe began accepting them as readily as gold. The practice gradually spread: paper money became a common form of legal tender and its use contributed to the establishment of the banking system, which was in full swing by the sixteenth century.

1781. The Air around us is not weightless. In fact, it can be weighed almost as accurately as iron or lead. A column of Air 1 Inch Square and 600 miles high, for instance, weighs approximately 15 pounds, about twice as much as of an average newborn baby. This weight is what creates the phenomenon known as 'atmospheric pressure'.

1782. Ten of the 105 known elements had been discovered and were in use in prehistoric times: gold, silver, lead, iron, copper, zinc, tin, sulphur, carbon and mercury. The largest individual contribution to the table of Elements was that of the nineteenth century English chemist Sir Humphrey Davy, who identified boron, barium, calcium, potassium, sodium and strontium in 1807 and 1808. He also demonstrated that diamonds are composed of pure carbon and discovered the hilarious properties of nitrous oxide — 'laughing gas'.

1783. If the chemical Sodium is dropped in water and a match is taken to the mixture, it will immediately and violently ignite. If Sodium is immersed in a pot of kerosene, however, it will not burn at all.

1784. Sound travels fifteen times more swiftly through steel than through air.

1785. According to the Theory of Relativity, the mass of an object increases with its velocity. In nonscientific terms, this means that things get bigger as they move faster. The process has been demonstrated in laboratories. In several experiments, objects accelerated to 86 percent of the speed of light have doubled in weight. The theory also postulates the rather incomprehensible notion that given enough speed, an object will become as large as the universe itself.

1786. A pipe 2 feet in diametre will allow four times more fluid to pass through it than a pipe 1 foot in diametre-the volume of a pipe varies as the square of its diametre.

1787. If you punch a series of holes in a paper cup filled with Water, the Water will squirt out farthest and fastest from the lowest holes. The reason is that Water Pressure is greatest at the bottom of the cup. For the same reason, dams are made thicker at the bottom than at the top'.

1788. Experiments conducted at several college laboratories demonstrate that hard rock music played to colonies of termites cause the insects to enter a kind of frenzy and to chew through wood at twice their normal rate.

1789. The following is a standard test used by many psychiatrists to determine if a person is susceptible to Hypnosis. The patient is told to stand in the centre of a room with his/her eyes shut. The tester stands behind him and asks the patient to fall back into his arms without resistance. The tester assures the patient that he/she will not be hurt and tells him to trust the tester completely. If the patient falls back without hesitation, he/she will be easily Hypnotized. It not, he/she won't.

1790. Females learn to talk earlier, use sentences earlier and learn to read more quickly than males. Males have a greater incidence of reading disabilities, stutter more, read with less speed and accuracy and by the time they reach maturity have a smaller vocabulary than females.

1791. Based on the total number of people tested since IQ tests were devised, women have a slightly higher average IQ than men.

1792. There are bullfights in Detroit. Twelve times a year, at the Cobo Arena, some of the best Spanish and Mexican matadors are featured, as well as several American Bullfighters who have been trained in Spain. Bullfights themselves are not illegal in the United States; the matador is simply not allowed to kill the bull. In Detroit, therefore, all fights are 'exhibitions', bloodless events that demonstrate the matador's skill, not his ability to make a kill. A sport practiced in ancient China consisted of placing two angry male quails in a large glass bowl and watching as the creatures clawed each other to death. In 1822 Timothy Dwight, president of Yale College, forbade all students to play Football. Violators were to be reported the dean and were to be penalised by a fine not to exceed fifty cents. In the 1905 Football season, eighteen men were killed in college games in the United States and 159 were permanently injured. At that time, Football players wore only light equipment. Punching, linking arms, gouging and kicking were all part of the action and the entire team was allowed to line up on the scrimmage line. At least a quarter of all games, reports tell us, ended in mob brawls. In 1905 the Reverend David Buel of Georgetown University reported that one unidentified team had been taught to 'strike their opponents in certain delicate parts of the body so as to render them helpless'. The large number of deaths and injuries that year prompted President Theodore Roosevelt to establish the National Collegiate Athletic Association, which instituted regulations designed to make college Football a less lethal sport. In 1910 a Football team was penalised 15 yards for an incompleted forward pass. Before 1850, Golf balls were made of leather and were stuffed with feathers. The Stanley Cup, emblematic of ice Hockey supremacy in North America, was donated in 1893 by Canada's then governer general, Frederick Arthur, Lord Stanley of Preston. Originally awarded to honour Canada's top amateur team, it eventually became the championship trophy of the professional National Hockey League. Stanley Cup playoffs have been held continuously since 1894, although in the 1918-1919 season the finals were halted by the worldwide influenza epidemic. Oddly, Lord Stanley himself never saw a Stanley Cup game. The Pittsburgh Pirates got their name as a result of bad publicity. In 1880 the Pittsburgh team allegedly 'Pirated' an important player away from Philadelphia and did nothing to smooth over ruffled feelings. Local newspapers angrily called Pittsburg 'a bunch of Pirates'. The epithet stuck and eventually became the team's official name. The Aztec and Maya Indians of Mexico and Central America played a complicated kind of ball game not unlike lacrosse. The game, played in a large stadium and witnessed by thousands of spectators, went on for several hours. When the game was finished, the captain of the losing team was slaughtered before the onlookers, his body torn limb from limb and pieces of his heart passed among the crowd for members of the audience to nibble.

No high jumper has ever been able to stay off the ground for more than one second. In 1866 the world record for the mile Run was 4 minutes 12 3/4 seconds, set by W. G. George in London on August 23. Today that time would be considered a pretty good achievement for a high school runner.

1793. Sports fans in Brazil sometimes become so impassioned that it was necessary to build a wide moat around the playing field of Rio's 180,000 seat Maracana Stadium. The moat keeps the crowd from running onto the field, molesting the players and attacking the referees. Lenin Stadium in Moscow has enough seats to accommodate more than 103,000 people. The practice of identifying baseball players by number was begun by the Yankees in 1929. In 1931, the practice became standard throughout the American League, the National League adopted it in 1933. Basketball is the only major sport entirely of American origin. It was invented in December 1891 by James Naismith, a Canadian instructor at the YMCA Training school (later Springfield College) in Springfield, Massachusetts.

1794. A Comet's tail always points away from the sun. Until the mid sixteenth century, Comets were believed to be not astronomical phenomena, but burning vapours that had arisen from distant swamps and were propelled across the sky by fire and light. There are approximately 10,000 pieces of equipment revolving around the earth. About 3,000 of these pieces are satellites, the rest are odd bits of Debris. According to scientists, gold exists on Mars, Mercury and Venus. A space vehicle must move at a

rate of 7 miles per second to escape the earth's gravitational pull. This is equivalent to going from New York to Philadelphia in about twenty seconds. A bucket filled with earth would weigh about five times more than the same bucket filled with the substance of the sun. However, the force of gravity is so much greater on the sun that a man weighing 150 pounds on our planet would weigh 2 tons on the sun. In 1910, when it was announced that Halley's Comet would once again pass the earth, hysteria broke out in Europe, based on the belief that the arrival of this comet always heralded catastrophe.

1795. There is a sea squirt found in the seas near Japan that digests its own brain. When the sea squirt is mature, it permanently attaches itself to a rock. At this point, it does not need to move anymore and has no need for a brain. So, waste not want not, it eats it.

1796. A male gypsy moth can smell a female gypsy moth in heat up to a mile and a half away.

1797. A squirrel cannot contract or carry the rabies virus.

1798. 1 in 5,000 north Atlantic lobsters are born bright blue.

1799. The brown myotis bats when born are equivalent to a woman giving birth to a 30-pound baby.

1800. If you keep a Goldfish in the dark room, it will eventually turn white.

1801. The Frilled Neck Lizard was pictured on Australia's two-cent coin. The coins are no longer in circulation

1802. Fairy Penguins live for an average of seven years.

1803. The Emu is the world's third largest bird. The Ostrich and the Cassowary take the top positions.

1804. The nest of an Emu can be up to 1.5 metres wide!

1805. The Emu can run at speeds up to 45 km/hr!

1806. The temperature of the saltwater crocodile's egg will determine the sex of the new born crocodile.

1807. Koalas can make an extremely loud and agressive growling noise.

1808. Shark's need to swim or they will sink!

1809. A mother dingo regurgitates food for her puppies.

1810. Platypuses can consume their own body weight in food in a 24-hour period!

1811. The male platypus has venom strong enough to kill a small dog or cause excruciating pain among humans.

1812. Quokkas recycle a small amount of their body's waste products.

1813. The box jellyfish is responsible for more deaths in Australian than Snakes, Sharks and Salt Water Crocodiles. The Irukandji jellyfish is only 2.5 centimetres in diametre, but can cause death to humans within days.

1814. The venom of a stonefish can kill a human in two hours.

1815. A horse has 18 more bones than a human.

1816. An elephant's trunk is equivalent to the human nose and upper lip - yet an adult elephant can carry nearly 270 kilograms with it. It can also store about 4 litres of water in it.

1817. Batology is the taxonomic study of blackberries. Batologists classify and categorise the 1000 different species of blackberry.

1818. Nearly one million earthworms can be found in a single acre of land.

1819. Chimpanzees in the wild chew medicinal plants when they feeli ill.

1820. American ground squirrels can tell how dangerous a rattlesnake is - just from the sound of its rattle.

1821. A vampire bat's teeth are so sharp; it can bite and suck blood without its victim even noticing. The bat is the only mammal that can fly.

1822. About 5,000 species of animal live in the desert. More than half of all desert animals keep cool by living underground.

1823. Reindeer are the only living deer in which both male and female have antlers.

1824. A penguin chick recognises its mother among thousands of almost identical penguins - by her call.

1825. An ant can lift up to 50 times its own weight.

1826. If humans had the grasshopper's jumping powers, we could leap one third the length of a football pitch.

1827. Instead of teeth, snails and slugs have rows of tiny bumps on their tongues, which act like a file to break up food.

1828. Some seals can dive to depths of over 250 metres and can stay underwater for more than 30 minutes.

1829. Camels originated in North America about 40,000,000 years ago. A camel can consume about 100 litres (22 gals) of water in one sitting. The camel's eyes are almost like slits, protected with heavy eyelids and long eyelashes that interlock to keep grains of sand out.

1830. There are 6 kilograms of gold per cubic kilometre of seawater.

1831. It doesn't matter when badgers mate - the cubs are always born around February. This can happen because the female badger controls when the fertilised egg begins to develop.

1832. The smallest mammal in the world is probably the pygmy shrew. It weighs just two grams. To stay alive its heart has to beat over 1,200 times a minute and it must eat every few hours, day and night or it will starve to death.

1833. Some Arctic and Antarctic fish have evolved proteins in their blood which act as antifreeze stopping their blood from freezing solid.

1834. The sperm whale is the largest predator that has ever lived.

1835. The blue ringed octopus, found in Southeast Asia, carries such a powerful neurotoxin that just one octopus contains enough to cause paralysis and death of ten adult humans.

1836. The tongue of a blue whale is the size of an elephant. The entire whale generally weighs the same as about 30 elephants.

1837. The pirate spider invades other spiders webs by creeping so slowly that the resident spider does not realise what is going on. The pirate spider can get close enough to bite, injecting very toxic venom.

1838. Fishes cannot live in the Dead Sea because the water has too much salt in it.

1839. A parrotfish makes its own sleeping bag to sleep in. It uses mucous (like spit) to make a see-through bag all around it's body to protect it from attack by other creatures in the ocean.

1840. The swordtail is the fastest swimmer of all the fish.

1841. Most animals don't eat moss. It's hard to digest and it has little nutritional value. But reindeer fill up with lots of moss because the moss contains a special chemical that helps reindeer keep their body fluids warm. When the reindeer make their yearly journey across the icy Arctic region, the chemical keeps them from freezing-much as antifreeze keeps a car from freezing up in winter.

1842. Camels are called 'ships of the desert' because of the way they move, not because of their transport capabilities. A Dromedary camel has one hump and a Bactrian camel two humps. The humps are used as fat storage. Thus, an undernourished camel will not have a hump.

1843. The Siberian Tiger is the largest cat in the world. It weighs up to 300kg (660 lbs) and can eat 27,2 kg (60 lb) of meat at one mealtime.

1844. Did you know moths are not really attracted to light? Moths fly towards the blackest point, which is behind the light.

1845. The rhino is a primitive-looking animal. They have looked the same for thousands of years. There are two species of rhino: the white (or square-lipped rhino) and the black (or hooked-lipped rhino). The black rhino has three toes on each foot. Both the black and white rhino have two horns.

1846. The rhinoceros's horn is made of the same stuff found in our hair and fingernails, which is called keratin. It also contains something called gelatin.

1847. Ancients Greeks believed giants fighting underneath the ground caused earthquakes. The Ancient Japanese thought there was a giant spider living under the earth and each time it moved, it caused the earth to quake.

1848. There are over 900 different types of bats and they can all fly.

1849. The Vampire bat has fewer teeth than the other bats because it doesn't chew its food. It lives on the blood of mammals. Bats do not need to see when they fly, they use sound to help them figure out where they are going. Bats always turn left when exiting a cave.

1850. An elephant's brain is about four times the size of a human's brain. Among all animals ever having lived on earth, the brain of the elephant is the largest known. Baby elephants have absolutely no idea what to do with their short trunks. It takes them many months of learning by example before they can even use the trunk to squirt water into their mouths for a drink. Elephants are strict vegetarians. African elephants have much larger ears than their Asian counterparts. Both male and female African elephants grow tusks; in Asian elephants, only the male grows tusks. Elephants have 'fingers' at the bottom of the ends of their trunks. The African elephant has two finger at the end of its trunk, whereas the Asian has one. An elephant can draw up to four gallons of water into its trunk before squirting it into its mouth for a drink. The elephant also uses the trunk to spray its body with water and dirt, protecting the skin from insect bites and exposure to the sun. An elephant's teeth are used for grinding vegetation. Six large ridged molars are located in each half of the upper and lower jaws, but only used one at a time. Forming a succession at the back of the jaw, the teeth move forward and push out teeth that are worn out or broken. When the last molar moves forward, at the age of 28-30, it must last the rest of the elephant's life (up to 60 or 70 years). Otherwise, the animal can no longer chew effectively and may starve. An elephant walks on its toes. The sole of each foot is made of thick elastic pads, which flatten to form a flexible pad with each step. Nails are located on the front of the foot.

1851. The Great Pyramid is a stone computer – if you take the lengths of the sides and their heights and angles, you can calculate many different things. The pyramid will tell you how to work out the distance round the outside of a circle if you know the distance across it. The Egyptians could use the Great Pyramid to work out the distance the Earth travels round the sun and the speed of light. The pyramid is a mathematical horoscope – you can calculate the future from it. The Institute of Pyramidology in London says the pyramid has already predicted the Crucifixion of Jesus and the First World War. It has also predicted that the world will end in the year 2979 A.D. The Great Pyramid is a sign to the world how much knowledge the Egyptian priests had – and how much power. They persuaded Cheops to have it built and made him pay all the bills. Then when he died they didn't want his body inside their wonderful creation. The Great Pyramid is an observatory for watching and recording the movement of the stars. The Great Pyramid is a giant calendar. The Egyptians could use it to measure the length of a year to three decimal places. The Great Pyramid is a sundial. The shadow fell on pavements and the pavements were marked with the day of the year and the hour of the day. The Great Pyramid is a landmark. All ancient maps could use it as the starting point for drawing and measuring their charts – rather like the Greenwich Meridian is today. The Great Pyramid is a perfect store for the weights and measures of the ancient world. The government needed a master set of weights to check if traders were giving proper value when they sold goods. But weights like the deben were made of copper and lost weight after a few years' wear and tear – sometimes they were even 'fixed' by crooked shopkeepers. The centre of the pyramid is the centre of tremendous forces of nature. Strange and wonderful things can happen there . Many tourists have gone into shock or fainted when they reached the centre. A pyramid was built as the huge stone tomb of a Pharaoh. The burial chamber in the centre was filled with awesome riches for the Pharaoh to take on into the afterlife. The riches were a temptation to robbers. The pyramid builders tried to fool the thieves by making false doors, staircases and corridors. The base of the Great Pyramid of Cheops is equal to the area of seven or eight soccer fields (754 X 754 feet). The burial chamber inside the Great Pyramid is as large as a small modern house. The pyramids are close to the Nile because some of the huge stones had to be carried from the quarries by boat. The pyramids are all on the West bank of the Nile – the side on which the sun sets. This is for religious reasons. The Pharaohs were buried with religious writings to help them in the afterlife. The earliest ones were written on the walls of the burial chambers. Later, they were written on the coffins. The last were written on papyrus and rolled up and placed in the dead man's coffin. The writings described different ways to get to the afterworld and are known as the Books of the Dead. Pyramids contained everything the King would need in the afterlife including a toilet. There are over 90 pyramids in Egypt. The pyramids of Egypt are the oldest stone buildings in the world. It is forbidden to climb the pyramids today. There have been too many accidents, so now you have to have special permission.

1852. The smallest frog in the world is from Cuba and is only 1/2' long. The largest frog in the world is from West Africa (Conraua goliath) and is about 12 inches long.

1853. In 1955 Switzerland became the first country to fluoridate salt, originally at 90 ppm. The amount was later raised to 250 ppm. France became the second country to do so in 1986, quickly followed by Jamaica and Costa Rica where there is now 'universal' salt fluoridation.

1854. In order for a rocket to leave the surface of Earth, it must travel faster than 25,000 miles per hour. This is called escape velocity. If the rocket has a speed less than the escape velocity of an object, the object's gravity will pull it back down. The escape velocity of a black hole is greater then 186,000 miles per second. That means a rocket would have to travel faster than 186,000 miles per second in order to leave the black hole. The speed of light is 186,000 miles per second, so light doesn't travel fast enough to leave the black hole, hence it is black.

1855. Oysters breathe much like fish, using both gills and mantle. The mantle is lined with many small, thin-walled blood vessels, which extract oxygen from the water and expel carbon dioxide. A small, three-chambered heart, lying under the abductor muscle, pumps colourless blood, with its supply of oxygen, to all parts of the body. At the same time a pair of kidneys located on the underside of the muscle purify the blood of any waste products it has collected.

1856. Butterflies evolved from moths sometime between 245 million years ago (when the oldest fossil moths were preserved in Triassic rocks) and 110 million years ago (when the oldest butterfly parts were preserved in Cretaceous amber). By 40 million years ago the major family groups of butterflies are found in Eocene rocks.

1857. Tigers are the largest living cat species in the world. Siberian tigers are generally the heaviest, with males often weighing more than 600 pounds. Sumatran tigers are the lightest, with males weighing only about 250 pounds. The average male Bengal tiger is nine feet to nine and one-half feet long. Females typically grow to eight and one-half feet in length. Males weigh 400 to 500 pounds and females average 300 to 400 pounds. Tigers that live in the Northern regions of India grow slightly larger than in Southern regions. They also are lighter in colour.

1858. An eagle can see a rabbit about 1 mile or 1760 yards away. Now the average person needs to be about 550 yards away to see the same rabbit. That's why when someone says 'you must have eagle eyes', they mean you can see really far.

1859. People who are colour blind just can't see things in as many colours as people who have normal vision and they cannot see certain colours like red, green and some blues. Not all colour-blind people see colours the same way, either. That's why when someone says 'you must be colour blind', they mean you didn't pick out your colours too well.

1860. There is no way of telling male oysters from females by examining their shells. While oysters have separate sexes, they may change sex one or more times during their life span. The gonads, organs responsible for producing both eggs and sperm, surround the digestive organs and are made up of sex cells, branching tubules and connective tissue.

1861. People who have nearsighted vision can see things that are near very well, but they have trouble seeing things far away clearly. The scientific name for nearsightedness is myopia. People who have farsighted vision can see things far away clearly but have trouble seeing things close up. The scientific name for farsightedness is called hyperopia. Now that's a mouthful!

1862. If you thought, 'Lightning!' then hats off to you. But I had a more illuminating answer in mind. The air around a lightning bolt is superheated to about five times the temperature of the Sun. This sudden heating causes the air to expand faster than the speed of sound, which compresses the air and forms a shock wave; we hear it as thunder.

1863. In a volcanic eruption, the violent separation of gas from lava produces a 'frothy' rock called pumice, loaded with gas bubbles. Some of it can float, geologists say. I've never seen this happen and I'm thankful for that.

1864. Yes, but observing the process is less interesting than watching paint dry. Rocks called iron-manganese crusts grow on mountains under the sea. The crusts precipitate material slowly from seawater, growing about 1 millimetre every million years. Your fingernails grow about the same amount every two weeks.

1865. USGS says at least 1,000 million grams or roughly 1,000 tons of material enters the atmosphere every year and makes its way to Earth's surface. One group of scientists claims microbes rain down from space, too and that extraterrestrial organisms are responsible for flu epidemics. There's been no proof of this and I'm not holding my breath.

1866. A 1999 study showed that African dust finds its way to Florida and can help push parts of the state over the prescribed air quality limit for particulate matter set by the U.S. Environmental Protection Agency. The dust is kicked up by high winds in North Africa and carried as high as 20,000 feet (6,100 metres), where it's caught up in the trade winds and carried across the sea. Dust from China makes its way to North America, too.

1867. The San Andreas Fault, which runs north south, is slipping at a rate of about 2 inches (5 centimetres) per year, causing Los Angeles to move towards San Francisco. Scientists forecast LA will be a suburb of the City by the Bay in about 15 million years.

1868. Because the planet rotates and is more flexible than you might imagine, it bulges at the midsection, creating a sort of pumpkin shape. The bulge was lessening for centuries but now, suddenly, it is growing, a recent study showed. Accelerated melting of Earth's glaciers is taking the blame for the gain in equatorial girth.

1869. The gravity on Mars is 38 percent of that found on Earth at sea level. So a 100-pound person on Earth would weigh 38 pounds on Mars. Based on NASA's present plans, it'll be decades before this assumption can be observationally proved, however. The red planet takes 687 Earth-days to go around the Sun — compared to 365 days for Earth. Taking into account Mars' different rotational time calendars on Mars would be about 670 days long with some leap days needed to keep things square. If you find one, please mail it to me. A Martian can sleep (or work) and extra half-hour every day compared to you. Mars days are 24 hours and 37 minutes long, compared to 23 hours, 56 minutes on Earth. A day on any planet in our solar system is determined by how long it takes the world to spin once on its axis, making the Sun appear to rise in the morning and sending it down in the evening.

1870. The Mauna Loa volcano in Hawaii the largest volcano on Earth. It rises more than 50,000 feet (9.5 miles or 15.2 kilometres) above its base, which sits under the surface of the sea. But that's all volcanic chump change. Olympus Mons on Mars rises 16 miles (26 kilometres) into the Martian sky. Its base would almost cover the entire state of Arizona. The world□fs deadliest recorded earthquake occurred in 1557 in central China. It struck a region where most people lived in caves carved from soft rock. The dwellings collapsed, killing an estimated 830,000 people. In 1976 another deadly temblor struck Tangshan, China. More than 250,000 people were killed. A 1960 Chilean earthquake, which occurred off the coast, had a magnitude of 9.6 and broke a fault more than 1,000 miles (1,600 kilometres) long. An earthquake like that under a major city would challenge the best construction techniques. The 1994 Northridge earthquake had a magnitude of 6.7 was responsible for approximately 60 deaths, 9,000 injuries and more than $40 billion in damage. The Kobe earthquake of 1995 was magnitude 6.8 and killed 5,530 people. There were some 37,000 injuries and more than $100 billion in economic loss.

1871. A place called Arica, in Chile, gets just 0.03 inches (0.76 millimetres) of rain per year. At that rate, it would take a century to fill a coffee cup. It is the driest place on Earth.

1872. Intense rainfall over a short period of time can trigger shallow, fast-moving mud and debris flows. Slow, steady rainfall over a long period of time may trigger deeper, slow-moving landslides. Different materials behave differently, too. Every year as much as $2 billion in landslide damage occurs in the United States. In a record-breaking storm in the San Francisco area in January 1982, some 18,000 debris flows were triggered during a single night! Property damage was over $66 million and 25 people died.

1873. The Grand Canyon is billed as the world's largest canyon system. Its main branch is 277 miles (446 kilometres) long. But the Valles Marineris on Mars extends for about 3,000 miles (4,800 kilometres). If added it to a U.S. map, it would stretch from New York City to Los Angeles. In places this vast scar on the Martian surface is 5 miles (8 kilometres) deep.

1874. Earth's diametre at the equator is 7,926 miles (12,756 kilometres). Venus is 7,521 miles (12,104 kilometres) wide. Mercury and Mars, the other two inner rocky planets, are much smaller. Pluto is rocky, too, but it's comparatively tiny.

1875. About 97 percent oceans make up about two-thirds of earth's surface, which means that when the next asteroid hits the planet, odds are good it will splash down. Nearly 70 percent of the Earth's fresh-water supply is locked up in the icecaps of Antarctica and Greenland. The remaining fresh-water supply exists in the atmosphere, streams, lakes or groundwater and accounts for a mere 1 percent of the Earth's total. The Pacific Ocean covers 64 million square miles (165 million square kilometres). It is more than two times the size of the Atlantic. It has an average depth of 2.4 miles (3.9 kilometres).

1876. Earth is more active, in terms of both geology and weather. Much of our planet's geologic history was long ago folded back inside. Some of that is regurgitated by volcanoes, but the results are pretty hard to study. Even more recent events evident on the surface — craters that can by millions of years old — get overgrown by vegetation, weathered by wind and rain and modified by earthquakes and landslides. The Moon, meanwhile, is geologically quiet and has almost no weather; its craters tell a billions-year-long tale of catastrophic collisions. Interestingly, some of the oldest Earth rocks might be awaiting discovery on the Moon, having been blasted there billions of years ago by the very asteroid impacts that rattle both worlds.

The majority occur along boundaries of the dozen or so major plates that more or less float on the surface of Earth. One of the most active plate boundaries where earthquakes and eruptions are frequent, for example, is around the massive Pacific Plate commonly referred to as the Pacific Ring of Fire. It fuels shaking and baking from Japan to Alaska to South America.

1877. The temperature of earth increases about 36 degrees Fahrenheit (20 degrees Celsius) for every kilometre (about 0.62 miles) you go down. Near the centre, its thought to be at least 7,000 degrees Fahrenheit (3,870 Celsius).

1878. The top three countries are Indonesia, Japan and the United States in descending order of activity.

1879. Groundwater comprises a 30 times greater volume than all freshwater lakes and more than 3,000 times what's in the world's streams and rivers at any given time. Groundwater is housed in natural underground aquifers, in which the water typically runs around and through the stone and other material.

1880. Scientists estimate that more than three-quarters of Earth'fs surface is of volcanic origin— that is, rocks either erupted by volcanoes or molten rock that cooled below ground and has subsequently been exposed at the surface. Most of Earth's volcanic rocks are found on the sea floor.

1881. If the earthquake originates under the ocean, yes. Near the earthquake's epicentre, the sea floor rises and falls, pushing all the water above it up and down. This motion produces a wave that travels outward in all directions. A tsunami can be massive but remain relatively low in height in deep water. Upon nearing the shore, it is forced up and can reach the height of tall buildings. One in 1964 was triggered in Alaska and swamped the small northern California town of Crescent City, moving train cars several blocks and killing several people there. Asteroids can cause tsunami, too.

1882. No, contrary to many artistic images of tsunamis, most do not result in giant breaking waves. Rather, most tsunamis come onshore more like very strong and fast tides. The water can rise higher than anyone along a given shore area has ever seen.

1883. The greatest known depth is 36,198 feet (6.9 miles or 11 kilometres) at the Mariana Trench, in the Pacific Ocean well south of Japan near the Mariana Islands.

1884. The fastest 'regular' wind that's widely agreed upon was 231 mph (372 kph), recorded at Mount Washington, New Hampshire, on April 12, 1934. But during a May 1999 tornado in Oklahoma, researchers clocked the wind at 318 mph (513 kph). For comparison, Neptune's winds can rage to 900 mph (1,448 kph).

1885. More than two million cubic miles of fresh water is stored in the planet, nearly half of it within a half-mile of the surface. Mars, too, appears to have a lot of water near its surface, but what's been detected so far is locked up as ice; nobody has estimated how much might be there.

1886. Our planet is more than 4.5 billion years old, just a shade younger than the Sun. Recent evidence actually shows that Earth was formed much earlier than previously believed, just 10 million years after the birth of the Sun, a stellar event typically put at 4.6 billion years ago.

1887. The Sahara Desert in northern Africa is more than 23 times the size of southern California's Mojave Desert.

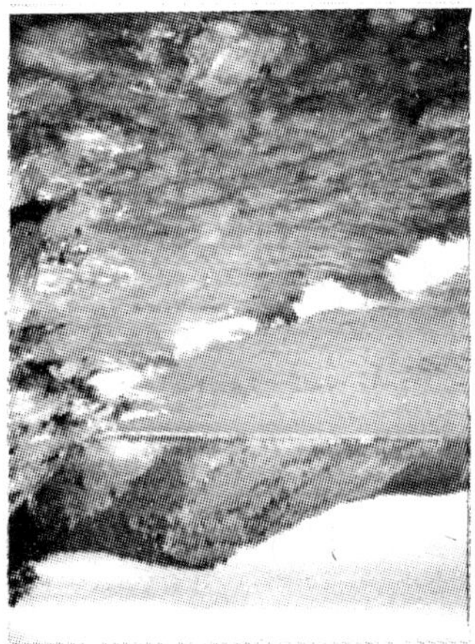

1888. Mars has two satellites, Phobos and Deimos. The earth has only one natural satellite, the Moon. The outer planets have lots of Moon, most of them found fairly recently and leading to the possibility that scientists might one day need to redefine what it means to be a moon.

1889. Lake Baikal in the south central part of Siberia is 5,712 feet (1.7 kilometres) deep. It's about 20 million years old and contains 20 percent of earth's fresh liquid water.

1890. Greenland covers 840,000 square miles (2,176,000 square kilometres). Continents are typically defined as landmasses made of low-density rock that essentially floats on the molten material below. Greenland fits this description, but it's only about one-third the size of Australia. Some scientists call Greenland an island, others say it's a continent.

1891. The most prominent topographic feature on earth is the immense volcanic mountain chain that encircles the planet beneath the sea — the chain is more than 30,000 miles (48,000 kilometres) long and rises an average of 18,000 feet (5.5 kilometres) above the seafloor. It is called the mid-ocean ridge and is where earth's plates spread apart as new crust bubbles up — volcanic activity. There are more volcanoes here than on land. The spreading, however, leads to scrunching when these plates slam into the continents. As a result more volcanoes and earthquakes take place in places like California and Japan.

1892. Like all living creatures, rivers have a life span. They are born, grow in size and they age. They can even die during the span of geological time.

1893. Speculation has existed for decades that ancient asteroid impacts might create hot spots of volcanic activity, which could give rise to mountains that poke up through seas that didn't used to be there. There's no firm answer to this question, but a recent computer model suggested Hawaii might have been formed in this manner.

1894. Louisiana loses about 30 square miles (78 square kilometres) of land each year to coastal erosion, hurricanes, other natural and human causes and a thing called subsidence, which means sinking. Much of New Orleans actually sits 11 feet (3.4 metres) below sea level. Parts of the French quarter have sunk 2 feet in the past six decades. The city is protected by dikes, but all experts agree that storm tides from a direct hit by a major hurricane would breach the system and swamp much of the city.

1895. The Antarctic Ice Sheet holds nearly 90 percent of the world's ice and 70 percent of its fresh water. If the entire ice sheet were to melt, sea level would rise by nearly 220 feet or the height of a 20-story building. Scientists know there's a melting trend underway.

The United Nations has said that in a worst-case scenario — depending on how much global air temperatures increase — seas could jump 3 feet (1 metre) by 2100.

1896. Talc is the softest of minerals. It is commonly used to make talcum powder.

1897. Mineral elements taken from earth provide the colours. Strontium yields deep reds, copper produces blue, sodium yields yellow and iron filings and charcoal pieces produce gold sparks. Bright flashes and loud bangs come from aluminum powder.

1898. Mars can whip up hurricane-like storms four times bigger than Texas. Dust storms on the red planet can obscure the entire globe! Jupiter has a hurricane twice the size our entire planet and it lasted for at least three centuries (another storm on Jupiter is even bigger). Venus is a living hell and Pluto is routinely more frigid than the coldest place on Earth (though may change one day and Pluto may in fact become the last oasis for life).

1899. In Burntcoat Head, Minas Basin, part of the Bay of Fundy in Nova Scotia, tides can range 38.4 feet (11.7 metres). The bay is funnel shaped — its bottom slopes upward continuously from the ocean inlet. The result is an extreme 'tidal bore', a wave-like phenomenon at the leading edge of the changing tide. Bores in Fundy can travel up feeder rivers at 8 mph (13 kph) and be more than 3 feet (1 metre) tall.

1900. Mt. Cotopaxi in Ecuador supports the only glacier on the equator.

1901. The Mid-Atlantic Ridge, which splits nearly the entire Atlantic Ocean north to south. Iceland is one place where this submarine mountain chain rises above the sea surface.

1902. The creosote bush, which grows in the Mojave, Sonoran and Chihuahuan deserts, has been shown by radiocarbon dating to have lived since the birth of Christ. Some of these plants may endure 10,000 years, scientists say. If only they could talk.

1903. Saturn has the most obvious rings. But Jupiter and Neptune both have subtle ring systems. And even Earth may once have been a ringed planet.

1904. Antarctica is the highest, driest and coldest continent on earth.

1905. Since the ocean floor is being continually regenerated as the continental plates move across the earth's surface, the oldest rocks on the ocean floor are less than 300 million years. In contrast, the oldest continental rocks are 4.5 billion years old.

1906. During the 9-hour period of most vigorous activity on May 18, 1980, Mount St. Helens dumped more than 540 million tons of ash over an area of more than 22,000 square miles (56,980 square kilometres). It was the most destructive volcanic eruption known to occur in the United States. Fifty-seven people were killed by the eruption including USGS scientist Dr. David Johnston, who was at a monitoring site 5 miles (8 kilometres) from the volcano. An estimated $1 billion damage was caused by the eruption, through mudflows and landslides as well as what fell from the sky.

1907. Astronomers know that over the next few billion years, the Sun will swell so large as to envelop Earth. If we're still here, we'll probably fry and the planet will be vapourised. There's a chance, however that the changing mass of the sun will cause earth to move into a more distant and pleasant orbit. One mathematical calculation shows it would be theoretically possible for humans to engineer such a move before it's too late.

1908. Ailurophilia is the 'love of cats'. The nose pad of a cat is ridged in a pattern that is unique, just like the fingerprint of a human. There are more than 500 million domestic cats in the world 50 different breeds recognised by one of the many cat-registering associations. The American cat population reached nearly 68 million in 1996. American Demographics magazine estimates that's about 200 million kitty yawns per hour and a whopping 425 million catnaps each day!

1909. A cat's heart beats twice as fast as a human heart, at 110 to 140 beats per minute. 25% of cat owners blow-dry their cats hair after a bath. Calico cats are almost always female. If your cat is near you and her tail is quivering, this is the greatest expression of love your cat can give you. If her tail starts thrashing, her mood has changed — Time to distance yourself from her. Cats wag their tails when it is in a stage of conflict. The cat wants to do two things at once, but each impulse blocks the other. For example: If your cat is in the doorway wanting to go outside and you open the door to find it raining, the cat's tail will wag because of internal conflict. The cat wants to go outside, but doesn't want to go into the rain. Once the cat makes a decision and either returns to the house or leaves into the rain, the tail will immediately stop wagging. Don't pick a kitten or a cat up by the scruff of its neck; only mother cats can do this safely and only with their kittens. Cats knead with their paws when they're happy. Your cat loves you and can 'read' your moods. If you're sad or under stress, you may also notice a difference in your cat's behaviour. The domestic cat is the only cat species able to hold its tail vertically while walking. All wild cats hold their tails horizontally or tucked between their legs while walking. An average cat has 1-8 kittens per litter and 2-3 litters per year. During her productive life, one female cat could have more than 100 kittens. Cats have 290 bones in their bodies and 517 muscles. A cat has five more vertebrae in her spinal column than her human does. There are three body types for a cat. Cobby type is a compact body, deep chest, short legs and broad head. The eyes are large and round. Muscular type is a sturdy body and round, full-cheeked head. Foreign type is a slender body, with long legs and a long tail. The head is wedge-shaped, with tall ears and slanting eyes. Sir Isaac Newton, discoverer of the principles of gravity, also invented the cat door. A cat will almost never 'meow' at another cat. If your cat is 3, your cat is 21 in human years. If your cat is 8, your cat is 40 in human years. If your cat is 14, your cat is 70 in human years. The average age for an indoor cat is 15 years, while the average age for an outdoor cat is only 3 to 5 years. The oldest cat on record was Puss, from England, who died in 1939 just one day after her 36th birthday. The weirdest cat on record was a female called Mincho who went up a tree in Argentina and didn't come down again until she died six years later. She managed to have three litters with equally ambitious dads. A cat's normal body temperature is 101.5 F degrees. This is slightly warmer than humans. People who own pets live longer, have less stress and have fewer heart attacks. Cats love to chew on grass, catnip, parsley or sage. There are two species of wild cats in Africa and Europe that still hunt. These two species both resemble the domestic tabbies. The behaviours shown by most house cats have a parallel in the wild. A cat will kill it's prey based on movement, but may not necessarily recognise that prey as food. Realising that prey is food is a learned behaviour. The greatest number of mice killed by one cat is 28,899! Towser, a tortoise-shell tabby in charge of rodent control in Scotland, killed 28,899 mice in her 21 years. This is about four mice per day, every day, for 21years. Towser died in 1987. The first cat show was held in 1895 at Madison Square Garden in New York City, New York. A falling cat will always right itself in a precise order. First the head will rotate, then the spine will twist and the rear legs will align, then the cat will arch its back to lessen the impact of the landing. 'Sociable' cats will follow you from room to room to monitor your activities throughout the day. The Giraffe, Camel and Cat are the only animals that walk by moving both their left feet, then both their right feet, when walking. This method of walking ensures speed, agility and silence. It is believed that a white cat sitting on your doorstep just before your wedding is a sign of lasting happiness. White cats are a symbol of good luck in America, while black cats are a sign of bad luck. Cats are partially colour blind. They have the equivalency of human red/green colour blindness. Cats don't see 'detail' very well. To them, their person may appear hazy when standing in front of them. Cats need 1/6th the amount of light that humans do to see. Their night vision is amasing! Cats can see up to 120 feet away. Their peripheral vision is about 285 degrees. Cats eyes come in three shapes: round, slanted and almond. The colour of a kitten's eyes will change, as it grows older. At birth, kittens can't see or hear. Cats open their eyes after five days and begin to develop their eyesight and hearing at approximately 2 weeks. They begin to walk at 20 days. Kittens begin dreaming at just over one week old. A cat's ear pivots 180 degrees. They have 30 muscles in each ear and use twelve or more muscles to control their ear movement. Cats rub up against other cats and people, in an attempt to 'mark' them with their scent glands. They most often use the scent glands between their eye and ear (near the temple area) or their scent glands near the base of their tail. Most cats prefer their food at room temperature and will boldly refuse any food that is too cold or too hot.

Many experts report that cats will purr when feeling any intense emotion (pleasure or pain). Give your cat fresh water at least once a day. If your cat refuses your tap water, it may be sensing (with it's superior sense of smell) the chlorine or other minerals in your water. Many finicky felines demand bottled water, just like their human counterparts. Don't put your cat on a vegetarian diet. Cats need meat to survive. Never routinely feed your cat dog food. Cats need five times more meat protein than dogs do and more taurine, not found in dog food.

1910. 'Pair bonds' can develop between two cats who live together or between a cat and a person. A cat that bites you after you have rubbed his stomach is probably biting out of pleasure, not anger. An adult cat has 32 teeth. Never leave your cat in a vehicle alone. On summer days, temperatures in an automobile can reach 160 degrees in just minutes. It is said cats use the earth's gravity to determine 'their place' in the world and to develop the ability to return there when necessary. According to myth, a cat sleeping with all four paws tucked under means cold weather is coming. He brew folklore believes that cats came about because Noah was afraid that rats might eat all the food on the ark. He prayed to God for help. God responded by making the lion sneeze a giant sneeze — and out came a little cat! Stings to the mouth can be very dangerous to cats. If your cat is stung or ever experiences any type of sting to the mouth, take her to the vet immediately. As her mouth swells from the sting, she may be unable to breath. Stings require urgent medical care. A cat cannot see directly under its nose. This is why the cat cannot seem to find tidbits on the floor. You can tell a cat's mood by looking into its eyes. A frightened or excited cat will have large, round pupils. An angry cat will have narrow pupils. The pupil size is related as much to the cat's emotions as to the degree of light.

1911. Abraham Lincoln loved cats. He had four of them while he lived in the White House. Julius Caesar, Henri II, Charles XI and Napoleon were all afraid of cats. Cats have an average of 24 whiskers, arranged in four horizontal rows on each side. Statistics indicate that animal lovers in recent years have shown a preference for cats over dogs! Cats can be taught to walk on a leash, but a lot of time and patience is required to teach them. The younger the cat is, the easier it will be for them to learn.

1912. Squirrels belong to the order 'Rodentia', with 1650 species; it is the largest group of living mammals. It also comprises forty percent of all present day mammal species. There are over 365 species of squirrels in seven families. They include the tree squirrel, ground squirrel and flying squirrel. Plus many squirrel-like mammals such as the gopher, ground hog and prairie dog. Squirrels are the most active in late winter, when the mating season begins. The males will chase females, as well as, chase off other suitors. This ritual of chasing, occurs through the trees at top speed. While they perform some of the most breathtaking acrobatics imaginable. The period of gestation varies from 33 days in the smaller species of pine squirrels, up to 60 days for the larger species such as the common gray and fox squirrels. Squirrels are usually born in the early spring. The average litter consists of four. This varies with climate and location. A second litter can occur in mid summer, if there is an adequate food supply.

1913. A female squirrel will choose the strongest male during mating season, but is unlikely to breed with that male again. This is natural way of reducing inbreeding and to preserve the species. A baby squirrel weighs approximately one ounce at birth and is about one inch long. They do not have hair or teeth and are virtually blind for the first six to eight weeks. Gray squirrels come in many colours. Shades of gray are the most common followed by shades of brown. There are also pure white and pure black squirrels, but both are variations of the gray squirrel. The common Red squirrel can have an all black coat. While the Kaibab squirrel has a black body with a white tail. Both are found in coniferous forests. In the summer squirrels are most active two to three hours after sunrise, then they'll rest in the afternoon. Resuming activity again two hours before sunset. The squirrel will retire to its nest well before dark and will rarely leave the nest in the dark. In the winter, the squirrel will complete its activities between dawn and mid- day and will remain in or around the nest until the next day.

1914. During winter storms or severe cold, the squirrel may not leave the nest for days. But, the tree squirrel does not hibernate! An adult squirrel normally lives alone. But will, in severe cold, share its nest with other squirrels to conserve body heat. Once the temperature rises, the guests will be on their way. Squirrels eyes are located high and on each side of their head. This allows them a wide field of vision, without turning their head. The gray squirrels diet consists of nuts, seeds and fruit. It will eat bird eggs, bugs and even an animal carcass if there is no other food source available. The gray squirrel requires some salt in its diet and may find this salt in the soil along roads where snow and ice may have been. Squirrels chew on tree branches to sharpen and clean their teeth. That's why you may see many small branches on the ground around large trees. They will also chew on power lines for the same reason; this has caused many major power outages throughout the country. A squirrel's brain is about the size of a walnut. The average adult squirrel needs to eat about a pound of food a week to maintain an active life. Squirrels communicate through a series of chirps. The frequency and the duration of the notes communicate everything from laughter to alarm.

Their frequency range is normally between .01 KHz. and 10 KHz. (kilohertz). These sounds when used in conjunction with tail gestures form the basis for squirrel communication. If a squirrel has taken up residence in your attic or crawl space, the only practical way to remove them is by trapping. A squirrel will break the shell of a nut with its teeth, then clean the nut by licking it or rubbing on its face before it is buried. This action applies a scent to the nut, which helps the squirrel find it later, even under a foot of snow. The sweat glands of a tree squirrel are located on their feet, between the foot pads and on their paws between the toes. When hot or excited a squirrel will leave wet tracks on a dry surface. This scent is also used to mark the trees in their territory. If a squirrel's nest becomes infested with fleas or other parasites, it will move to or build a new nest. This is why there may be more nests then squirrels in a given area. The gray squirrel has been known to build a nest in many unusual places, in an attic or a crawl space seems to be the most common. Squirrels have also built nests in automobiles, chimney's, barbecue grills and under porches. When a squirrel senses danger, its first instinct is to stand motionless. If on the ground it will race to the closest tree or other climbable object to escape. If it is in a tree, it will circle the trunk with its body pressed tightly to the bark. The squirrel's erratic path while crossing a street is an attempt to confuse the oncoming vehicle thereby causing it to change direction. This is obliviously the squirrels biggest and often last mistake. The male tree squirrel takes twice as long, as the female, to groom itself. They are the cleanest animals in the rodent family. A squirrel□fs teeth grow continuously. Their incisor's will grow six inches per year, but stay short due to the constant wear they receive. The most common type of squirrel bite is a result of feeding a squirrel by hand. Never hold the food between your fingers; chances are very good you will be bitten. A squirrel's eyes are always looking for predators and they rarely focus on what they are eating.

1915. A chicken will lay bigger and stronger eggs if you change the lighting in such a way as to make them think a day is 28 hours long! The chicken can travel up to 9 miles per hour. There are seven distinctive types of combs on chickens: rose, strawberry, single, cushion, buttercup, pea and V-shaped. Unrelated to the chick, the male cock-of-the-rock bird earned the name 'cock' because of its rooster-like appearance and combative behavior. The female of the species influenced the word 'rock' being added to the name because of her habit of nesting and rearing the young in sheltered rock niches. There are four places in the United State with the word 'chicken' in their name. Chicken, Alaska; Chicken Bristle; in Illinois and Kentucky; and Chicken Town, Pennsylvania. The largest chicken egg on record was nearly 12 oz., measuring 12 1/4' around. The greatest number of yolks in one chicken egg is nine. The record for laying the most eggs: seven in one day. There are more chickens in the world than any other domesticated bird. More than one chicken for every human on the face of this earth. The longest distance flown by any chicken is 301 1/2 feet. Some breeds of chickens can lay coloured eggs. The Ameraucana and Araucana can lay eggs coloured in shades of green or blue, depending on the breed and it's ancestry. In 1994, 73,866 million eggs were produced in the U.S. proving once again the U.S. has the best darn chickens in the world. China not only has the most people in the world, but also has the most Horses with 10,000,000 and chickens with over 3,000,000,000 of them. Chickens and turkeys are known to cross-breed, these breeds are known as 'Turkins'. The term 'Chicken Pox' didn't come from people believing that they came from chickens; it came from the Old English term 'gican pox' - which means the itching pox. Alektorophobia is the Fear of chickens. There are approximately 450 million chickens in the United States. Chickens make sounds with actual meaning. They give different alarm calls when threatened by different predators. A rooster will attack anything that he thinks will harm the hens (that includes humans). Their spurs (located at the back of their leg) can cause a very painful puncture wound. If a rooster is not present in a flock of hens, a hen will often take the role, stop laying and begin to crow. In Gainesville, Georgia - the chicken capital of the world - it is illegal to eat chicken with a fork! McDonald's in India doesn't serve beef — only chicken, mutton and fish. The closest living relative of the t-rex is the chicken. The waste produced by one chicken in its lifetime can supply enough electricity to run a 100-

watt bulb for five hours. The longest recorded flight of a chicken is thirteen seconds.

1916. The annual Leonid meteor shower has long been a favourite of serious skywatchers. Last year, when it produced a stupendous storm of shooting stars, it became the doorstep-astronomy darling of the masses. Since the Moon ambles through the same region of space as planet Earth, it too is showered by small particles every November. However, there is a difference: the moon has no atmosphere to gobble up the grains. So the tiny bits of comet debris slam into the surface and explode.

1917. Seismic recorders left on the moon in the Apollo era recorded these Leonid strikes in the 1970s and scientists first confirmed they occurred with visual observations during the 1999 Leonid meteor shower. Last year, three separate skywatchers saw one of these lunar Leonids, using telescopes and looking for such events. They observed a brief flash of light equal in brightness to a dim star that would be visible to the naked eye under reasonably dark skies. Leonids travel so fast relative to the Earth and Moon – more than 160,000 mph (72 kilometres per second) – that the impact per unit of mass is 10,000 times greater than dynamite. Moon dust for a few yards around the impact area is vaporised. Leonids donot hit the ground. The heat created by a meteor (or meteoroid, if you prefer) vaporises most of them high in the air. Even larger space rocks, up to basketball size, typically burn up and donot survive to the ground, though a handful – those made of dense material – do. However, comet material – the stuff of the Leonids – is 'fluffy', astronomers say. It fragments and disintegrates easily. Leonids are much faster than your average shooting star (or meteor, if you prefer) because they slam into Earth's atmosphere head-on in relation to the planet's movement. A Leonid doesn't stand a chance of reaching the surface, no matter what you call it. The myth that meteors shine because they rub against air molecules can be found in many news stories and reference articles about the Leonids and meteors in general. In fact, a meteor moves so fast that the air in front of it is compressed and heated by a phenomenon called ram pressure. It is the same thing that warms a hand-held pump when you work it to fill a bike tire. The heated air, in turn, scorches the meteor. Temperatures can exceed 3,000 degrees Fahrenheit (1,650 Celsius). When a comet takes 33 years to go around the Sun (compared to one year for Earth), it goes way out there and tends to get lost. Comet Tempel-Tuttle, responsible for the Leonids, gets lost a lot. It also gets found now and then. Tempel-Tuttle was 'discovered' by William Tempel in late 1865 and independently by Horace Tuttle in early 1866. Astronomers then figured out it had been observed in 1366 and 1699, too. An orbit was calculated and they determined that the comet was connected to the annual Leonid meteor shower. Nobody saw Tempel-Tuttle again until 1965, however. Then on March 4, 1997, armed with great orbital data, Karen Meech, Olivier Hainaut and James Bauer at the University of Hawaii 'recovered' the comet yet again. Tempel-Tuttle will next return to the inner solar system in the year

1918. The Leonids are bits of comet debris, boiled off comet Tempel-Tuttle every 33 years when it rounds the Sun. Scientists think comets formed along with the solar system's generation, some 4.6 billion years ago, when the Sun condensed out of a cloud of hydrogen, helium and some dust. Tempel-Tuttle built itself out of some leftovers and has been looping around the Sun ever since, presumably and its heart is pristine. Until corrupted on each pass by solar radiation that boils some of the comet into space. The streaks of light you will see as these meteoroids strike the atmosphere probably represent the best glimpse you will ever have at the brimstone that ruled the solar system in the early days, before the planets had swept most of the leftovers up. Back then, stuff small and large hit Earth all the time. Comets like Tempel-Tuttle do strike Earth now and then and always will. Meanwhile, the ephemeral Leonids (or any meteors) are prized targets of scientific study and scientists have used airplanes to examine a few at pretty close range in recent years. What did they find? Nothing less than the seeds of life, chemical precursors to biological activity that might long ago have survived inside a comet during a plunge into Earth's initially barren womb.

1919. Antarctica is actually a desert, receiving about the same precipitation (less than 2 inches a year), as the Sahara Desert. Dogs have been banned from Antarctica to protect the seal population. If Antarctica were to melt, the sea level would rise over 200 feet. The coasts of Antarctica are some of the windiest places in the world, with gusts reaching nearly 200 miles per hour. Antarctica represents about 9 percent of Earth's continental crust and has been in a near-polar position for more than 100 million years. The Adelie penguin was named after Jules-Sebastien-Cesar Dumont d'Urville's wife. D'Urville was the first man to set foot in Antarctica. The temperature in Antarctica once dropped 65°< F in 12 minutes. Because of the extremely cold temperatures and low absolute humidity, dry skin and cracked lips are continual problems in Antarctica. Visitors must drink frequently to replace the water they exhale with every breath. The Land of the Midnight Sun exists in the south, too: during the summer, the interior of Antarctica enjoys almost continuous daylight. As sea ice gets older, it becomes considerably stronger. In first-year sea ice, most of the salts remain in tiny pockets that prevent a more rigid crystalline ice structure from forming. As the ice ages, the salts slowly leach out, leaving a much stronger crystal. Antarctica is the size of the United States Of America and Mexico combined. Through December to March there is 24 hours of daylight. June to September means 24 hours of darkness.

1920. Cinnamon was the attar used by Queen of Sheba to captivate King Solomon. Because of the shape, cloves are considered an aphrodisiac for males, especially in Asia. Indonesian parents plant a clove tree when they bear a son, so both will prosper as they grow up together. A cousin of the gladiola, the ginger's pure white blossoms are thought to be a love potion because a woman wearing the aromatic bloom is so alluring. Egyptian traders originally brought it to Rome as an aphrodisiac. Samson courted Delilah with fragrant almond branches. Ancient Persians perfumed almonds in jars with flower petals before using them in desserts. Hindu males say Basil is an aphrodisiac because it resembles the female organ. In mythology, the dainty nymph Mente was turned into greenery by her envi-

ous rival, Persephone, wife of Pluto. Pluto found Mente irresistible, particularly her aroma. Hence, mint was thought to be an aphrodisiac. Contrary to popular belief, the tomato received this appellation not because it was originally considered an aphrodisiac, but because of a hearing problem. The Spanish brought the tomato back from the New World and called it 'manzana' or apple because that is what they thought it was. Early tomatoes were yellow, so Italians called them pomo d'or - apple of gold. Around that time, tomatoes, like eggplant, were thought by some to be poisonous because they happen to be botanical members of the nightshade family, which includes some toxic relatives. So, to disassociate the tomato from its poisonous reputation, the Italians changed the name to pomo d'Moro (apple of the Moors, of the Spanish). Later, a Frenchman touring Italy asked for the name of this unusual ingredient and misunderstood it to be pomme d'amour - love apple. The misnomer rapidly spread throughout Europe and became synonymous with the juicy red fruit ever since.

1921. The largest bone is the pelvis or hipbone. In fact, it is made of six bones joined firmly together. The longest bone is the 'femur', in the thigh. It makes up almost one quarter of the body's total height. The smallest bone is the 'stirrup', deep in the ear. It is hardly larger than a grain of rice. The ears and nose do not have bones inside them. Their inner supports are cartilage or 'gristle', which is lighter and more flexible than bone. This is why the nose and ears can be bent. After death, cartilage rots faster than bone. This is why the skulls of skeletons have no nose or ears.

1922. A dog's heartbeats 70 to 120 times a minute; a human heart beats 70 to 80 times a minute. The largest breed of dog is the Irish wolfhound. The Chihuahua is the smallest, while the St. Bernard is the heaviest. Dogs and men are the only animals with prostate glands. There are about 700 types of pure breed dogs. Dachshunds were bred to fight badgers in their dens. The most intelligent dogs are said to be Border Collies, Poodles and Golden Retrievers. A Bloodhound can identify several smells simultaneously. Dalmatian puppies are usually pure white when born. The smallest dog in history was a tiny Yorkie from Blackburn, England. At two years of age and fully grown, this little canine was an Fascinating6.35cm tall by 9.5cm long and weighed only 113grams! Most domestic dogs are able to reach speeds of 30.5kms per hour, when running flat out. The greyhound, the king of canine speedsters, is capable of reaching speeds of up to 64kms per hour! The oldest dog on record was an Australian cattle-dog named Bluey. He was put to sleep at the ripe old age of 29 years and five months! All dogs, from the German Shepherd to the tiny Poodle, are technically of the same species and can breed together and produce fertile offspring. The world's heaviest (and longest) dog ever recorded was an Old English Mastiff named Zorba. In 1989, Zorba weighed about 155kg and was 3.1m long from nose to tail! The tallest dog on record was named Shamgret Danzas. He was 1.06m tall, at the shoulder and weighed 108kg. A frightened dog puts its tail between its legs to cover the scent glands in the anal area. Since the anal glands carry personal scents that identify individual dogs, this behaviour is the canine equivalent of insecure humans hiding their faces. Dogs can very easily regurgitate. In fact, after eating, wolves can travel significant distances back to their dens and regurgitate their food at will to feed their pups! Dogs can see colour but it is not as vivid as the colour humans see. Dog colour is similar to what we see at twilight. The average city dog lives three years longer than the average country dog! The smallest dog in history was a tiny Yorkie from Blackburn, England. At two years of age and fully-grown, this little dude was an incredible 2.5 inches tall by 3.75 inches long! He weighed only 4 ounces! He was approximately the size of a matchbox. The oldest dog that has been reliably documented was an Australian cattle-dog named Bluey. He was put to sleep at the age of 29 years and 5 months!

1923. Our eyes can distinguish up to one million colour surfaces and take in more information than the largest telescope known to man. Our hearing is so sensitive it can distinguish between hundreds of thousands of different sounds. Our sense of touch is more refined than any device ever created. When we touch something, we send a message to our brain at 124 mph. Our brain is more complex than the most powerful computer and has over 100 billion nerve cells. Our nose is our personal air-conditioning system: it warms cold air, cools hot air and filters impurities. In one square inch of our hand, we have nine feet of blood vessels, 600 pain sensors, 9000 nerve endings, 36 heat sensors and 75 pressure sensors. We have copper, zinc, cobalt, calcium, manganese, phosphates, nickel and silicon in our bodies. In one hour, your heart works hard enough to produce the equivalent energy to raise almost 1 ton of weight 1 yard off the ground. Scientists have counted over 500 different liver functions. In 1 square inch of skin there lies 4 yards of nerve fibers, 1300 nerve cells, 100 sweat glands, 3 million cells and 3 yards of blood vessels. The structural plan of a whale's, a dog's, a bird's and a man's 'arm' are exactly the same. Nerve impulses to and from the brain travel as fast as 170 miles per hour. Your stomach has to produce a new layer of mucus every two weeks otherwise it will digest itself. Your left lung is smaller than your right lung to make room for your heart. You use an average of 43 muscles for a frown. You use an average of 17 muscles for a smile. Every two thousand frowns creates one wrinkle. The average human blinks his eyes 6,205,000 times each year. You burn 26 calories in a one minute kiss.

1924. Among the first known 'dentists' of the world were the Etruscans. In 700 BC they carved false teeth from the teeth of various mammals and produced partial bridgework good enough to eat with.

1925. Ophthalmic surgery was one of the most advanced areas of medicine in the ancient world. Detailed descriptions of delicate cataract surgery with sophisticated needle syringes is contained in the medical writings of Celsus (A.D. 14-37).

1926. A sneeze zooms out of your mouth at over 100 m.p.h.

1927. If you were freeze-dried, 10% of your body weight would be from the microorganisms on your body.

1928. When you eat meat and drink milk in the same meal, your body does not absorb any of the milk's calcium. It is best to have 2 hours between the milk and meat intake.

1929. The tooth is the only part of the human body that can't repair itself.

1930. One human brain generates more electrical impulses in a single day than the world's entire telephones put together.

1931. Everyone knows that the male African Ostrich is the world's largest bird. But did you know that they have recorded to stand 9 feet tall and weigh 345 lbs! These fat daddies's are also the fastest land bird and can run at speeds up to 40 MPH. The wandering Albatross has the largest wingspan of any living bird. One very old male specimen had a span of 11 feet and 11 inches. There is a poisonous bird from New Guinea called the Pitohui. The Pitohui contains a toxic alkaloid similar to that of the poison arrow frog on its feathers and skin. It is the only example known of a poisonous bird. The fastest wing-beat belongs the Sun Gem, a Hummingbird found in South America, is 90 beats per second. The greatest age for which a bird has been reliably recorded is 80 years old in the case of a Sulfur- Crested Cockatoo. 'Cocky' lived and died at the London Zoo.

1932. A Ruppell's vulture collided with a commercial aircraft over the Ivory Coast at an altitude of 37,000 feet! The plane was damaged but managed to land safely. The vulture didn't make it. Feather remains were used to make a positive ID. A mallard collided with a jet over Nevada at 21,000 feet. The jet crashed killing all aboard.

1933. The largest chicken egg was laid by a Black Minorca in England. The 5 yolk egg weighed nearly 12 ounces. It was 12 1\4 inches around the long axis and 9 inches around the short axis. The heaviest chicken egg was laid by a White Leghorn in NJ. The double yolk and double shell egg weighed 16 ounces.

1934. Bees beat their wings 200 times per second.

1935. Swifts fly non-stop for their first two or three years until they are old enough to breed. They eat and drink while flying.

1936. Arctic terns fly a distance of 35,000km while going from the Arctic to the Antarctic and back.

1937. Fish hear through their bodies. The loudest animal in the world is the Blue Whale. It can make sounds as loud as 188 dB that can be picked up 850 km away. Electric eels store enough energy in their tails to light up 12 light bulbs. A shock from it could kill a person.

1938. Leeches vary from a size of 25 cm to 1 metre. Grasshoppers hear with their legs, waving them in the air to tell where a sound is coming from.

1939. Bananas have been grown and cultivated as a food source for a million years, but only recently the banana's full potential become widespread. Bananas, the economical delicious fruit, is easy to peel, which makes it a great lunch box item even for the very young. Ounce for ounce, the fruit of a banana is a good source of Vitamin C, fiber and potassium, which also adds to its appeal. The banana is the most popular fruit in North America and is one of the few fruits that must be imported. About four million bananas, grown and harvested year-round, are imported to North America each year. The banana, believed to have originated from the jungles of Asia, is grown on the world's largest herb plant. Because banana plants reach heights of 15-30 feet and the stem is not make of wood, the plant is susceptible to damage by winds. Wind traveling at 25 mph can damage or destroy a banana field within minutes. For this reason, each banana plant is supported by a sturdy pole. The fruit of the banana plant grows on a stem. On average, some 150 bananas grow on each stem. The fruit is ready to be harvested 8-10 weeks after its appearance on the plant. Bunches of bananas are referred to as hands, while a single banana is called a finger. A cluster of bananas is anywhere from four to eight individual fruits. The fruit is harvested green, then shipped to special ripening facilities where it will take anywhere from three and a half to seven days to finish ripening. It takes about two and a half weeks for the fruit to be harvested, ripened and placed on supermarket shelves.

1940. Once in the home, bananas should be keep at room temperature or hung on a banana hook for the best results. Bananas can be placed in the refrigerator for slower ripening. The peeling will darken, but the fruit will remain firm for several days. Bananas also can be frozen. Remove peeling and store in airtight bags or containers. Green or green-tipped bananas are best for cooking and/or broiling. The fruit actually ripens best off the plant; so don't be afraid to purchase green bananas. When left on the plant too long, the fruit tends to split open and become tasteless. Yellow bananas are perfect for eating fresh or adding to your favourite salad or sandwich. Brown-speckled bananas or ripe and overripe fruit are still good for baking. In order to ripen a green or green-tipped banana in your home, place it in a brown paper bag for a couple of hours. It's possible to hasten the ripening process of other fruits and vegetables by placing them in a brown paper bag overnight with several ripe bananas. To keep them from ripening too quickly, keep them at a temperature of 57 degrees. Other interesting fact about bananas include: propagation of the banana plant is done through shoots from the rhizomes; banana seeds are sterile; in order to grown and propagate, the banana plant must have tropical sunny temperatures, rich soil and lots of water. Banana peel has its uses as well. The peeling makes a good fertiliser for rose bushes. Simply dig a hole near the rose bush and bury the peeling. Since bananas have made their appearance in North America, the only time they have been conspicuously absent was in 1941 when both American and British governments requisitioned all large ships–including boats transporting bananas— to aid in WWII war efforts.

1941. The name coffee comes from the Arabic word qahwah, meaning wine and not from the town of Kaffa, in Ethiopia (Abyssinia), as many writers have supposed. There are twenty-four steps in the 'Coffee Process'. Our knowledge of coffee is about 1,000 years old. Coffee was first mentioned in literature by Rhazes, an Arabian physician. The use of coffee as a beverage is about 700 years old. Pope Clement VIII was the first to baptise coffee and make it a true Christian beverage. 'Coffee Smellers' were discharged wounded soldiers employed as spies to 'smell out' unlicenced coffee roasting during the coffee monopoly in Germany. Goats actually discovered the coffeeplant. Their shepherd noticed that hey were getting very hyper; therefore, one day, he followed their every move and found out that they were eating a strange berry that was keeping them awake all day and night. Monks used coffee to stay awake and concentrate on what they were doing.

1942. 40.000 different kinds of spiders exist and only 850 species of bird spiders are known. In one year, spiders consume as many insects as the whole weight (in kilogram) of the population of England and Wales. The name 'bird spider' comes from the fact that some bird spiders feed on small birds. The first explorers in Latin America discovered a spider eating a small bird (Avicularia avicularia = bird-eating spider). Another reason to use this name could be that some tree spiders allow themselves to drop to the ground when there is danger and then spread their legs that are covered with hair and then glide like a little bird from branch to branch. Spiders are no insects. Insects have 6 legs; spiders have 8. A lot of insects can fly, spiders can never fly. The body of an insect consists of three parts, the body of a spider of two. Spiders possess 6 to 8 eyes; insects only have one pair of eyes. Spiders have an open blood circulation system and a primitive heart on the back. A spider does not have a skeleton like a human being. The spider body is totally or partially covered with an external, hardened skeleton made of chitin. This is an armature for the protection of the inside of the spider. The chitin-skeleton provides strength and a place to attach the muscles. It also prevents spiders from dehydration. The size of bird spiders can range from 3 cm (a Spanish variety) to the biggest bird spider (the Theraphosa blondi) with a span of 25-30 cm at the most. Female bird spiders can become as much as 25-30 years old. Males only become 4 to 7 years old. Usually they do not live to be that age because after the mating the female sometimes tries to kill the male for an easy meal. There are also bird spiders that brush their hair from their abdomen, the bombing spiders (mainly Brachypelma- species). These are bird spiders that brush their hair with their hind legs (when they feel threatened) from their abdomen towards the attacker. The hair then floats through the air and irritates the airways and the skin. What remains is a bare spot. Bird spiders live in all tropical and subtropical areas. When a spider loses a leg, this lost leg will grow again bit-by-bit. After every moulting the leg will grow a little bit: regeneration (this takes about 2 or 3 times moulting). When a bird spider moults, it loses its skin. In English, bird spiders from the New World are called tarantulas. African species are called baboon spiders. This creates a lot of confusion. The real tarantula is a wolf spider that lives in Southern Europe and is therefore not a bird spider! The wolf spider and the bird spider are not related. Sometimes there is also confusion with the American black widow spider or Australian black widow, but this is a small orb-web spider and does nowhere near resemble a bird spider.

1943. A mosquito's wings beat 500 times a second. The animal responsible for the most human deaths worldwide is the mosquito. Mosquitoes dislike citronella because it irritates their feet. Mosquitoes prefer children to adults and blondes to brunettes. A mosquito can detect a moving target at 18 ft away. The average life span of a female mosquito is 3 to 100 days. The male lives 10 to 20 days. Mosquitoes lay up to 300 eggs at a time, fly across 150 miles in their lifetime, range from sea level to altitudes as high as 10,800 feet (3,600 metres), develop from egg to adulthood in 4 to 7 days. There are 2,700 species of mosquitoes. A mosquito weighs about 2 to 2.5 milligrams. A female mosquito drinks about 5-millionths blood of a litre. Mosquitoes find new hosts by sight (they observe movement); by detecting infrared radiation emitted by warm bodies; and by chemical signals (mosquitoes are attracted to carbon dioxide and lactic acid, among other chemicals). A mosquito can fly at an estimated speed of 1 to 1.5 miles per hour. A mosquito can smell you or a cow or another host from a distance of 20 to 35 metres. A film of oil on water kill mosquito larvae because the oil clogs up the snorkel that the larvae use to breathe. Mosquitoes don't see very well, but they zoom in like a heat-seeking missile. In the spherical arrangement of their compound eyes, blind spots separate each eye from the next one. As a result, they can't see you until they are 30 feet (10 metres) away. Even then, they have trouble distinguishing you from any object of similar size and shape: tree stump, 55-gallon drum, etc. When they are 10 feet (3 metres) away they use extremely sensitive thermal receptors on the tip of their antennae to locate blood near the surface of the skin. The range of these receptors increases threefold when the humidity is high.

1944. The elements oxygen and hydrogen are 96.5% of ocean water. The other 3.5% is dissolved elements, such as chlorine, sodium and other salts. About 97% of all of the Earth's water is saltwater. The oceans cover about 71% of Earth's surface. The thermocline is an ocean zone in which the temperature drops very rapidly. It is usually found at around 300 to 800 metres deep, between the relatively warm surface zone and the cold deep zone. The thermocline blocks sonar, so it is a favourite hiding place of submarines. The temperature of most ocean water is about 39 degrees Farenheit (4 degrees Celsius), which is just above freezing! The longest mountain range on Earth is really the Mid-Ocean Ridge. It extends from the Arctic Ocean, down the middle of the Atlantic, winding into the Pacific Ocean. The largest waterfall on Earth is actually underwater. It is found in the Denmark Strait and slowly cascades downward for 2.2 miles. This is over three times as tall as Angel Falls, in Venezuela, which is the tallest land waterfall. The tallest mountain on Earth is also partly underwater. Mauna Kea, an inactive volcanic island in Hawaii, stands 33,465 feet tall when measured from ocean floor to summit. Given their sheer volume, ninety-nine percent of the living space on the planet is found in the oceans. Biologists estimate that somewhere between 500,000 and 5,000,000 marine species have yet to be discovered and described. The Mid-Ocean Ridge stretches 46,000 miles (74,000 km), more than four times the lengths of the Andes, Rockies and Himalayas combined. A slow cascade of cold water beneath the Denmark Strait between Greenland and Iceland sinks 2.2 miles (3.5 km), over three-and-a-half times farther than the tallest waterfall on land, Venezuela's Angel Falls. The average depth of the oceans is 2.5 miles (4 km). The deepest point lies in the Mariana Trench, 6.8 miles (10.9 km) down. By way of comparison, Mount Everest is only 5.5 miles (8.8 km) high. Earth's longest mountain range is the Mid-Ocean Ridge, which winds around the globe from the Arctic Ocean to the Atlantic, skirting Africa, Asia and Australia and crossing the Pacific to the west coast of North America. It is four times longer than the Andes, Rockies and Himalayas combined. Canada has the longest coastline of any country, at 56,453 miles or around 15 percent of the world's 372,384 miles of coastlines. At the deepest point in the ocean, the pressure is more than 8 tons per square inch or the equivalent of one person trying to support 50 jumbo jets. At 39 degrees Fahrenheit, the temperature of almost all of the deep ocean is only a few degrees above freezing. If mined, all the gold suspended in the world's seawater would give each person on Earth 9 pounds. In 1958, the United States Coast Guard icebreaker East Wind measured the world's tallest known iceberg off western Greenland. At 550 feet, it was only 5 feet 6 inches shorter than the Washington Monument in Washington, D.C. Although Mount Everest, at 29,028 feet, is often called the tallest mountain on Earth, Mauna

Kea, an inactive volcano on the island of Hawaii, is actually taller. Only 13,796 feet of Mauna Kea stands above sea level, yet it is 33,465 feet tall if measured from the ocean floor to its summit. If the ocean's total salt content were dried, it would cover the continents to a depth of 5 feet. Undersea earthquakes and other disturbances cause tsunamis or great waves. The largest recorded tsunami measured 210 feet above sea level when it reached Siberia's Kamchatka Peninsula in 1737. The Antarctic Ice Sheet is almost twice the size of the United States. The Pacific Ocean fills nearly a complete hemisphere of the Earth's surface.

1945. Unless forcibly separated, pigeons mate for life. Male pigeons have the rare ability to lactate, producing milk for the babies just like the females do!

1946. A grown pigeon has nearly 10,000 feathers. In the 17th century, King George I of England, decreed all pigeon droppings to be property of the Crown—and the 'lofts' were policed to enforce the law! With the ability to beat its wings up to ten times per second and maintain a heart rate of 600 beats per minute for up to 16-hours without rest, the racing pigeon is the unequalled athlete of the air! A famous WWI homing pigeon named 'Cher Ami' finished his distinguished career by delivering a vital message: The location of the famous 'Lost Battalion'. That mission alone is credited with saving nearly 200 human lives! 'Cher Ami' was awarded the French Croix de Guerre with Palm for his heroic service. He died of his extensive battle wounds. One WW II homing pigeon named 'GI Joe' saved over 1000 allied soldiers lives in a single mission! He was awarded the Dickin Medal, equivalent of the Victoria Cross. His average speed on that flight was 60 mph! Despite enemy fire, pigeons achieved a 98% success rate in missions flown in WW II—often with mortal injuries to themselves. The French, Swiss, Israeli, Iraqi and Chinese armies still use homing pigeons today! Pigeons proved valuable in the Gulf War, as their messaging was not affected by electronic jamming. The pigeon has the rare ability for a large bird to be able to fly nearly straight up. Pigeons have been taught to use 'tools' and were found to retain that knowledge! Pigeons have a visual memory that can store at least

300 objects or images indefinitely! The pharmaceutical industry in Australia 'employed' pigeons trained to identify anomalies in pills and capsules on a moving conveyor and remove them from production. The birds did outstanding work but authorities quickly put an end to the practice! Racing Pigeons routinely maintain flight speeds of 50 to 60 mph! Some pigeons reverse-commute, feeding on grain in the country, while living in the city.

1947. All dolphins and whales belong to the scientific order of Cetacean. All Cetacean are marine mammals that have adapted marvellously to water and lost the faculty to come back on land again. Dolphins have colonised all oceans and seas of the planet, from polar to tropical regions. They are true mammals. They must get oxygen from air and not from water such as fish; their infants are born underwater and must be brought up to the surface immediately to survive. Another dolphin is often present to help the mother when birth is taking place. Presence or non-presence of dolphins is a good indication of the state of the seas in many parts of the world. Climate or change in currents or sea temperature can also make dolphins disappear or come back after many years, the most remarkable case of this is the Monterey Bay in California where the Risso Dolphin reappeared in 1970 after a non presence of 70 years.

Dolphin species vary in their degree of curiosity and interaction with humans. Individual dolphins vary to the same degree. Some species are very shy, others will approach humans with great curiosity. One solitary dolphin, interact with humans more than with any pod. Jean Louise, a solo dolphin who lived in Brittany for many years, seemed to enjoy swimming with people but did not allow physical contact. If dolphins have spent time in captivity, they can become very use to people touching them, riding along with them, etc. But they also can become mildly aggressive; nipping, pushing, etc. These are strong creatures with territorial interests. It is also known of one dolphin in Italy that they didn't known what to do with because he was so aggressive with humans and other dolphins. Dolphins seem to enjoy playing games with humans; they invent them if you don't. We all heard of the famous stories about the dolphin rescues where a human is pushed to the safety of the shore by dolphins. A bottlenose dolphin seems to enjoy pushing items. Man is the greatest predator of dolphin's, more than 100,000 dolphins die each year because of man, either in nets or for gastronomy (being eaten). The Pacific Tunas and Dolphins follow the same routes, for years they were both captured in the nets aimed at the Tunas, the Dolphins were either drowned or slaughtered. From 200,000 to 500,000 dolphins were killed this way between 1960 and 1972. Now under pressure of common citizens, new legislation, actions of nature and wild life organisations, fishing industries in many countries have adopted new nets so that dolphins can escape. Tuna is now guaranteed to be 'Dolphin Safe' in many regions of the globe (not all). Despite ecologist actions Dolphins are still being served as meals in many parts of Japan and hundreds are massively slaughtered each year in the Faeroe Islands. Pollution of rivers, seas and oceans by human activities is also a great danger for many species of dolphins, at the end of the food chain this mammal will concentrate all the poisons and chemicals man does release in its habitat. The second predator of Dolphin after man is the Shark, the worst areas for these encounters are South Africa and Australia. Bottlenose dolphin survival rates for the Sarasota population (the only one studied in enough detail) are 0.961. This means that at least in the Sarasota Bay (and also in captivity) the life expectancy (the average age they can be expected to reach) is about 25 years. The maximum age (which only a few will reach) is more than 40 years. Survival rates in other populations may be different. Some species of dolphins are reported to swim up to 40 km/hr, due to special structures in the skin that reduce turbulence. They spend the least amount of energy when swimming at speeds of about 8 km/hr. The distance a dolphin travels depends very much on its food supply. The optimum swimming speed (the speed at which a dolphin spends a minimum of energy and hence can maintain for a long time) is about 8 km/hr. Dolphins sleep about 8 hrs/day, which would leave 16 hours for travel. This would mean they can travel up to 128 km/day. The dolphin is capable of diving for up to 20 minutes at 300 metres, this is considered to be a maximum for a bottlenose dolphins. Although in some experiments they have dived to about 500 metres (a dolphin that was especially trained for this). Usually, bottlenose dolphin will not dive very deep (some populations live in areas that are 1 to 10 metres deep (Sarasota Bay). The Dolphin respiratory system can renew 90% of its lungs at each inhalation (where only 15% for the human). In order to extend the stay under water its blood circulation, capable of variable geometry, will concentrate in vital organs only. Dolphin respiration is not a reflex such as with human being, it is a voluntary act. It can be blocked when caught in a fishing net to prevent from drowning immediately.

1948. All dolphins and whales can produce complex sounds, both for communication among them and for navigation under water. The common dolphin can hear sounds upwards of 150 kHz but generally produce sounds ranging from 1.5 to 11.0 kHz. Patterns of sounds can be observed, mostly clicking, moans, whistles, trills and squeaks. Males can whistle to get the attention of females or to warn the group of imminent danger (so does man, we are all mammals too). Dolphin sounds are believed to be emitted by the 'nasal sac', an area just behind the melon (the rounded region of a dolphin's forehead). The melon itself might be used as a acoustic lens to focus these sounds. Low frequencies are emitted to locate far away objects as they travel far under water due to their long wave length. High frequencies locate objects at close range with high precision but don't travel far due to their short wave length. Dolphins can determine size, direction, speed, distance and some of the internal structure of any objects under water. A female dolphin can detect that a swimming human female is pregnant (and will often in reaction tend to protect her). As the produced wave of sounds bounce off distant or close objects, the Dolphin receives in echo an acoustic 'image' that is send to the brain in the form of nerve impulses for interpretation and action. Dolphin can detect a band of fish more than a hundred metres away.

1949. Cranberries are sorted for ripeness by bouncing them; a fully ripened cranberry can be dribbled like a basketball.

1950. Hummingbirds are the only animals able to fly backwards.

1951. If you stretch a standard Slinky out flat it measures 87 feet long.

1952. There are more living organisms on the skin of a single human being than there are human beings on the surface of the earth.

1953. Your body contains enough iron to make a spike strong enough to hold your weight.

1954. The amount of carbon in the human body is enough to fill about 9,000 'lead' pencils.

1955. One square inch of human skin contains 625 sweat glands.

1956. When you blush, your stomach lining also reddens.

1957. The human body has less muscles in it than a caterpillar.

1958. The typical housefly cruises at 8 km/hr.

1959. 93% of a watermelon is water.

1960. The most abundant metal in the earth's crust is aluminium.

1961. If you could save all the times your eyes blink in one lifetime and use them all at once you would see blackness for 1.2 years!

1962. A bee sting is acidic and a wasp sting is alkali. To treat a sting by one of these you should use the opposite type of chemical.

1963. The space shuttle Columbia, USA in 1981 was the first spacecraft that could be used again.

1964. The amount of energy liberated in the form of light in a supernova explosion is so much that the explosion can be seen even during day!

1965. The first machine to carry people up in the air was a balloon. It was built by the Mongolfier brothers and first flew in Paris in 1783.

1966. In 1969, the Concorde was the first passenger plane to fly faster than sound.

1967. The solar challenger was the first solar powered aircraft to cross the English Channel in 1981. It's 262 km journey took 5.5 hours.

1968. The longest pipeline in the world is 2856km long and is used for carrying crude oil. It runs from Edmonton, Canada to Buffalo, USA.

1969. The world's largest hovercraft can carry over 400 passengers and 60 cars and can travel at the speed of 120kmph.

1970. The largest machine in the world is a coal digger in Ham Bach, West Germany. It is 220mts long and 85mts high, i.e. as tall as a 30-storey building.

1971. One of the world's most powerful fire engines is the Oshkosh fire truck, used for aircraft fires. In just 3 minutes, it can spray enough foam to cover a football pitch.

1972. Moving waves were used to produce electricity by Japan about 30 years ago.

1973. The largest hailstone ever, was found in Kansas, USA. It was the size of a melon, 19cm wide and weight 758gms.

1974. The first metal bicycle was called the High-Wheel or Penny Farthing. People had a hard time keeping their balance on this type of bicycle.

1975. Of the 35-40 million tonnes of flyash generated annually by thermal power plants in India, only 2-3 percent is productively utilised.

1976. The worst industrial disaster in India occurred in 1984 in Bhopal the capital of Madhya Pradesh. A deadly chemical, methly isocyanate leaked out of the Union Carbide factory killing more than 2500 and leaving thousands sick. In fact the effects of this gas tragedy is being felt even today.

1977. Every year some 50million cars are added to the world's roads. Car making is now the largest manufacturing industry in the world.

1978. In India the number of motorised vehicles have increased from 0.2 million in 1947 to 36.3 million in 1997.

1979. The number of registered vehicles in Delhi is more than the sum total of registered vehicles in Mumbai, Calcutta and Chennai.

1980. One of the most important measures to counter pollution is planting trees. With neem and peepal being the largest emitters of oxygen, planting them in the gardens purifies the surrounding air and helps in maintaining hygienic conditions. While champa, mogra and chameli have better chances of surviving pollution in summer, bulbous varieties do better in winter.

1981. The fear of water is called hydrophobia. The fear of words is called logophobia. The fear of a particular word or name is called onomatophobia.

1982. Before the first spacecrafts flew to Mercury to take pictures of its surface, some astronomers believed that the planet would have a smooth surface. When Mariner 10 took pictures of Mercury during its flyby of Venus and Mercury in November 1973, scientists discovered that Mercury is the most cratered planet in the solar system with a surface similar to earth's moon. Mercury has no atmosphere at all. Sunlight reflects off its surface, similar to how light is reflected directly off the moon's surface. The lack of atmosphere means that sunlight cannot be spread through the atmosphere. The planet's sky is dark, just like the moon's and, if you were able to stand on the side of the planet not facing the Sun, you would be able to see billions of stars in the sky. A year on Mercury is only 88 days long, but a full day (from sunset to sunrise) takes 176 days, even though the planet takes 59 days to rotate on its axis. This causes the Sun to rise above the horizon at the beginning of a Mercurian day in the east (as on earth), then move higher into the sky, move back down towards the horizon at the East and then quickly move over to the western horizon to set, after about 60 days! Mercury (4,878km wide) is slightly bigger than earth's moon (3475.6km wide) and is smaller than Ganymede (5,270km) and Callisto (4,890km), two of Jupiter's moons and Titan (5,150km wide), a moon of Saturn. Mercury can only be seen just after the Sun has risen and just before the sunsets. If you were to stand on Mercury, the Sun would appear two and a half times bigger than it appears on earth. Mercury is about 100 times closer to the Sun than Pluto, the most distant planet in the solar system. Mercury's speed is caused by the Sun's strong gravitational pull. Hold a short piece of string with something tied to the end of it and spin it around. Try it again with a longer piece of string. Notice how much longer it takes for the object tied to the end of it to spin round. Your finger acts like the Sun and the object acts like a planet orbiting the Sun. Despite being the closest planet to the Sun, Mercury is not the warmest. Venus is warmer. In fact, Mercury can be one of the coldest planets in the solar system. By the time one year has passed on Pluto (after 248 years), 1028 years have happened on Mercury!

1983. A quarter of the world's population is without safe drinking water. Less than 1% of the water treated by public water systems is used for drinking and cooking. Water makes up 75% of the human brain. 75% of trees are also made from water! Water expands by 9% when it freezes, making it less dense, which is why ice floats on water. You could live for a month without food, but you would be dead after a week without water! Once it evaporates, a water molecule spends around ten days in the air. 97% of the world's water is salty or otherwise undrinkable, 2% is stored in glaciers and the ice caps, the remaining 1% is left for humanity's needs.

1984. World corn crop is 600 million ton per annum. Nearly 10% is made into starch or starch-derived sweeteners making corn starch the largest starch commodity in the world. Over 3,000 products in the supermarket contain corn in some form, including cereals, snack foods, margarine, oil, puddings, soda and soap. Corn is a member of the grass family. An ear of corn has about 800 kernels in its 16 rows. A good acre of corn might have up to 25,000 plants. A bushel of corn weighs 56 pounds. A bushel of corn can provide 2.5 gallons of ethanol fuel or about 32 pounds of sweetener or cornstarch. Corn as a combination of starch, germ fibre and gluten and wet milling is their means to separate them. The single largest consumer of modified starch is the paper industry. Indian corn has white, red, purple, brown or multicoloured kernels. It was the original corn grown by the Indians and is known by the scientific name Zea Mays. It is many times seen in harvest time and Halloween decorations.

1985. Rocketdyne's Space Shuttle Main Engine (SSMEs) operates at greater temperature extremes than any mechanical system in common use today. The liquid hydrogen fuel is -423 degrees Fahrenheit, the second coldest liquid on Earth. When the hydrogen is burned with liquid oxygen, the temperature in the engine's combustion chamber reaches + 6000 degrees Fahrenheit - that's higher than the boiling point of Iron. The maximum equivalent horsepower developed by the three SSMEs is just over 37 million horsepower. The energy released by three of Rocketdyne's Space Shuttle

Main Engines is equivalent to the output of 37 Hoover Dams. Although not much larger than an automobile engine, the SSME high-pressure fuel turbopump generates 100 horsepower for each pound of its weight, while an automobile engine generates about one-half horsepower for each pound of its weight. Even though Rocketdyne's SSME weighs one-seventh as much as a locomotive engine, its high-pressure fuel pump alone delivers as much horsepower as 28 locomotives, while its high-pressure oxidizer pump delivers the equivalent horsepower for 11 more. If water, instead of fuel, were pumped by the three space shuttle main engines, an average family-sized swimming pool could be drained in 25 seconds. The SSME high-pressure fuel turbopump main shaft rotates at 37,000 rpm compared to about 3,000 rpm for an automobile operating at 60 mph. The discharge pressure of an SSME high-pressure fuel turbopump could send a column of liquid hydrogen 36 miles in the air. The Space Shuttle flies about 200 miles (330 km) above the earth's surface (equivalent to roughly half the distance between Los Angeles and San Francisco). In contrast, geostationary (stationary with respect to the Earth's surface) communications satellites have to be lofted approximately 21,500 miles (35,800 km) above the earth's surface and the Apollo spacecraft were approximately 227,000 miles (378,000 km) above the earth's surface when they reached the moon. NASA's Compton Gamma Ray Observatory, launched in 1991 aboard the Space shuttle Atlantis, is the heaviest spacecraft ever deployed by a space shuttle. Each of the Space Shuttle's solid rocket boosters burns 5 tons of propellant per second. A space shuttle and its boosters ready for launch are the same height as the Statue of Liberty but weigh almost three times as much. The space shuttle main engine weighs 1/7th as much as a train engine, but delivers as much horsepower as 39 train engines. It only takes the space shuttle about 8 minutes to accelerate to its orbital speed of more than 17,000 miles per hour.

1986. The smallest species of crocodile is the dwarf caiman of South America. Females rarely grow beyond 4 feet and males rarely exceed 5 feet.

1987. The king cobra is the longest venomous snake in the world. The longest specimen ever was kept at the London Zoo and measured 18 feet and 9 inches. Zookeepers killed it in 1939 due to the outbreak of war. They feared it would escape the zoo and pose a threat to the citizens of London. The world's most venomous snake is probably the species of sea snake Hydrophis belcheri. The snake that is responsible for the most deaths of humans is the saw-scaled or carpet viper. It resides from West Africa to India. The world's fastest reptile (measured on land) is the spiny-tailed iguana of Costa Rica. It has been clocked at 21.7 mph!

1988. The largest pig on record was a Poland-China hog named 'Big Bill'. He weighed a portly 2,552 lbs and was so large that he dragged his belly on the ground. He had a shoulder height of 5 feet and a length of 9 feet. The smallest breed of pig is the Mini Maialino. Pigs of this breed average only 20 lbs at maturity. The largest piglet ever farrowed was a stillborn 5 lb 4 0z male. Average weight for a piglet is 3 lbs.

1989. The peanut is otherwise known as a groundnut or 'goober nut' from the Congo name 'nguba' and is actually a legume. The US president Jimmy Carter is one of the world's most famous peanut farmers. There are about 50,000 peanut farms in America. An American botanist is known to have developed over 300 different uses for the peanut ranging from the dull to the utterly spectacular including shoe polish, shaving cream, toothpaste, grease and ink. An Australian inventor is said to have devised a car, which runs on peanut butter. The famed butter spread based on peanuts was invented by an American doctor back in 1890 to provide a nutritious and easily digestible food for his elderly patients.

1990. Surveys have revealed that men prefer smooth peanut butter while women prefer crunchy. Peanut butter is responsible for over half the consumption of US peanuts. The world record for eating 100 peanuts, one at a time is 59.2 seconds. Peanuts are adaptable and can be used whole, flaked and ground in sweet dishes, cakes and biscuits, whilst nutbutters can be added to soups and stews to thicken them, as well as eaten raw or roasted or made into the famous peanut butter. Peanuts contain about 40-50% oil and peanut oil is used in cooking as salad oil, in margarine's and the residue is fed to animals.

1991 . The heaviest insects are the Goliath Beetles family.

1992. The Anopheles mosquito, which carries the malaria parasite Plasmodium is estimated to have been responsible for half of the human deaths in history outside of war and accidents since the Stone Age. This claim is always debated by those who would say, 'Well the parasite is causing the deaths, not the mosquitoes!' However, the parasite must be delivered by the mosquito vector to infect its host. It is harmless to humans without the mosquito.

1993. A female house mouse gives birth to 6 young about 19 days after mating. She is ready to mate again in two days. She can produce 6 to 10 litters a year. Each of her young is ready to mate in two month. Remarkably, all her children, grandchildren, great grandchildren and great, great grandchildren can have offspring in the same year. Two mice, starting to breed on New Year's Day, could theoretically have as many as 31,000 descendants by December 31. Rats can jump 3 feet straight up and four feet outwards, from a standing position. They can burrow three feet straight down into the ground; chew through building materials, glass and cinder block; swim 1/2 mile in open water and against current in sewer lines; and, climb up inside the pipes with diametres between 1-1/2 and 4 inches. A rat's teeth are so strong; it can bite through aluminium, lead and other metals.

1994. Though bats are hated and feared, they may also be the single best controller of the insect kingdom. Bats may eat as many as 600 mosquito-size insects in an hour. An average size bat colony may eat 1/2 million insects in one evening.

1995. A tagged Monarch butterfly was released near Ontario, Canada and was recovered 4 months later in Angangueo, Mexico. The straight-line distance between these two sites is 2,133 miles. However, the actual distance traveled could be double this figure.

1996. Cockroaches will nibble at book-bindings, photographic film, starched linen, leather goods, almost anything...fouling them with strong smelling scents.

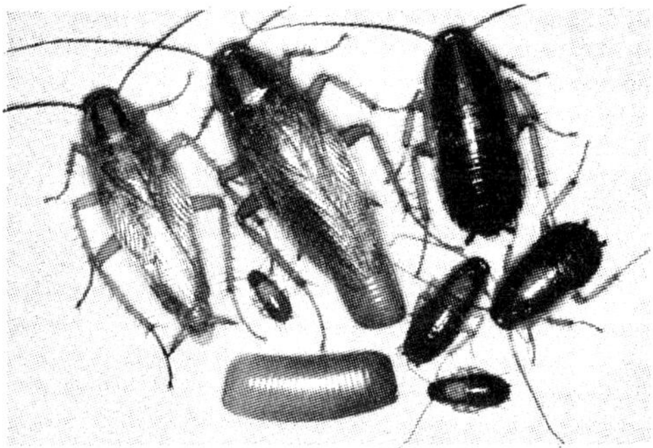

1997. Cockroaches favourite food is the glue on envelopes and on the back of postage stamps. A German cockroach can survive a month or more without food...but less than two weeks without water.

1998. Caterpillars make juicy meals for birds, so they protect themselves by devising various disguises. Some look like bird droppings, others disguise themselves as twigs and some match the colours of leaves.

1999. The stings of ants, bees and wasps are modified (egg laying tools), used to inject poison in defence or to paralyze prey. More than 50

different chemicals have been identified from various species. Some cause itching, pain, swelling and redness; others destroy cells and spread poison. Honeybees cannot pull their barbed stingers from human skins and will eventually tear themselves away leaving their stingers behind, dying soon afterwards.

2000. The tallest as well as the heaviest horse ever recorded was a Shire gelding named 'Sampson'. He measured 21.2 1\2 hands (7 feet 2.5 inches) and weighed 3,360 lbs! The smallest horse in history was a stallion named 'Little Pumpkin'. He stood 14 inches and weighed only 20 lbs! The oldest reliably documented horse was named 'Old Billy'. He died at the ripe old age of 62! The fastest race speed ever recorded was 43.26 mph, by 'Big Rackett', 20.8 seconds in the 3/4 mile. 'Big Rackett' was four years old and carried 114 lbs.

2001. The oldest cow ever recorded was a Dremon named 'Big Bertha' that died 3 months after her 49th birthday on New Years Eve, 1993. 'Big Bertha also holds the record for lifetime breeding as she produced 39 calves. The heaviest live birth of a calf is 225 lbs for a British Friesian cow in 1961. The highest lifetime yield of milk for a single cow is 465,224 lbs by the creatively named cow No. 289. The highest milk yield for a single day is an unbelievable 241 lbs by a cow named Urbe Blanca. Dairy cows can produce 125 lbs of saliva a day. Fast food hamburgers come from culled dairy cattle. Dairy cows can produce up to 200 lbs of flatus (farts and burps) a day!

2002. A Kangaroo is a marsupial mammal. It is a macropod, which means 'big foot'. When European explorers first saw these strange hopping animals they asked a native Australian (aborigine) what they were called. He replied 'kangaroo' meaning 'I don't understand' your question. The explorers thought this was the animal's name. And that's how the kangaroo got its name. The Kangaroo moves by hopping on its powerful hind legs. It uses its thick long tail to balance its body while hopping. A kangaroo can hop at up to 60kmh (40mph). It can also leap over obstacles up to 3m (10ft) high. Because of the unusual shape of its legs and its bulky tail a kangaroo can't walk or move backwards very easily. A male kangaroo is called a boomer and a female is called a flyer. If you lift a kangaroo's tail off the ground, it can't hop. Kangaroos use their tail for balance. Male kangaroos do not have pouches. There are 47 varieties of kangaroos, ranging in size from the two-pound rock wallaby to the 6-foot, 300-pound red kangaroo. Kangaroos live up to 20 years in captivity, but only six in the wild.

2003. Kangaroos are found in Australia, Tasmania and New Guinea. Most are terrestrial and all are herbivorous, grazing and browsing for their food. Each long, narrow hind foot has four toes. The short forelimbs are used almost like human arms, but the thumb is not opposable. Kangaroos possess soft, wooly fur and some have stripes on the head, back or upper limbs. All kangaroos have a chambered stomach that is functionally similar to those of such ruminants as cattle and sheep. They regurgitate the vegetation they have eaten, chew it as cud and then swallow it again for final digestion. Kangaroos need very little water to survive and are capable of going for months without drinking at all. When they do need water, they dig 'wells' for themselves, frequently going as deep as three or four feet. Kangaroos travel in groups (mobs) under the leadership of the largest male ('old man' or 'boomer'), which dominates younger rivals by biting, kicking and boxing. Kangaroos usually have one young annually. The young kangaroo or joey, is born alive at a very immature stage, when it is only about 2 cm long and weighs less than a gram. Immediately after birth, it crawls up the mother's body and enters the pouch. The baby attaches its mouth to one of four teats, which then enlarges to hold the young animal in place. After several weeks, the joey becomes more active and gradually spends more and more time outside the pouch, which it leaves completely between 7 and 10 months of age. Female kangaroos enter into heat within a few days after giving birth; they mate and conceive, but after only one week's development the microscopic embryo enters a dormant state that lasts until the previous young leaves the pouch. The development of the second embryo then resumes and proceeds to birth after a gestation period of about 30 days.

2004. One of the world's rarest and most sought after collector coins, the 1933 Double Eagle, was sold at Sothey's auction house in New York on Tuesday 30th July 2002 for the record sum of $7.59 million. The coin, featuring a standing Liberty on one side and an eagle on the other, was minted in 1933 at the height of the Depression but never circulated as President Roosevelt abandoned the Gold Standard. All 445,500 coins, each with a face value of $20, were put into storage and ordered to be melted down in 1937, but it was not until the 1940s that it was discovered ten coins had not been returned. Nine were subsequently recovered but one coin got away and ended up in the collection of King Farouk of Egypt. It disappeared again in the mid 1950s and resurfaced in 1996 when a UK coin dealer attempted to sell it to undercover Secret Service agents in New York. After protracted legal wrangling, it was agreed that the coin be sold at auction with the proceeds split between the dealer and the US Mint's enterprise fund.

2005. The earliest gold jewellery dates from the Sumer civilisation in between the Tigris and Euphrates rivers in southern Iraq around 3000 BC. A major archaeological find of early jewellery was in the Royal tombs of Ur, in Mesopotamia, dated to around 2,600 BC where gold articles made by lost wax casting included a wild ass on the rein ring of a chariot. Copper and bronze inlaid with gold also date to this period, demonstrating the craft skills in metalworking that existed. A beautifully modelled bull cast in gold dating to 2,300 BC was found in the Caucasus in eastern Europe. In Egypt, gold jewellery and other artefacts have been found in Pharoah's tombs dating to around 1500 BC and later.

2006. The face mask of the boy-king of Egypt (1361-1352 BC), Tutankhamun was discovered in his tomb in 1922 by Howard Carter. This tomb preserved some of the greatest treasures of the goldsmiths art. This face mask is normally on display in the Cairo museum.

2007. Ramses the Great of Egypt had 8 official wives and nearly 100 concubines. He was over 90 years old when he died in 1212 BC. Amenhotep III dug a pleasure lake for his wife, which was over 5,500 ft long, in only 15 days. Hatshepust was referred to as 'His Majesty', despite being a woman. After her succession, she was depicted as a man, without breasts and wearing the costume of a ruling pharaoh, complete with false beard. Cleopatra seduced Julius

Caesar and bore him a son. Later the 'temptress of the East' married Mark Antony, by whom she had more than three children. The pyramids were built not by slaves, but largely by peasant farmers conscripted during their 'off-season', when their fields were flooded by the annual inundation of the Nile. The true pyramid shape may have been inspired by the spreading rays of the sun. The 'Book of the Dead' was not an actual book but a collection of up to 200 chapters or spells written on a papyrus scroll to assist the soul on its journey to the afterlife. A popular scene from the Book of the Dead was the so-called 'Opening of the Mouth' ceremony. A statue or mummy could be brought magically back to life if the foreleg of a bull was extended towards it and the face was touched with a fish-tail knife blade and other objects. The crocodile monster was another nightmarish apparition in the Book of the Dead. Called the 'devourer of human hearts', it lay in wait for the deceased in the Hall of Judgment. The Arab produced a volume known as The Book of Buried Pearls specifically for tomb robbing, with detailed lists of hidden treasure and magic formulae for outwitting the guardian spirits. The mummy of Ramesess I, after its discovery at Thebes, was kept lying so long in the sun that the resins grew warm and the king's arm began to lift, terrifying the workmen nearby.

2008. Thousands of dinosaur bones can be found where they were washed together by violent floodwaters and buried under mud, sand and rock. Many of the animals were torn apart and their bones broken and jumbled-up. The muds and sands hardened like concrete to form the great layers of fossil rocks we find today. Quick flood burial would be the only way that so many dinosaurs and other things could have become fossilised in the way scientists have found them. Animals and plants will fossilise only if they are buried quickly and deeply - before predators, decay and weather destroy them.

2009. Volcanoes emit huge amounts of steam and underwater lava creates hot water/steam, which dissolves minerals, adding salt to the water. Furthermore, erosion accompanying the movement of water off the continents after the flood would have added salt to the oceans In other words, we would expect the pre-flood ocean waters to be less salty than they were after the flood.

2010. The problem for fish coping with saltiness is that this fish in fresh water tend to absorb water because the saltiness of their body fluids draws in water (by osmosis). Fish in saltwater tend to lose water from their bodies because the surrounding water is saltier than their body fluids.

2011. The Tarsier is one of the smallest primates and lives in the forests of Borneo and Sumatra and the Philippines. Tarsiers have a maximum body length of 6-1/3 inches and a 10-1/2 inch tail. Their eyes are so large that they would be equivalent to grapefruit. Tarsiers, along with animals from the genus Galago, are the only primates able to turn their heads through 180-degrees in each direction. Galagos, known as bush babies, also share the Tarsier's large eye-to-body ratio. They can be found in sub-Saharan African forests.

2012. There has never been a book written in the same way as the Bible! Over 40 authors wrote the Bible. Authors wrote from 3 different continents Asia, Africa and Europe. It was written at different times; covering a span of 1,500 years. They all wrote about the same thing and without any contradictions!

2013. One incredible thing about kangaroos is that the mother (called a doe) can determine the sex of her babies. How she does this is unknown, but she tends to put off bearing males until she is older. Males move away after about two years, but females stay with their mothers longer and benefit from mother's help more. A doe is nearly always pregnant. All her life, she is rarely without three offspring — an embryo in the womb, a Joey in her pouch and a larger youngster at her heels. The Joey can survive only a few minutes unless it reaches the pouch and attaches to one of the four nipples. Once there, its mouth swells on the nipple so that it cannot be removed without injury. A ring of strong muscles, similar to human lips, seals off the opening to the pouch to protect the Joey from bouncing out and keeps the pouch waterproof if mother goes for a swim.

2014. There are at least two possibilities as to why flightless birds such as ostriches and emus have wings: Either the wings are indeed 'useless' or derived from birds that once could fly. Loss of features is relatively easy by natural processes, whereas acquisition of new characters, requiring specific new DNA information, is impossible. Loss of wings most probably occurred in a beetle species that colonised a windy island. Again, this is a loss of genetic information, so it is not evidence for microbe-to-man evolution, which requires masses of new genetic information. The wings have a function. Some possible functions, depending on the species of flightless bird, are balance while running, cooling in hot weather, warmth in cold weather, protection of the ribcage during falls, mating rituals, scaring predators (emus will run at perceived enemies of their chicks, mouth open and wings flapping), sheltering of chicks, etc.

2015. Clouds may seem to defy gravity because they float. But gravity does affect clouds. Gravity influences the shapes and sizes of clouds and causes snow and rain to fall from them. Clouds form from water that evaporates from lakes, rivers, oceans and soil. When warm air and sun cause evaporation, the warm air full of water vapour rises. As air rises, it expands and cools, forming clouds. Cooler air can't hold as much water vapour as warm air. The extra vapour changes into water droplets and ice crystals, which gravity pulls to earth as rain and snow.

2016. It's hard to imagine, but 95% of all the animal species on the earth are insects! Millions of insects can exist in a single acre of land! Scientists have discovered over one million species and they think that there might be ten times that many that hasn't been named yet!

They are divided up into 32 orders or groups of insects. The largest order is the beetles (Coleoptera) with 125 different families and around 500,000 different species. In fact, one out of every four animals on earth is a beetle. Scientists estimate that 10% of the animal biomass of the world is ants and another 10% is termites. This means that 'social insects' probably make up an incredible 20% of the total animal biomass of this planet! Insects eat more plants than all the other creatures on earth! They are also so important in the breakdown of plant and animal matter that without them, we would have a world covered with dead plants and animals! In addition to all of this, insects are a major food source for many other animals. Insects are incredibly adaptable creatures and have evolved to live successfully in most environments on earth, including deserts and even the Antarctic. The only place where insects are not commonly found is in the oceans.

2017. In Peru, one researcher reported seeing 43 species of ants on a single tree. Some researchers believe that 30% of the animal biomass of the Amazon Basin is made up of ants. A single ant colony can include over 5-million busy members - soldiers and workers (undeveloped females; never have wings; cannot mate), males (can mate with the queen) and the queen. Her majesty is one busy bug, laying up to 100-million eggs a day! She only needs to mate once in her lifetime to be able to produce at least 15 years of eggs. Although she is called a 'queen,' she is more of an egg factory than a leader. Somehow, the Creator has designed ants to be highly efficient and organised as a group without a leader. Ants have a communication 'language,' and each colony member has a task, working together to keep the colony fed, safe and healthy. Ants can lift 20 times their own body weight. An ant brain has about 250 000 brain cells. A human brain has 10,000 million so a colony of 40,000 ants has collectively the same size brain as a human.

2018. Most of the tropical rain forests straddle the equator. One-third of the world's total is in the Amazon basin of Brazil. Rain forests usually experience high humidity and daily rainfall. The vast areas of trees have been called the 'lungs of the earth'. The forests 'breathe' by removing large amounts of carbon dioxide from the air and giving off oxygen. It is feared that the loss of rain forests will increase CO_2 levels in the atmosphere and result in global warming. On a more local level, the clearing of rain forest land diminishes the amount of evaporation. As a result, the rainfall decreases and the ground dries out, reducing its ability to support vegetation. Loss of rain forests also reduces the absorption of solar energy. Sunlight reflects off the barren ground instead of being absorbed by trees. This would tend to cause earth cooling, an opposite result from the carbon dioxide increase. If the cooling effect dominates, rainfall and air circulation might decrease worldwide. Rain forests covered about 30 percent of the earth's land surface in 1950; the 'greenbelt' is now at 7 percent and still declining. The trees are being cleared for timber, underground minerals and farms. In the process, the great diversity of plants and animals in the rain forests is destroyed. Many conservationists consider deforestation the planet's greatest environmental problem. Clearly, the ultimate results are uncertain at this time.

2019. Sound always originates as a vibrating object, whether a violin string, vocal chords or a hanging leaf. The sound is carried to you by oscillating air molecules, which in turn set your eardrum vibrating. There are several ways in which wind makes itself heard. Trees provide a natural outdoor instrument. As branches and leaves shake, they cause vibrations in the surrounding air. The faster the object moves, the higher will be the pitch that is heard. The willow has been likened to a flute, the pine to a violin.

2020. Mt. Waialeale in Kauai, Hawaii, averages 460 inches (11,685 mm) of rain (38 feet / 11.58 metres) each year. Northern Chile is one of the driest places on earth. Cold ocean currents prevent the formation of clouds and in places there is no recorded rain in over 400 years. Central Uganda in Africa averages 242 thunderstorm days each year. The highest air temperature ever recorded was 136°F (58°C), in Libya. This occurred in 1922, in the shade. Death Valley, Califor-

nia, has recorded a temperature of 134°F (56.7°C). The lowest temperature reading ever measured was -129°F (-89.2°C) in Antarctica, 1983. In 1921, 6.3 feet (approx. 1.9 metres) of snow fell at Silver Lake, Colourado, in 24 hours. Holt, Missouri, experienced 12 inches (approx. 30.5 centimetres) of rain in just 42 minutes, in 1947.

2021. Isaac Newton first analysed the technical details of rainbow formation in 1665. A rainbow occurs when raindrops and sunshine cross paths. Sunlight consists of all the colours of light, which add together to make white illumination. When sunlight enters water drops, it reflects off their inside surfaces. While passing through the droplets, the light also separates into its component colours, which is similar to the effect of a glass prism. Each falling water drop actually flashes its colours to the observer for just an instant, before another drop takes its place.

2022. A rainbow is usually seen in the opposite direction in the sky from the sun. The rainbow light is reflected to the eye at an angle of 42 degrees to the original ray of sunlight. The bow shape is actually part of a cone of light that is cut off by the horizon. If you travel towards the end of a rainbow, it will move ahead of you, maintaining its shape. Thus, there is no real end to a rainbow and no pot of gold waiting there. Because the 42-degree angle is measured from each individual observer's eye, no two people see exactly the same rainbow. Every person is at the centre of his or her own particular cone of coloured light. From the high vantage point of a mountaintop or an airplane a complete circle of rainbow light sometimes can be seen.

2023. The bright, primary rainbow has red on the outer edge and blue within. Higher in the sky there is always another, dimmer rainbow with the order of colours reversed. This secondary rainbow results from additional reflection of sunlight through the raindrops. It is most visible when there are dark clouds behind it.

2024. Even though there are more than 10^{22} known stars in the universe, each one is unique. No two stars have exactly the same properties. This may sound like guesswork, since we have analysed very few stars in detail, but the conclusion is a certainty. A star has so many variables in its makeup that the probability of two identical stars is zero. These variables include the total number of atoms, exact chemical composition, size, temperature and motion. Some stars show obvious colour and brightness differences. Others require spectroscopic study to detect their particular identity or fingerprint.

2025. The world's highest cricket ground is in Chail, Himachal Pradesh. Built in 1893 after levelling a hilltop, this cricket pitch is 2444 metres above sea level.

2026. The World's first university was established in Takshila in 700 BC. More than 10,500 students from all over the world studied more than 60 subjects. The University of Nalanda built in the 4th century was one of the greatest achievements of ancient India in the field of education.

2027. The Baily Bridge is the highest bridge in the world. It is located in the Ladakh valley between the Dras and Suru rivers in the Himalayan Mountains. It was built by the Indian Army in August 1982.

2028. The air around a lightning bolt is superheated to about five times the temperature of the Sun. This sudden heating causes the air to expand faster than the speed of sound, which compresses the air and forms a shock wave; we hear it as thunder.

2029. Scientists estimated that volcanoes posed a tangible risk to at least 500 million people.

2030. Groundwater comprises a 30 times greater volume than all freshwater lakes and more than 3,000 times what's in the world's streams and rivers at any given time. Groundwater is housed in natural underground aquifers, in which the water typically runs around and through the stone and other material. More than two million cubic miles of fresh water is stored in the planet, nearly half of it within a half-mile of the surface. Mars, too, appears to have a lot of water near its surface, but what's been detected so far is locked up as ice; nobody has estimated how much might be there.

2031. A place called Arica, in Chile, gets just 0.03 inches (0.76 millimetres) of rain per year. At that rate, it would take a century to fill a coffee cup.

2032. Astronomers know that over the next few billion years, the Sun will swell so large as to envelop Earth. If we're still here, we'll probably fry and the planet will be vapourised. There's a chance, however that the changing mass of the Sun will cause earth to move into a more distant and pleasant orbit. One mathematical calculation shows it would be theoretically possible for humans to engineer such a move before it's too late.

2033. On average, about 400 billion gallons water is used worldwide each day.

2034. Pluto's is only about half the width of the United States. Charon is the largest moon compared to its planet of any moon in the solar system. Charon is about half the size of Pluto. Almost all the other planets travel around the Sun in nearly perfect circles. Not Pluto! It takes an oval-shaped path with the Sun nowhere near its centre. What's more, its path is quite tilted from the nice orderly plane where all the other planets orbit. If you lived on Pluto, you'd have to live 248 earth years to celebrate your first birthday in Pluto-years. If you lived on Pluto, you would see Charon from only one side of the planet. Charon's orbit around Pluto takes about six and one-half earth days. Pluto's day (that is, one complete rotation) takes exactly the same amount of time. So, Charon always 'hovers' over the same spot on Pluto's surface and the same side of Charon always faces Pluto. At Pluto's current distance from the Sun, the temperature on its surface is about 400 degrees below zero Fahrenheit! It will get even colder as it moves farther from the Sun. From Pluto, the Sun looks like just a bright dot in the sky, the brightest star visible. The light from the Sun is as bright on Pluto as the light from the full moon is on earth. If you weigh 100 pounds on Earth, you would weigh only 7 pounds on Pluto! Pluto orbits in a far-out region of the solar system called the Kuiper (rhymes with viper) Belt. There are lots of icy, rocky objects out there. But they are so far from the Sun that they are really hard to see, even with powerful telescopes.

2035. An earthworm can grow only so long. A well-fed adult will depend on what kind of worm it is, how many segments it has, how old it is and how well fed it is. A Lumbricus terrestris will be from 90-300 millimetres long. A worm has no arms, legs or eyes. There are approximately 2,700 different kinds of earthworms. Worms live where there is food, moisture, oxygen and a favourable temperature. If they don't have these things, they go somewhere else. In one acre of land, there can be more than a million earthworms. The largest earthworm ever found was in South Africa and measured 22 feet from its nose to the tip of its tail. Worms tunnel deeply in the soil and bring subsoil closer to the surface mixing it with the topsoil. Slime, a secretion of earthworms, contains nitrogen. Nitrogen is an important nutrient for plants. The sticky slime helps to hold clusters of soil particles together in formations called aggregates. Charles Darwin spent 39 years studying earthworms more than 100 years ago. Worms are cold-blooded animals. Worms can grow a new tail, but not grow a new head if they are cut off. Baby worms are not born. They hatch from cocoons smaller than a grain of rice. The Australian Gippsland Earthworm grows to 12 feet long and can weigh 1-1/2 pounds. Even though worms don't have eyes, they can sense light, especially at their anterior (front end). They move away from light and will become paralysed if exposed to light for too long (approximately one hour). If a worm's skin dries out, it will die. Worms are hermaphrodites. Each worm has both male and female organs. Worms mate by joining their clitella (swollen area near the head of a mature worm) and exchanging sperm. Then each worm forms an egg capsule in its clitellum. Worms can eat their weight each day.

2036. Men can read smaller print than women can and women can hear better.

2037. The state with the highest percentage of people who walk to work is Alaska.

2038. The youngest pope was 11 years old.

2039. The first novel ever written on a typewriter was Tom Sawyer.

2040. The San Francisco Cable cars are the only mobile National Monuments.

2041. Each king in a deck of playing cards represents a great king from history

2042. Spades - King David, Hearts - Charlemagne, Clubs - Alexander the Great, Diamonds - Julius Caesar.

2043. Bullet-proof vests, fire escapes, windshield wipers and laser printers all have one thing in common. All were invented by women.

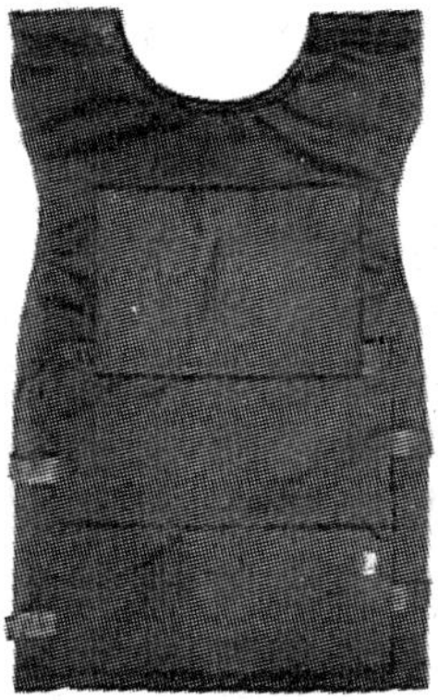

2044. The practice of mounting a horse from the left side began in ancient Greece. Warriors always carried their weapons on their left side, which made mounting on the right side impossible. The first people to tame and ride horses were from central Asia in 1519 AD. 1.9 million people own horses in the United States that's more than 3 horses per person. Many white and grey horses are born black and turn grey or white as they mature. Most horses are right or left handed just like people. They have a good side and a bad side. Hopefully their bad side is your good side and vice versa. A horse should have his shoes set at the angle of his leg and according to the way he moves. This does not always mean they are straight in their angle.

2045. Vetiver grass is an amazing plant. Its aromatic oil is used in expensive perfume. It's one of nature's pollution busters. Recent studies in Queensland have found this grass removes chemicals from water and sediment. It's particularly good at getting rid of atrazine. One of the most common agricultural herbicides in Australia. Dense vetiver grass acts as a 'bio-filter' to trap chemical residues. This hardy grass is ten times more tolerant to herbicides than other plants. It also reduces erosion caused by rainfall runoff. Future scientists believe vetiver grass could be used in artificial wetlands to dramatically improve water quality in agricultural areas.

2046. Tablecloths were originally meant to be served as towels with which dinner guests could wipe their hands and faces after eating!

2047. The Nobel Peace Prize medal depicts three naked men with their hands on each other's shoulders!

2048. A Boeing 747 airliner holds 57,285 gallons of fuel!

2049. A lightning bolt generates temperatures five times hotter than those found at the sun's surface!

2050. Almost half the newspapers in the world are published in the United States and Canada!

2051. The Stethoscope was invented by Dr. Rene Laennec in 1816 because he was too embarrassed to listen to a young pretty woman's heart.

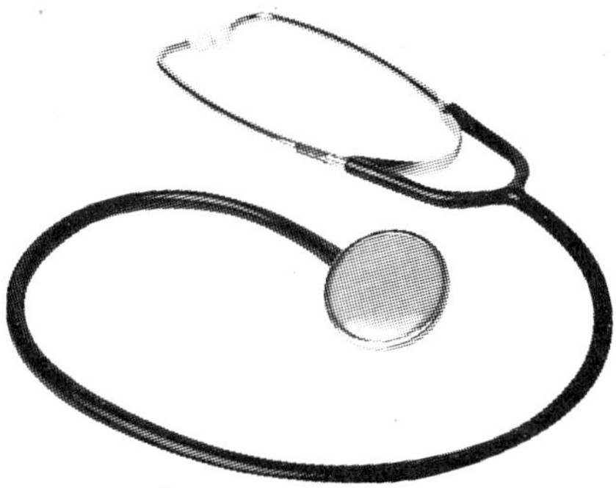

2052. Morris Michtom invented the Teddy Bear when word got out that President Teddy Roosevelt refused to shoot a bear cub on a hunting trip.

2053. Levi Strauss invented jeans during the Gold Rush when he noticed that miners needed stronger pants. Levi's first jeans were made out of tent canvas.

2054. Ruth Wakefield invented chocolate chip cookies in 1930 at the Toll House Inn. She substituted broken pieces of chocolate instead of baker's chocolate.

2055. A 19-year-old French boy named Blaise Pascal invented the calculator in order to help his dad who was a clerk. The first calculator was a wooden box with 16 dials on it.

2056. Donkeys are very social animals. They are most active in the evening and in the wild they travel in herds of up to one hundred individuals. At one or two years of age, a male donkey is sexually mature and leaves the group to search for a mate when the group disbands during mating season. By the time he reaches three or four years of age, he achieves an adult position within his group. Donkeys are very observant and cautious animals. They will refuse to do anything that seems dangerous to them. Donkeys can hear several octaves higher and lower than a human. It has been documented that donkeys 'rumble' to each other in tones too low for the human ear to detect.

2057. In 10 minutes, a hurricane releases more energy than all the world's nuclear weapons combined.

2058. The Main Library at Indiana University sinks over an inch every year because when it was built, engineers failed to take into account the weight of all the books that would occupy the building.

2059. 'Go' is the shortest complete sentence in the English language.

2060. Ketchup was sold in the 1830s as medicine.

2061. Leonardo da Vinci could write with one hand and draw with the other at the same time.

2062. Because metal was scarce, the Oscars given out during World War II were made of wood.

2063. Upper and lower case letters are named 'upper' and 'lower' because in the time when all original print had to be set in individual letters, the 'upper case' letters were stored in the case on top of the case that stored the smaller, 'lower case' letters.

2064. Back in the mid to late 80's, an IBM compatible computer wasn't considered a hundred percent compatible unless it could run Microsoft's Flight Simulator.

2065. Some calculators can spell out 'GO2HELL' after typing in 1134206, then looking at it upside down.

2066. Disney was once sued because a child noticed that in one scene, flying leaves spelled out the word 'Sex'.

2067. The Boston University Bridge (on Commonwealth Avenue, Boston, Massachusetts) is the only place in the world where a boat can sail under a train driving under a car driving under an airplane.

2068. Montpelier, Vermont is the only U.S. state capital without a McDonalds.

2069. The word 'hippopotamus' means 'river horse'. The animal got this name because it spends much of its time in the water and its wide nostrils and ears look like that of a horse.

2070. Snakes have no ears so they cannot hear air-borne sounds. But snakes can feel vibrations on the ground hence when someone approaches them they can make it out due to the vibrations of the feet on the ground.

2071. The cat's eyes are adapted for seeing in the dark. During the day, the pupils contract, but at night they open wide letting in every bit of light possible. The back of the eyes is coated with polished silvery pigments called Eumelanin and Phaeomelanin, which reflects every bit of light that falls on the eye. That is why cat's eyes glow in the dark.

2072. Parrots do not talk; they only imitate sounds that human beings make. They can't express themselves and are definitely not sharing any thoughts, they 'talk' simply because they enjoy imitating sounds. Parrots do not learn human speech easily. The words must be repeated slowly and clearly, many times over. Once it learns a word or phrase, it probably never forgets.

2073. Only male peacock have feathers. The females don't have these beautiful feathers. Peacocks display their feathers and dance to attract peahens.

2074. There is a species of hyena, who are called laughing hyenas. But actually hyenas don't laugh. When this creature is on the prowl or becomes excited, it makes a howling and chuckling noise that sounds like a laugh.

2075. The king cobra can live up to 20 years. It lives longer in captivity than in the wild! The king cobra can deliver up to 12 oz. of venom in one bite! The king cobra can eat a three-year-old cow! In one bite because it can pop its jaw out of it's socket! The king cobra loves the water it tries to find the closest spot to it to make its nest! The king cobra can get up to 18 feet long and slither up to 13 mph.

2076. The zoos feed the king cobra veggies. The king cobra has two fangs about 3 inches long each.

2077. Rats can't vomit. That's why rat poison works so well.

2078. A blue whales heart only beats nine times per minute.

2079. A chameleon's tongue is twice the length of its body.

2080. A shark can grow a new set of teeth in a week.

2081. The penguin is the only bird that can swim but can't fly. The cheetah is the only cat that can't retract its claws.

2082. Emus and kangaroos can not walk backwards.

2083. A mole can dig a tunnel 300 feet (91 m) long in just one night.

2084. A cow gives nearly 200,000 glasses of milk in her lifetime.

2085. The orca is the largest member of the dolphin family and is not really a whale. Due to its size, however, the orca is frequently included in discussions of whales. Orca eats smaller dolphins.

2086. Flies jump backwards when they take off.

2087. The largest dinosaur, Argentinosaurus, was estimated to weigh 110 tons.

2088. It's against the law to have a pet in Iceland.

2089. In 1681, the last dodo bird died.

2090. The snail mates only once in its entire life.

2091. The waste produced by one chicken in its lifetime can supply enough electricity to run a 100-watt bulb for 5 hours.

2092. Scorpions can withstand 200 times more nuclear radiation than humans can.

2093. The average garden-variety caterpillar has 248 muscles in its head.

2094. Cats sleep 16 to 18 hours per day.

2095. No other animal gives us more by-products than the pig. These by-products include pig suede, buttons, glass, paintbrushes, crayons, chalk and insulation to name a few.

2096. A kangaroo can jump up to 10 feet (3 m) high and leap up to 26 feet (8 m).

2097. The Queen termite can live up to 50 years and have 30,000 children every day.

2098. The cockroach's favourite food is the glue on the back of stamps.

2099. Tuna swim at a steady rate of 9 miles (14 km) per hour until they die and they never stop moving. Some Scientists estimate that a

15-year-old tuna must have traveled 1,000,000 miles (1,609,000 km).

2100. At full speed, a Cheetah takes strides of 26 feet (8 m).

2101. Of the 4,000 species of mammals on the planet, there are 900 different species of bats.

2102. The Australian Antarctic Territory is 5,896,500 square kilometres (42% of Antarctica). The total coastline of Antarctica is 23,358 kilometres. The south magnetic pole is at latitude -68.682, longitude 138.6 and is moving at the rate of 4.9kms a year. In winter when the sea ice reaches its maximum extent an additional 20,000,000 square kilometres band of pack ice surrounds the continent. Ninety percent of the world's ice-29 million cubic kilometres-and 60 to 70 percent of its fresh water, is locked up in the Antarctic icecap. Only about 0.4 percent of Antarctica is not covered by ice. The mean thickness of the icecap is 2.16 kilometres (4.7 kilometres at its thickest point). If all the ice were to melt, the level of the world's oceans would rise by 65 to 70 metres and if the weight of the ice were removed it is estimated that the underlying rock would rise on average by 1000 metres. This process - known as isostatic uplift - would take many tens of thousands of years. Without the ice we would see the single mass of East Antarctica and a smaller archipelago of rugged mountainous islands - West Antarctica. The continent of Antarctica has yielded some of the world's most ancient rocks, with the older ones being over 3 billion years. Because of the continent's remoteness, Antarctic ice is very pure and small traces of impurities are readily detectable. The world's largest glacier, the Lambert Glacier, about 40 kilometres wide and 400 kilometres long, is in the Australian Antarctic Territory, near the Prince Charles Mountains.

2103. The staple food of the Kanembu, a tribe living on the shores of Lake Chad in Africa, is Algae. The Kanembu harvest a common variety known as Spirulina from the lake, dry it on the sand, mix it up into a spicy cake and eat it with tomatoes and chilli peppers.

2104. Eighteen ounces of an average Cola drink contain as much caffeine as a cup of coffee.

2105. Rennet, a common substance used to curdle milk and make cheese, is taken from the inner lining of the fourth stomach of a calf.

2106. There are 15,000 different kinds of rice.

2107. Rice is the chief food for half the people of the world.

2108. Everyone knows about Vitamins A, B, C, D and E. Few are aware that there are also Vitamin K (promotes proper liver function and vitality), Vitamin T (helpful in treating anaemia), Vitamin H (also called biotin) and Vitamin U (promotes healing of ulcers).

2109. In ancient Rome it was considered a sin to eat the flesh of a Wood-pecker.

2110. Arriazia means the complete absence of breasts.

2111. Athetosis indicates constant involuntary movements of the fingers and toes. In advanced stages of this disease sufferers continually wave their hands about in slow, languid motions and are totally unable to keep the fingers still. Often this disease is confined to one side of the body.

2112. Harlequin foetus - A newborn child emerges covered with fatty epidermic plates about a sixteenth of an inch thick. These plates cover the entire body and face like a loosely built stonewall. The skin is so stiff and contracted that the eyes cannot be opened (or if they are open, they cannot be shut) and the lips are too stiff to suck. The child soon dies from starvation and loss of body heat.

2113. Mercyism - The need to regurgitate after each meal and then im mediately to eat another full meal. For some reason, this disease was at one time observed to be common among physicians.

2114. Naevus pilosus - Enormous moles or birthmarks with great amounts of hair growing out of them. The 'bearded woman' and 'orang-utan man' seen at circuses and carnivals are usually victims of this disorder.

2115. Plica polonica - The skin and nails turn spongy and black, the hair follicles exude a gluey liquid and the hair itself becomes painful to the touch. Oddly enough, this disease is found almost exclusively among Polish people.

2116. Polyorchidism - The presence of more than two testicles. This is the opposite of the condition known as anorchidism, in which a male is born with no testicles at all.

2117. Saltatoric spasm - Spasmodic muscular contractions of the calves, hips, knees and back that cause the sufferer to spring up or jump about uncontrollably every time he or she attempts to stand.

2118. Xeroderma pigmentosun - Small yellow warts cover the entire body. The skin is wrinkled and abounds in strange white scales. This disease, quite rare, usually attacks children.

2119. Ninety percent of all teenagers suffer from some form of acne.

2120. In 1971, at Memorial Hospital in New York City, a woman weighing less than 100 pounds ran a fever of 114 degrees and survived without brain damage or physiological after effects.

2121. The oldest known books in the world were made of clay. Actually earthen tablets on which written symbols were imprinted and baked, these 'books' were used for recording land deeds and business transactions by the Babylonians five thousand years before movable type was invented in the West.

2122. Johannes Gutenberg was not the first man to produce a book printed with movable type. Printed books were made in China five hundred years before their appearance in Europe. These books were set in movable type made with metal or porcelain characters, were printed on paper (which also was invented in China centuries before it reached the West) and were bound in a manner much like contemporary volumes, complete with title page and cover.

2123. There are 10 million books in the Russian Public Library in Leningrad, enough to supply every man, woman and child in the city with two free books. Remarkable as this may sound, however, the statistic is dwarfed by the book-count at the Library of Congress in Washington, D.C., which has 72,466,926 books on its shelves or more than seventy-two free volumes for every person in Washington.

2124. The average person in America spends fifty-two minutes each day reading the newspaper. This means that in a seventy year lifetime (subtracting the first fifteen years as nonnewspaper reading time), the typical person spends a little less than two years, about 687 days of his or her life reading the paper.

2125. In every hour that one listens to the radio in America, one hears approximately 11,000 spoken words.

2126. In a single human cell, there are between 10,000 and 100,000 coded messages known as genes. If all the directions contained in all these genes were written down, the words would fill the equivalent of 10,000 volumes of the Encyclopaedia Britannica.

2127. In the seventh month of foetal life the Adrenal Glands, located just above the kidneys, are about the same size as the kidneys. At birth they are slightly smaller and they continue to shrink throughout life. By the time a person reaches old age, the Adrenals are so small they can hardly be seen.

2128. In one year, the average human heart circulates from 770,000 to 1.6 million gallons of blood through the body, enough fluid to fill 200 tank cars, each with a capacity of 8,000 gallons. The Ketchua Indians of the Andes Mountains in South America have 2 to 3 more quarts of blood in their bodies than people who live at lower elevations. Human lips have a reddish colour because of the great concentration of tiny capillaries just below the skin. The blood in these capillaries is normally highly oxygenated and therefore quite red. This explains why the lips appear pale when a person is anaemic or has lost a great deal of blood. It also explains why the lips turn blue in very cold weather. Cold causes the capillaries to constrict and the blood loses oxygen and changes to a darker colour.

2129. The brain of Neanderthal man was larger than that of modern man.

2130. An adult sitting in a relaxed position inhales approximately one pint of air with every breath.

2131. The lens of the eye continues to grow throughout a person's life.

2132. The hair of an adult man or woman can stretch 25 percent of its length without breaking. If it is less elastic, it is not healthy. Apart from its vulnerability to fire, human hair is almost impossible to destroy. It decays at such a slow rate that it is practically non-disintegrative. It cannot be destroyed by cold, change of climate, water or other natural forces and it is resistant to many kinds of acids and corrosive chemicals. This is why it clogs sinks and drain-pipes.

2133. If one were to unravel the entire human alimentary canalesophagus, stomach, large and small intestines, it would reach the height of a three-story building.

2134. There are 35 million digestive glands in the stomach.

2135. An average of 400 million sperms are contained in a single human ejaculation.

2136. Men reach the peak of their sexual powers in their late teens or early twenties and then begin a slow decline. Usually, they are past their sexual prime by their late forties. Women, on the other hand, do not reach their sexual peak until their late twenties or early thirties and they remain at this level through their late fifties or early sixties.

2137. The human sense of smell is so keen that it can detect the odours of certain substances even when they are diluted to 1 part to 30 billion.

2138. Even if the stomach, the spleen, 75 percent of the liver, 80 percent of the intestines, one kidney, one lung and virtually every organ from the pelvic and groin area are removed, the human body can still survive.

2139. A person cannot taste food unless it is mixed with saliva. For example, if a strong-tasting substance like salt is placed on a dry tongue, the taste buds will register nothing. As soon as a drop of saliva is added and the salt is dissolved, however, a definite taste sensation results. This is true for all foods.

2140. A loss of 20 percent of the body's water would result in certain and painful death. Ordinarily the body cannot go more than a week and a half without water. The longest recorded time anyone has gone without water is eleven days.

2141. When astronauts remain weightless in space for prolonged periods, scientists have discovered, their bones lose a measurable amount of weight and thickness. This means that weightlessness actually causes human beings to shrink.

2142. A Crocodile weighing 120 pounds exerts a force of about 1,540 pounds between its jaws. A human's jaw exerts a force of about only 40 to 80 pounds.

2143. The Chow is the only dog that has a black tongue. The tongues of all other dogs are pink.

2144. At birth, baby kangaroos are only about an inch long, no bigger than a large waterbug or a queen bee.

2145. A full-grown moose may be 8 feet high at the shoulder and weigh almost a ton.

2146. A newborn polar bear cub weighs only twice as much as a newborn human, about 15 pounds. Yet when fully-grown, polar bears reach weights of up to 1,600 pounds.

2147. Lanolin, an essential ingredient of many expensive cosmetics, in its natural form, a foul smelling, waxy, tarlike substance, is extracted from the fleece of sheep.

2148. Alligators, dolphins, crocodiles, frogs, porpoises, turtles, water snakes, whales and several other water going creatures will drown if kept underwater too long. Unlike fish, these animals require a certain amount of air in order to survive.

2149. A bridge built in Lima, Peru around 1610 was made of mortar that was mixed not with water but with the whites of 10,000 eggs. The bridge, appropriately called the Bridge of Eggs, is still standing today.

2150. Japanese farmers, after removing the hulls from their rice crop and sorting out the white kernels, take the hulls from the leftover rice, mix them into a kind of paste, mould the substance into brick-shaped blocks and build houses with them. Such buildings are known in Japan as 'houses of rice skin'

2151. The Escorial, the famous palace located outside Madrid, was built in the shape of a gridiron because Saint Lawrence, to whom the palace was dedicated, was roasted on one.

2152. The I-Ching, practised by Taoist scholars since one thousand BC, uses coins (of which tails value 2 and heads value 3) to create a process of divination that views past, future and present as a whole. Central to the philosophy is the realisation that current reflection and meditation will affect the course of events. The I-Ching provides no set predictions but shows a possible course on one fractal arm of the future. The 23rd hexagram of the I-Ching signifies Chaos, Disintegration. It's a timely reminder that if you create order and take it too far you set the store for it to implode and wipe out what you have been working for, sound familiar? Thus 23 has a strong theme of rejection of modern materialistic values.

2153. December 23, 2012 is the day the classic Mayans said the world would end.

2154. The human biorhythm cycle is 23 days long.

2155. The Harmonic Convergence occurs every 23,000 years.

2156. Geosynchronous orbit occurs at 23,000 miles above Earth's surface.

2157. It takes 8 minutes 17 seconds for light to travel from the Sun's surface to the Earth.

2158. 10 percent of all human beings ever born are alive at this very moment.

2159. The Earth spins at 1,000 mph but it travels through space at an incredible 67,000 mph.

2160. Every year over one million earthquakes shake the Earth. When Krakatoa erupted in 1883, its force was so great that it could be heard 4,800 kilometres away in Australia.

2161. Every year lightning kills 1000 people.

2162. In October 1999, an Iceberg the size of London broke free from the Antarctic ice shelf.

2163. If you could drive your car straight up you would arrive in space in just over an hour.

2164. 'Wireless' communications took a giant leap forward in 1962 with the launch of Telstar, the first satellite capable of relaying telephone and satellite TV signals.

2165. The dinosaurs became extinct before the Rockies or the Alps were formed.

2166. Female black widow spiders eat their males after mating.

2167. When a flea jumps, the rate of acceleration is 20 times that of the space shuttle during launch.

2168. The earliest wine makers lived in Egypt around 2300 BC.

2169. If our Sun were just inch in diametre, the nearest star would be 445 miles away.

2170. Astronauts cannot belch - there is no gravity to separate liquid from gas in their stomachs.

2171. The air at the summit of Mount Everest, 29,029 feet is only a third as thick as the air at sea level.

2172. The tallest tree ever was an Australian eucalyptus. In 1872 it was measured at 435 feet tall.

2173. Christian Barnard performed the first heart transplant in 1967 - the patient lived for 18 days.

2174. Human tapeworms can grow up to 22.9m.

2175. The Ebola virus kills 4 out of every 5 humans it infects.

2176. Giraffes often sleep for only 20 minutes in any 24 hours. They may sleep up to 2 hours (in spurts - not all at once), but this is rare. They never lie down.

2177. There are 60,000 miles of blood vessels in the human body.

2178. On the day that Alexander Graham Bell was buried, the entire US. Telephone system was shut down for 1 minute in tribute.

2179. The low frequency call of the humpback whale is the loudest noise made by a living creature. The call of the humpback whale is louder than Concorde and can be heard from 500 miles away.

2180. A quarter of the world's plants are threatened with extinction by the year 2010.

2181. The Universe contains over 100 billion galaxies.

2182. More germs are transferred shaking hands than kissing.

2183. The fastest speed a falling raindrop can hit you is 18mph.

2184. A healthy person has 6,000 million, million, million haemoglobin molecules.

2185. Inbreeding causes 3 out of every 10 Dalmation dogs to suffer from hearing disability.

2186. The world's smallest winged insect, the Tanzanian parasitic wasp, is smaller than the eye of a housefly.

2187. If the Sun were the size of a beach ball then Jupiter would be the size of a golf ball and the Earth would be as small as a pea.

2188. The grey whale migrates 12,500 miles from the Artic to Mexico and back every year.

2189. Each rubber molecule is made of 65,000 individual atoms.

2190. Quasars are the most distant objects in the Universe.Quasars emit more energy than 100 giant galaxies.

2191. The saturn V rocket which carried man to the Moon develops power equivalent to fifty 747 jumbo jets.

2192. Light would take .13 seconds to travel around the Earth.

2193. Males produce one thousand sperm cells each second - 86 million each day.

2194. One in every 2000 babies is born with a tooth.

2195. Every hour the Universe expands by a billion miles in all directions. Even travelling at the speed of light it would take 2 million years to reach the nearest large galaxy andromeda. The temperature in Antarctica plummets as low as -35 degrees celsius. At over 2000 kilometres long The Great Barrier Reef is the largest living structure on Earth. A thimbleful of a neutron star would weigh over 100 million tons. The risk of being struck by a falling meteorite for a human is one occurence every 9,300 years.

2196. The driest inhabited place in the world is Aswan, Egypt where the annual average rainfall is .02 inches.

2197. The largest meteorite craters in the world are in Sudbury, Ontario, Canada and in Vredefort, South Africa.

2198. The largest desert in the world, the Sahara, is 3,500,000 square miles.

2199. The African Elephant gestates for 22 months.

2200. The short-nosed Bandicoot has a gestation period of only 12 days.

2201. The mortality rate if bitten by a Black Mamba snake is over 95%.